RINGS OF ANUBIS

RINGS OF ANUBIS

E. CATHERINE TOBLER

MASQUE

RINGS OF ANUBIS

Cover art by Timothy Lantz.
www.stygiandarkness.com
Cover design by Sherin Nicole.

ISBN: 978-1-60701-520-8

Masque Books
www.masque-books.com

Masque Books is an imprint of Prime Books
www.prime-books.com

For more information, contact:
publisher@masque-books.com

For my mother and Liz Ann, two ladies who always believed.

CHAPTER ONE

Paris, France ~ October 1889

Virgil Mallory came into Eleanor Folley's life during the autumn of her thirtieth year, a time when she should have been perfectly content to be with her father, books, or specimens from the field. Hers was not the life of a nun, she assured people (indeed, many presumed she had been packed off to a convent school, considering her Unfortunate Youth), but that of a librarian. No difference, her adviser and fellow librarian Juliana had argued.

"Would you look at that?"

Juliana's voice beckoned, and Eleanor looked up from the collection of Senegal shells she was sorting, a fine and disorganized mess after yesterday's hordes of younger Exposition *visiteurs*. She peered over the table at Juliana, at the gold ribbons that wrapped her auburn hair into a perfect Psyche knot. The woman's interest seemed captured by something more than the airships passing over the clear glass roof of the Exposition Universelle all morning.

"Is it another elephant?" Eleanor asked, her voice thin after a restless night. Two elephants had already passed through the Galerie des Machines that morning—one of living flesh, one of cleverly engineered clockwork. Eleanor was hard-pressed to say which beast was more remarkable, as each was astounding in its own way. Both beasts had responded to the commands of their handlers—*abattre, debout, révérence*—though the living elephant had been less amused at the idea of showing a leg than the clockwork creature had.

Eleanor placed a cowrie shell back in its proper bin and stood, brushing dust from her skirt as she straightened it. She longed for her trousers, but had made a promise to her father: trousers were permissible for adventuring, but skirts were required in public. The Exposition Universelle in Paris was as public as anything could be, Eleanor supposed, with citizens of almost every nation coming to gawk at Eiffel's tower, the Negro village, and the Galerie des Machines, in which they now found themselves. The gallery was massive, constructed of glass and iron, hinged arches vaulting above to enclose the largest interior space in the world. The way the light filtered through the glass intensified the colors of frescos, burnished the gleam of machines, and even seemed to make people glow—everything and everyone appeared gilded, as if having emerged from the pages of an illuminated manuscript

Though the Folleys had been in Paris five months, it remained a daily wonder for Eleanor to work among the other exhibitors. The opportunity to show their research, inventions, and collection was something that might not come again. Eleanor appreciated, too, the chance it gave her to soak in the variety of languages and attempt to bend her tongue around them. While French was second nature to her, there were other less common languages she longed to explore.

Such conversations rained down from the elevated track that circled the gallery above the exhibition space. Visitors could walk, or ride in carriages, above the machines but also among them, as a variety of flying beasts flaunted their lavish designs. Mechanical pterodactyls, owls, and sparrows reeled in the sunlight that streamed through the glass ceiling. More than one of the miniature mechanical dodos had found itself entangled in a lady's hat or hair, and it soon became a desired distinction. If you hadn't had an encounter with a dodo, your Exposition experience was not complete.

Folley's Nicknackatarium had never known such an honor. Eleanor tried to remind herself that it *was* an honor, even as other exhibitors tried to turn their inclusion into something else; most felt the Folleys didn't belong here or with them—surely it could be only chance or pity that found them within these circles. Her father's reputation as an archaeologist had never been sterling, and marrying an Egyptian only deepened the tarnish. In the wake of Dalila Folley's disappearance, his status in archaeological circles dropped even lower. The Folleys were Irish, after all, people murmured; even his daughter had gone a-roving, so what precisely could one expect? Eleanor often wondered which straw would break him, but his love of the field never faltered.

"*Not* an elephant," Juliana said as Eleanor joined the older woman at the edge of the main display table within the Folley booth. "Nor a dodo."

What Eleanor saw might well have been another extraordinary clockwork creature, so little sense did it make at first. Her father was speaking with a young man, and in an environment where people the world over had come to witness the marvels of science and industry, one man speaking to another should have been in no way exceptional.

Yet her father did not speak to young men, and indeed went out of his way to avoid them. According to her father, men aged fifty or older were the only people who made for decent conversationalists; there was no sense in wasting words on anyone—save daughters, he would add with a wink to Eleanor.

The only young men he might exempt from his strict policy were those who chanced to unearth a mythical tomb or bring him a piece of sand-crusted evidence to add to his life's research. Had you discovered the intact head of the Winged Victory of Samothrace, Renshaw Folley would see you straight away!

This young man was not Moorish, Indian, or Javanese, so it wasn't his origin that her father found interesting, but something else. His features were unremarkable from a distance, skin pale and features drawn, as if he had not been out of doors in years. He appeared average in every way, clad in a simple ditto suit of coal black, black cravat tied haphazardly beneath the beard that covered his chin. His hair was cut to his jawline, longer than fashion dictated, and rather disorderly, unable to settle on one color; bits of blond curled in the midst of darker brown. The brown matched his eyes—something in his eyes . . . he was not as young as she had first thought. Her attention flicked to the bright pin he wore in his lapel: a gold letter *M* curled within a copper twist of clouds. Eleanor's mouth flattened into a thin line at the sight of the symbol.

"Do you know him?" Juliana whispered.

"Only his kind," Eleanor said somewhat hoarsely, her mouth having gone dry. She did not wish to know why an agent of Mistral was here, even as she very much *did* want to know. She had always felt the organization could be more than it was—if only someone cared to take the time to make it so. Had he come to escort them out, to remind them they were Irish and should, at the least, go back to Dublin if they could go no farther? "And he smells odd."

Eleanor could not name the scent that rose even above the gentle lily fragrance Juliana wore; perhaps the young man had walked through Professor Twine's Miracle Steam Bath before he'd come here. The scent could be anything, for the petite professor claimed he could enhance his steam with any scent from past or present. Eleanor wished to smell her mother once more—bergamot, black tea, sun-drawn sweat from days on digs—but had yet to visit Twine to see if it might be possible. She closed her hand into a fist within the folds of her skirt, making an effort not to reach for the comforting lump of the ring she wore on a chain hidden beneath her blouse. Even so, her mind whispered the poem in which she often sought shelter: *Backward, turn backward, O time, in thy flight; Make me a child again, just for to-night.*

Her father gestured across the aisle to their booth now, past the glass-encased statues of Horus and Osiris, to Eleanor. The young man's gaze settled on her, entirely too curious and lengthy as he assessed her. Eleanor straightened and turned away, preparing to disappear into the back of their booth and slip into the neighboring one if her bustle allowed. She could lose herself in the Exhibition for the rest of the day, walking the maze of it as confidently as she could any ancient tomb. Maybe the Miracle Steam Bath could hide her from the curious eyes of young men from Mistral. At the very least, she could distract herself. Eleanor grabbed a book, but her father's voice caught her before she could vanish within its pages.

"Eleanor, a moment please. Surely that text can wait, and"—his mouth twisted in a vague smile as she turned back toward the shells—"the children will be here in an hour's time to make the shells sing yet again."

Her father crossed the aisle and tugged the book from Eleanor's grasp, his hands closing around it as if they were the best kind of old friends. Without the book, Eleanor felt strangely naked under the continuingly curious regard of . . .

"Eleanor, this is Agent Virgil Mallory. With . . . Mistral." He gestured to the young man who had followed him.

Eleanor did not miss the slight pause before her father mentioned Mistral. Nothing good had ever come from that quarter in Eleanor's opinion, and she doubted anything would. Covert agencies never seemed to care about desires beyond their own.

Eleanor forced a smile at the young man and took a closer look at him. What had rumpled his suit and left his hair disorganized? He smelled both bitter and sweet and, beneath that, another layer that felt somehow *old*. He must have been accustomed to people staring at him, for he did not stir under her study—not even when Eleanor's eyes widened in final recognition of the scent. Opium. He smelled like opium smoke.

"My daughter, Miss Folley," her father said. "Librarian for the

Nicknackatarium, but she was there that day, all of twelve, I think, when those men appeared out of the dust." Folley lifted his fingers to his mouth.

That day, all of twelve.

No matter the reasons this young man had for approaching her father, Eleanor told herself that speaking of the day her mother vanished could not be chief among them. Just as her father did not speak to young men, neither did people speak of the day Dalila Folley vanished. It wasn't done.

Eleanor's attention followed her father's motion to his mouth. She could remember the blood on his lips that day, could remember how bright it was in the swirling, obscuring sand. Renshaw dropped his hand and shook his head, as if he were trying to *not* remember. He extended a hand toward Juliana.

"Mrs. Juliana Day. Also a librarian of ours, but not there. That day."

"That day" was never far from Eleanor's thoughts, although she had tried to lock it away for her father's sake. Now she couldn't understand why her father was speaking of it—almost casually—in the presence of a Mistral agent. Dread should have bent her shoulders, fear pricking every finger, but instead it was hope that buoyed her up. Hope was decidedly worse.

Their entire world had been turned upside down "that day," and while she had sought to right it, her father begged her to leave the memories be. She had been but a child, had surely misunderstood what she saw. Eleanor could not deny that possibility, but neither could she stop trying to understand. She had lost her mother that day, but Renshaw had lost his wife. Which was worse?

In the eighteen years between then and now, Eleanor hadn't found a single satisfying answer to the strange occurrences of that day. Her father's solution was to leave the field entirely and open his Nicknackatarium to allow the people of Dublin a glimpse of ancient Egypt. His every action told her to seek no answers, even though they were what Eleanor most wanted. Could she find them now?

She looked again to Mallory, wishing for her father's sake she could send him away, wishing to smother the small flame of hope his presence had inexplicably lit.

Mallory inclined his head the merest bit to Eleanor and Juliana, a strand of gold-brown hair slipping free along his temple. He brushed it back and Eleanor noticed the tarnished silver ring encircling his right index finger. Skulls peered from the metal. A *memento mori*?

"Mr. Mallory," Eleanor said.

"Agent," he corrected, and his long fingers delved into his worn jacket to withdraw a neatly kept silver badge imprinted with a number.

The lapel pin he wore did more to prove his position to Eleanor. Where might one inquire as to the legitimacy of a badge number for a mysterious organization few even knew existed? Mistral did not make its offices or officers public.

"Miss Folley."

"Agent, what brings you to our booth today?" She gestured toward the device sitting in the center of the main table, the squat machine that had gained them entry into the Exposition. "Have you need of Folley's Extraordinary Efficient Extractor? The Triple E, able to pinpoint priceless artifacts beneath even the densest soils and ensure a clean, intact extraction?"

Mallory grinned at her practiced pitch. Juliana gestured toward the small marvel of science, her hands gently drawing invisible circles and waves in the air. The machine, with its exposed tubes and cogs, was ugly even in the golden light of the hall. A panel of switches and lights stretched across the machine's surface; bright blue extensions—resembling braces that would hold a man's pants up—allowed the machine to be supported by one's shoulders. Hideous.

Still, Eleanor knew one did not have to be beautiful to serve science. The device had to do with magnetic fields—not that she fully understood it. She could have taken the time, but it was her father's invention and Eleanor found little use for it. She preferred to make discoveries on her own, with fingers and shovel, dirt packing every fingernail. Why allow a machine to attempt what she could better accomplish?

"Agent Mallory has come with distressing news," her father said. He clutched the book to his chest like a shield.

Her father could rarely resist when it came to telling a distressing tale—as long as *he* was not the main character.

"Distressing?" Juliana's gestures ceased and she reached for Eleanor's arm.

Distressing coupled with the mention of "that day" made Eleanor's attention waver. *Distressing* for her father may well mean *exultant* for her. She forced herself to be still, to be the deferential daughter her father longed for her to be.

Agent Mallory, unaware of her father's penchant for telling distressing tales, delivered his news. "The ring has been stolen from the Egyptian

Museum," Mallory said. He slid his badge back in a vest pocket, and then opened a portfolio Eleanor had not noticed he was carrying under his arm.

"The ring?" Eleanor asked while Mallory shuffled through pages and loose papers. She wanted to leap at the papers, spread the pages out and devour what they contained. It was the same feeling that always claimed her before entering an unknown tomb. "Surely the Egyptian Museum possesses more than one ring, Agent Mallory." But for Eleanor Folley, there could be only one ring within that museum. She could feel the ring she wore on a chain beneath her blouse pressing between her breasts, almost insistent, as if asking if one of its three siblings had been found.

Mallory's brown eyes flicked from his papers to Eleanor, annoyance plainly writ in the fine line atop his straight nose. "Your 'Lady's' ring, Miss Folley," he said and produced, without looking away from Eleanor, a small photograph. He offered it to her.

Eleanor thought the photograph felt much heavier than it should. Memory, she supposed, could make even an image hard to hold. The mummified arm was as she remembered it, still wrapped in crumbling fabric. The desert had preserved a goodly portion of the desiccated skin, though at the delicate wrist and hand, it had shredded to reveal bone thin as winter twigs. Eleanor had last cradled the arm on a sandy plain outside Cairo. Her mother had pressed it into Eleanor's protective embrace, saving it from being trampled by metallic hooves mere moments before her mother . . . vanished? Was taken?

"She's not *my* Lady," Eleanor whispered, but could not release the photograph. Her fingers tightened until her thumbnail gleamed white. She thought she could smell the dust of Egypt: could taste it again on her tongue, a drug as strong as Agent Mallory's opium, heady and capable of carrying her backward in time.

Backward, turn backward . . .

The story of the Lady and her rings was supposed to be fiction, a tale told to child-Eleanor to carry her into sleep. But sleep had never come easily after the discovery of the *real* Lady and her four rings; the appearance of her horses, her guards. The memory of unearthing the mummy's arm with her mother had the power to make her feel all of twelve again; it made her remember everything her father so desired her to forget.

In the photograph, the wooden crate housing the arm had been crudely broken. A crowbar, Eleanor thought as she studied the deep bite marks that scarred the edge of the box. The arm, lying on a bed of muslin, had not been injured and still appeared to be colored with the fingerprints of Eleanor's own blood—but the Lady's fingers were bare. The single ring left to her was missing.

"Some of the museum's contents have been in transit of late," Mallory said in a low tone as another group of exhibitors passed them down the aisle, speaking exuberant French. "The Nile flooded the museum this past summer, leaving things unsettled."

"Unsettled" seemed an understatement. The flood damage had been a subject of great interest among Egyptologists and archaeologists. Her father had offered to shelter items needing housing in the Nicknackatarium in Dublin, but the curator scoffed. The great museums of the world had made similar gestures, and Renshaw Folley was but a discredited archaeologist whose wild tales of his wife's disappearance—which he now so wished to forget—had tarnished his credibility. He would forever be considered little more than a dabbler, a purveyor of knickknacks, never a serious archaeologist who meant to preserve artifacts before time swept them away.

"It is believed to be the work of a single person," Mallory continued after glancing behind him to ensure they were still alone. "A person with intimate knowledge of the museum and its security. A person who knew the Lady remained when so much else had been moved."

Eleanor's head came up sharply and she looked at Mallory, surprised to find his eyes on her. She knew the conversation was about to take a fateful turn. Mallory would know about her past—he was with Mistral, was he not? He would ask for her help and dredge up everything Eleanor had tried to leave behind for her father's sake. She wanted to tug Juliana away before Mallory could say more, for there was much her friend did not know.

"Miss Folley—"

"No, Agent Mallory."

A person with intimate knowledge of the museum and its security procedures. A person who knew the Lady remained when so much else had been moved. Eleanor could picture the steady hands bypassing locks, the shadowy form slipping past any guard. Fear whispered *Christian* in her ear, but she refused to believe him responsible for the theft.

Surely he would not—

Yet he so easily could.

How many valuable artifacts had she discovered with Christian Hubert? How many dangerous situations had they been in during their time together— and managed to get out of? She could not count. Could he have slipped into a museum, silent as snow, melting into shadows when the need arose?

Eleanor returned the photograph to Mallory and reclaimed her book from her father. The leather cover held the heat of his embrace, familiar and safe the way it had been that long-ago day. *"Eleanor, to me!"*

Her mother crying out for the arm. Men on mechanical horses, clockwork steads stronger than their living counterparts, emerging from the desert sands. Her mother running with the arm until those horses caught her. Until those men dismounted and—

Their mouths were not human . . .

"My reply to anything you may have to say is *no*," she added when Mallory appeared as if he were about to speak again. She set her jaw, an ache winding through her. "The Lady was lost to us years ago. Let her rest."

This was the line her father asked her to walk, the path from which she tried not to stray. But how could she not stray with that body still lost under ancient sands? With a ring now stolen, how could she not leap wholeheartedly from that path?

Eleanor left the men and Juliana to their own devices, too conflicted to stay. She hated the hope she felt—that all the mysteries could be solved; that, with answers, she might be able to put it all at last to rest. Her father would tell her no, please don't, as he ever had.

She left the gallery on trembling legs, to take deep, steadying breaths of the crisp October air outside. The Exposition would close at month's end. Why did Mallory have to find them now?

She pressed herself against the glass-and-iron flank of the building and stared down at her scarred hand. The worst of the marks were hidden beneath her sleeve, but every day they reminded her of the Lady, her mother, and the loss of both. Eleanor looked at Eiffel's tower rising against the blue sky. Only then did she decide that her father was right. Young men were not worth the trouble.

━◆━

Giza Plateau, Egypt ~ October 1881

Egypt tasted as Eleanor remembered: gritty, dry, and full of a hundred thousand secrets. She licked her lips and peered down the long corridor before her. A shadow moved across the ancient tomb walls.

Her grip closed hard on her lantern handle. The shadow did not come again, so she took a step toward the corridor's end, where according to her map it intersected with another long corridor. Eleanor had paid good money for the map and hoped it was accurate; she had no desire to get lost in this home of ancient bones. She reasoned that if another person were already in the tomb, she could follow them as easily as she could her map. But to what end? Who were they and what did they want here? This tomb was small, supposedly not well known. Foolish to follow them, she decided, studying her map once more before tucking it into her trouser pocket. She wasn't about to have come all this way only to have a shadow spook her. She was determined to sketch the hieroglyphs of the tomb's limestone walls, another step in her quest, and exit as neatly as she had entered.

"Imagination," she said, and her voice echoed back to her. "That's all. Only—" The shadow came again, resolving into the unmistakable shape of a body large enough to be male. "—imagination."

Eleanor lowered her lantern flame and stood in the half-light, listening. She heard the crunch of boots. As quietly as she could, she withdrew her revolver from its holster and moved down the shadowed corridor, toward the flicker of light that glowed around another corner.

At the corridor's end, the god of eternity, Heh, crouched above the doorway with open arms. In one hand he held the looped cross of an *ankh*, the symbol for "life," while the other clutched palm reeds. The *shen* ring— sign of infinity—was carved beside his head. Eleanor could not help but stare; the carving was flawless, blackened by time but otherwise untouched.

The man—were it such a creature rather than a minotaur or other beast of myth—had headed left, and Eleanor followed, foolish though it was. East, toward the sun and the burial chamber of a simple artisan. Simple perhaps, but still revered, for his tomb was beautiful and sparked Eleanor's imagination at every turn.

She could not imagine, however, what she discovered in the final chamber. The hieroglyphs were ruined, the walls defaced, history pummeled into small fragments, the floor strewn with debris. The man—quite solid, no longer a shadow—crouched beyond the sarcophagus with his lantern in front of the only untouched section of wall. He was prying out a section of the inscribed stone.

"No," Eleanor whispered.

The man turned to appraise her, his eyes colorless within the lamplit room. "Took you long enough," he said in a rumble of French. He turned back to his task. Large hands well suited to the work moved around the jagged slab of stone, working with hammer and chisel.

Despite her anger, Eleanor easily understood the French, even if she didn't immediately understand what he meant—took her long enough to what? Her anger clouded everything. Had he destroyed every marking, only to take the surviving panel with him? Eleanor looked at the carved desert hare beneath his hands, the word for "open," and the shining sun, "illumine." She saw no more, for the stone crumbled with his next chisel. He clicked his tongue.

"How could you?" Eleanor rushed forward as his hands came away, broken stone cascading over his boots, dust clouding the air between them. "Did you destroy *everything*? Is it all—"

"Gone."

He sounded as defeated as Eleanor felt. He stood and angled his lamp upward, the light slanting across the ceiling. Eleanor followed its path to see only a few gold stars remaining amid chipped blue paint. She looked to his lamp-brightened face and realized who he was.

Christian Hubert was well known in archaeological circles, an explorer beyond compare. He was the stuff of legends: wealthy, highly skilled, arrogant, and apparently leaning toward Egypt rather than Greece when it came to unearthing the ancient world. Knowing who he was, Eleanor rejected the idea that he'd meant to demolish the carvings, or inflict the rest of the damage around them. Then who had? His earlier words settled in.

"Took me long enough?" she asked.

Hubert tucked hammer and chisel into his rolled leather pack. If he was still disappointed by losing the final panel of stone, he didn't show it. "What's a little girl like you doing in a place like this? You should be at a tea party." His tone was balanced on the edge of laughter.

Eleanor's entire body trembled, not from anger, but despair. She looked away from Hubert, to the destruction of the chamber. Symbols remained here and there, but only in partial. Heads of horned vipers, tails of winged owls, nothing that would ever read as whole again. The words Eleanor had sought, the words that might explain where her mother had gone were rubble and dust around them.

Her father's words crept back to her, even in this place. *She's dead, Eleanor, she went where the dead go.* Eleanor could not believe that.

Hubert laughed when she didn't answer him, and soon the light around Eleanor faded. He had left and taken his lamp with him. For a long minute, she didn't care, could hardly muster the energy to turn the flame up on her own lantern to search the walls again, for something, anything. Even the broken sarcophagus in the center of the room was empty. Nothing remained of the artisan who had once made rings for a lady's hand.

Eleanor drew her notebook and pencil out, forcing her hands to steady, to at least make a record of what little remained. What had Flinders Petrie said—that Egypt was like a house on fire and one must preserve her before she vanished entirely, as though she had never been? Would this bit help Eleanor find what she sought? Her shaking fingers traced the fragment of a horned viper upon the wall, then fell away.

Outside again, the sunlight was dazzling and almost painfully warm compared to the cool shadows of the tomb. She was relieved to find her camel where she'd left it and no sign of Hubert. Eleanor hadn't thought *he*, the Great Explorer, would stoop so low as to steal the beast, though many in the desert would. She pressed her gauze-draped pith helmet back onto her head, but still found herself squinting against the sunlight as she mounted the camel and left the tomb site. She had placed too much hope within it.

⊰—⊱

She sought the smoky dimness of a tavern, numbing herself with cool draughts of black, foamy Egyptian beer. The men in the tavern paid her no attention, not even when she lit a cigarette. She was on her third when a large hand covered hers and drew the cigarette down from her lips.

"Those are bad for you, little girl."

That same amused and mocking tone. Christian Hubert spoke again in French, and while Eleanor was not yet fluent, French was coming easier than Greek or Latin. He lowered himself onto the bench beside Eleanor and stamped out her cigarette before helping himself to a long drink of her beer. He gestured to the bartender for another round while Eleanor tried to slide away from him. There was nowhere to go, save the end of the bench that led to a corner of the wall.

"What do you want?" she asked, keeping to French.

"I was going to ask you the same." The waiter arrived with more beer and Hubert paid, dipping his head in thanks. The thin shaft of sunlight snaking through the carved screen of the high window illuminated Hubert's golden hair; his eyes were revealed as green and not colorless as they had been within the tomb.

Eleanor closed her eyes and drank more beer. "Why couldn't you have sailed to Greece?" she asked. "There is plenty of marble left to unearth and cart away."

"How poetic you are with beer in your mouth."

She looked at him, wishing he were the dust of a thousand years. She was both impressed and repulsed by him—would he help or hinder her quest? Was he also on the path of the rings? If so, why? She sat a little straighter.

"How old are you?" he asked. "And a woman, at that." His eyes skimmed over her, taking in blouse and trousers, boots and weapons. "Folley's girl, hmm? They talk about you, raised amid the tombs. Some say you have more in common with the dead than with the living."

People talked about her? Good Lord. "And you?" she asked, feeling the sting of his words. Fresh from schooling at her father's side, she knew what she was doing, at least, unlike so many tomb robbers who destroyed much in their effort to reach gleaming gold. "Forty?"

Hubert tipped his head back and gave such a pleased laugh that many in the bar turned to look at them.

"Such poetry." He finished his beer and poured more from the clay pitcher. Dark and foamed at the edges, like old rivers, Eleanor thought.

"Age doesn't matter," Hubert said and clinked his mug against hers. "But may you live to catch me in years."

They sat in silence, Eleanor content to watch him drink while she tried to make sense of things. Why had he been in the tomb? Before she could ask—

"What *were* you doing in that tomb?" he asked. "The tomb is small, and you . . . Well."

Eleanor flinched. That single word felt like a barb in her skin. "Why were *you* there? No one cares about it. What does an artisan matter, when the pyramids of Giza could be visited?" That only made the destruction of the tomb more confusing. If the artisan didn't matter, why destroy his burial place?

"Exactly." Hubert touched the bracelet around Eleanor's right wrist, hemp and shells. She withdrew her hand before he could look closer and see the scars beneath it. "Tell me that you've come to see firsthand what you learned. Lectures weren't enough. You needed to see it for yourself."

"If that story pleases you, by all means."

His mouth moved in a smile, one that made Eleanor think of jackals. He was enjoying this game. "But it doesn't. That's not why you were there."

Eleanor wanted very much to leave the tavern, but she could not escape the table without Hubert moving. With a steady hand, she reached out to touch the long fall of golden hair against his cheek, tucked it behind his ear, and let her fingers linger. This was more foolish than following his shadow, she thought, noting that his neck was smudged with dust. She suspected her own was as well.

Took you long enough, he had said. *He knows what I'm doing . . . but why?*

As she thought it would, her touch spurred him to motion, but not away from her, rather toward. She should have been shocked, but men were confusing creatures. She slid her hand down to his neck in an effort to keep him at bay.

"I don't think you had better—"

Hubert's mouth closed over hers in a kiss tasting of dust and beer. Eleanor leaned forward, as if to return the kiss, but her hand tightened on him and her teeth dug into his lip. Hubert pulled back, laughing. He stood from the bench and lifted his nearly empty glass to her.

"To your next raid, little girl," he said. "May it be more profitable."

Eleanor could only agree with the sentiment as Hubert left the tavern for the relative cool of an Egyptian evening. Her heart hammered madly in her chest and she shook her head. Entirely foolish.

Paris, France ~ October 1889

Eleanor brought her father his evening tea and settled into the patchwork-covered wing chair across from him. Their rented rooms were comfortable, and they had burrowed deeply in, having been there since May for the start of the Exposition Universelle. Juliana had retired to her own room some time ago, leaving Eleanor and her father to while away the evening as they were accustomed. Eleanor wished Juliana would join them more often, but understood why she didn't; it was difficult to spend time with a man one might be falling in love with when that man's mind was constantly either on his work or occupied with memories of his dead wife.

Eleanor moved one of her pawns on the chessboard between them, which drew a grunt from her father as he sipped his steaming tea. Needing something to do with her hands while he planned his next attack, Eleanor picked up her needlework, but could not concentrate on the innumerable stitches before her. It was ridiculous, making patterns on fabric when she should be quizzing Agent Mallory on the missing ring. Her mind could not let go of the image of the Lady's hand without its ring.

Beyond the fourth-story windows, the Paris rain poured. Eleanor wanted to vanish within the storm; perhaps it would silence her mind to the Lady and Christian, to her mother and Egypt. She wished she could take her own advice and allow the Lady to rest, wished again that Juliana had lingered, for she could have excused herself from her father's preoccupied presence and talked to the woman long into the night about such matters.

Juliana would save her from herself as she had so many times before in the small hours when she could not sleep. Juliana would hold Eleanor's hands so Eleanor wouldn't be tempted to slide her fingers into the ring she wore about her neck and ask it to carry her away.

Her father captured one of Eleanor's knights and she stared at the board, angry with herself. It was a mistake she had made as a child. She discarded her needlework and saw only defeat on the chessboard battlefield before her. The ancient game of Senet was more to her liking, but that board stood dusty in a far corner of their home in Ireland, neglected since her mother's disappearance—as so much had been.

"You're distracted," Renshaw said. He added his tea cup to the flotsam on the table: a bookmark without a book, a worn notebook with a fraying bind, a handful of shelled almonds, a tea strainer, a pencil chewed nearly to its core. Renshaw steepled his fingers and considered Eleanor over them.

"Don't study me as though I'm a tomb. I've set everything aside that you asked me to."

Having changed into more comfortable trousers earlier, Eleanor drew her knees to her chest. As always, there hung over her the feeling that her father's eyes could look into her very soul. He would see every minuscule crack, would pry each open and peer inside to discover what she did not want him to see. Eleanor moved her bishop to claim a pawn, but there was little to gain from the move.

"Even the most hidden tomb eventually gives itself up," he said. "The ground shifts, the sands part, and there is the past laid clean before us." He exhaled and reclined into the chair. "I wish Mallory had not come to us today."

"No, he is—" she drew a breath, conflicted again "—the last thing we needed."

"His is not the first disturbance into this little life of ours." Her father pushed his glasses from the tip of his nose back to the bridge and did not consider the chessboard, though Eleanor hoped his attention would fall there. "I know you, and you have not let the Lady rest. The lady—*you*, dear Eleanor—protests too much."

Even if he didn't immediately understand something he saw, Renshaw Folley filed it away until the day came that he did understand. Had he seen Eleanor reading the books he asked her not to read? Had he leafed through her notebooks?

"How *could* I let it rest?" Eleanor watched at her father in the low lamplight. "I don't believe Mother is dead."

"Eleanor." Renshaw pushed away from the chessboard and rose from his chair. They were perhaps the worst words she could have said to him. She possessed a singular talent for being the fly in someone's otherwise perfect soup.

Her father braced his hands against the windowsill and stared at the wet night. Beyond the reflections in the windowpane, Eleanor could see the lights of Paris gleam under the new coat of rain. Across the Seine, Eiffel's Exposition tower stood as a smudge against the sky; the buildings of the Exposition were momentarily quiet and still. Their rooms overlooked the length of the Champs de Mars, a perfect witness to all Exposition activities, but tonight it could not occupy Eleanor's mind the way it usually could. Mallory and the missing ring occupied her attention.

Agent Mallory would come back. Eleanor believed that as firmly as she believed her mother was not dead. Mallory was not the kind to let something rest; she had seen that in his eyes. He would return and ask Eleanor the thing he must ask. And she—she would say yes, despite the pain it would bring her father. Eleanor would help him recover the ring because she hoped it would lead to her mother. She had to know.

"Have you read my research then?" she asked when he said nothing more.

"Yes, and it's better relegated to one of Mr. Verne's fantastical novels if you ask me." He didn't turn from the window, but Eleanor could see his reflection: his creased forehead, the tears that shone behind his glasses. He drew them off and began to polish the lenses with the hem of his untucked, wrinkled shirt.

Eleanor felt all of eight years old and wanted to apologize. Her research had hurt him, as she had known it would. Still, she let the apology go unspoken, because it wouldn't get them where they needed to go. If they didn't solve this now, then when? "It's why I never shared it with you. I knew it would hurt—"

"Not hurt," he said as he again pushed his glasses back into place. He looked at Eleanor once and then back at Paris. "I'm angry and sad."

A bad combination in a Folley, Eleanor knew all too well.

"You've shut yourself away from the rest of the world, Eleanor, and continue to dream of something impossible. Your mother is dead. I have prayed for you to accept this. How can you not? How can you cling to this fancy? I asked you to give this up years ago."

"I tried." Eleanor shuddered, feeling cold again as she recalled coming home from her journeys, unannounced and soaked to the bone with cold Dublin rain. The rain dripped to the stone floor, droplets leaving a trail behind her as she admitted her failure to learn anything new about her mother's disappearance. As she'd traveled deeper into Egypt, into Israel, and Greece, Morocco, the path she had once so clearly seen dissolved like sugar under rain.

The longing to know, to understand, was reborn in Paris that spring, surrounded as Eleanor was by a wealth of information on Egypt and its peoples. The Louvre's Department of Egyptian Antiquities brimmed with thousands of treasures, and she had spent hours studying, sketching. As wonderful as it was to see the crypt of Osiris or read the countless stèlae housed in the museum rooms, it was heart-wrenching that the items were no longer in Egypt. Even the Luxor obelisk in the Place de la Concord seemed to reach back toward Egypt, where it belonged with its sibling. Egypt ran like blood in her veins; she could taste it on her tongue even now. Agent Mallory sought to draw her into the past the way she believed her mother had been drawn. Men on mechanical beasts, ripping Dalila Folley from the quiet of an archaeological dig, perhaps wanting only the body they'd found, the rings the Lady possessed. There had been a glimmer against the horizon, like the waver of light on moving water, a shimmering heat mirage, and then— Nothing. Quiet, dust, her mother gone, her own blood in the sand. Eleanor could not refuse the opportunity to know the truth of that moment.

Eleanor crossed to her father, taking him by the shoulders to draw him from the window's chill and back to his chair. She tucked his favorite wool blanket around his knees and offered him the tea again. He took the cup and sipped, looking a hundred years old, as fragile as any of the papyri in their small collection. His eyes were heavy with sorrow and regret and a dozen other emotions Eleanor did not want to name. She did not want to know how deeply she had hurt this man, but she could not help but see it in the vulnerable lines of his face.

She drew his glasses off and placed them on the untidy table. She pulled the blanket to his chin and dropped a kiss on his forehead while nudging the ottoman closer for his feet.

"Sleep and don't worry," she said.

"If Mallory comes back—"

"I'll send him away." It was a lie. As much as she wanted to honor her father's wishes, Eleanor knew she could not send the agent away. Not if she were ever to understand her mother's disappearance. Not if she meant to put the past firmly to rest. She turned the lamp down and squeezed her father's hand before moving away.

"Eleanor?"

She looked back at him. He lifted his feet onto the ottoman and she wished she could not count the times he had slept in chairs rather than the single bed in his room. The bed, narrow and meant for one, was still too large for him, he said. Though he wished to deny it, his grip on Dalila Folley had not lessened these many years, either.

"Father?" she asked.

"Checkmate in two."

CHAPTER TWO

Everyone carried secrets. Virgil Mallory knew this better than most. He was reluctant to pry Miss Folley from the comfortable world she knew, reluctant to expose her past when she appeared to set it behind her. Still, he would. If Hubert or anyone else thought to muck about in the past to change the future, he meant to prevent that.

He ducked as he stepped into the four-in-hand, fingers already ripping at his tie as the carriage moved into the streets, away from the Exposition Universelle and Eiffel's god-awful tower. He had not worn a tie since Caroline's memorial, but today, venturing into the much-loathed public, he felt it was best to look like what he was.

"What I am," he muttered. "Agent. Only that."

The tie unknotted with a whisper. He pulled the length of it loose and crumpled it between shaking hands. The beast inside him clawed to be let out, and Virgil closed his eyes, sinking into the cushioned bench. His fingers itched for the opium pipe, the one thing certain to quiet the creature within. No pipe was at hand, so he stroked the ring of silver around his right index finger, rubbing the worn skulls along its smooth circle, praying for calm. *Viver disce, cognita mori.* The words engraved on the band bade him to learn to live, yet remember death; he had difficulty with the former, though the latter came easily enough now.

By the time he reached the townhouse that Mistral used for its Paris offices, he was only somewhat more composed. Stepping into the building provided another measure of calm, as he preferred places he knew to those he did not. It was easier to control the beast when he knew he could control his surroundings. The Exposition Universelle had been a small horror with its countless people, machines, and glassed ceiling. The townhouse, with its walnut doors and carpeted stairways, was home as well as workplace; the building boasted meeting rooms, offices, and private residences. Virgil knew each and every room, each and every hall.

So too did he know Miss Baker, a fixture in the Paris office for as long as he could remember. She greeted him in the foyer as she always did and offered to take his coat.

"Are they waiting?"

Miss Baker nodded, and Virgil stepped past her with a muttered thank-you before taking the stairs by pairs. He heard conversation even before reaching the upper drawing room and let himself in without knocking. Half a dozen agents milled about the room. The director himself was distracted, which allowed Virgil to move, almost unseen, toward his usual high-backed chair beside his partner, Michael Auberon.

Auberon looked every inch the gentleman Virgil wished he himself were. His posture was straight, shoulders broad. His brown eyes conveyed only a sense of ease and confidence. His tie was impeccable, his waistcoat without wrinkle, a riot of gold vines and birds scattering over the indigo fabric. He appeared wholly comfortable in such attire—the collar not pulling too tight, another self not attempting to subdue the face he showed everyone.

"Don't say it," Virgil said as Auberon's attention dropped to Virgil's own loosened collar. Virgil placed the remains of the bow tie on the table before him.

Auberon, his skin as dark as the mahogany table they occupied, cleared his throat and studied the mangled fabric before he began to neatly fold it into thirds. His hands were steady, broad, and sure. "I did tell you," he said in a low tone.

Virgil inclined his head, silently allowing that Auberon was right. He shouldn't have attempted the tie. Later, in his own rooms, he would have to look in the mirror, would have to admit what it truly was, that Auberon was right when it came to Virgil no longer denying his true self. A wolf in gentleman's clothing.

"Agent Mallory spent the morning with the Folleys at the Exposition," Director Walden said.

Virgil sat a little straighter in his chair, as the other agents settled into their own and the meeting came somewhat to order.

"Has progress been made?"

"Mister Folley seems to understand the gravity of the matter," Virgil said. Should the ancient portal be opened once more, the damage one might inflict upon the world was unknowable, and Mistral preferred to hedge all bets.

"And Miss Folley?" a fellow agent asked.

Virgil didn't like the edge to the man's voice. Virgil had no doubt Miss Folley understood the situation as well, if not better than, her father. It was rumored she had seen the portal, but he remained reluctant to admit to the committee that this was the case. Virgil held his silence.

"What if she doesn't cooperate?" another agent asked.

"She *will* cooperate," Virgil said and stood up from the table, the animal inside him lunging forward. He drew it back with an effort that left his hands shaking. What made it worse was that every man at the table knew what he struggled with.

He looked at the men gathered around the oval table with its small green lamps, each man a near reflection of the other with their black suits and perfectly knotted ties. Auberon alone might understand Virgil's perspective— that of the outsider—being the only Negro in the room. Otherwise, Virgil felt as though he was, for the first time, not truly part of this group.

"There are no guarantees," one of the men said.

"No, but she . . . " Virgil's voice trailed off. He didn't feel he could explain to them what he sensed of Eleanor Folley, but he attempted to. "She is not a typical woman, gentlemen," he said. "Read her file." *Not the way I read it, going to bed with it every night. Perhaps that's why I feel protective of her.* "She was raised in a non-traditional household, schooled in archaeology from a very young age by an Irish father and an Egyptian mother, *in the field.* She worked with Christian Hubert, of all people." *And, rumor also says, fiercely loved him.* "She has a connection to this that none of us do. I believe she will come around."

"You'll meet with her again," Director Walden said.

Virgil thought of Eleanor Folley, little more than a librarian at first glance with her dust-coated skirts, smudge of dirt on her cheek, nutmeg curls speared through with two pencils. A closer look revealed umber eyes that held both old hurt and lingering fears; a mouth that likely knew a curse or four, yet kept silent in deference to her father. Hard-worn boots beneath her skirts: dusty and not dainty or laced with ribbons. She smelled of Pear's Soap, which made him hungry, and bore a faint scar along the bottom edge of her chin. He knew too much about her and yet nothing at all. The person he had come to know on paper had managed to surprise him in person.

What had she seen in tombs she raided with Hubert? What truths had they unearthed about the Lady's ring? That information was most vital to Virgil, for with Eleanor's knowledge, he might further his own understanding of Caroline's activities in Egypt. Might understand if it were linked to the strange properties Director Walden had mentioned in association with the Lady. He absently touched his own ring.

"Virgil."

Auberon's gentle voice drew Virgil from his thoughts. He looked to his partner and then Walden. Even though it hadn't been a question, Virgil answered the director. "I will meet with her again." Even if it meant going back to the Exposition's cacophony.

As soon as the words left Virgil's mouth, the men around the table began to rise and disperse. The matter was now in Virgil's hands, and while they would hold him accountable for the good or ill that followed, they wouldn't harp too much at this stage.

Auberon lingered, and Virgil was grateful. Looking at Auberon was often like looking at himself, for they were such strange creatures to everyone else. A wolf and a Negro, loose in Paris. What was the world coming to?

The room emptied, leaving them amid the gloom of the afternoon, faces from the oil paintings on the walls barely swimming through the lamplight to look upon them. The building was old; Virgil could almost feel the years pressing down on him. Had Miss Folley felt the same inside a museum or tomb?

"I don't envy you this," Auberon said.

Virgil smoothed his hands over the wrinkled tie on the table. "I don't envy *her* what's to come. My part is small." Small, but if it served to finally unite the various bits of information Virgil had collected over the years, important.

Auberon's hand curled over Virgil's shoulder and gave a firm squeeze. Confidence always flowed from those hands, and Virgil took comfort in it. Familiar.

"You only have to convince her that reclaiming what may have taken her mother's life is a good thing," Auberon said.

And that, Virgil thought, might be as simple as leaving his own wife's death behind. Which was to say, not a simple thing at all.

Kharkov Governorate, Russian Empire ~ December 1885

Fat, wet snowflakes swirled down from the night sky to land on Virgil's face and hair. The wolf inside him wanted unleashing so that he could run in the snowstorm, but the agent he was wouldn't allow it. He stared in dismay at the derailed train on the tracks below the low rise where he and his partner crouched. Come sunrise and God willing, he would be en route to Athens to drop the requested satchel into the hands of Gregale agents, and then rendezvous with his wife Caroline after too much time apart. But first, there was an intelligence satchel to retrieve, the world to save.

"This was unexpected," Joel Abernach said.

Virgil looked to his partner and snorted. The German, who was untroubled by the snow or cold, had a way of understating everything. "Unexpected, but of use to us," Virgil said.

He didn't care that the royal train carried Russia's tsar; their goal was a Crimean scientist and his satchel of research into the organs of the mind. Phrenology fascinated some, Virgil supposed, but he didn't believe there were countless organs rolling about his skull. He divided his mind cleanly in two: man and beast.

Virgil looked toward the train. "Come on." His breath fogged in the cold air, and the wolf inside relaxed as he finally slipped into motion and headed toward the train. The scent of spilled coal saturated the night air, sharp and oily, but Virgil became aware of another scent as they neared. There were freshly dead bodies inside the wreckage. The beast within him gave a sudden start.

There was enough activity within the wreck to cover their approach. Steam poured from the derailed train, over the rails, and provided good cover as well. The cries of the trapped and injured reached Virgil's ears and he felt only a moment's hesitation. He and Joel could assist the rescuers or center in on their assignment, the satchel. He preferred the latter, mostly to not muddy the waters; Russia was not their normal territory, and he had no desire to upset the balance of matters that didn't wholly concern him. He gestured Joel to the left, while he circled right.

His mind turned to Athens, to clear blue waters licking ivory sand, to sunlight, and to Caroline. The long absences were only one reason Virgil had been reluctant to marry. How could a marriage thrive when he was often on one side of the world and she the other? No spouse should have to endure such a thing. When both parties were Mistral agents, it only further complicated matters. Virgil saw more of his partner Joel than his wife, and while Joel was enjoyable to work with, he wasn't the one Virgil had married. Wasn't the one he wanted to come home to at the end of a mission.

Joel vanished into another train car ahead while Virgil paused at the rear, waving a hand to disperse a billow of steam. The caboose sat half on and half off the rails, black window blinds drawn. The metal door hung open, its latch broken from the impact of whatever the train had hit.

Virgil climbed onto the car. Metal creaked under his weight, the hiss of escaping steam from broken pipes mingling with the distant cries from the passengers-turned-rescuers.

It will get easier, Caroline was fond of telling him. Virgil wanted to believe her, wanted to believe that the separations would become a normal part of their routine, but in six years of marriage, nothing had changed. The time away from her didn't feel normal, even if Caroline seemed to thrive with the mishmash of schedules. She adored their brief reunions and, after planning lavish dinners and hard lovemaking, would rest content in his arms. Her white-blond hair would spill loose from its usual bun, and she would smile a smile he so rarely saw but loved even so. He had no doubt Caroline would say that was *why* he loved it.

"If we had this every day," she would say, stroking slim fingers down Virgil's bare arm, "it wouldn't be the same."

And Virgil would think, no, it would be better. He kept his silence, because there was little point in arguing the same matter for the hundredth time.

But this time was different; she had sent an urgent telegrapheme. Caroline had something urgent to share. After his current mission, could he meet her in Athens?

She had never asked to meet him. What had changed? He didn't want his mind to wander, because the list of what he hoped for was long. Had she come around to his way of thinking, that they needed more time together? He knew that neither of them would leave Mistral for the sake of their marriage, and perhaps that spoke loudest of all. They were both dedicated to the organization before they were dedicated to each other.

Virgil's eyes swept the train car and, finding it lacking what he sought, he moved through the toppled and smoking debris to the next car. The windows had been blown inward from the impact here, glass covering every surface in a glittering veil. A pair of well-worn shoes peeked out from under a desk. Virgil circled the desk to find their Crimean scientist flat on the floor, neck slashed by a shard of window.

"Bad luck," Virgil murmured and closed the unseeing eyes before he began to search for the satchel.

The train car was a collection of debris and overturned furniture. With every step Virgil took, the car creaked and tipped further on the tracks. Chairs dangled out windows, books spilled across the polished wood floor through more broken glass, a small set of assay scales lay crushed beneath a metal globe.

Seeing little else of immediate interest, Virgil backtracked to the dead body with the good shoes. He knelt in the glass and lifted the man's hands. Shaking back the jacket sleeves, he discovered a metal cuff ringing the left wrist. A short length of chain dangled without a matching cuff on its opposite end. Virgil's eyes went to the man's neck, and a closer look revealed the manner of the injury: a clean sweep that looked intentionally made.

"Hell," Virgil whispered and straightened from his position. He reached for his revolver. It was too much to ask that a mission go smoothly.

It was also too much to ask that they reach the satchel first, for, as Virgil stood, a black-clad figure approached him from the neighboring car, carrying the satchel with its dangling handcuff. The train car shifted again, metal groaning in angry protest, and Virgil reached for the crooked desk to steady himself. The approaching figure let out a startled cry and grabbed the splintered doorframe.

"Impassable, then?" Virgil asked.

The person's head jerked up in surprise, clearly not expecting company within the demolished train. He aimed his revolver at the figure, steady and true. The scent that rolled from the stranger proved their sudden, desperate fear. Virgil smelled blood, too, and noted the crimson staining the hands that clutched the doctor's case. Carrion stench and something else, something familiar. Something feminine.

"Mallory—"

Joel's voice rose from behind the woman, startling her again. She moved like lightning thrown from a stormy sky, bright and swift. She drew her own revolver from the belt at her waist and turned to fire before Virgil could react; when he did, it was with a savage snarl.

The first shot caught Joel in the jaw, and he crumpled in a splatter of blood. Virgil dropped low to avoid the second and third shots, then plowed his shoulder into the woman's knees, dropping her into the broken glass.

The satchel tumbled free, but she held fast to her revolver. Virgil dropped his own, covering her hand as she attempted to angle the barrel into him. Her hand felt somehow familiar beneath the blood covering her. Her free elbow pistoned into his ribs.

Virgil's hand closed hard around her revolver, trying to wrest it from her grip. Beyond their struggle, he caught sight of Joel, motionless in a spreading pool of blood. The woman's arm snaked around Virgil's neck and she pressed her cheek to his. They had danced this way before, hadn't they? The thought was abrupt.

Ah God—don't ask this of me.

"He's already dead," she said as her free hand fisted into his hair to hold him firm, to keep him from looking away from Joel. Beyond the neat point of blood against Joel's jaw, Virgil spied the blossoming wound at the top of his skull, blood and brain soaking his hair.

The wolf within him had been close all night, but never so close as this. At her words—that voice held familiarity, too—and Joel dead in his own blood, Virgil could feel the claws, could feel his human flesh part to give way to the thing inside him, that which he hated above all things. It wasn't always the moon that controlled the wolf; anger was an equally powerful force in this equation. Virgil allowed the anger to consume him; his human form was ripped away.

It was no gentle transformation and never came any easier. The shedding of one form for another might have provided solace for some, but it was not so for Virgil Mallory. Blood and other viscous fluids spilled as flesh gave way to chocolate-colored fur; bones twisted and reformed as the wolf consumed the human. Arms rippled with corded muscle, turning to legs; clawed paws devoured hands, and his once-fine suit fell to shreds.

The woman in his arms screamed. It was primal and went to the core of the beast he had become. He drew in the scent of her again—too familiar, no matter the terror and disbelief—and then ripped into her. His claws delved beyond her mantle, into breast and belly to spill flesh and blood to the glass-strewn floor around them. The scent of her blood hit his nose and a strained growl escaped him before it turned to a full-fledged howl.

Some part of his animal brain begged for quiet, or maybe it was a lingering shred of the human within him. Humans: he didn't want them here, didn't need them discovering this. *No.*

He bowed his bloody head and pressed his nose to the silver ring that gleamed within the fur of his paw. The beast used the ring as a focus, to calm himself and draw backward, before he tore the entire train from the tracks.

Virgil pulled himself out as if emerging from a tar pit, bones piecing themselves back together, goosebump-riddled skin replacing the brindled fur. He took a shuddering breath as reason intruded where only violence had reigned before. Naked but for his old silver ring and shaking, he moved toward Joel, to ascertain what he already knew.

"Vir . . . gil."

Virgil blinked. *Let me be wrong.* He turned from Joel's body to the ravaged woman on the floor behind him. She reached a bloody hand toward him, crooking her fingers once.

"Virgil."

No. The denial was swift inside him; how expert he had become at denying everything these past years, denying the wolf, denying what he did while his body was given up to it. It wasn't him, it was a thing he couldn't fight, a thing beyond his control.

Virgil reached for the hood that covered Caroline's face and he drew it off. White-blond hair spilled over the glittering shards covering the floor, the green eyes that had looked into his on their wedding day already growing distant and unfocused. She tried to hold her hand up, but it dropped against her slashed belly.

There had been signs, Virgil supposed as he lifted Caroline's hand into his own. Her blood was still warm. There had been signs that something wasn't right with her; too many secretive meetings at work, too many middle-of-the-night airship flights to destinations unknown. "Work" only covered so much.

She sputtered blood. Virgil folded Caroline's arm across her chest, but kept hold of her hand, his mind leaping in an effort to understand what was before him. There were questions, accusations, but he forced them away, knowing that this, that Caroline's betrayal, answered all questions and explained all accusations.

A ragged laugh escaped him as he realized how much they had in common after all. It wasn't easy, leading such a life, but Caroline always flourished under a challenge. She loved it—*this* was the life she loved, the life that kept her away from Virgil.

"God, no. No."

He repeated the word like a litany, as if it would mend what the beast inside him had torn apart. His free hand trembled as he pressed it against her ruined belly. Logically he knew there was no putting her back together, but still he tried to gather her up and put her right.

"Caroline."

Her fingers twitched in Virgil's grip. "Wanted to tell . . . you."

Hell. He'd wanted to tell *her* about the thing inside him, but had never taken the time to find the proper words. In all these years, both of them had denied and hidden so many things. And now, the thing inside him had taken her life.

"Sweet bird," he whispered and stroked shaking fingers across her pale cheek. He left strands of scarlet there, her own blood. "Caroline—no." The taste of her in his mouth made him want to retch.

Caroline blinked once, trying to concentrate on him again. "Don't . . . let go."

Virgil held firm to Caroline's hand until it went limp, until her eyes rolled to the side and went blank. Only then did he turn and retch into the mess around them. He screamed until he was hoarse and empty of all things, until there was only ice in the center of him.

Virgil extracted his bloody hand from hers and forced himself to pat her body down. This was the job. A distance. He didn't expect to find anything of use on her body; agents went in clean, whatever agency they worked for. *Who was she with? Good Lord, who?*

An unfamiliar growl intruded into the whirlwind of his mind. Virgil's head snapped up, senses coming back to the here and now, mindful again of the unfamiliarity of the landscape around him. A jackal crouched in the train wreckage, lips curled back from gleaming, ragged teeth. Another five jackals approached from behind. The longer Virgil kept his hand on Caroline, the more insistent the warning growls became. Jackals this far north? Virgil couldn't fathom it, but knew he didn't have the time.

Virgil closed Caroline's eyes and reached for his revolver in the debris. He rose on bare feet, naked and bloody, to face half a dozen jackals that appeared intent on eating him alive. As the wind shifted, he could smell others coming and the rotting carrion stench of vultures.

He reached for the creature inside him, and disgust consumed him. The idea of allowing it to resurface after it had killed Caroline was a thought he could not endure. He lifted his revolver and managed to get one shot off, but the jackals did not fully retreat. The closer they came, the stranger they smelled to Virgil. They were not wholly animals, he thought; they were like him.

He took a surprised step backward, able to claim Joel's body if not Caroline's as the jackals crept ever closer. They didn't look vested in Joel as they did Caroline. Was she with them? Virgil stared at her, knowing to his marrow that she was not wolf or jackal, but he couldn't explain the creatures' behavior.

Virgil hefted Joel over his shoulder, grabbed the satchel, and staggered out of the wreckage. Naked, bloody, hauling his dead partner—not exactly the way he had envisioned the mission. He moved swiftly toward the shadowed airship that hovered across the murky plain.

No Athens, he thought numbly, but opium's blessed haze? Soon. *Soon.*

⟨⟩

Paris, France ~ October 1889

He was always careful, exceedingly so.

He never brought opium to the townhouse—though his first choice would have been to partake of the smoke within his private rooms—and always made certain that no one followed him to the den he did favor. If anyone did, he was not aware of it. Word never reached his superiors; so far as they knew, Virgil Mallory was not a habitué of any such place. He was a wolf, indeed, and often kept odd hours because of that, but he was not suspect.

Thus it was in his usual comfort that Virgil accepted the pipe from Clementine, a small Chinese girl with a gleaming black braid worn over her right shoulder. The idea that she was too young to be in a place such as this crossed Virgil's mind again, but he would not judge. When she offered to stay and assist as she always did, he shooed her away as *he* always did. She bowed, braid whispering over her brocade robe, and backed out of the low-lit private room. She closed the door and allowed him to lock it. He paid extra for the privacy, but then many did.

The couch was covered in brocade, a deep blue that recalled the color of his mother's eyes. Virgil stroked his fingers over the fabric once, then set to the task before him. The pipe was his favored ivory, pale against his long fingers, while the bowl was a jade shaded toward the color of Caroline's eyes. How many eyes would haunt him, because he recognized Miss Folley's in the spill of umber pillows around the couch, in the gleam of the blanket draped over the curled couch arm.

He set flame to the opium lamp. The oil caught and funneled heat upward, a perfect channel to warm the jade bowl of his pipe. He packed the opium with care and never minded going slow, for the entire process had become ritual to him. Virgil held the long pipe in his left hand and crossed himself with his right, over lips and brow and heart.

"Holy Virgin Mary," he said in the silence of the room, "you are reigning in glory with Jesus your Son. Remember us in our sadness. Look kindly on all who are suffering or fighting against any difficulty."

He brought the pipe to his mouth and took a long draw, bringing the vapors slowly into him. It was a curious thing, like the trespassing of a small hand inside his chest, a hand that took hold of the beast and kept it happily caged.

"Have pity on those who are separated from someone they love." Smoke curled from his mouth as he whispered, pale tendrils of sweetness glancing over him. He followed the smoke trail, mind turning to Eleanor Folley, to the glimpse of her scarred hand and the buried warmth in her eyes. Like called to like, he thought, and didn't try to push the images aside. "Have pity on the loneliness of our hearts."

He reclined into the spill of brocade and opium-soaked silk. His gaze drifted to the ceiling, where more fabric billowed. It resembled a cerulean sea bottled in this small room, but as the opium began to have its say, the walls seemed to dissolve. He was no longer in the den, but floated on a sea of blue, which merged with a golden sky.

"Have pity on the weakness of our faith and love," he whispered and inhaled another long draw of vapor from the pipe. He felt the wolf within him retreat, massive head lowering in complete submission.

But as the wolf withdrew, Virgil felt a hollow sensation he had never known before. The wolf bowed, and in the space he had occupied, there was nothing. There was a strange void where Virgil could not find purchase.

He continued his prayers in murmurs, half-formed words falling from careless lips. "Have pity on those who are weeping." He pictured Caroline, afloat on the same blue waters, pale hair spilling about her. "On those who are praying." These words, wreathed in opium smoke, were still a prayer to him: a connection to a thing he felt beyond the wolf. "On those who are fearful."

Fearful. Virgil's head reeled and the wolf rose up. So fearful, but not him. *God, that was not me,* and he gasped for air. The pipe tumbled from his hands and claws appeared before his eyes. Not me. *Not me.* It became a chant in his head, over and over, until well-known hands wrapped round the clawed paws and drew him back to the safety of the couch.

"Holy Mother," he whispered, seeking an anchor in the prayer. There came a laugh, a low thunder that Virgil reached for. "Please obtain for all of us hope," he continued.

"And peace, with justice," said the thunder, a voice that was both familiar and not as the smoke seeped into Virgil's mind.

"Amen."

He drifted, a boat without shore. He didn't know how long, but when he came back to himself Auberon was there, crouched across from the lacquered tray with its pipes and the still-burning lamp. The flame was low, nearly gone. Virgil blinked, trying to erase the sight, for Auberon should not be here witnessing this. Had he picked the lock? Virgil knew it was not beyond him, nor beyond Clementine's tender heart to lead Auberon to this room.

"Ah, God."

Auberon's slash of a mouth moved in a smile. "No, not that, my friend." He poured water into a cut crystal glass, offering it to Virgil.

Virgil took the glass and drank, which cleared his gummy mouth if not his mind. Friend, Auberon called him, not partner. "You should not be here."

Michael Auberon: named for an archangel, but always preferring to be called by his surname—which he shared with the magical king of fairies.

Virgil supposed it would have been easy for Auberon to tell him that *he* should not be here, either, but he didn't.

"I have tried to respect your needs as I watch you leave the townhouse most evenings." Auberon poured himself a glass of water as well and took a sip, his Adam's apple working above the precisely tied fabric at his neck. "But in so doing, I have neglected my need to keep you clear-minded and an asset to Mistral."

Enough of the opium still held sway with Virgil that it didn't occur to him to be cross with his partner—his friend. Was Auberon sent to watch over him? Virgil didn't care. He looked at the man who had never attempted to replace Joel Abernach, but had only tried to be a good partner in his own right. The man who had succeeded in doing such from the beginning.

Virgil gestured to the opium tray. "Will you join me?"

"I cannot." That silence again, as Auberon cupped the glass in his large hands and watched Virgil with fathomless eyes. "You will never silence the wolf," he said. "Surely you know this and yet you persist? The wolf is part of you, my friend."

"It is *not*." The denial was swift.

Auberon moved swiftly himself, throwing his water glass to the side and batting Virgil's away next. Still becalmed by the opium, Virgil did little when Auberon charged. The large man bore Virgil back to the couch, his hand fisting into Virgil's shirt collar. Auberon pulled hard, ripping the shirt open to expose the vicious scar that marked Virgil from neck to belly.

"Part of you," Auberon said. "Look upon yourself!"

It was the one thing Virgil did not wish to do. It was the reason he came to this place, to forget himself and silence the creature inside. He bucked Auberon off and slid backward over the low couch, crouching in a tangle of blanket and pillows. One hand came up, to touch his scarred chest. His fingers curled deep, aching, and he thought of Eleanor's own scar around her wrist, across her hand. Another on her chin.

"Have pity on the weakness of our faith." Auberon spoke the words of the prayer in a resonant voice, refusing to back down from Virgil.

Virgil felt the wolf inside him *leap*, though the beast should have been well and truly asleep. His lips curled back over his teeth. "Do not do this." It was close to a plea. Fear curled in Virgil's belly. What if the opium no longer worked? What if his anger devoured him even so? God, no. *No.*

"And you, do not do *this*," Auberon said. "Accept that this creature is you." He kicked the lacquered opium tray over, spilling pipes and matches and the lamp, the flame of which smothered in its own oil. The flames of the other lamps in the room stuttered. "You were but a child, Virgil. Savaged and scarred, but still alive and now whole and miraculous. If this is not the doing of God, what can it be?"

Virgil said nothing. How many times had he asked that question? What did God want of him? Had He meant *this*? What God could? By all rights, he should have died in the wreck of his own flesh and broken bones, but he hadn't. He hadn't.

"How alike we are," Auberon whispered. "Wretches who wish they were anything but that which looks back upon them in the mirror."

Virgil bowed his head, digging his fingers hard into his hair, against his scalp. Wretches both, he thought. Not yet saved; still lost. "Have pity on those who are fearful," he whispered, clinging to the words of his faith despite the sins that cluttered around him.

In the flickering light of the room, Auberon crossed himself. "Amen."

CHAPTER THREE

"And then Naville told me in no uncertain terms that the Rinaldi Codex was a forgery! Can you imagine? Of all things. Claimed that I had brought an illicit document to the Fund and should be expelled!"

Eleanor watched Juliana shelve another stack of books, her own mouth pressed into a thin line. Had Juliana encountered difficulty because she was a woman or because she was a known associate of Renshaw Folley? The Egypt Exploration Fund had been welcoming enough to women in the beginning, but as they regulated policies on artifacts from Egypt, everything else bore greater scrutiny as well.

"What was his basis for that conclusion?"

Eleanor closed the book she had been staring at all morning, unable to concentrate. The night before had been largely sleepless as she found herself unable to put the day's events behind her. The memories dredged up by Agent Mallory fed into her dreams, contorting them into nightmare landscapes of rippling portals of light that threatened to carry her away. Eleanor had seen neither portal of light nor Agent Mallory in the waking world, but felt that either might be lurking nearby.

The occasional screech from clockwork pterodactyls circling the gallery's high ceiling didn't help set her at ease.

Juliana turned from the bookshelves and brushed her hands together. "The seal on the frontispiece. He claimed one marking to be a stork, when everyone knows Rinaldi House favored herons. Anyone with two eyes could see it was a heron." She laughed, strangely happy despite her obvious annoyance. "A stork! Preposterous."

Eleanor's mouth quirked in a grin, which faded as a throat was cleared nearby and a voice asked, "Excuse me, ladies?"

It was Mallory's voice, and Eleanor scowled. His quick appearance gave credence to the idea that he had been lurking, and she cast a glare to a passing pterodactyl, wishing it had warned her as to his approach. Eleanor spied a smudge of dust on Mallory's otherwise flawless black coat. She pictured him crawling around machinery displays all morning and found the idea oddly comforting.

Juliana took a surprised step backward at Mallory's arrival, upsetting a stack of books on the floor. One arm flailed in an effort to steady herself as Eleanor and Mallory stepped toward her. Each grasped one of Juliana's arms, balancing her as she came to rest atop the disheveled pile of books.

"You would think, with all the loud machinery in here, and—" she cast a hand toward the ceiling and the metal forms that glided below it "—flying beasts, I wouldn't be quite so unsettled." As Juliana spoke, one of the pterodactyls gave a monstrous cry. It sounded as though the entire gallery of iron and glass had broken apart above them. "Agent Mallory, you do have a way about you."

Mallory pressed his free hand to his chest. "My mother says so, yes." He nodded, rough-cut hair brushing his cheek.

Juliana's face filled with color and Eleanor laughed, a sound nearly lost under the wail of another pterodactyl passing above them.

"Mothers are notoriously biased," Eleanor said, giving Juliana's arm a squeeze before releasing her. She noted Mallory wore no tie today, even though his shirt collar was fully buttoned. She didn't ask, especially when Mallory's fingers fluttered to his collar, as if he were already keenly aware of the curiosity.

"If you're looking for Mister Folley," Juliana said, "he's not presently here—" she gestured to the booth they stood in with its cases, shelves, and table "—though he may well be somewhere in the hall."

"I was actually looking for Miss Folley," Mallory said and inclined his head toward Eleanor. He gestured to the bookcases around them, a library in miniature. "Would she be shelved under foolish or impudent?"

Juliana's giggle sounded like something that might come from a twelve-year-old at the telling of a bawdy joke. Eleanor glared at her traitorous friend before she looked to Mallory.

"I would place her under *absurd*, myself," Eleanor said and turned away from them both, moving into the depths of the booth and the trio of shelves there. Her father had thought that in addition to the machines, some Exposition attendees might like to see his ancient volumes. He had thus far been proven incorrect. Eleanor's fingers trailed over languages (dead and living) and sciences (natural and seemingly not).

"Eleanor, come back." Juliana's voice was laced with her laughter still. "We meant no harm. This nice young man would like to speak with you."

"Nice young man," she muttered and rounded the shelf to find Virgil Mallory at its opposite end. She had known he would come back, had hoped he would even as she struggled with her father's wants lying in direct opposition to her own.

"I really am quite nice," Mallory said.

"So your mother says?"

She enjoyed the faint tipping of his mouth and the way it brightened his eyes. She was beginning to get the impression that he didn't like his task any more than she did, for Eleanor could not remember tales of Mistral agents being this delicate in the wrangling of their prey.

"I don't mean to complicate your life," Mallory said with what sounded like a hint of apology as he stepped toward her. Something about the agent lent an edge to him today, something she couldn't pinpoint. He came close enough that she could smell him again, though his scent was different today: there was no sweet scent of opium.

"I think *your* life is already rather too complicated," she said in return. "The last thing you need is such a folly."

His smile broadened. "You have researched the Lady's ring, Miss Folley," he said. His voice dropped and the smile faded. "You know what we're up against with its theft. You must."

Eleanor feared she did know. If she paired her research with Mallory's, what would it show? How much closer would that place her to her mother? She took a gamble, to see how much he thought he knew.

"You think the thief means to open a portal to the past?" Eleanor asked, her voice as low as his, though they had only Juliana and passing mechanical beasts to overhear them.

She thought Mallory would laugh it off, as if she was making a joke at his expense, but he didn't. His eyes held hers in a way that told her he might have been asking himself the same question. The idea that their notions about the theft might not be so dissimilar gave Eleanor hope.

"It sounds foolish when spoken aloud," he said.

"It does," she agreed, but the idea still chilled her. She fell into trivialities to keep the feelings of loss from overwhelming her all over again. "There is no way to verify the ring's theft. Being that the Egyptian Museum has always denied being in *possession* of the Lady's arm, how could the Lady's *ring* be stolen from them?"

Mallory nodded, conceding the point. "You have only my word and the photograph, Miss Folley."

"And the half dozen or so men on the roof!" Juliana cried as she stepped behind the shelves and took refuge between Eleanor and Mallory.

Men on the roof? Eleanor swept her skirt aside as she emerged from the shelter of the bookcase. Mallory came around the opposite end, peering up with her. Beyond the gleaming wings of a pair of pterodactyls, black-clad people stood atop the iron-flanked windows that constituted the gallery's roof. Each wore a short mantle, their faces effectively covered with metallic masks that had been shaped like birds' heads: long pointed beaks, short hooked beaks, gleaming gem-colored eyes. Eleanor tried to put this in perspective of the Exposition, that it was a demonstration, but when the windows shattered, Eleanor knew it was not.

Glass rained into the Folley booth, and both Eleanor and Mallory lifted hands to shield their faces from the shower of debris. The metalwork wings of one pterodactyl seized up, the creation plunging to the gallery floor with a squawk.

"Oh, the wretches!" Juliana cried, appearing from the shelves behind Eleanor and Mallory. "The books! Renshaw's *machine*!"

Ropes uncoiled into the gallery and the bird-faced people began to descend, drawing guns. Some of the pterodactyls were still flying, their controllers heedless of the intrusion; one intruder kicked one of the winged beasts to the floor, where it shattered. Eleanor pulled Juliana back from the table and tucked her once again into the space between the bookshelves.

"The books have survived floods and fires," Eleanor said. She looked back to see a bird-headed interloper land atop one of the bookcases; Mallory had drawn his revolver and fired before the man could get further. The report of the gun was startling within the confines of the booth and, Eleanor hoped, lost to other exhibitors under the hum of machinery. The intruder's body snapped around, feet caught snugly in his rope, hanging dead against her father's ancient texts.

"A little blood won't be their undoing." Eleanor tried to reassure Juliana, but when Mallory joined them between the shelves and pressed a second revolver into Eleanor's hand, all reassurances died in her mouth.

"It won't be *your* undoing, either," Mallory said, a growl edging his voice. "Four remain. You know how to use it."

Eleanor shook her head, not in denial of his words but at what holding and using the gun would mean. This was the line, she thought; the line she would cross where everything would change. Her hand hadn't known a gun's weight in years; she had thought to never know it again. But Mallory's revolver felt good in her palm, familiar, and that terrified her. "I don't want to go back there—for *his* sake."

"I know," Mallory said, and she thought she heard the understanding in his voice, the regret.

Unlike Mallory, the three men advancing on them didn't care what Eleanor wanted. They unsheathed their weapons, short thick-barreled rifles, and fired in rapid succession. The shells from one gun impacted the shelves, throwing a thick, wet substance across the books. The shell from another gun ignited the liquid. The fire was sudden and intense; a glowing fireball expanded through the Folley booth, flames touching every wetted surface. Eleanor jerked Juliana to the floor, watching as Mallory hit the ground, too. Instinct took over.

"Crawl away, Juliana—*away!*" But the woman did not move.

The masked men were shadows to Eleanor, a memory from her past. Like the people in the desert strangely illuminated amid the dust, they represented a danger to those she loved. These men flickered in and out of her vision thanks to the flames that sought to consume the chemical that had doused the books. They drew revolvers next.

Eleanor pressed Juliana behind her and lifted Mallory's revolver. She fired without thinking twice. The first shot took a man in the chest, while the second flew wide and lodged into a passing pterodactyl. Eleanor adjusted her aim and caught another man in his neck, while Mallory hit the third. Each of the men toppled from their ropes to hit the floor with muffled thumps.

"Eleanor!"

Juliana's cry drew Eleanor's attention from the dead men. Looking into Juliana's wide eyes was little better. Eleanor lowered the revolver and reached toward Juliana. But Juliana, friend and surrogate mother these long years, came to her feet and fled the booth, pushing aside the approaching security guards who tried to stop her.

Eleanor dimly registered that Mallory moved to intercept the guards, showing his Mistral credentials. He insisted his people were on their way, that the scene must remain intact for them, but allowed a pair through with fire extinguishers to subdue the flames. Eleanor moved, pressing Mallory's revolver into his hands before she traced Juliana's steps, and found her cowering in Professor Twine's booth, closed into his Miracle Steam Bath contraption.

"Juliana."

The woman turned away. Through the cut-glass panes of the domed device, steam that smelled like violets swirled, a strange contradiction to the scent of burning books a few booths down. Eleanor circled the device, trying to meet Juliana's eyes, but the woman refused to look at her. Professor Twine watched this strange dance from his stool, arms crossed over his chest.

"I wouldn't have let them hurt you," Eleanor said.

"They didn't want me, did they?" The words came choked between sobs, and at last the woman looked at Eleanor. Juliana's face was flecked with blood, her dress splattered with chemicals and soot.

"No," Eleanor said.

Juliana stepped to the edge of the glass, steam swirling with her movements. "I never wanted to know what you did all those years ago."

"I never wanted you to know." She withdrew a folded handkerchief from her skirt and offered it through the slits in the glass to Juliana. Juliana took it, then turned away, stepping deeper into the violet-scented steam as she wiped her face clean.

Eleanor left her, knowing she would need time and want to be alone. Eleanor attempted to accommodate her, eyes flitting to the glass ceiling of the gallery as she made her way back to the Folley booth. She saw no one up there, but that didn't mean these were the last.

The Folley display had been roped off, but the guards recognized Eleanor and let her through. She found Mallory kneeling near the first of the bodies, edging his fingers under the bird mask to reveal the human face beneath.

Eleanor didn't recognize the person and exhaled, realizing only then she had worried Christian's face might peer back at them. If he was responsible for the museum theft, was he now trying to reclaim the ring she possessed? She crouched beside Mallory.

A muscle in Mallory's jaw flexed, but he met Eleanor's gaze as his fingers slipped from the mask's edge. "I know these men."

Eleanor touched Mallory's arm at the crook of his elbow. He leaned into her briefly, but Eleanor found a sliver of solace there, in the heat and scent of him—not the sweetness, but the darker thing that stretched beneath the gunpowder. She leaned into him, unbalanced but supported, as Mistral agents began to arrive.

Eleanor's eyes sought his, a small reflection of herself hovering in their brown depths. She suspected he had as many questions as she did, but they would have to wait. He looked past her, to the tall Negro man who was speaking with the guards in harsh tones. Mallory's hand slid over Eleanor's and he set her back on both feet before he moved away.

Mallory had sketched the scene in his notebook, but another man arrived to photograph the wreck of the booth. Once his work was done, the bodies were removed. Eleanor had never seen dead bodies removed with such efficiency, but the Galerie des Machines was a public venue, and the last thing Exposition officials wanted was to admit such an attack had befallen one of the exhibitors. Others were already looking at the Folley booth with great curiosity—what did Folley possess that would trigger such interest? Eleanor wished they would look elsewhere.

The precise cleanup work of the Mistral agents both fascinated and chilled Eleanor. Not even during her time with Christian had she seen such a thing. Even with Christian, there was a respect for a life that had passed, even if it were the life of an enemy. The Mistral agents who worked to clear the scene within the Galerie were dispassionate, as mechanical as any invention in the hall, as they lifted the sheet-wrapped bodies onto stretchers and carried them carefully away.

Across the aisle, Mallory spoke in hushed but angry tones to the tall Negro, his hair in more disarray than usual. Gesturing with both hands, it appeared Mallory would prefer to punch something or someone than attempt a conversation. The Negro attempted an explanation and tried to rest a hand on Mallory's shoulder, but Mallory threw it off.

"Ellie!"

Eleanor's father pushed past the guards. A word from Mallory and the guards let him through. Eleanor watched her father take in the destruction, the broken glass, the burned spines of the books, the gooey control panel on the otherwise-intact Triple E.

"What the hell is this?" he asked in a whisper. He grabbed Eleanor's hands and pulled her to the edge of the central table.

"I don't know," Eleanor said. It was utter truth. She couldn't give credence to the idea Christian was involved or was trying to reclaim the ring she wore. He wouldn't go to these lengths. And, she reminded herself, Mallory had said he'd known the men. Was this Mistral's doing? She looked at Mallory, to see that he had allowed the Negro agent's hand upon his shoulder, allowed himself to be led to a bench.

"If the ring has been taken, why an assault here, on us?" her father whispered.

Did he have a theory of his own, one that didn't involve Christian and the ring she wore? Did the attack mean whoever took the ring knew of their initial discovery and involvement?

His face creased with his frown. "You are an authority on the ring," he admitted with reluctance. "Perhaps whoever took it means to reach you next, to help them use it."

Eleanor tilted her head and allowed herself a little relief at his words. "But you don't believe it to be anything more than a ring." He certainly did not know about the ring she wore, either; his head might shatter like a toppling mechanical pterodactyl if he did.

"What I believe does not matter." Her father shook his head, and his scientific mind turned to the problem at hand. "What matters is what the *thief* believes. You unearthed the Lady with your mother. You were there when she vanished."

"When the riders took her, you mean." *Vanished* was a vague word, one her father had never used before. It had always been his belief that the riders abducted and later killed Dalila when they discovered they lacked one of the Lady's rings.

"I don't know what I mean." Renshaw hung his head and scrubbed his hands through his thinning silver hair.

"Miss Folley."

She looked up to find Mallory before her, appearing recovered from his tirade. His jacket hung open, his gun holstered at his side; the revolver she had used was tucked into his waistband.

"Is there somewhere private we could speak?"

Her father gestured beyond the back of the booth, to a much-worn door in the far wall. "Take the storage room," he said, and before Eleanor could say another word, Mallory claimed her arm and escorted her there. She felt the prick of curious stares as they progressed toward the door. Even Professor Twine stared, shaking his head when Eleanor nodded as they passed by.

The storage room door fell shut behind them with a *thump*, the room colored in shades of gray. While little expense had been spared in the main hall, a storage room was a storage room, the windows here small and miserly. Eleanor drew the door shut behind them.

"Hell," Mallory said and took in the extra displays and crates from exhibitors that packed nearly every bit of space within the room. A path wound its way through them, narrow but navigable. "The Holy Grail might be in here."

"No, that's under lock and key in the States," Eleanor said, and before Mallory could make another quip, took his hand and dragged him deeper into the room. She wanted to ascertain both that they were alone and that no one might eavesdrop from beyond the door. Somewhere between her father's extra crates and those of Professor Twine, the aisle made a neat loop, leaving a small island of low crates in the center. Eleanor stopped and turned to Mallory. "You said you knew those men. How?"

"They were Mistral agents, Miss Folley," he said, eyes not meeting hers. He looked up one stack of crates and down another.

His answer only further confused her. "Presently in Mistral's employ? Are agents so expendable then?"

"No." Mallory's fingers slid against the worn edge of a crate. "These agents were on probation, which seems to have been revoked. Miss Folley—"

Whatever he meant to say, he stopped himself. Eleanor hadn't known this man long, but he was clearly as bothered and confused by what had happened as she was, if not more so. Mistral agents on probation; Mistral agents who had now been eliminated?

Eleanor thought of the Negro in the display hall, his calm face and steady hands. Of the way he had tried to calm Mallory down.

"The Negro in the hall," she said, and only then did Mallory meet her eyes. "He knew they were Mistral agents when he arrived, didn't he?"

"That man is Michael Auberon, my partner, and yes, he knew. They all knew." Mallory pushed away from the crates, stalking a few steps before turning back to Eleanor. Did he snarl, or did she imagine it? "It would appear my own agency no longer trusts me, Miss Folley. I told them you would comply, for what choice did you have?"

"You told them I would . . . *what*?"

Mallory closed the short distance between them, his eyes flashing with an anger that made Eleanor swallow hard. She wanted to take a step backward, but held her ground.

"What choice do you have? You are haunted by your mother's disappearance and think the ring holds the answers. That ring is stolen and you—what?— *ignore* it and go on with this half-lived life?" He growled those words—she didn't imagine it. Mallory gestured to the crates around them. "This place is not you. I told Mistral I felt you would assist in the ring's recovery, but they felt the need to threaten, to make certain you understood what's at stake. You know what's at stake—I've seen it in your eyes—but they didn't believe me."

The defeat in Mallory's voice sounded familiar to Eleanor. She stiffened her spine and her resolve. She thought of the way he had been sure she was on her feet before he walked away in the hall, but not even that could wholly sway her to his side. He felt she would assist? How could he know anything about her? He was Mistral. He was too dangerous by far.

"Librarian saves world from ruin," she murmured, trying to make light of it, trying to make this something it wasn't.

"You are *not* a librarian," Mallory said.

He straightened from the crates and came at her, forcing her to step backward now, and round the low-stacked island of crates.

"You have ties to Christian Hubert, raided with him for a good two years in a desperate attempt to discover what became of your mother. Or—" Mallory's head cocked. "Was it love, Miss Folley? Was it love that kept you bound to his side?"

There was something curious in his voice at that question, something that made Eleanor's stomach drop into her boots. He either knew or had made a well-placed guess. "You have no right—"

"What *did* happen, Miss Folley?" Mallory advanced on her, but as he came around the left side of the crates, she skirted to the right, keeping the solid mass of wood between them. "You were there—by all accounts given in your file, you saw the portal. Was there a hand? Did you see the dark god?"

Eleanor faltered, surprised by the line of questioning. His questions reached beyond taunting, for he sounded interested in her answers even as he pressed her. And the things he said—What he knew, he shouldn't know, by God!

By all accounts in her file . . . Her file? Good God, what did Mistral know? Or worse, what did they presume? Eleanor held her silence as Mallory strode forward and grabbed her right hand. She flinched, thinking he meant to peel her sleeve back and expose her scars.

"Your mother stepped backward in time, didn't she?" Mallory asked. "Unlucky her, the ring was left here, which trapped her there. Can you imagine what might happen if the wrong person went back?"

Mallory pulled Eleanor to his side and, again, she found comfort in his solid warmth. She found herself shaking, unhinged by the idea that he knew what she believed of her mother. How could he? Staring into impenetrable brown eyes gave Eleanor no answers.

"Hubert took the ring and means to go back to that ancient time," Mallory said, pressing Eleanor into the stacked crates.

She shook her head and in order to keep her eyes on his, found herself looking upwards more than she had a moment ago. Had Mallory grown? "No."

"He means to change the entire future, Miss Folley—for *you*."

Ridiculous. "No!"

"Do you think he means to bring you every treasure this world has to offer? Lay them at your feet so you and your father might receive the recognition you deserve? Perhaps the portal allows one to move forward as well. What treasures of the distant future might he bring you? Things we cannot even yet imagine, Eleanor."

Her given name on his tongue jolted her into motion. "No."

She shoved Mallory from her and moved a few steps away, placing the island of crates between them. She couldn't think with her heart pounding in her ears, could only stare at him even as she knew he was wrong. Christian would never do such a thing, and certainly not for her.

Mallory turned and headed toward the door and, although little had been resolved, Eleanor exhaled, thankful for the reprieve. Christian Hubert didn't burn for her today the way he had all those years ago; nothing could be further from the truth.

⊲━━⊳

Marrakech, Morocco ~ September 1884

Eleanor watched Christian slide into the chair opposite the woman they had met earlier that morning. It remained a mystery: How had the woman known of the remote ruin when she and Christian had only spied it from his airship? As curious as it was to have met someone else in the uninhabited area of their first encounter, it was less surprising to find her here, the only tavern for miles.

The rickety building crouched behind rough trees and scrub between the Wad Tensift River and the Atlas Mountains, a desolate place few came to willingly. This woman looked completely out of place, even with Christian's attention on her. The woman's hair, pale blond and bobbed at her ears, spiraled into gentle curls under the guidance of Christian's fingers. The woman's expression moved from annoyance to interest in a heartbeat.

Eleanor could not hear Christian's words, but she had once been in that woman's position, angry at coming away from a tomb empty-handed. Eleanor could almost hear him calling the woman "little girl," could picture him sipping from her beer before he ordered his own. When he finally did lift the woman's glass and drink, Eleanor looked away. His hands were coated in Moroccan dust this time, not Egyptian.

It wasn't the first time Christian had played someone to get what he wanted. Eleanor had seen it time and again, but this time, this woman had nothing they needed. The rest of the trip was to be pleasure only—just them and the airship and whatever they might find to explore. As they had journeyed to the tavern, Christian had betrayed his interest in the woman. And now he made his play for her, as Eleanor had known he would. It was his way.

Eleanor still lived with the vague idea that she and Christian would marry, as society expected them to. It would, if nothing else, stop the press from clucking like old crotchety hens when word of their exploits reached civilized shores. Living an unconventional life was one thing, but romping about old ruins in the midday sun—in trousers—with her supposed lover was a scandal Renshaw Folley shouldn't have to endure, and what a cruel, heartless daughter she was to force him. So sayeth the newspapers.

Eleanor didn't want to think about how long it had been since she had spoken to her father. She took a sip of cool beer and closed her eyes. Thinking of her father made her think of Dublin, and Dublin made her think of rain. Out here, rain was a luxury they didn't have.

She peered over her shoulder at Christian and the woman. Neither had noticed her. His interest in Eleanor had waned these past months; it was easier to pay attention to the next adventure than it was to her.

It wasn't her; Eleanor understood that. It was very much *him*. Wanderlust filled Christian the way breath filled normal men. He was not the kind of person to be tied to any one life. That they had stayed together this long was surprising to her even now.

As she watched the pair, the woman withdrew a small muslin pouch from her vest. She offered it to Christian, but he refused. The woman tugged the drawstring open and dipped a finger inside.

That finger came out encircled by a ring but Eleanor didn't have to be any closer to recognize. She could picture it all too easily on the hand of the Lady.

Christian took the woman's hand to study the ring, then slipped it free. He held it into the stream of light that pierced the wooden window slats. Even in the dusty air, the gold caught the late afternoon sunlight and revealed a scarab upon the ring's face. It was the kind of thing that could have been used as a seal, pressed into liquid gold or wax.

Eleanor forced herself to calm as Christian tucked the ring into his pocket. She turned away, paid for her beer, and left the bar, trying not to look like she was hurrying as she moved to their shared room above the tavern. The cramped space smelled like warm beer, but the real bed and bathtub more than made up for it.

Christian stepped into the room moments later. Eleanor looked up from her bag and worried over what to say, if he would tell her. But his hands were gentle on her shoulders, his mouth likewise as he kissed the back of her neck.

"Ready to go, then? I saw that woman in the bar—the one from the ruin?" Relief flooded her, sweeter than any Dublin rain. He meant to tell her. He would tell her about the ring, they would laugh at their luck and—

"She knows of another, a few hours north of here," he continued as he readied the last of his own bags. "It's Roman, and she says no one goes there, but she'll guide us."

"She's a guide?" Eleanor watched Christian grab his pack, unease creeping up her spine. "She doesn't look like a guide."

It wasn't jealousy but confusion that colored Eleanor's voice. Random women encountered in distant ruins didn't simply happen to possess a ring Eleanor had last seen the day of her mother's disappearance.

Christian drew on his coat. "She knows who I am. I think she means to impress me. Us. At the worst, we give her a little ride northward, mmm?"

Eleanor wanted to say no, she would not go. She wanted to demand the ring from Christian because it was more hers than his. Why had he not shown it to her? Why had he not told her? Another part of her wanted very much to go. Wanted to see this woman and the ruin she supposedly knew of; wanted to talk with her in an effort to understand how she possessed one of the Lady's rings.

And so Eleanor found herself smiling at the woman when they met her at Christian's tethered airship a few paces from the tavern. The *Remous* was not a pretty ship by modern standards; she had been used well and it showed in her every line. This was not to say the ship was ugly, for Eleanor found beauty in all things old. The airship was smaller than her modern counterparts, capable of precise maneuvers while over a city, and swift among the clouds. Her copper-trimmed iron hull still managed to gleam despite its dings and scratches, and her wooden deck was sturdy, polished to a deep glow by Christian himself. The *Remous* had seen them from Egypt and Paris to deeper parts of the Sahara, to the mountains of Switzerland and the rivers of Russia.

"Miss Folley, this is Miss Irving," Christian said in introduction and welcomed both of them aboard. "Our intrepid guide."

"Intrepid guide," Eleanor echoed as she shook Miss Irving's hand. The woman was not dressed for desert exploration; dust coated her bustle and dirtied her gloves.

"The location is Roman, then?"

Miss Irving nodded, causing the ridiculously small hat with its blue satin flowers pinned atop her pale curls to bob. "Roman ruins, not entirely explored, so goodness knows what awaits us, and please, call me Caroline." She squeezed Eleanor's hand, then stepped onto the deck of Christian's airship. "This ship is amazing. I've never seen its like."

Eleanor tuned Caroline out as she praised the ship and kicked her own bag down into the hold. Caroline trailed after Christian, blue skirts sweeping the wooden deck while her petite gloved hands reached up in an effort to touch the inflated balloon above them. Eleanor pondered Christian's lack of . . .

"Common damn sense," she muttered and turned to examine the lines, to be sure the *Remous* was sky-worthy. When Christian queried her as to the readiness, Eleanor only nodded. The sun was nearly gone, so, one by one, Eleanor lit the glass lanterns rimming the deck, and drew a delighted laugh from Caroline as she did. The lanterns expelled their light through metal hoods cut with images of birds. Sparrows, pelicans, and owls of light danced across the iron hull, some lifting into the sky. The ship followed after.

Two hours into the flight, a lamp near Eleanor went out and she startled at the sudden lack of light. She was about to relight the globe when Christian's gloved hand stayed her motion.

"Look at that, little girl," he said and gestured to the horizon.

Christian had taken a course as close to the coast as he could without losing the proper trail to the ruin Caroline wanted them to see. Without the lantern's light, the starlit sky spread everywhere, making a neat seam against the black ocean water. Pinpricks of light gleamed on the water, turning its surface into another sky.

"I've never seen a thing like it!" Caroline exclaimed as she wedged herself against Christian's side, as if being closer would enable her to see better. "Haven't been on a ship like this in my life."

Eleanor said nothing, but tried to gauge Christian's opinion of the woman at his side even so. His face was closed to her, thoughts shuttered away. What was he planning? When would he tell her about the ring?

Likewise, she considered Caroline, who surely knew more than she pretended to. Eleanor learned to tune out Caroline's voice, to watch eyes and body instead. Both said that she had done this before. She had been on an airship, for she walked steadily; she had sought ruins, for her eyes lit up when she spoke of stones and marvels she had wandered. That was something Eleanor understood. Whatever Caroline was actually doing, she loved the exploration.

The night air stayed clear, and by the time they began their descent, Caroline had grown silent. It was hard to tell if she had run out of things to discuss, or was simply captivated by the view of the world above. She lingered by Christian's side, her arm threaded through his as he let enough air out of the balloon to take them to the ground.

"We'll stay here tonight," Christian said.

The airship touched the ground with a gentle bump. He and Eleanor leaped the rail as they had dozens of times before, and secured their anchor lines around sturdy old trees. "We'll scout more at dawn, but for now, let's see what there is to see." His expression was more confident than Eleanor felt. She was thrown off balance with the addition of Caroline to the group.

Christian offered Caroline a lamp and another to Eleanor, before he finished securing the ship.

Eleanor turned the flame on her lamp low while Caroline scampered ahead as best she could in her abundant skirt. Every now and then, a small cry of surprise would arise from her, but Eleanor turned her attention toward the vestiges of buildings before them.

There was a strange beauty to the place, a beauty shared with ruins across the world. Eleanor stepped between fallen stones, letting her eyes adjust to the night; across the far horizon, lightning sparked, briefly throwing columns and architrave into sharp relief. A scattering of columns dotted the land farther out. It was easy for Eleanor to imagine this place as a thriving community, columns still supporting walls, stones aligned into roadways, men coming and going on horseback. She walked deeper into the debris, until she found a broken column to rest her lantern upon. The light illuminated a rectangular space of columns, most tumbled down to their plinths. Beyond the columns, stones spilled over the hilly ground. On the far hills, a light sparked. A campfire? Eleanor shivered at the idea of someone out there. She turned to find Christian nearby.

His hands slid around her waist and he pressed a soft kiss against her mouth. Eleanor opened her mouth to his and slid her arms under the drape of his coat. Her fingers smoothed over his vest, over the lump within one pocket. She did not pause but wrapped her arms fully around him.

"Not here," Christian murmured.

"No, not here," she agreed and stepped away from him. This time, her fingers did skim into his vest pocket, scooping the pouch carefully into her hand. She had learned to pick pockets as a child, for her father usually carried interesting things he didn't want anyone else to see. Eleanor palmed the pouch and let it vanish into her own trouser pocket as Christian stepped away. His eyes were on the crumbling columns and not her.

"Can you imagine this place?" he asked her and turned in a slow circle to look around them. "Of course you can—it's what you do."

If he smiled, Eleanor missed it, her attention straying to the bit of bright light on the otherwise black hillside. Her heart beat a steady rhythm inside her chest, and she slipped her hand into her pocket, feeling the item inside the leather pouch. It could only be a ring.

"Will you draw this place for me, Eleanor?" He kept his voice low, reverent.

She looked back at Christian and said, "Yes." She wanted very much to add the image of this place to her book. It would almost be easy to forget about the ring, to forget how he'd obtained it. It was also easy to lie to herself.

"Isn't this breathtaking!" Caroline crossed to them, her lamp still bright, illuminating an arc of space around her. To Eleanor, she looked like an angel dropped down from the starry heavens, one angel bent on mischief which Eleanor couldn't fully name.

Eleanor bade them both goodnight and hoped Caroline proved a distraction for Christian. At the sound of his rumbling laughter, it seemed guaranteed. In the *Remous*, Eleanor slipped into a single bunk along the wall, pulled the blanket over her, and withdrew the leather pouch. She had almost hoped she was wrong, but the gold ring that fell into her palm was the Lady's scarab. Eleanor closed her trembling hand around it. Part of her thought the world would shimmer away, that the ring would carry her back to her mother—or at least the moment of her loss.

She could not see her mother for all the dust that churned. Every way she turned there was another horse, the complaint of sandy gears, the whinny of a creature bound inside the clockwork, the slap of a tail or a rein . . .

The *Remous* stayed solid around her, no portal of light opening to carry her away, no mechanical horses to knock her to the ground. She would have welcomed that portal, no matter where it led. To her mother or elsewhere. She was growing weary of the search, of the idea that those closest to her were compounding the difficulty.

Eleanor turned the ring over in her fingers. What the hell was Christian about? Had he planned to meet Miss Irving here all along? How had she come to have a ring at all?

These answers, she decided, didn't matter. Not tonight. Tonight there was a ring, a ring she hadn't seen in more than a dozen years. She fought between anger and sleep, until she heard Christian and Caroline return to the ship. To Eleanor's surprise, Christian denied Caroline when she made an intimate advance and directed her to a single bunk rather than drawing her into his own.

Eleanor stayed in her bunk until the pair fell asleep. Christian didn't take long, and Eleanor found it amazing Caroline didn't get up and prowl the ship after he dropped off. Clearly she had need of Christian for a while longer.

Eleanor returned the ring to its pouch and slid it into her vest, where it pressed against her ribs. She crept out of the *Remous* with her pack and dropped onto the ground, listening for any signs of pursuit or discovery. All stood silent, and she took the time to retrieve her lamp from the column before leaving.

Christian was a creature of habit and would wake with the first sunlight of the new day. Eleanor took advantage of the habit now, feeling a twinge of regret. Without him, she couldn't have covered nearly so much ground in her search, having no funds to secure a ship of her own. But with him— Was he using her for his own ends?

Without another thought for him, she moved through the broken stones beyond the ruin, toward the flickering light on the distant hillside.

CHAPTER FOUR

Paris, France ~ October 1889

It was Virgil's fondest desire to seek shelter in the opium den and lose himself to the bliss of the drug, which was why he suspected Auberon stayed by his side all evening after leaving the Galerie des Machines. A new wave of guards stood outside the main doors, alert for further incursions. Virgil felt it both foolish and useless. Mistral had made its point, such as it was. If Eleanor failed to cooperate, her family would become a target.

He didn't see Eleanor Folley bending to threats. She had likely experienced worse in her travels, and the most regrettable aspect of today's attack would be whatever became of her friendship with Mrs. Juliana Day. The woman hadn't known of Eleanor's exploits, nor did Eleanor want her to know. Virgil chewed on that as he and Auberon stepped into the night, for he knew what it was to hold a secret and pray no one discovered it.

"I think we have a firm duty to remain here," Auberon said.

Virgil looked at Auberon, reading from his voice that rather than it being a duty, it would be a delight to spend the evening at the Exposition Universelle. Auberon grasped Virgil by the arm and pulled him deeper into the eighty-some-odd buildings that clustered at the base of the Eiffel Tower. Did light gleam off the surface of a lagoon? Was it was deep enough to drown his friend in?

Evening crept closer, but many of the buildings displayed their mastery over electricity, to tempt the crowds into staying well past sunset. Even the tower supported a beacon at its topmost point, spreading brilliant light across the whole of the Exposition.

"Ah—eels! Come on, old man."

Auberon pulled a reluctant Virgil across the cobblestone walks toward a profusion of vendors, around which clustered parents and their children. Outside of his sister's flock, he and children didn't usually get on, but neither did he get on with the eels Auberon enjoyed.

"Why is it always eels with you?" Virgil murmured and drew his arm free from Auberon's hold. The scents of potatoes, pea soup, and spice cake assaulted Virgil's nose and awakened his own appetite.

Auberon grinned, a bright flash of teeth in his dark face. "You don't know what you're missing."

Perhaps it was the wolf in him that refused something as wriggly and slimy as eels. Virgil's nose wrinkled as they neared the vendors and Auberon set to ordering. The eel vendor tipped his head toward Virgil and Virgil shook him off, also trying to dislodge a child who stepped upon his foot.

"Sebastian!"

Sebastian's mother grasped him by the arm and pulled him back to her side, though not before the cup of cider in the youngster's hand tipped and spilled a warm shower all over Virgil's shoe.

"Oh, sir, forgive him, please."

Virgil stared at his shoe and only realized he was growling when Auberon nudged him and insisted to the woman that no harm was done. Auberon thrust a meat pie into Virgil's hands and took him by the arm once more to lead him away from the vendors.

"Your hackles are up, old man," Auberon said. "Vendor mentioned something about a Cairo Street. Thought we could look."

A path of cider footprints trailed in their wake as they moved deeper into the Exposition. Virgil was aware that Auberon continued to talk, but he registered few of the actual words. Hunger had taken him over. He devoured bite after bite of meat pie, trying not to look at the fried fish and hot eels that Auberon tore into.

They walked in companionable silence for some time, observing the Exposition and its crowds around them. The walkways were mostly themed: an Italian street flowed into a Grecian scene, which then melted into Egypt. Virgil followed Auberon into what purported to be Cairo, a street populated by Egyptians and smelling of exotic spice and oils. Youths in brightly colored robes called for people to come ride the donkeys; several finely dressed Parisians attempted it, though one lady could not coordinate her dainty boots and voluminous skirts, and one gentleman found himself entirely too tall, feet dragging on the street to the delight of the Egyptians. Auberon laughed out loud, though before Virgil could find any humor in it, he discovered something else.

Eleanor Folley stood a distance down the street, studying what looked like a fragment of a column propped against one of the manufactured stucco walls of the Cairo scene. Hieroglyphs and a faint splash of paint covered the column, but Virgil's attention stayed on Eleanor, taking in the curl of her hair against the nape of her neck, the cut of her vest and the way it fitted against her waist, the sudden new curve of her bottom in trousers. It was like discovering a new land, of sorts. Virgil tried to take note of anything that might give him a clue as to what she was about this evening, but he kept coming back to her trousers.

"Virgil."

He forced himself to look at Auberon, who stood a few steps away. Virgil had come to a standstill with what remained of his meat pie dripping juices down his hand. The scents of cider and meat pie twined around him until his own nose twitched in revulsion, but he straightened and stood taller. Forced his attention from Eleanor's trousers. Less wolf, more gentleman.

"A remarkable tweed," Virgil said and stepped once more to Auberon's side.

Auberon's mouth twitched, but he said nothing. Virgil withdrew his handkerchief to clean up the mess of his pie, then consumed the last few bites. His eyes strayed back to Miss Folley as, beside her, Mrs. Day gave a tentative smile. Eleanor looked annoyed, and Virgil wondered how she'd been lured from protecting the Folley booth. Perhaps her father remained there yet.

"It's quite possible," Virgil said, "Hubert may try to deliver the ring to Miss Folley."

"That's our best-case scenario, for we have only to watch her to capture him and reclaim the ring," Auberon said, and then it was he who stopped to gape at something farther down the Cairo street. "*God's trousers.*"

"What is it about trousers this evening?" Virgil looked, but didn't immediately see what had caught Auberon's attention. It was difficult enough to drag his own from Miss Folley.

"Miss Barclay is here."

Those four words from Auberon caused Virgil to look anew at the crowds before them, and this time he found with ease the source of Auberon's distress. The corner building of the Cairo scene was edged with brightly painted columns, between which stood dancers on shorter podiums. Short beaded bodices of magenta and copper and gauzy flowing skirts of scarlet left midriffs quite bare. Were it not for the golden chains that draped over their bellies, they would be wholly exposed. The women didn't move their legs to the music, but rather their bellies, causing the chains to shimmer in the light.

Among these dancers was Cleo Barclay, a woman who worked for Mistral's sister agency, Sirocco, in Cairo. While Virgil knew Cleo was well versed in all things Egyptian (he presumed her given name had cursed her with an interest from a young age), he had no idea she could belly dance. Judging by the half-strangled look on Auberon's face, neither did he.

The light from three nearby lamps spilled over her sepia skin and gilded her curling, ebon hair from root to tip. She was draped in gold jewelry around belly and neck, these metals emphasizing the amber of her eyes even from a distance, but nothing was quite so fabulous as her mechanical arms. From the elbows down, her arms gleamed in gold and copper, a collection of gears, cogs, and other fine metalwork. Her fingers were miniature masterpieces that now worked to click brass castanets in accompaniment to the small band of musicians nearby. Drums, a flute, the rhythmic rattle of a tambourine; it was a cacophony one could not ignore.

"I see no trousers," Virgil said. The idea of trousers brought his thoughts back to Eleanor, who appreciated the dancers as well.

Auberon's elbow met Virgil's ribs, hard.

"Mmmph." Virgil took a step away, trying not to chuckle. The last he knew, Cleo was confined to Sirocco's private hospital in Cairo after an accident on the site of a temple dig. Cleo had been lucky to escape with her life. When they managed to extract her from under a fallen statue, it had been at the expense of her arms. Doctor Peregrine Fairbrass had been convinced he could save her and clearly had.

Virgil's face brightened. "Did you eat a bad eel? It's good news, you fool." He gave Auberon a nudge. "She's alive and she'll love Paris—won't she?—and likely even Eiffel's god-awful tower. If she doesn't demand to visit the upper levels, I'll buy your next eels."

Auberon grunted, his mouth set in a firm line. "Did you say you have a map? With the Lady's excavation marked?"

"Indeed I do." Yet Virgil made no move to withdraw the map from his pocket. He took his time in, once again, cleaning his hands on his handkerchief, watching the dancers, and grinning broadly when Cleo picked him out in the crowd. He lifted a hand to her and she waved, her expression faltering when she noted Auberon.

Some matters, Virgil decided, were painfully obvious to those who were not so close to the subject. Auberon loved her and she him, and they were both thick-headed clods to continue denying it.

"She'll appreciate you more than the tower, I wager," Virgil said and at last drew the map from his jacket pocket. "Could be good to have Miss Barclay's input on this matter, you know. She and Eleanor—Miss Folley—might work well together."

"Eleanor, is it?" Auberon looked away from Cleo's dance and snatched the map from Virgil.

"Entirely too familiar of me, I would agree." Virgil clasped his hands behind his back, forcing himself to watch Auberon unfold the map. He wanted to look at Eleanor again, but didn't, and the wolf inside him growled. This evening needed to end so that he might sink into tranquil opium vapors and escape his battle for a little while. In the meanwhile, he touched the ring he wore, hoping for a little balance.

"You know, you have my apologies."

As the musicians wound down and the crowd applauded the dancers' efforts, Virgil thought he had misheard Auberon. He looked at his partner, who had unfolded the map but whose attention was still on Virgil.

"I knew they meant to send those agents and said nothing."

"And you could have done what? Overstepped the line the director drew around you?"

"For the sake of my partner, yes."

The guilt in Auberon's voice was plain. Virgil touched Auberon's arm. "All things considered, Miss Folley may well have needed that extra push." Still, he didn't relish that he and Eleanor had been positioned by Mistral to take the lives of those agents. "If Hubert doesn't attempt to return the ring to Miss Folley, there's no telling what he might be about."

He showed Auberon the small mark on the map in the stretch of desert where Dalila Folley had discovered the Lady. The Lady had been fully unearthed the following week by Sirocco archaeologists and carted away in secrecy. Cleo Barclay had a hand in that, and in seeing the Lady stayed safe all these years.

Had Caroline known about the Lady? About Mistral's involvement with her? During their time together, she had always been vague about her duty stations. The research Virgil had done after her death had shown she spent most of her time in Egypt. All things considered, it wouldn't make sense for her not to know.

"We need her," Virgil said as the dancers swayed into motion at the beginning of another song. "Miss Folley knows things it would take us years to unearth." *And she may hold information about Caroline.*

"She has put it all behind her—the tomb raiding, I mean."

It was Auberon who looked toward Eleanor this time. Virgil watched his eyes swing that way, but didn't follow it. He stayed focused on the map. The map didn't involve difficult things like curves of tweed.

"I don't think she's the kind of person to spend her entire life behind walls," Virgil said underneath the thrum of the music. "While she enjoys working with her father, she would rather be in the field." He knew that much from her file, but he had also seen it clearly in her eyes. She loved her family, but she loved being in the wide world, breaking it open to see what it contained.

Auberon looked to Virgil. "Not that her father has a shred of true respect among his peers, and her ties to Hubert don't exactly place her in a good light."

"We can't know what that relationship was," Virgil said, and now did look for Eleanor in the crowd. She and Mrs. Day continued to watch the dancers, Mrs. Day laughing when one of the girls demonstrated a dance movement to her and suggested she imitate it. He suspected he knew exactly what Eleanor's relationship with Hubert had been. Was his theft of the ring part of an elaborate courtship? "But why wait eighteen years?"

"What's that?" Auberon drew his attention from the dancers again.

"Eighteen years." Virgil looked up. "Since Dalila Folley unearthed the Lady and disappeared. And now Hubert's stolen the ring that might open that portal again."

"Egyptians," Auberon said as if it explained everything, and gestured to those around them in the street. "Align this with that on a certain date— maybe eighteen years had to pass before it *could* be opened—and then, magic." He wriggled his fingers in the air, and added in a more level tone, "That *portal* is conjecture."

Virgil allowed that was true, though he sensed that to Eleanor it was anything but conjecture.

"So why take it at all? In an effort to woo Ele—Miss Folley back into his life?" While other men might resort to flowers or chocolates, Hubert might prefer to present a priceless artifact to the object of his affection. Hubert and Caroline would have gotten along famously, for she would have loved the unique gift, something another woman could not buy or otherwise possess.

"From the records we've found, Eleanor loved that life. Hubert wants her back, so he claims the one thing that remains from the day Eleanor lost her mother. What woman wouldn't swoon into his arms at that?"

"You're mocking me now." Virgil couldn't imagine Eleanor swooning for anyone, but surely she would feel *something* if Hubert brought the ring to her.

"Maybe you're right, nodcock. Hubert will bring her the ring." Virgil sought Eleanor in the crowd again, but this time did not find her and felt a shred of disappointment. "We observe Miss Folley and when Hubert arrives, we do what we do."

Virgil prayed this would not involve bodies falling dead at their feet, though he rather suspected, considering how things had gone thus far, it would.

Loire Valley, France ~ June 1879

"She's so . . . shiny."

Virgil looked from his younger sister, Imogene, to Caroline Irving Mallory, his new bride, who indeed shone as she spoke with her father. She had chosen to follow in Queen Victoria's footsteps and wore a glimmering gown of white and cream, which made her the focal point of the post-wedding reception at the Mallory vineyard.

"You say that as if she doesn't suit me," Virgil said. Caroline looked like a creature from another place and time, wrapped in a froth of organdy, lace, silk, and linen. Her white-blond hair was caught up in a profusion of roses and peonies, the scent of which carried clearly to Virgil.

"It's not that," Imogene said.

Imogene was shiny in her own right tonight, wrapped in sky-blue silk, her hair twisted up with their mother's glittering sticks. A line of eight piercings marked her left eyebrow; each earring was a pale blue stone, like cool lake water: the work of Dr. Fairbrass, or so she claimed when she'd attempted to smother their parents' ire at the jewelry. Virgil pictured his sister in a Bohemian's tent smoking while the work was done.

Imogene struggled to explain. "She looks nothing like a Mistral agent. Her father, now, he looks like one, no matter what kind of clothing you dress him up in."

"He's Mistral's director. Today, *she's* a bride and should look like nothing else." Virgil swallowed the last of his champagne and handed off the glass to a passing waiter. The waiter asked if he would have more and Virgil shook his head. The more he drank, the more this elaborate reception would blur, even if the creature inside him would keep its silence a little longer. On one level, the idea appealed, but he wouldn't make an ass of himself simply because he and Caroline had argued over the style of their reception.

"I think it's strange," Imogene continued, "that you've never brought her home. Mother and Father should have met her before today."

"I couldn't agree more." Virgil took a flute of champagne from a passing tray, his point of view on losing focus turning in a heartbeat. Maybe making an ass of himself would feel good. His grip tightened on the glass, but he didn't yet drink.

That he hadn't been able to introduce Caroline to his parents before their wedding still shamed him. There was never time, Caroline always said. She didn't want to spend her few free days with his parents; she would much rather spend it with him, tangled in bed if they weren't arguing over how little they saw one another. Mistral kept them both busy: why should he want to make her life even busier?

His parents liked her well enough, but what else might they say on this day of all days? Virgil knew they would say nothing that might make him doubt. Deep down, he worried he did doubt, but more champagne easily smothered that idea.

"She is nice," Imogene said. "Not that I know her. At all." Imogene took Virgil by the shoulder. He looked down at her, into brown eyes that were worried under the winking blue gems. "Do *you* know her?"

It wasn't at all the question he expected from his younger sister. He looked back at his wife—such a strange word, that. In truth, he feared he didn't know Caroline as well as he should. And she didn't know him—didn't know the creature inside him, nor did anyone in this room. He wanted to tell Caroline, had wanted to tell her before this day of all days.

Virgil dropped a kiss on his sister's upturned nose and ruffled her hair. He smoothed the blond strands back into place before she could fuss too much. "I love her, Im, enough to make her my bride."

But that, Virgil knew, didn't answer his sister's question. He did love Caroline; he loved her *shine*, for lack of a better word. She was utterly alive, throwing herself into the world and daring it to catch her if it could, and the past two years had been some of the best he could remember.

When he stopped to recall the promotions and missions to unimaginable corners of the world, he was also mindful that he had been alone for most of them. Caroline didn't know the heart of him, the things he feared. That she would leave him if she did know was chief among them.

God, what have I done?

He lifted his glass to empty it when it was abruptly taken from him. Their older brother, Adrian, held the glass, blocking Caroline from view. He, like Virgil, favored their father: dark of eye and hair, whereas Imogene took their father's eyes and their mother's gold hair. To Virgil, they were similar coins thrown into a fountain, glimmering differently depending on how the sun cut through the water.

"Becoming a drunkard won't do, my dear brother," Adrian said and handed the glass off to another passing waiter.

Virgil didn't fuss over the glass. The creature inside wanted to upset Caroline's reception, and while arguing with Adrian would accomplish that, Virgil refused to give in to the desire. It was more important that his brother was here at all, given their rocky history.

"She's quite lovely," Adrian said, turning to look at Caroline. "And that dress."

Virgil made a vague sound, somewhere between a grunt and a growl, and looked at Caroline—his *wife*. She did look lovely and shiny and all those things, and that dress . . . *God, the dress.* Virgil wanted to pay the tailor so that he might never make another creation like it, to save other men from looking upon its loathsome beauty. The back of the dress was a marvel, topaz-encrusted lace draped in a way that allowed bare skin to be glimpsed. Even the edge of her corset could be seen, butter-yellow ribbons rising in a froth against her back. Virgil didn't appreciate that every man in the room, including his brother, had ogled his new bride. He prayed that in fifty years, it would not be what he remembered of this day.

"Once again, you are goodness incarnate," Adrian said.

There it was. The quiet had passed. Virgil looked at Imogene. She looked elsewhere, knowing—as Virgil did—what was coming. He had the silly idea they might escape it, but fleeing the room with his sister in hand would only raise eyebrows. Caroline couldn't abide raised eyebrows.

"Always good, wherever you are."

Color stained Adrian's cheeks. How much champagne had his brother consumed? "No need for drunkards, brother."

It was the wrong thing to say. Adrian turned on Virgil. There was a line between his eyes and a sneer on his lips, as though one had been cued by a stage manager to assume them. Virgil knew it would never change. The words would come next, the words Adrian always used as though he followed a script.

"The jewel of their lives. Why, Mother and Father don't even care that they have not previously met your bride. Of course, it was such a *short* engagement, Virgil, but still—not a moment to introduce your love? Not even a dinner party to acquaint the families? That isn't how it's done—and yet, you still shine. Golden Boy."

Imogene stepped into their small circle and placed her hand against Adrian's arm. "Adrian, can we not—"

Adrian threw her hand off, never looking away from Virgil. Virgil held the angry gaze, hoping to contain the explosion rather than prevent it. If his work with Mistral had taught him anything, it was that bombs were made to explode.

"What's next? Youngest director in the history of Mistral?" Adrian bit off a rough laugh. "Director at twenty-four."

"Adrian, stop it."

But Imogene's words went ignored. In Adrian's eyes, she was the youngest and a woman and didn't matter.

"It's fine, Im," Virgil said. He felt the beast inside him rise. That beast wanted to tear Adrian's throat out, brother or no; wanted to taste his blood and watch his body fade into death. "We're all used to it, aren't we?" Virgil looked from Imogene to Adrian. "But dear brother, I will not have you spoiling Caroline's day. She will not look back on this and remember you facedown in the cake." *Won't remember you in a pool of your own blood, my own chin dripping with it.*

Virgil studied the cake, a glittering four-tier confection that would make quite a mess were he to shove his brother into it. Virgil pictured Adrian with sugar roses in his hair and wasn't amused. He kept coming back to his brother dead by his own hand. Pulling the beast backward was a feat that left him shaking.

"I'm not golden," Virgil whispered.

"Leave be, Adrian," Imogene tried again. "If you are unhappy at the vineyard, you can change that. It isn't Virgil who keeps you tied there. It isn't even Father. And do not tell me it's the family legacy. That vineyard will thrive with or without you."

Adrian raised his hand to slap Imogene, but Virgil caught and held it.

"Don't." Virgil's voice was low and edged with a growl. He felt the beast rise up, claws pressed to skin as if to a window, looking at all he could not have. The darkness was so close Virgil felt it slide around his neck and run Stygian fingers through his hair. His tie grew tighter and so, too, his waistcoat. For one terrifying moment, he felt himself slip. His jaw began to lengthen.

"Virgil."

It was Imogene's voice, small and bright like a candle in utter darkness, that brought him back to himself. Virgil released Adrian's hand. Adrian stepped back with a low moan. Imogene's light touch on Virgil's arm kept him grounded in his human form.

"I think you should fetch your lady and head home," Virgil whispered.

Adrian bowed his head, then met Virgil's furious expression. "Happy honeymoon, brother."

He turned and crossed the ballroom to collect the young woman who had been waiting for him near the staircase. Virgil knew Adrian wouldn't take his anger out on her, because only those he loved most were subject to such wrath. With her, Adrian would stifle his rage. Not family, not her concern.

"You okay, Im?" Virgil looked at his sister.

"It's good Caroline didn't meet us sooner," she whispered. She kissed Virgil on the cheek. "See you in a little while."

Virgil let her go, eyes drifting to Caroline again. She had missed Adrian's tantrum, and Virgil exhaled in relief. No bride should have to deal with such madness. He watched Caroline's father slip a small box into her hand. Caroline opened it, but at this distance Virgil could not see what she'd been gifted with.

She would show him later, he thought, but when later came, Virgil had forgotten the gift and was drunk enough to fully appreciate the lace and topaz concoction that was the back of his wife's wedding gown.

* * *

Paris, France ~ October 1889

It was before sunrise, and the Galerie des Machines stood quiet. There was a cathedral silence to the space as Eleanor worked to unshelve the books burned in Mistral's attack. Mistral had left them on her father's insistence that they and they alone handle them, being that the books were old and required a careful hand. Eleanor didn't mind the work, but hated that it was necessary.

Working in the quiet of the Galerie—the booth illumined by lamplight—didn't bother her either. It was better than falling asleep only to dream of that day, of the plumes of dust, the riders within, the light and the hand. The voice.

It was like being inside a silhouette whirligig, turning and turning until she couldn't tell left from right, shadows thrown tall around her. The light shimmered, and a large hand moved within it from a great distance off. Eleanor tried to take hold of the swirling light, the shadowed hand. Both were warm like Cairo sun and smelled of orange blossoms.

"Not yet, Eleanor." That voice was a rein around her wrist, holding her back.

Eleanor drew a burned volume off the shelf. These books were irreplaceable, but she supposed it was a small price for Mistral to pay in an effort to convince her to help them. The idea they would be so careless with another person's treasure—not to mention lives—bothered her, even if it didn't surprise. Mallory wasn't half so careless, even if he was with the agency.

As if she had summoned him, she looked up to find Virgil Mallory watching her from the corner of a case containing a statue of tall, falcon-faced Horus.

Eleanor offered him a smile as she set the burned book on the center table. There was no question Mallory's strings were also being pulled by Mistral, considering the nature of the agents they had dispatched yesterday. This entire endeavor was costing him something, too, but what she couldn't say.

"Agent Mallory," she said.

Today he wore a smudged green suit that reminded her of the hills of home. As a child, her father had dared her to count all the colors of green that made up Ireland; Eleanor felt she was still counting, for she always managed to find a new shade whenever they returned.

Today's Mallory looked unassuming, not the man who had drawn so quickly during the assault, and surely that worked to his advantage. How many weapons were hidden on him today? He was certainly the one to be most wary of.

Weapon or not, she was coming to believe she could share her beliefs with Mallory; he would not judge them or her. In the storage room, she felt he understood exactly what was at risk if they pursued this course. If one opened a portal to the past, the future itself might be transformed. Her father always put her off, telling her how foolish the idea was, how foolish *she* was—forever the child.

"Miss Folley," he returned, with a nod. He didn't move from his position against the case.

Eleanor drew another book from the shelf. "Did I see you on Cairo Street last night?"

Mallory's smile was crooked. "I don't know. Did you?"

Eleanor blushed and she turned back to the shelf of damp books. *A Thousand Miles Up the Nile*, *On the Origin of Species*, and *The Great Pyramid* were all damaged, smelling heavily of oil and soot. She tried to concentrate on that smell and the loss of the books, but it was Mallory her mind turned to, the glimpses she'd had of him and his partner in Cairo Street. Mallory eating a sloppy meat pie, Auberon looking entirely too content with . . .

"Was it eels?" she asked when she turned back to the table, adding the trio of books to the stack.

Mallory laughed. He pushed away from the glass case. "Auberon has an undue fondness for them."

"I'm glad you got to see some of the Exposition—or perhaps you'd seen it before? Being that it's been open since May. But then, are you stationed in Paris?"

Mallory closed the distance between them. "We haven't had time prior to this, despite being headquartered here." Glass crunched under his feet nearer to the table.

"I should sweep again," she murmured. "You'll still find glass in the most unnatural . . . places . . . " Her voice trailed off as Mallory opened a book and a glitter of glass sifted out of it and onto the floor.

Mallory carefully closed the book and set it aside. "That's the best place to find things," he said.

Eleanor shook her head in disagreement. "I like things where I expect them to be. Books on their proper shelves. The sun rising in the east. The tea in the right cupboard. The Sphinx at Giza, not Luxor, and please don't move my hairbrush."

"In all your time raiding, didn't you ever welcome something unexpected?" Mallory perched against the edge of the table, crossing his arms over his chest.

She didn't like that word, *raiding*. It carried too many ugly possibilities. It implied she wasn't a proper archaeologist. Her gender was an issue among most of the men in the field (if not the world), but that had never held her back; had never stopped her father from giving her the best education he could.

"When *exploring*, the unexpected can kill you. And to clarify, I never raided. That might imply the theft of artifacts rather than their recovery."

The easy smile on Mallory's face slipped away. "I never said—"

"It's only a short step away, though, isn't it?"

A frown flickered over Mallory's face as if she had struck at some buried truth. Mallory had mentioned her file the day before. What skewed point of view filled the pages Mallory was familiar with? Eleanor turned back to the burned books and pulled another few free.

"What can I do for you today, Agent Mallory?"

"It's actually what I can do for you." At Eleanor's doubtful expression, he continued. "Whether you like it or not, the Lady's ring has been stolen—"

"Agent—"

"My research tells me the ring may open, for lack of a better word, a portal. I suspect Christian Hubert played a part in the theft. You are connected, Miss Folley, by your prior acquaintance with him and your mother's disappearance. You were with her when she discovered the Lady—"

Oh, to be five again. *Five again and Mother alive and whole and Egypt only a bedtime story, not a living, breathing place that could carry someone away.*

"—and were then attacked by men who attempted to claim the arm for themselves. But your mother was already lost, wasn't she? She had already *gone back.*"

It was strangely intimate, her ideas conveyed by him. She didn't ask herself if he believed it; he believed that she believed and that was enough. The memory of that day pressed near again as Mallory's hand closed around her arm. She recalled the way the riders had grabbed her, remembered the stench of the man who pulled her into the sand in an effort to get the arm. His mouth had not been human.

In the shaded space between the tall bookshelves, Eleanor looked into Mallory's eyes and found she hadn't far to look at all. He was too close. His eyes, intense and flecked with gold, held the look of a man who would not be deterred. One who needed her help and who somehow believed in the very thing she did. It was a look she knew too well; the look of someone who was hunting for a thing he would have no matter what stood in his way. She had seen the same look on her own face countless times.

"I think she stepped into that portal, Eleanor," he said, her name soft on his tongue. It rested like a secret between the two of them, in this dim, hushed place. "And I think *you* believe that too."

The riders trampled Eleanor into the sand as Dalila fled with the Lady's arm. Eleanor's hands dripped blood, but it was more the loss of her mother she felt, as brilliant gold light stabbed rays through the dust, as that black hand beckoned and swept her mother away.

"I need your help, Eleanor," Mallory said, "but there's something I can do for you also."

"What do you mean?"

"I can arrange for you to see the Lady."

"What?" She tensed in his hold. "She's— They buried her, Agent Mallory, and took the arm. They left her in the desert." It was something almost as painful as her mother's disappearance, the idea that a body would be abandoned to the desert waste.

"Mistral unearthed her and brought her to Cairo," Mallory said, his voice still low. "Part of what Sirocco—our sister organization—does in Egypt is preserve artifacts. Almost like you."

The idea of seeing the Lady again sent a chill through Eleanor. What would it be like, to look upon the woman she had found with her mother in the Egyptian sands? All proof of the Lady's existence had been denied, yet Mallory was telling her the Lady had been unearthed. Had it been Mistral that had attacked? Mistral had rescued them, yes, but had they also been the assailants? The idea nauseated Eleanor.

Or had Mistral intervened for its own purposes? Had they learned of the assault and provided aid only in order to return and excavate the Lady? There was no doubt they would want her. She was too strange not to take.

"What do you want from me? Exactly." Eleanor didn't move away from Mallory, for fear she would discover the rest of the Galerie waking up, her father arriving. This pleasant fiction that she and Mallory could solve the riddle of what happened to her mother might evaporate if she moved.

Mallory squeezed her arm, as if he feared she would run when he spoke the truth. "I want you to help me stop this person—even if it's not Hubert. I believe your mother stepped through that portal and that she was trapped without the ring. Whatever Hubert means to do—and I do think it's him, even if you may not—we can't allow it. Mistral can't. The entire world could be changed."

"That's impossible."

Mallory laughed, low and unconvinced. "I don't pretend to know how temporal mechanics work, but think of it." He gave her arm a slight shake. "A single person could be killed and that might be enough to change the entire course of history."

"It *can't* happen," she said.

"It *can*."

Eleanor reached into the neck of her blouse. She fumbled with the fine gold chain around her neck and drew it out to show Mallory the small gold ring.

Mallory stared at it for a long time, saying nothing. He finally grasped it with his free hand and squinted as he took a closer look at the scarab.

"I don't know how much you know about the Lady," Eleanor said. Mallory's reply was silence, apparently too taken with the ring. She watched as he studied the gold, taking small delight in the way his eyes appreciated every line.

"There isn't only one ring," Eleanor said. "There are four rings."

Mallory's eyes snapped to Eleanor's. "*Four* rings?"

Eleanor couldn't tell if he was more surprised or angry or horrified. "When my mother and I unearthed the Lady, there were four rings. The story says: *she wore four rings to mark her stations, for she was respected and honored among her people.*" Eleanor remembered the countless times her mother had told her the tale. "The arm was broken by a horse stepping badly."

She could still hear the snap of the ancient bone and could still feel a man's mouth as it closed around her arm. Biting. Tearing. And the memory of that hand from her dream, closing around to draw her toward . . . what?

"Three of the rings were lost in the struggle," Eleanor continued, "but the carnelian remained. It's the only ring the museum had."

"And this one?" Mallory slid the ring over his index finger, where it lodged against his middle knuckle and went no farther. The gold chain glinted between them. His silver ring looked even more tarnished when compared to the bright gold.

"I recovered it a few years ago." *Stole it straight from Christian's pocket, if you'd rather. That makes me a thief, doesn't it?* "So you can stop worrying about someone opening the Glass of Anubis tonight. I believe all four rings must be together—"

"The Glass of Anubis?" Mallory whispered. "Better than 'portal' at any rate, isn't it? So—all together, a certain time and place?"

"I don't know, but all four rings were there when my mother vanished. I don't know where the other two rings are, but if Christian took the carnelian as you believe, it's only a matter of time before he comes to me, to reclaim this one." Mallory gave her a quizzical look and Eleanor forced herself to say, "I took this one from Christian."

"You said you weren't a thief."

Eleanor reached out to take the ring off Mallory's finger. Her own hands trembled and she was aware of the intense warmth of him when she touched him. She pulled the ring free from his finger and tucked the chain back into her blouse, at last stepping out of his hold. "I don't rob tombs."

"That's a rather fine line, isn't it?"

Eleanor said nothing. He was right, for she felt like a thief. She stepped back to the bookcase and returned to the work of taking the burned books off the shelf. She was thankful for Mallory's silence, not knowing what else to say. But at last, he said: "Tell me about the Glass of Anubis?"

"It's what my mother called it," she said, telling herself to calm after their talk of fine lines. Mallory's tone stayed reconciliatory, so Eleanor continued on that path. She handled the books as she considered where to begin. How much did he know? Had he been to Egypt? Seen the temples and their markings? "Do you know who Anubis was to the Egyptians?"

Mallory's head dipped in a brief nod. "One of their gods." His fingers rasped over a book as she added it to the table. "Something to do with death?"

"Mummification and afterlife," Eleanor said, but was pleased Mallory had come as close to the truth as he had. Maybe they could work together after all. "They portrayed Anubis with the head of a jackal, colored black to speak to rotting flesh, the Nile soils."

"Why a jackal?"

There was a curious weight to Mallory's voice, but Eleanor appreciated the question. She had asked it of her father as a child. "Jackals are known scavengers—what better place to scavenge than a graveyard?" Mallory grunted, as if he had something to add, but at his continued silence, Eleanor went on.

"When a person died, they came before Anubis so their heart could be weighed against a feather. In this way, he could determine if they were worthy of the afterlife." This, too, drew a curious look from Mallory; it wasn't so far removed from Christian traditions, someone barring the way to heaven. "If you led a good life, your heart was no heavier than the feather. If you led a misguided life, your heart was heavy and Anubis gave you to the monster Ammit for eating rather than sending you to eternal life." She added a book to the stack, and Mallory met her eyes again.

"And the glass?"

"My mother's theory was that Anubis looked at a person's life in detail. He used the rings to open windows into other times and places the way we might page through a diary. My mother thought of them as looking glasses, reflecting something Anubis couldn't otherwise see. He did this to better understand a person before sending them to their fate."

Mallory lifted a book, fingers sliding along the sooty spine. Eleanor wished she could share his thoughts in that moment, so intense was his expression. When he looked at her, she could not read his face. Would he tell her it was nonsense?

"With a window," he eventually said, plainly choosing each word with care, "much as with a door, one can both enter and exit."

The suggestion rested between them, an invitation for Eleanor to explain more without worry of being judged. Still, she kept her silence, only nodding, not ready to fully trust.

"This, then, would hold with your belief that your mother stepped back in time, rather than perishing that day in the desert."

Eleanor's head came up. "How do you know *what* I believe?"

Mallory cleared his throat, as if about to confess to a host of sins. "Mistral has watched you, Miss Folley. Because of Hubert, yes, but for your own doings as well."

Eleanor turned to take another book from the shelf before she channeled the resurgence of her anger in another way. "I told you, I'm not a—"

"I know," he interrupted, and Eleanor let him. "Miss Folley, I need your help. You and Hubert know the most about this Glass of Anubis. Of the two, you are my one hope. Even if he needs a host of other rings, we can't allow him to keep the one."

Eleanor stared at him across the stack of burned books. "And you're offering the Lady in exchange?"

"I think for a thorough and successful investigation, we need to consider *all* evidence available to us. These are her rings, after all, and she may lead us to the others."

Eleanor leaned against the table. The sun had risen enough to slide through the windows of the far end of the building, beginning to turn every machine inside to gold.

"Cairo," Eleanor said.

"Cairo," Mallory echoed.

Only one word between them, but an accord nonetheless.

CHAPTER FIVE

Dublin, Ireland ~ September 1880

"Eleanor?"

Eleanor folded another jacket into her leather case and looked at the doorway where her father stood. She couldn't bear the look on his weathered face. She turned back to her wardrobe, grabbing trousers and blouses, then stockings from an open drawer.

"Ellie, I have asked you not to do this. Please."

Her father stepped into the room, a place that normally thrived on order, but this afternoon it lay in shambles. Bureau drawers hung open, discarded clothing haphazardly tossed on bed and floor; books and traveling cases yawned equally wide, the latter soon to be filled by the former. Eleanor hated the sight of her room; not simply its unusual disorder, but the room itself. She could still imagine traces of her drawing pencils on the walls, though they were longsince worn away. Too many years, time to go.

"I did as you asked." Eleanor grabbed her favorite boots and set them near her bureau; she would wear them tomorrow and all the days to follow. They held the good luck of prior journeys to Egypt, dust rubbed deeply in. "I finished my schooling—"

"But Ellie—you wanted more, said you wanted to be an archaeologist—"

There was a hopelessness in his voice, and Eleanor couldn't hold back her laughter. She pushed another blouse into her pack. "I've studied it for years with you. Where else do you think I might study? It's a foolish dream. I'm a woman, and you—"

When Eleanor didn't continue, he prompted her. "I what?"

Eleanor stopped fussing with her clothes to look at her father. "You know what I mean to study."

His mouth thinned. "Your mother's death."

"Her *disappearance*. How can you not want me to understand what happened that day?" Her leaving would be good for both of them, she reasoned. If she stayed, she would only make him unhappier. Would only make herself unhappier, too.

"She didn't die. It was something else—I don't know what." The men and the dust, the panicked horses, and the light, ah *God* that light and the hand, so dark and warm, like the desert as soon as the sun had gone down. "I mean to find out."

"Eleanor, I ask you again to leave this be. Please."

"I can't. As much as you want me to, I need to know. You believe she died, but I don't believe that. I can't." *Not after what I felt.*

Her father had no answer, and Eleanor didn't expect he would. Their arguments had only grown more circular in the many years since her mother's disappearance, bettered in no way when Renshaw admitted Dalila had left Eleanor the very thing that would enable her to travel where she would, find what answers she may. Eleanor would have gone even without the inheritance, even if it had come to stealing from her unyielding father. She needed to leave, regardless of how.

She continued packing, essentials only. She would begin in Egypt, at the dig site if she could find it. The very idea caused a shiver to claw up the length of her spine. What would it be like to return?

"It isn't forever," Eleanor said, though if she meant to reassure herself or her father, she didn't know. "I'll be back and I will write. You could come with me, you know." She wanted to share this journey with him, wanted his experience alongside her, but she knew he would refuse.

Her father laughed, a sound she hardly recognized. She watched as he removed a stack of blankets and sank into the much-patched chair in the corner of her room.

"I said the same to my family, but once Egypt was in me, there was no staying in touch with anyone but her."

There was something different in his voice then, and Eleanor knew he understood. He didn't want to admit it was the same for his daughter. "Egypt has been in me since my first visit to Cairo—do you remember?"

She could see he did; his eyes grew damp and distant and he sank a little deeper into the chair, holding the blankets close. Eleanor recalled the huge camels, their long legs and precise feet, and the sight of Giza at sunset, thrown into shadow as the sun vomited gold into the sky. There was nothing quite like it, her first glimpse of the place that would consume her life.

"I stood you on the ground," her father said.

"And rubbed Egypt into me." Eleanor closed her eyes and felt her father's hands pass over her cheeks that day, rough with Egypt's dust.

When she looked at him again, he looked stricken. She tossed aside the blouse she held and crossed to her father, where she knelt and took hold of his hands.

"As much as you don't want me to go, that's how much I *must* go. I will make us both miserable if I stay." The sight of tears slipping down her father's face gave her pause. "I only want you to understand."

"And I you," he said with more venom than she had ever known from him. "Your mother is dead, Eleanor. She died six years ago. She would—" His voice hitched. "She would be ashamed to know you're carrying on like this."

Eleanor jerked her hands out of her father's. "There is no shame in dedication."

"Dedication to a futile hope." He stood and grabbed Eleanor's case. He began to empty it, throwing clothes, notebooks, and pencils to the floor. "You are throwing your life away!"

"Stop it." Eleanor grabbed at his hands, but he wrenched free and continued to upset what she had packed. "Da! It's my life to throw. Mine!"

Her father dropped the empty leather case on the floor and stared at Eleanor without saying a word. She saw the deepening lines around his eyes and mouth, the hard-carved line between his eyes. None of them could be wiped away, nor would she want that; they stood as testament to his own experiences. Eleanor wanted to take his hand, wanted to make him understand, but the days when she could work such magic were gone. Instead, she picked up her case to begin packing again.

"The ship leaves early," Eleanor said. "I should finish this."

But when she looked up to ask if he would see her off, even though she knew he would not, he was already gone.

Come morning, Eleanor left the rooms above Folley's Nicknackatarium alone and, in the light fog, made her way to the station. She boarded the passenger airship with countless others, lighthearted and eager to be on their journeys, whereas she felt only a creeping doubt. She had never gone against her father's wishes before. This was a new landscape entirely.

She took a window seat and stared down at the platform; she looked forward to Egypt and the answers it might provide, but a piece of her was still anchored here, and it tugged her attention to the people in the fog.

She imagined her father there, his scarf fluttering in the wind, desperate eyes searching the crowd. Eleanor pressed her hand to the window and the thickening fog erased the figure, if he'd ever been there at all.

⟩⟨

Paris, France ~ October 1889

Long hempen lines tethered the airship *Nuit* in the public shipyards near the Exposition Universelle, the ship unlike any Eleanor had seen before. Its size and lines impressed others in the shipyard as well; small groups clustered about its berth, marveling at the construct.

The *Nuit* was larger than most of the ships there, at least two hundred feet in length if Eleanor had to guess, and made chiefly of metal. Its patina-bronze balloon gleamed under the cold morning light, not the fabric Eleanor had known from Christian's *Remous*, but metal, with loops of more metal ringing it from top to bottom to stabilize the craft. Gleaming metal had been shaped into cloth-like ripples around a blue female figurehead, the cuts and whorls within the metal strands seeming to move under unseen winds. As Eleanor drew closer, she could see silver stars sprinkling the blue body. She was delighted to recognize it as Nut, the Egyptian goddess of the sky.

Eleanor had flown a great deal in her life, but never on a ship such as this, and she wished her father and Juliana had come, if only to see this marvel. But Juliana could not be swayed any more easily than her father; she would stay with Renshaw and the library, allowing Eleanor to give the Sphinx her regards.

It wasn't Mallory who greeted Eleanor at the airship; it was his partner, Michael Auberon. He ducked out of the bronze entry hatch and waved her up the stairs. The sight of him gave Eleanor pause, for she hadn't thought of other Mistral agents accompanying them to Egypt. It made sense, but Eleanor was both relieved and torn about the idea. She didn't want her past exposed to countless strangers, but if they were with Mistral, they likely already knew.

"Miss Folley?"

"Mister Auberon? Please, call me Eleanor." While the idea of Mistral being involved in such a personal matter still vexed her, she reminded herself to try. Perhaps being on familiar terms with one another would help.

"Simply Auberon," he said.

His hand enfolded hers and Eleanor felt unsteady, as though she had taken hold of the dark hand from her dream. A whispered voice told her not to fear what was to come.

"Eleanor?"

Auberon's voice drew her back to the present like an anchor being dropped. "Surely you have flown before?"

Eleanor had looked beyond him, to the upper height of the *Nuit*, where a host of flags fluttered. The fabric flapped on the morning's breeze, as though they rather wished to snap free. Auberon's coat also flipped under the wind to reveal his scarlet waistcoat and the butt of the revolver he carried. Eleanor concentrated on these simple things, allowing the scarlet to draw her fully out of the memory of the gleaming hand.

"I have. My apologies, Auberon."

She extracted her hand from his and decided to blame her reaction on a lack of sleep, with which he sympathized, saying the past few days could not have been easy, all things considered. She let him lead her inside, past an impressive walnut staircase, to the main sitting room where Mallory occupied a chair at a broad table.

Mallory looked up as she entered, but did not look at her. His eyes were far distant, seeing something beyond the room.

"I thought you could regale us with all you know about the ring—rather *rings*—over the course of the flight," Mallory said. He was out of sorts, more nervous than she had seen him before. Could it be he didn't enjoy flying?

"Good morning to you, too, Agent Mallory," she said and stepped deeper into the cabin.

It was a streamlined space, though not so narrow people couldn't move comfortably. Polished wood gleamed in low lamplight, smaller nooks and sitting areas giving way to the larger space where Mallory's table squatted, a fireplace nearby.

The table's surface was strewn with papers, books, and a tea service. The room was nearly cozy, curved walls decorated with artwork that spoke of many distant countries. Where there were shelves, they were crafted to fit the sway of the walls, each laden with books and artifacts Eleanor wanted to explore. She felt almost at home in the space. The *Nuit* had seen the world and brought pieces back with her.

"I am—" Mallory pushed the stack of papers before him back and stood up. He gave her a short bow. He had forgone the tie again today, his jacket draped over the back of the chair. His black waistcoat was unbuttoned, the sleeves of his shirt rumpled as though he'd rolled them up and back down again only recently. "Forgive me, Miss Folley. Good morning."

"Never up with the larks, him," Auberon said, and moved easily past Eleanor, toward the tea service. "Tea, Eleanor?"

"Please," she said and allowed her scrutiny to slide from Mallory to the papers he had been studying. She saw many familiar images: photographs and sketches of the Lady, of her hand and carnelian ring. She had similar sketches in her childhood sketchbooks.

Mallory offered her a slim book. Its pages had been divided into sections, labeled with precise markers and a careful hand. *Discovery, Folleys, Christian Hubert, The Ring, The New Kingdom (Dynasties 18-20).*

"It's so thin," Eleanor said, listening to Auberon pour the tea. "You aren't—" She broke off, the accusation dying on her tongue.

"Holding out on you?" Mallory's voice was rough, and he sat back down. He sorted through more pages and photographs as if some of the information were new to even him. "I had hoped we would try to work *together*, Miss Folley."

Eleanor set the book down and accepted the cup of tea Auberon offered. She found herself making another apology to Mallory. She told herself that if she meant to make the effort to work with Mistral, she could not grow defensive at the smallest perceived slight. "I'm sorry."

"You really will have to forgive him," Auberon said, nodding Eleanor toward the chair beside Mallory, while he took one across from them. "He isn't known for his manners."

Eleanor looked to Auberon, curious as to the man's insights when it came to Mallory. "What is he known for?"

"His ability to get the job done, no matter the circumstances."

The honest affection and pride in Auberon's voice was a strange contrast to how drawn Mallory's own face became. It clearly wasn't a compliment in Mallory's opinion. What circumstances had those jobs drawn him to? Maybe they had more in common than they thought.

"Like a dog worrying at a bone," she said.

"Slobber flying every which way," offered a new voice.

Eleanor turned to look at the woman who entered the sitting room, recognizing her as one of the Cairo Street dancers from the Exposition. She was better dressed here, the marvel of her mechanical arms covered by a travel duster. Leather gloves protected her hands. "One of the dancers?"

The woman made a quick bow, something curious in her eyes. She extended her hand to Eleanor. "Cleo Barclay. I work with Sirocco in Cairo— the Egyptian branch of Mistral. It's a pleasure to have you with us."

"It's reassuring to know how you see me, Cleo," Mallory said. "And you will have to forgive me my poor manners this morning. I spent the night reading about the dead. They were far less critical of how one dresses or acts."

"Didn't mind your snoring in the least bit, did they?" Auberon said.

Eleanor watched the agents interact and sipped her tea, her attention coming back to Mallory as he extended his hand, offering her something small and metallic. It was a pin like the one that adorned his own jacket and those of Auberon and Cleo.

"You've been designated as a special consultant," Mallory explained, "so if you would wear that . . . " He nodded to the pin in her palm. "Once we reach the Cairo offices, it should prevent people from stopping you every five minutes to ask your business should you be without one of us." Mallory waved a hand toward Cleo and Auberon, and they snorted.

"He won't let you out of his sight, don't worry," Cleo said and poured herself a cup of the fragrant tea. "Ever since you explained that there are *four* rings, he won't stop talking about you." Cleo's mouth twitched upward. "All the way to the second level of the Eiffel Tower, Miss Folley this and Miss Folley that and the Lady had four rings—*four* rings!—to mark each of her stations and—"

Mallory cleared his throat. "Miss Barclay."

Cleo slid gracefully into the chair next to Eleanor's. "He's even allocated more agents to assist in what will be a longer mission than we planned." She tilted her head as she studied Eleanor. "Collect one ring and done. But no, hmm?" She didn't appear too upset by the change of plans.

"How many agents in all?" Eleanor asked.

"Only a dozen or so," Cleo said.

Perhaps it was a small contingent for Mistral and its sister agencies, but to Eleanor, it sounded like too many. She was used to having one or two on a mission. The fewer people along, the fewer could muck it up.

"And *their* purpose?"

The leather of Mallory's chair whispered as he shifted. "Being that we have three rings to recover, they will assist in that aspect. We can't be everywhere at once, Miss Folley, though neither can your Christian."

Eleanor stared at Mallory, the sense of distrust returning. She didn't want to take offense, but the words prickled like a needle drawn against bare skin. Cleo and Auberon didn't break the silence; the *Nuit* made a low creak as the wind picked up and she strained against the tethers which kept her from soaring where she wished.

"I think we need to establish something," Eleanor said as calmly as she could. She set her teacup on the table. "He isn't *my* Christian and I'm not *his* Eleanor. Walking away with the scarab ring could not have endeared me to him."

But had it? Christian taught her many things, and without that instruction, she wouldn't have succeeded in claiming the ring at all. Was he proud?

The silence after she spoke seemed thicker than before. Eleanor heard distant voices outside the ship, but from within the curved walls there was only the spark of the fire until Cleo spoke.

"Do you have that ring with you?" she asked.

"I never take it off." Eleanor touched the lump of the ring beneath her vest and blouse, but didn't withdraw it. Showing it to Mallory had been one thing; showing it to Auberon and Cleo was something else entirely. She wasn't ready to let them that close to her or the memory of her mother. "Have you gathered proof that Christian has the carnelian?"

Cleo answered, "No. Imagine the scene: the museum flooded, workers striving to clear artifacts before they can be damaged. It's chaos. I suspect the ring isn't the only item missing. When the collection is returned to its proper place, we'll find more lost. Not," she stressed, "that Hubert had anything to do with that, but this was honestly a thief's playground."

"Agents, Ma'am."

At the sound of yet another voice, Eleanor looked to the doors leading from the chamber. A thin man filled the space, his reddish-blond hair barely contained in a queue. He didn't look in any way an agent: dressed in a rumpled suit that bore stains of what she hoped was tea, he emitted an odor akin to fried cod. Eleanor's nose wrinkled and she couldn't help but notice that Mallory withdrew somewhat as well, leaning *away* from the young man.

"We're ready to get underway, agents. Estimated time of arrival . . . " And here, he looked uncertain, biting his bottom lip as he pondered times and destinations. " . . . tomorrow morning. Cairo time."

"Thank you, Gin," Auberon said and began to collect the papers covering the table. Cleo set to picking up the tea service.

Someone outside closed the exit hatch, and only then did Eleanor realize Mallory had pulled on his coat and was offering her his hand. "Come up top with me?"

Eleanor took his hand and the mantle that Cleo offered. Cleo grinned and only said, "You'll see," as Mallory pulled her away.

He led her past corridors that twisted elsewhere into the main level and up the grand staircase. Eleanor wasn't certain what she expected of the *Nuit*'s second level, but it wasn't what she saw. Sweeping windows followed the curve of the cabin, reinforced with steel every six feet. Chairs and tables were bolted to the floor, allowing small groups to partake of the wide views as they traveled. It was colder up here than down below, and Eleanor was thankful for Cleo's mantle.

"The cabins below are windowless, as they wrap the core of the ship— for increased security," Mallory said as he guided her toward the stretch of windows near the bow. "But this entire floor makes up for it."

"I've never seen a room like it." Eleanor moved toward the edge of the floor where it met the windows. When she looked down, it was like standing in the sky itself, above the whole of the shipyard. She gasped and reached for Mallory's arm.

He anchored her with a firm grip. "Should have mentioned that."

Paris spread out beneath them as the ship lifted from its berth. Eleanor never had trouble gaining her sky legs, so the motion didn't unsettle her, but the continued impression that she was flying amused her.

"It won't make you queasy to watch?" Mallory asked.

"I feel like a child again, dreaming of flying," she murmured. "I've never had a problem with heights. Sometimes the only way to really see a thing is to get above it."

Mallory kept his silence as the ship skimmed through the low-gathering clouds above the city. The *Nuit* gained speed then—too much speed—and appeared headed directly for the Eiffel Tower.

"Mallory—"

He laughed, a sound that was half disbelief. "Ah, hell. Gin!" He shouted the pilot's name. "You've forgotten—"

Cleo's voice carried upward to them. "—about the—"

Followed promptly by Auberon. "—bloody damn tower!"

The *Nuit* made a quick move, graceful considering her size, and Eleanor lurched into Mallory. His firm presence beside her kept them both upright.

"Gin is . . . " Mallory paused, as if searching for the correct word while the *Nuit* righted herself and likely made a stunning display above the early Exposition crowds. "Cleo would call him a unique treasure in God's collection."

"And you?"

Mallory considered that as the *Nuit* picked up another measure of speed and left the tower behind. "In some ways, the younger brother I never had. Gin's always been a part of Mistral. Director Walden adopted him as a kid. He only ever wanted to fly."

Mallory guided Eleanor to a small sitting area not far from where they'd stood, into lapis- blue seats that reminded her of tomb vaults painted for the goddess Nut. It eased her mind somewhat that Mistral had a sister agency in Cairo. She thought back to what Mallory had said, about them trying to preserve artifacts much as archaeologists did, and she found comfort in that idea, too.

For a time they were quiet, enjoying the show outside the windows as Paris slid past. They shared the sky with a handful of balloons, their occupants waving to the *Nuit* as she went. Farther out, a few airships skimmed the clouds, but soon enough, the *Nuit* was alone in the sky, steaming south toward the azure spread of the Mediterranean and Egypt beyond.

"Have you been to Cairo before?" Eleanor asked Mallory, and he turned his attention to her with a nod.

"I have. My work with Mistral has taken me a good many places, but Cairo is special, isn't it?" He settled into the chair, lacing his fingers together across his chest. "I've never seen it with someone who was essentially raised there."

Eleanor thought of the book downstairs, with the collected intelligence on her family and the ring. Was it only that, intelligence, or did it strive to reach beyond and draw conclusions as to why certain things had happened? Before she could ask, Mallory went on.

"I don't mean to make you uneasy, but you're not entirely a stranger to me, Miss Folley. I've read a great deal about you, but much of it is conjecture. Have you heard of deductive reasoning?" he asked and, when she shook her head, continued. "It's taking known facts about a person and using them to build a foundation toward the facts you may not know."

"Agent Mallory—"

"Virgil, please."

"*Agent* Mallory."

Eleanor stood up, but there was nowhere to go. She looked around the glass room, spying Auberon and Cleo at the stern, a far enough distance away that they could not be heard. Rather than storm downstairs, Eleanor sat back down, feeling like a jack-in-the-box.

"I'm presuming Mistral is willing to go to any length to recover this ring, but I dislike the idea that agents have been watching me."

Eleanor found the idea of Mallory watching her less troubling than other agents doing so. However, his expression as she spoke was not one of recrimination but of plain, outright study; she decided it was troubling all the same.

His hand slid over hers—too familiar, but she did not move away. Something within his expression compelled her closer. Something inside her recognized him.

The shadow of his eyes deepened and then flared gold, like sunlight on the edge of Egyptian sands. Then, a growl. It was a low sound, startling, rising from deep inside him. He dipped his head closer to her and appeared to smell the air between them; he took a long draw through his mouth, as he might from an—

Opium pipe.

She watched, transfixed. He inhaled, his hand clenched hers, and that low snarl rumbled out of him again. It was the sound of a large predator, a wolf scenting prey, and Eleanor shuddered.

He came closer, so close that his rough-cut hair brushed her cheek. Any closer and his cheek would skim hers. Part of her wanted that, wanted to know the way his slight beard would feel against her skin.

"Mallory," she whispered.

He blinked and the moment passed. He drew his hand away from hers and looked almost in pain as he stood.

"If you will excuse me."

He didn't wait to see if she would excuse him; he simply left, and Eleanor sagged into the blue velvet of the chair, relieved he had gone.

CHAPTER SIX

Loire Valley, France ~ August 1868

The first time he changed into a wolf, Virgil Mallory believed he was dying.

The afternoon sun had begun to wear on him, and he dragged an arm across his sweaty forehead, trying to push back the nausea.

His day had been spent working in the vineyards, a bucket of live toads at his side. At the base of each grapevine, he knelt and dug a small hole in which he would bury the toad alive. His grandfather and father prayed for a miracle from the toads, that they would stave off the blight that was claiming vines across the country. The illness and the insects that seemed to bear it didn't appear to have reached the Mallory crop, but they took no chances, and thus Virgil found himself with bucket, spade, and toads.

The toads were as confounded with the idea as Virgil was. Early in the day, Virgil hadn't dug the hole deep enough, which meant escaping toads. Early in the day, Virgil hadn't covered the bucket with a piece of cloth, which meant escaping toads. Now, as the afternoon wore on, the toads had grown too tired to flee and Virgil too disinterested to give chase.

Virgil jabbed his spade into the rich earth and flopped on the ground. He squinted against the bright blue cloudless sky and wished he were anywhere but here. He didn't want to be a vintner and was relieved the responsibility would fall to Adrian as the eldest. Virgil wanted to be an explorer, for it implied a romantic life, flitting about the world as he would, carried by ship, train, or balloon. The idea of staying here was death.

It was then the first pain overtook him. Virgil rolled to his side, jabbing a knee into the bucket. Toads and smelly water sloshed out. The toads flopped much like Virgil, half-unaware of their surroundings, until at last they righted themselves enough to escape.

Virgil was vaguely aware of the sodden ground beneath him; he dug his fingers into the mud in an effort to set himself upright, but he could not stand. He managed to get to his knees before doubling over again. His jaw came down against the edge of his spade, and he reeled back in pain before his body once again jerked forward. He splayed into the mud, into the last of the fleeing toads.

"God!"

He cried out, but there was no answer. When he cried again, he felt his jaw slip loose, expanding impossibly outward. Virgil lifted a shaking and muddy hand to his jaw, trying to put it back, *put it back, oh God put it where it belongs*, but his body was a thing separate from his mind. His hand was no longer his hand; his fingers curled inward to his palm and his nails cracked apart, sharp claws gleaming in their place.

Inarticulate sounds erupted from him as clothing tore; his skin came next, splitting and peeling back as though something vile sought escape. He tried to get away, but there was no escaping himself. His legs felt twice their normal length, tangled in snapping grapevines.

No, snapping bones, my bones.

His leather boots burst around his growing feet, trousers ripped and fell into the mud, and his hair—*Oh Lord, his hair. It was everywhere.*

The human boy was gone, and soon after, all human thought fled. All he saw and heard was transformed; his eyes were more readily able to discern motion, his ears picking up even the slight rustle of toads moving through grapevines. He could smell the toads, sharp and rich, and the lake in the distance. The water called to him, for the day was warm, his belly empty.

He loped straight through the grapevines, mindless of the trellises, the spade, or the bucket. He trampled one toad, then scooped the next into his mouth. He chewed, content with the crunch of bones and flesh against his teeth and tongue. Then he coughed it up. The thing tasted foul, sharply bitter in his mouth. He spat it out as best he could and ran on to the lake.

The lake was not beautiful or ugly to his eye; it was simply a pool of water into which he leapt after taking a good look around the bank to ensure a lack of predators. The cool water closed over him and he thrashed, easing the warmth that had encased him. He drank and paddled back to the bank, where he caught another toad and consumed it whole. He caught another and though they stayed bitter, another, and only then did the nausea and pain come over him again.

When human reasoning returned, Virgil lay naked on the bank of the lake, covered in mud and debris, a toad leg caught in the corner of his mouth. Virgil rolled over and vomited everything he'd eaten, everything he'd drunk. Once empty, he crouched there shaking. The low drone of toads farther down the bank made him close his eyes.

He was unsure how much time passed as he finally roused enough to pick himself up. His bare toes dug into the ground as he gained his balance. He staggered to the water, to wash with stiff motions before he headed back to the grapevines.

His clothes were destroyed. Where they were not shredded, toad-fragrant mud matted them. He picked up his clothes and the flattened bucket and stared at the ravaged length of grapevines before him. His father would kill him—if his mother didn't first over the ruined clothing. He didn't know which was worse, but neither was punishment compared to what he had turned into.

A glimpse at the darkening sky told him he didn't have enough time to repair the trellises. He didn't want to tend this vineyard for the rest of his life, but neither did he want to see it fall to pieces. He was responsible for this destruction, so tossed his shredded clothes aside and reclaimed his spade in an effort to set the trellis to rights. By the time he finished the sun burned low against the horizon, the last rays winking through the trees along the hillsides.

Virgil felt steadier, but was no clearer as to what had happened. He retrieved his clothes once more and held them in a muddy bundle against his bare chest as he traced his way back to the house. How to explain it to his parents? He chewed his bottom lip and watched the house before he moved closer. It didn't look as if anyone was about.

"Saint Michael, give me strength," he whispered, and then made a dash for the back garden.

A spreading elm rose in the center of the garden, a stone wall enclosing the entire space. Virgil had climbed the tree countless times, though his hands and feet found better purchase now than they had before. He wedged his tattered clothing under one arm and climbed until he could reach the small balcony to his room. The doors stood ajar, likely his mother's doing since she often told him the room needed airing. Considering the stench he brought with him this time, he couldn't argue the point.

He dropped his muddied clothing on the balcony and caught a glimpse of himself in the cheval mirror that stood inside. He looked a mess, his hair matted with mud and blood, leaves clinging to his legs. His pale skin blossomed with bruises, as though he'd been in a fight. A fight with a monster. He wrapped his arms around himself, afraid they come apart again, but they didn't.

"Saint Michael, give me strength," he whispered.

The skies over Northern Africa ~ October 1889

Virgil prayed to Mary more these days than Michael, though he was unsure why, for both remained important to him. They had given him strength and solace and provided guidance when there was no other to be found. When he woke from bad dreams and ached for opium, as on this night, it was the image of Mary he reached for, her comforting hand.

He traded whiskey in his cabin for the *Nuit*'s moonlight-flooded second deck. The ship made a pleasant hum, the halls dim and quiet, everyone else closed into their rooms for the night. He pictured Gin asleep at the controls and the co-pilot guiding the ship toward the African coast. For now, the windows looked down upon the Mediterranean, calm and silvered under a waning quarter moon.

"Mallory?"

He startled at the sound of Eleanor's voice and pulled his robe around him. He scolded himself, for he should have smelled her, and now that he knew she was here, he did. That now- familiar scent of old books and soap, which carried with it a combination of rosemary and another herb he did not know. He was certain if he stood close enough, he could also smell the dust of Egypt on her, as though it had been rubbed into her skin enough times to become a part of her. He had let his guard down on this familiar ship, and found it hard to raise again as Eleanor made her way to him.

"Trouble sleeping?" she asked before he could ask her forgiveness.

He grunted and moved on bare feet toward her. "Yes," he said and came to stand at the edge of the window, so that he could look down and find himself in apparent flight above the water. "You?"

This near, yes, he could smell Egypt on her. It was pleasant in this close space, and he wanted nothing more than to take Eleanor to his cabin where they could burrow for the rest of the flight, talking of distant lands. Not so he could learn more of Caroline, but so he could learn more of Eleanor. Eleanor of the rings, he thought, spying the line of the gold chain she wore.

"Yes," she said, and he could see smudges under her eyes, proving she hadn't slept well either. "My childhood haunts me."

Virgil couldn't have been more surprised unless Eleanor had confessed to being the Virgin Mary. He saw in the moonlight the pale tracings of the scars on her hand, the scars that reminded him of those marking him. They were not even, but ragged, as though made by an angry mouth. As his had been.

He wanted to confess that he, too, had woken from dreams of his own childhood, but didn't. Wanted to ask her about her hand, for it was not in her file. But this remained complicated.

"Mistral won't hurt you," he said instead. "You have my word." It was easier, perhaps, to come back to this, their earlier conversations which did not involve lingering childhood horrors.

"I want to believe that," she whispered.

Virgil also wanted to believe it, though his inquiries into what had happened at the Exposition left him unsettled. Something was moving behind the scenes, but he couldn't yet pinpoint what. Perhaps it was more accurate of him to say he wouldn't let Mistral hurt Eleanor—that he could control somewhat more.

"I confirmed that the men who attacked your display at the Exposition were on probation from Mistral—agents whom no one would exactly miss were they dispatched." Surely whoever sent them knew exactly how Virgil would respond to such an advance. They would have known, too, how Eleanor would react, given her history.

"Have you been on probation?" she asked, still whispering, as if she were afraid to ask personal questions. He also wanted to know more, wanted to share more, and yet these things never came easily. Not after Caroline. Not after the wolf.

"After my wife and partner died, yes." Probation was a hell he never wanted to experience again. In those days, he'd had only his work, and the reduction of it left him reeling. Mornings were spent organizing Mistral paperwork, but afternoons were left to him to fill. He had acquainted himself with far too many opium dens.

"Virgil."

His name was made new and strange in her mouth, and he felt then as though they crossed a line on a map. Here be dragons and wolves and squirming beetles buried in sand. In the moonlight, her eyes were bottomless, iris and pupil smudged into one vast pool.

"Both were agents, killed in the line of duty. Mistral thought I needed time. I spent a few months off active duty and was then saddled with Auberon."

While he needed the time, he also needed to stay busy. He could admit now that staying busy hadn't solved the problem. Joel and Caroline still intruded upon his thoughts whenever they pleased.

Virgil came back to their earlier conversation, meaning to keep Eleanor at ease with him and the idea of their working together. "Your file, the one Mistral has assembled. It isn't you, Eleanor. It is pieces of your life, yes, but dwindled to impersonal facts. It's like someone transcribing, say, a circus performance—"

Eleanor stared at him, something in her expression causing him to falter.

"I am not comparing your life to a circus—"

"Well, it's partially accurate, no?"

They shared a low laugh, and Mallory found himself thinking of the attack at the Gallery, the men on ropes and the pinwheeling pterodactyls. Such a circus.

"Imagine a performer in a circus looking at a transcription of the event. It was nothing like that, the performer would say, because for them it was an act of muscle and balance, where everyone else saw only the lights and the fall. What you will find in your file mostly relates to the Lady and your mother's disappearance."

He slipped his hand into his robe and withdrew the thin black book. It was tied shut with a scarlet ribbon. He offered it to Eleanor, and if fingers could be cautious, hers were, as if plucking a bone from sand. She wouldn't like the record, he thought as she untied the ribbon. No one he knew would like to look at their life spread impersonally on a page.

She moved to a dimly lit lamp mounted on the nearby window frame. "These are the impersonal facts, then?" she asked as she began to skim the pages. When she came to the passage he hated, she read it aloud, low and private between them. " 'She journeys because her mother cannot, because she has lost the connection to the womb, because she fears the dissolution of her very self. To search the world is to avoid the one truth she cannot face, that her mother will never return. The death of the womb is the death of the daughter.' "

"I don't believe that, Eleanor," he said.

"My father would agree with it." She offered him the book back, not bothering to tie the ribbon. "What if it's true? It's easy to doubt oneself."

"I do it every day," he said, and tucked the book into his robe pocket.

While his disquiet over his earlier dream had passed, he wasn't clear if Eleanor's had, and he wasn't ready to return to his cabin. Sleep felt far away. He took a chance.

"You say your childhood haunts you."

Eleanor shifted the hold of her robe, from her right hand to her left, then extended her right hand for him to see. The robe's sleeve slid up her arm, revealing the ragged scars in their entirety.

"This happened the day we found the Lady," Eleanor said. "I dream of it often, the men on their horses. I was trampled by hooves, but this . . . one of the men bit me." There was the briefest pause before she added in a strained voice, "His mouth was not human."

This admission was a surprise, and very like events in his childhood. Strange creatures with monstrous appetites. Virgil reached for her hand and when she didn't object, he turned her hand over to look at the network of scars running up the inside of her arm.

"Not human?"

"I think time has made what it will of that memory. My dreams certainly do. I saw them as monsters, so monsters they became." And while this explanation was neat and tidy, Virgil didn't care for it; there was more beneath the surface, more she was afraid to explore. Eleanor looked up from her arm. "Earlier, you smelled me."

Virgil wanted to take a step backward, but there was nowhere to go. "It was too forward of me," he said, not remotely an apology. He released his hold on her hand, thinking of earlier that day, when she had felt threatened and the beast inside him responded. He had wanted to protect her, still wanted that. He knew he would harm any who meant to harm her.

"In my dream, I dreamed of finding the Lady again. I dreamed of those men who attacked, but in the dream it was you who bit me, Virgil." Her look dropped to his mouth. "You."

The notion of biting her wasn't a terrible one, if ill-timed. Virgil went still, speaking around the tension in his throat. "Tell me more of what happened after you were bitten. How old were you? How was the bite treated?"

"I was twelve. Mistral came; they took me and my father to a hospital in Cairo. I never thought to ask where. It was a British doctor, though. He cleaned my wound and stitched me back together."

Mistral and a British doctor in Cairo: it wasn't difficult for Virgil to piece that puzzle together. "It's likely you saw a Mistral doctor. Do you remember if agents spoke with your father or you afterward?"

Eleanor's intent expression told Virgil she was back in that past moment even now, remembering. "I'm not certain. As injured as my hand was, they doused me with chloroform before beginning work, and my father . . . " There was a pause, another slight shake of her head. "I don't know if he was there the entire time or not."

Virgil, if pressed to guess, would say yes, given all that had happened. Renshaw Folley wasn't the kind to abandon his only child after the sudden and violent loss of his wife. The appearance of Mistral soon after might have encouraged Eleanor's own distrust in the agency, even if on a level she didn't understand.

"And the nightmares began after?"

"Every child has bad dreams, Mallory," she demurred.

Virgil allowed that was so and carefully changed the course of conversation; it felt like a new book, thick with stories he hadn't yet read. With endings they had yet to write. "What was it like, to find the Lady?"

"It had always been a bedtime story," she said. "Never real until all of a sudden, it was." Eleanor stared out the windows and moonlight traced a pale, rippled line along her jaw. "I had been on countless digs with my parents; they were always digging somewhere, but this was different. My mother *knew* the Lady would be there."

"And you said four rings?" Virgil told himself to slow down, to address the rings, which they knew were fact. He told himself to not indulge in a fantasy that may or may not be true. But did Eleanor harbor a monster inside her the way he did? If she did, he was fairly certain she did not know.

"Four rings," she echoed. "One flat gold disk with a scarab engraving." She lifted her scarred hand to touch the chain she wore. "The carnelian is also set in gold. The third is gold with lapis. I can't picture it or the fourth very well. The Lady's hand was curled against her chest, the last two fingers curving inward." She demonstrated with her own hand now. "I think the fourth was plain silver or electrum, but you're relying on the memory of a twelve-year-old girl."

A twelve-year-old girl whose mother was torn away from her after the discovery of the Lady. That might linger when other specifics faded. "Seeing the Lady may bring some things back."

Eleanor looked as if she might be sick. Virgil could not stop himself from touching her arm, fingers digging into her shoulder.

"All shall be well," he murmured. He wanted her to believe that as much as he did.

"I think—"

But what Eleanor thought would remain a mystery, because the *Nuit* gave a sudden jolt beneath their feet, as if she had been struck by something. Eleanor lurched into Virgil's arms and they both fell against the window. For a moment, Virgil feared the glass would shatter, sending them spiraling to the distant earth below. But there came only the groan of the ship around them; the windows, made for such potential bumps, held. Virgil waited for an announcement from Gin, from Auberon, from someone. He could feel the *Nuit* trying to right herself, but the ship continued her downward trajectory. He didn't have to look out the window to know they were closing in on the water that lapped the African coastline, but still saw the moonlight against that shore, licking and hungry.

"Eleanor, hold on."

And then the rear cabin exploded in flame and glass as a host of fiery cannonballs careened inside.

CHAPTER SEVEN

Port Elizabeth ~ Cape Colony, 1884

Eleanor didn't want to be here. Rain poured from the sky in drenching sheets, and her wet fingers slipped against the doorknob of St. Augustine's as she pushed her way inside. She closed the door, then stepped into the nearest shadows in case eyes turned toward her; the hush of the cathedral was startling in comparison to the downpour. She became aware of the steady drip, drip, *drip* from her jacket onto the stone floor and she slipped it off, folding it twice and tucking it into the nearest pew. She pushed her revolver farther down into the waistband of her trousers.

On the run and pursued, she was still mindful of where she was. She dipped a knee to the floor and crossed herself, eyes on the altar at the far end of the aisle. The calming scent of beeswax candles reached her; no matter what was outside, there was only this in here. Only this sense of peace.

She slipped into the pew beside her jacket and clasped her hands together, expecting Christian to enter the church behind her. He did not. Eleanor counted only five other patrons, occupied with their own prayers. Still, she listened for him, knowing he couldn't be far. Ever since her abrupt departure from Morocco, Christian had trailed her. He turned up in the most curious places; sometimes it was as though he could read her mind. But then, if he were following the same trails she followed, it made perfect sense. Port Elizabeth wasn't on any trail, yet here she was, stranded.

The Empress had begun experiencing difficulty over Mozambique, and Eleanor found it remarkable they hadn't ended up in the channel. The pilots were experienced enough and welcoming to the point of over-booking their airship. While *The Empress* might have comfortably held twelve, she hadn't been made for twice that number, even if most of them were children. The memory of those young, wide eyes as the ship started losing altitude hung in Eleanor's memory and sent a chill down her spine.

She slid off the pew, onto the kneeler. "Thank you for seeing us all safely down," she said into her hands, and then jumped when the door to the church flew open.

Only the storm, she told herself, then caught sight of the long shadow thrown down the aisle of the church. Someone too slight to be Christian. Eleanor fought to keep her eyes on her hands, but when the person stepped into the pew Eleanor occupied, she had to look.

Caroline crossed herself and then her legs, blocking Eleanor's access to the main aisle.

"It was dreadful," Caroline said in a voice low enough so as not to disturb the other worshippers, "watching *The Empress* lose altitude like that. I truly believed we would all end up in the water."

Caroline had been on *The Empress*? Eleanor mentally rifled through the passengers, the suited men, the overdressed mothers, and all those children. She couldn't pick Caroline's face from any of them at first, then thought of the slight man who occupied a seat near a portside window. Short cropped hair hidden under a hat, the shadow of stubble against his jaw. Eleanor looked at Caroline now, spying a trace of makeup, like that an actor might wear on stage.

"It is equally dreadful," Caroline continued, "what we only see in retrospect. I should never have offered that ring to Christian for any price, because it goes beyond that, doesn't it? Thinking I could hide it with him . . . "

Caroline's voice took on an edge, her eyes resting on the altar. Eleanor studied her. How close had this woman been before—how many disguises did she wear? Eleanor and Christian had taken on a disguise or two during their time together, but none so outwardly seamless as the one Caroline had donned on *The Empress*. It made Eleanor question everything.

Eleanor tried to calm herself. She knew Caroline was skilled at hiding. The woman who chased her now was not the woman Eleanor had met in Morocco, wrapped in fussy blue satin with a ridiculously small hat perched atop her head. *Purposeless hat*, Eleanor snarled inside. Caroline was never the same woman twice.

"It's simple, Miss Folley. You give me the ring and we go our separate ways."

The idea made Eleanor recoil. Something deep inside said *no* and caused her to bristle. It *was* simple on the surface—it was but a ring, wasn't it? Not to Eleanor. The idea of the ring in Caroline's possession again was like death, giving away a piece of herself, a piece of her mother. Eleanor bowed her head and reached for her sodden jacket, stuffing arms back into it, made awkward as her blouse and vest were likewise damp.

"That looks like a refusal, Miss Folley." Caroline moved enough to draw her revolver. "I would hate for this to turn ugly, especially in such a beautiful place. And these people? All as innocent as those children, but *The Empress* had to come down, you understand."

If Caroline was bluffing, it worked to slow Eleanor's progress with her jacket. Caroline had a hand in taking the ship down? She was capable of that? Eleanor eyed Caroline's steady grip on the revolver, not caring that her own blouse sleeves rucked up inside her jacket sleeves. She felt the fabric tear and still didn't care. *Get the jacket on and run. Go. Go.*

"This is why I never deal with amateurs."

Eleanor laughed at that, unable to stop the sound before it rose. Caroline didn't take kindly to the suggestion within that laugh. She moved with ease, wet trousers sliding against the wood pew so she could angle her revolver into Eleanor's ribs. Eleanor flinched and made to move away from the weapon, but Caroline's other arm wrapped around her shoulders.

"Don't do this here," Eleanor said.

"At least your soul won't have far to go."

Something stirred inside of Eleanor, something that took hold of her and guided her with the intent of getting out of harm's way. Eleanor slammed the heel of her palm into Caroline's chin, and Caroline went slack enough that the revolver came away from Eleanor's ribs. Eleanor snaked out of Caroline's remaining hold and dropped to the stone floor, rolling under the pew, between the slight space afforded between floor and seat.

When Eleanor came up, Caroline was in motion and screaming. She lifted the revolver, tracking Eleanor's movement along the back of the pew. The first bullet bit into the old pew wood, sending splinters flying. The sound in the cathedral was deafening, and Eleanor flinched again. The *instinct* moved inside her once more. She wanted to leap for Caroline, throw the woman to the floor and beat her bloody.

Keep moving! Her mind screamed the direction, but the inner part of her wanted to confront Caroline, wanted to understand exactly why *she* wanted the rings. What did she know? Or was it simply a game to her? She had been bested and that couldn't stand?

"Caroline—"

"I have five more bullets, Miss Folley."

Eleanor had no doubt that Caroline envisioned each one buried within her. Eleanor looked up the length of the aisle, to the patrons who cowered silently in the pews—save for one woman who screamed for the priest.

"If you don't want that woman silenced in an awful way, you *will* give me that ring."

Absurd. Eleanor peered around the column at Caroline, who stood near the pew, revolver raised in Eleanor's direction. "Who *are* you?" The question was out of Eleanor's mouth before she could consider the words.

"I'm the one about to make you miserable."

Caroline shifted her aim, sighting down the length of the aisle toward the screaming woman. The woman was perhaps sixty, her hair silver and held at the nape of her neck with a gold clasp that gleamed in the candlelight. For one terrible instant, Eleanor imagined the woman's white blouse soaked through with blood. She leapt for Caroline.

They went down in a tangle and the revolver spat another bullet, which knocked into a pew. Patrons screamed and sought sanctuary while Eleanor scrambled to get on top of Caroline, clawing her way toward the weapon.

She didn't expect Caroline to bring her shooting arm down. Caroline's elbow cracked into Eleanor's head and the room swam. The candles blurred and there were four sets of windows where there had only been one before.

The impact brought Caroline's arm within Eleanor's grasp and she held on for dear life—if not her own, then for the patrons of the church. Eleanor grabbed for the revolver, but Caroline wouldn't relinquish her grip. Caroline shoved the revolver beneath Eleanor's chin, pressing hard. The barrel was still warm, yet Eleanor felt only cold. Every part of her stilled.

"There is no reason *not* to kill you," Caroline said, bringing her face within inches of Eleanor's. "Kill you, take the ring, and—"

Caroline's threats ended in a squawk as the male patrons of the church set upon her. They pulled the women apart and wrestled Caroline's gun free, turning it on her.

The priest looked aggrieved over the scuffle in his church, the threat to his congregation, and the damage to his pews. He demanded that the men take

Caroline to his office—he had already sent a boy to bring the authorities to handle her.

When the priest turned to Eleanor, she picked herself up from the floor. She took a step backward, looking to the lady in her white blouse. *Still white. No blood.* But she *wanted* blood, God forgive her—the instinct inside her was nearly salivating for it. Eleanor felt as though she would be sick.

She brought her eyes back to the priest.

"Forgive me, Father," she whispered.

And then, she fled.

Northern Africa ~ October 1889

Eleanor came to consciousness amid a mess of debris. She lay unmoving, not clear where she was or what had happened. Trying to sort her thoughts led her to the whiskey smell of Virgil Mallory in the moonlight, but that memory was inconsistent with her current state.

She tried to draw her right hand to her chest because her fingers ached with cold, but the hand wouldn't budge. Her left hand was plastered against her breast with something cold and tacky, her hair spread unbound across her eyes. This gave a strange impression of what lay around her, everything shrouded in gossamer strands. She moved slowly, feeling ground beneath her, not floor, along with sharp, broken fragments of the *Nuit*. And then, she felt the curve of a cheek. Cold, metal, perhaps the goddess Nut herself.

"Damn."

A gentle shake of her head cleared her hair from her eyes, allowing her to see the slanted, splintered wood burying her. It looked like she was inside a casket that had exploded. Two wooden slats trapped her right wrist; pressing on one allowed her to pull her arm free. She didn't feel broken anywhere and calmed.

"Mallory!" There came no reply, and Eleanor wriggled to free her feet next. "Auberon? Cleo?"

There was no reply to any of her queries, so Eleanor concentrated on getting herself free. She picked out bits of paintings amid the debris, charred canvases;

glass glittered in the waning moonlight, proof to her that the beautiful upper deck of the *Nuit* was entirely gone. Chair cushions had exploded into fluff, candles lay in melted pools, and over everything there lingered the smell of burned wood. She recalled the ball of fire, the shattering glass, and the downward arc of the ship.

When she came free of the debris, she staggered. She was slow to lift her eyes to the destruction around her. The great balloon of the *Nuit* was broken open like an egg, bits of her spilling a trail across the desert.

"Eleanor."

Mallory's arms closed around her from behind, gentle and yet firm, and warmth settled around her as he drew her away from the wreckage. She hadn't realized she was cold until he was there. There was a great measure of comfort in his heat, in the now-familiar scent of him. She let Mallory support her and drew a shaking hand to her chest, seeking the line of her gold chain. Relief poured through her when her fingers found it and the ring still there.

"Here, sit."

Eleanor sat on the remains of a sofa perched crookedly on a lump of other debris. Perhaps the sofa had been crimson; now, it was charred black, its cushions missing.

"Ah, God, are you injured?"

Eleanor rested against the arm of the sofa while Mallory pulled at her blouse, searching for a wound. The cold and tacky wetness she'd felt *was* blood, she could see that now, though she viewed it from an emotional distance. She could feel no injury and should have felt *something* at the too-familiar touch of Mallory's hands on her—outrage, shock, upset, astonishment. She could hear Juliana making a list. But Eleanor felt nothing.

His long fingers moved up her arms, into the tangle of her loose hair, pressing along her scalp. She closed her eyes briefly—a little rest, she told herself. She couldn't help but look at Mallory when his fingers slid down her neck and came to lie against her collarbone, over the line of her gold chain.

Warm fingers, she thought, feeling those without a doubt. She fancied she could feel the whorl of every fingerprint. Mallory's forehead was gashed, and she imagined she could smell his blood on the night air too. His hair was a matted tangle, his collar speckled with what looked like ink.

"Someone wrote on you," she murmured, her fingers lifting in an effort to touch the ink, though it seemed impossibly far away.

"Something grazed you, but it doesn't look bad. Eleanor? Eleanor, stay with me."

The world vanished, blackness draping everything. Funerals, she thought; pack everything away. Was it the sight of her own blood that had her swooning? She refused to believe she was capable of a swoon. She was made of sterner stuff.

"Mallo—"

She tried to swim up through the layers of pitch and thought she was succeeding when something gleamed. She reached for it, watching her own pale hand slide into a darker one. It smelled like an animal. Eleanor tried to lift her head, tried to open her eyes. When at last she did, she saw only a pair of black eyes looking back at her. Onyx, framed with strokes of gold.

"Daughter," a voice whispered.

"Father," she replied.

"—anor!"

The world snapped back into place at Mallory shouting her name. She stared at him without speaking, without letting go of him.

"Where did you go?" he asked in a whisper.

She shook her head in answer—she didn't know. "Someone called me 'daughter.' I—Virgil, what hap—"

"Come on." He helped her up from the couch and began to lead her away from the wreckage. "Let's move while we talk. Gin is all right, and Cleo, but Auberon broke an arm."

Eleanor was cautious about every step she took, because of the debris and her bare feet, but also because she didn't feel truly *present*. She still felt the embrace of that hand and she didn't like it. She stared in silence at the world around them. Auberon, Gin, and Cleo were gathered some distance away from the *Nuit*, with Gin running back and forth with salvaged supplies. Cleo was splinting Auberon's arm. Her mechanical fingers gleamed gold in the light from a lamp.

"Should be in northern Africa," Mallory continued. One hand slipped down Eleanor's arm, to cup her elbow. "Damned lucky we didn't hit the water, if you will forgive my language."

Although they hadn't landed in water, Eleanor could hear it, so they weren't that far from it. She imagined the hulk of the *Nuit* in the ocean and a low shudder rolled through her. They could have been killed, drowned, and she took an uneven step into Mallory. Her bare foot came down against his own.

Water closing over them, trickling into mouths . . .

"Eleanor—Stop."

She did as he said, feeling she had no direction of her own, and looked into his eyes. Fathomless and rimmed in strokes of gold—no.

"Breathe," he said.

She breathed and felt the slow retreat of the hand. At its leaving, she felt cold again and burrowed her face into Mallory's chest. He tensed only briefly before wrapping his arms around her.

"Who did this?" she whispered.

"I was hoping you would have some idea."

Eleanor laughed and peered up at him. "Me? I would have said Mistral."

"Still suspicious of us, then? I thought we worked past that. I told you I won't let them hurt y—"

"Why be suspicious of an international organization of spies?"

"I'm not a spy—"

"And I'm not a tomb raider. Fine lines, remember?" She exhaled, and while propriety said she should step out of Mallory's embrace, she was content to stay where she was. The heat of him was too intoxicating. "You admitted Mistral took the Lady, unearthed her, and locked her away. Perhaps they were the attackers too."

She heard his voice rumble in his chest when he replied. "I don't believe it was Mistral who attacked you at the dig, Eleanor, but yes, Mistral was responsible for restricting access to the Lady afterward."

"Why *not* be suspicious, then?"

"Mistral wouldn't take down its own ship."

"Mistral would dispatch its own agents to be killed, but wouldn't attack its own ship? Another fine line?"

Mallory considered the question in silence, then offered another question instead of a direct answer. "What do you know about the Defenders of the Protectorate?"

Eleanor pulled back a little to look at him. "Entirely fictional."

"Entirely?"

"A secret group of warriors, from the time of the first pharaohs, sworn to protect Egypt and its treasures no matter the sacrifice? Granted, various groups have *claimed* to be the Defenders, but I've found no evidence that they ever existed, let alone continue to exist." She had never thought that it might have been Defenders who attacked her and her parents at the dig site—they were fiction, but wasn't the Lady, too? Her heart skipped.

He pressed the idea. "No evidence of a *secret* group?"

"We could talk in circles all day." She looked upward. "Night."

"That we could. Come on."

He guided her toward Auberon, Gin, and Cleo, who gave them tired smiles as they approached. Mallory kept an arm around Eleanor.

"Found her sleeping under the debris," Mallory said, and a laugh rose from them all. "Here."

He guided Eleanor to the burned ottoman next to the broken chair Auberon occupied. She sat, thankful to rest on something steadier than her own bare feet.

"There's no sign of anyone," Gin reported when he returned, arms laden with more supplies. "The radiotelegraphy unit is destroyed." He had managed to find a variety of shoes, slippers, and a pocket watch that was still ticking. He gestured to the sky. "Haven't seen anyone up there, either."

A glance at the yawning black sky only made Eleanor feel ill. She pictured that hand, and heard that voice calling her *daughter*, and felt the world tip out from under her again. Her hand tightened around Mallory's and he sat beside her, brushing loose hair back from her cheek.

"You've got a scratch or three."

"Here."

Cleo passed a damp handkerchief to Mallory and he stroked it carefully across Eleanor's scratched cheeks. "I'm no doctor," he said as he worked to clean her up, and Cleo and Auberon both laughed.

"He's better with a gun than a needle," Auberon said.

"Do you need to be shot?" Mallory asked him.

"Not that far gone. Yet."

Still, Eleanor thought Auberon looked ready to pull away from Cleo as she continued to wrap a length of cloth around his arm and splint.

Eleanor closed her eyes. The darkness behind her lids was no better than that which arced above them. She sought grounding in Mallory and the other agents, but her attention returned to the debris littering the ground. The idea that someone had taken the *Nuit* out of the sky sent a chill through her. The attack called to mind the assault on the Galerie, and she decided Mistral was hammering another point home.

"Any idea where we are?" Cleo asked. She tied a knot in the fabric at Auberon's wrist to secure the splint, then nudged him back against the broken chair. Gin offered up a bottle of whiskey that had survived the wreck, but Auberon shook it off.

"Should have been . . . " Gin cocked his head. "Hundreds of miles west of Cairo yet." His voice held a questioning lilt, as if he weren't entirely sure where they were.

"Any ideas, Eleanor?"

The question came from Mallory, and she looked around the vast expanse of desert in which they found themselves. There was nothing to immediately distinguish it from any other stretch of Egyptian desert, but she closed her eyes and listened.

"I can hear the ocean," she said and flinched when Mallory drew the handkerchief away, "but this desert looks like any other." Still, this close to Cairo, her thoughts couldn't help but take an uncomfortable turn. "If your theory is right, Mallory, that the Defenders shot us down, what are the odds that they'll be on us to be certain we're dead?"

"If such a group exists, I would say pretty good odds." Mallory folded the handkerchief into his pocket and withdrew his revolver, checking its ammunition.

"Wait." Cleo raised her hands as though she could slow everyone down. "We're in the middle of who knows where, without transport, limited supplies, an injured man, and now you're telling me the Defenders of the Protectorate may have shot the *Nuit* down and are on our trail?"

Eleanor was pleased at the tone of Cleo's voice. She was annoyed, but also sounded eager to get going. Eager to be moving and doing something. Anything was better than sitting still, and Eleanor shared the sentiment. This was her old life, laid open and bared once again. This was the world rushing to meet her, and her opening her arms to it.

"It's a working theory," Mallory said.

"I *hate* your theories," Gin said as he returned with more supplies.

"Almost like Moscow."

Auberon didn't bother to stifle his groan. "At least it's not snowing."

⇒

Snow might have been preferable to the desert heat they would soon know, Virgil thought two hours later as they crested another mound of sand and yet another stretch of desert spread endlessly before them.

Mistral policy dictated that in the event of a crash, if agents believed themselves in imminent danger, they were to secure, destroy, or collect anything of value before evacuating the site. Contact was to be made as soon as reasonably possible.

If they were hundreds of miles out of Cairo, it would be a long damn time before they could make contact. They carried the remains of the radiotelegraphy machine with them, but Virgil had no hopes they would be able to fix it.

He didn't have much hope at all as they walked on. The beast inside him clawed for escape and, having no opium, he fought to keep the thing contained. Be still, he told it, but every step was agony and the farther into the desert they walked, the more he shivered.

He should have found it amusing, five adults crossing the desert in their nightclothes, mismatched shoes and slippers for footwear. Robes and bed linens draped their shoulders, and each person carried several canteens of water. They had taken the entire cache of water, knowing it was their most important possession. Virgil ranked the bed linens as second most important, for they would provide shade when the sun rose. He hated the idea of sunrise, of traveling in the day's heat. It was likely that whoever shot them down would seek the remains of the ship, which eliminated the wreck as a place of safety and shade.

He prayed they would find a settlement soon. A small oasis, one tree to grasp so his arms could stop shaking. He turned his attention to the others in an effort to ignore himself and the monster inside.

Gin and Cleo helped Auberon by turns, while Virgil kept an eye on Eleanor.

109

She maintained a good pace despite the overlarge slippers she had inherited. It was fortunate none of them had broken a leg, and Auberon only an arm. Arms were more expendable when it came to trekking a desert.

At least none of them were barefoot.

Earlier, his eyes had lingered on the curve of Eleanor's foot. Small and pale and probably cold, smudged with soot and dust, and he'd wanted nothing more than to protect her from everything that had befallen them this night.

Ahead of them, Gin dropped to his knees and splayed full out, nearly unconscious by the time Virgil and Eleanor reached him. Virgil couldn't have asked for a better distraction; the sight of Gin's downed body made him momentarily forget the claw of the wolf inside.

Virgil uncapped his canteen and dribbled water over Gin's lips as Eleanor supported his head. Gin sputtered water everywhere.

"Think I . . . need to rest," Gin whispered.

"If you say so, boss," Virgil said, hoping his concern didn't show through. Gin was a Mistral agent and while he had trained for such circumstances as these, he had never actually crashed an airship and found himself on the run. In this situation, reality was entirely different than theoretical preparation.

"We'll all rest a bit," Auberon said, and nodded to Cleo.

She drew a length of linen from her bag and set to making a tent to shield Gin from the cool night breeze and the dust it lifted into the air.

"Why would the Defenders shoot down an airship?" Cleo asked as they got the makeshift camp together, and Gin settled. "Presuming they exist. Sirocco has no evidence they do."

Virgil knelt by Gin's side and smoothed the young man's hair back before offering him another sip of water. The light breeze teased the fabric around Gin's shoulders, making it whisper. The low voices of the others rose above the whisper, giving Virgil another anchor. The beast lay down, not content but also not pressing.

"Prescribing motive is never entirely accurate," Auberon answered, his eyes on Virgil, "but think of the *Nuit*. If they looked up and saw such a ship, perhaps they thought to bring her down for her treasures."

"Presuming they exist," Eleanor said. "According to legend, the Defenders are said to swear at a very young age to protect the whole of Egypt, from whatever source of incursion. Be it by land, air, or sea."

Eleanor's mention of incursions guided Virgil's thoughts to his first invasion by the beast, and he bit off a short curse. He looked at Auberon, who was still staring at him. Because he knows, Virgil thought; *found me in that awful den and he knows. Knows what my body craves—the cloying embrace of the dragon or the bittersweet dissolution as the beast inside claws its way out.*

"Wasn't—"

Virgil turned his attention to Gin as he fought to speak. Virgil hushed him, but Gin struggled to push himself up on his elbows. He stared at them through gummy eyes. Virgil settled for supporting him, since he wouldn't lie back down.

"Didn't come from below," Gin managed.

Cleo shifted her attention from Auberon to Gin. "What didn't come from below? The attack?"

"Was . . ." Gin took the canteen Eleanor offered him. "Up there, with us." He drank deeply, water trickling down the corners of his mouth to course through the dust coating him and wet his collar.

A cold dread settled in Virgil's belly, and even the beast retreated. "Another airship," he said.

"Defenders aren't known to *have* airships," Cleo said as she folded an extra bundle of linen into a pack. "They protect the land and remain on the land, at all times."

"So, if it wasn't the Defenders," Eleanor asked, "then who?"

Virgil appreciated Eleanor's restraint in asking only that. He didn't want her coming back to the idea it had been Mistral. That answer didn't make sense to him. Yes, they had threatened once, but destroying the *Nuit* was surely beyond their scope. He knew the investment such a ship demanded. Yet once, he would have sworn the same of Caroline: that she was incapable of betrayal.

That there existed people who enjoyed wreaking havoc for the sake of havoc remained senseless to Virgil. Caroline possessed some of that spiteful spirit, living life for only what she could gain. But in the end, what had it brought her? Little good. And still, not every memory of Caroline was tainted—and that sometimes made her more challenging to remember. It might have been easier had she been fully criminal, and not a person who had laughed and cried in his arms.

"Here."

Virgil looked down to find a canteen in front of him. He peered up at Eleanor. She pressed the canteen into his shaking hand.

"You need to drink," she said, and settled onto the ground beside him. She pulled her robe and bed linens around her, as graceful as any woman Virgil had ever seen. Tangled hair and mismatched slippers only added to her charm.

"If you think Cleo and I are hauling Auberon and Gin to Cairo on our own, you're mistaken." She grinned at him then and Virgil laughed, bringing the canteen to his mouth. Gin had settled back down. Cleo and Auberon were in conversation across from them, debating how fictional Defenders could fund the acquisition of an airship.

Virgil drank slow and long. His mind turned back to wolf-him at the lake, taking long drinks of cool water. The water had tasted strange against that queer tongue. Water lilies, there had been water lilies.

"You could carry Gin over your shoulder, make good time," he eventually said.

"Have you seen her?"

The sudden shift in topic made Virgil shake his head in silent question. He waited for Eleanor to elaborate.

"The Lady," she said.

"Should have guessed." Before he could reply, Eleanor charged ahead, so he kept his answer to himself that, yes, he had seen the Lady.

"The museum wouldn't even admit that she existed," she said. "They didn't care who I was—mocked me, in fact, when I mentioned my father. Didn't care that I helped find her. They always denied it, which only fueled my theory about her, that she was too dangerous to admit to."

"How long did you look?"

The night breeze caught her nutmeg curls, throwing them across her cheeks. "Not long enough. If I'd kept on a little longer, if I'd pressed a little harder—looked a few more places . . . "

Virgil recognized the regret in Eleanor's voice. He felt the same thing with Caroline. If only he had looked a little closer, had listened to the voice whispering in his ear. He might have known she worked for another agency and meant to twist every Mistral mission to her own benefit.

"And Hubert?" He was too curious after reading the half-stories within her file. Had they been lovers? Deep inside, the beast snarled. Virgil wondered if she would dodge the question, or take it to mean other than what it did.

"Originally the means to an end, eventually more than that. In the end, nothing what I had thought."

The admissions surprised Virgil. "I would like to hear more about it sometime, if you are so inclined," Virgil said and screwed the lid back onto the canteen. "When we're not sitting in the middle of the desert. In our nightclothes—" He broke off as dust kicked up along the horizon and then streamed away, revealing shadowed riders on horseback. "With a dozen or so riders approaching."

Virgil recognized the expression that crossed Eleanor's face, equal parts exhilaration and horror as he fitted his revolver into her palm. He moved past her, toward Gin who was trying to pick himself up from the ground.

"Bloody—" Gin sputtered. "I did find revolvers in the wreckage—I did! Cleo, did you—Oh, thank you, God."

The quintet moved as if they had worked together before, to face the approaching riders. Their weapons were meager and their number small compared to the fierce riders thundering out of the barren desert, but Virgil didn't question any of them. They were injured, but each was trained for this.

"Surely we've all been in worse," Eleanor said.

Her grin caught Virgil by surprise. Was it for the coming conflict or the second revolver Cleo offered her? They were old friends, Eleanor and that gun. When Eleanor offered his own back to him, he shook her off; the dual wield would give her twice the ammunition. He envied the apparent ease with which Eleanor stepped back into this life and wished he possessed the same when it came to reaching for the beast inside him; it wanted out.

"Chances are, we'll see worse before this is done," Auberon said. He shifted a revolver into his left hand, and while not his shooting hand, Virgil knew it would more than suffice.

Virgil caught and held Eleanor's gaze as the ground seemed to tremble beneath them with approaching thunder. "We ride it out?"

The question went beyond this moment; it spoke to the entire mission. Was she in this? Was she with them? Virgil could taste Egypt on his lips now, ancient and dry and deeply mysterious, the group of riders nearly upon them. He saw only confidence in Eleanor's eyes, the same as he would see if he looked to Auberon or Cleo, or any other agent he had been partnered with. The beast inside him strained at the leash. It wanted to run.

"We ride it out," she said.

Alongside Eleanor, Virgil turned with guns drawn to face the coming horde.

CHAPTER EIGHT

Eleanor Folley was not a lady—leastwise not a lady polite society would acknowledge as one of its own. She was reminded of this as the cloaked riders came out of the desert and she trained her revolvers on them. Her arms were steady, her stance the same, even if she looked like she belonged in the circus Mallory had mentioned. Wrapped in nightclothes and bed linens, her hair all aflunters, the circus could be the only proper society for her.

The horses were something out of a nightmare for Eleanor, the familiar sound of creatures bound in clockwork. Metal hooves struck the ground with a ceaseless fury. Eleanor concentrated on one target, but noted the rider carried only a spear. She looked at another to see he had but a sling. While the men held their weapons aloft, they made no move to use them.

She eased her fingers off the triggers and pointed her revolvers to the sky, walking slowly backward as the riders closed around them. Mallory did the same, and they now stood with backs braced together. Auberon and Cleo traced a circle around them, keeping the mechanical horses at bay with raised rifles. Gin was doing good to keep his feet, a revolver waving from one rider to another; he was the color of old paste in the wan desert light.

It felt strangely natural to have Mallory at her back as the horses closed in around them. No matter that her knees began to shake as old questions and fears rose up—*did they have the rings, would the portal open and whisk them back in time?*—she knew Mallory would be there. Wouldn't let it happen. She told herself this over and over as one rider separated himself from the others. The rider ducked under the joined spears of his men and came into the circle's confines.

Eleanor kept her revolvers raised. Mallory turned behind her, his chest flush against her back, and trained his revolvers on the man, over Eleanor's shoulders. Eleanor didn't stop him.

"You offend the oldest gods," the old man said to them in Egyptian. He pointed his spear at them, and Eleanor realized it was actually a staff. A small jackal perched at the staff's head, while its base was sharply forked. A scepter of Was? A cold chill slid down her back. This man might be a priest, someone with great power among his people.

"It is our place to remove you, to defend the homeland."

The rider spoke in Arabic, a language Eleanor had learned at her mother's side. While its familiarity might have comforted in other situations, the words themselves told her this would not end well.

The riders surged forward as if under some silent command, and Mallory never got off a shot. There were too many spears, horses, and bodies. The men slid from the horses to wrestle their group to the ground. Grasping hands and pressing bodies reminded Eleanor too closely of that day long ago and she screamed.

His mouth was not human.

Eleanor jerked away and pulled the trigger of her revolver. Three men leapt back and she rolled, clumsy in her nightclothes. Panic flowed over her.

That these men were like those from long ago settled so firmly into her mind she expected to be tackled and bitten. Expected her hands to run with blood until sand coated them. She felt a strange disquiet inside of her— something wanted *out*, but she couldn't pinpoint what.

At the swipe of a spear across her already-scratched face, she yelped. Another spear came at her, striking her across the legs. She crumpled into the dirt, panting as a coarse black sack was yanked over her head.

Not yet, Eleanor.

The bag, coupled with the voice in her head, was overwhelming, suffocating. She thrashed in panic and lifted both revolvers. Doubled fists slammed the guns from her grip and the bag pulled taut against her neck.

Eleanor spat out a curse and drew her arms to her chest, still trying to twist out of the man's hold. Every attempt she made, whether it was a twist or a stomp aimed at his feet, only served to increase his grip on her.

Another pair of rough hands grabbed her and dragged her into the sand. She kicked out, but her legs tangled in the mess of her nightclothes and didn't connect. The sudden knee in her back was sharp, although not as sharp as the blade under her chin. Eleanor went still, clasping her hands together as they tied her wrists with a length of rope.

They hauled Eleanor back to her feet and pushed her forward even as they kept hold of the rope around her neck. She found a halting, shuffling gait that allowed her to keep pace.

"Mallory!"

Eleanor was cuffed by her captor, and if Mallory heard her, he gave no reply. Perhaps he could give none. Eleanor didn't like that idea and lunged into the man who held her, trying to throw him off balance. His steps faltered, but he held firm, kicking her feet out from under her. Eleanor went down and the cord drew even more firmly around her neck. Blackness bled around the edges of her vision and she feared she would die right there. She jerked her hands up, remembering too late they were bound. The rope burned into her wrists.

"You will walk nicely," her captor rumbled and he yanked her back to her feet. The rope around her neck loosened as she stood up, and Eleanor took a shaky, dust-filled breath.

The strange metallic whinnies from the horses and the sound of sand grating in their gears unsettled her. It was too like the past, and when one rider tried to lift her onto a mount, she lurched free. She had no idea where she would run, bound and blind as she was; *away* sounded good in and of itself. But struggling proved useless; the men hauled her up and tied her to the saddle. Moments later, they were galloping.

She tried to tell herself a story as they traveled, couching it the way her mother would have. Defenders of the Protectorate, patrolling the desert wastes on their mechanical steeds. Her mother would have made it romantic—riding sepia oceans into ageless sunsets, seeking shade in unknown tombs, writing their names upon the sands so the winds would carry them to every corner of the land.

She called for Mallory again, but could only hear the hooves thundering over the rocky ground. It was a hellish ride; Eleanor glimpsed bits of sunlight as they poked through her hood, but nothing more. The sensation of being on the horse yet out of control sickened her, and by the time they pulled her down from the horse, she could do little more than drop to the ground.

When at last her captor drew the bag off, she squinted at the blinding sunlight. They appeared to be in the bottom of a canyon, walls rising high and ragged on either side of them. Three terraced levels of dwellings were carved into the cliff sides. Square doorways and smaller windows were covered in the same fabric the riders wore. In some places, children's faces peeked around corners to stare down at the riders and their captives.

Eleanor found these faces fascinating, but her attention was also caught by the images of the Egyptian gods on nearly every wall. Kneeling Ma'at and her infinite wings covered more than one door lintel, while Isis stood guard with her ankh near others.

What Eleanor didn't see were the other members of her party. There was no sign of Mallory or the rest, and the deeper into the canyon they walked, the more worrisome this absence became.

Some distance into the canyon, a woman in ochre robes approached them, shouting and gesturing. Her silver hair was wrapped into a high, braided column atop her head, and cowrie shells decorated her sleeves, making a bright music that was at odds with her demeanor. Eleanor took a step backward, meaning to avoid her, but she walked past Eleanor and her captor, still shouting. The woman moved toward another cluster of men who had somehow appeared behind Eleanor. They held Cleo in their midst! But no sign of the others.

The woman grabbed Cleo by the hair, pulling her from the group.

"Leave her be!" Eleanor shouted, but her captor jabbed her in the side, and Eleanor fell silent.

The woman forced Cleo to her knees and Cleo, with her arms bound before her, had no choice but to go down. It was Cleo's arms the woman had an interest in; she lifted them and peered intently at the assembly of gears and cogs, sticking a brown finger into them. She continued to mutter and gesture to the men, and Eleanor caught the Arabic word *tabiba*, which meant the woman might be a doctor. A doctor of what was unclear.

"I want this one," the woman said in Arabic.

Every inquiry met with denials from the men, and denials from Cleo herself.

"I want to take these apart," the woman continued as she plucked at Cleo's intricate fingers. She murmured words over the fingers, as though speaking an incantation.

Cleo closed her mechanical fingers hard over the woman's hand and tried to wrench herself away. The old woman shrieked as the fingers gripped. She backhanded Cleo, who went sprawling into the dirt.

The man who appeared to be their leader, with his manner and staff, put a gentle hand on the woman's shoulder and moved her away, murmuring. She was not easily placated, but eventually she turned and vanished the way she had come, but not without a scowl directed at Eleanor.

The men roughly hauled Cleo back onto her feet, and their group continued deeper into the canyon. Eleanor said nothing as they pulled her in the opposite direction.

Faces still peered from windows; others of the tribe were bold enough to step from their homes and stare. Among these people, Eleanor saw no children, and the only women she saw were outfitted as the men were, in simple clothing that would not hinder in battle. Trousers and tunics, hair kept short or pulled back in braids. Shells and bracelets layered atop tattooed arms.

A temple façade filled the far end of the canyon. Whether this was a natural end to the canyon or manmade, she could not say; she only knew she had been intentionally paraded through the entire settlement.

The air inside the temple was cool and smelled vaguely of jasmine, a sharp contrast to the dust outside. Eleanor coughed, nausea roiling inside her. She forced it down as she was pushed inside, beyond columns holding up a carved stone ceiling.

Three columns stood on either side of her, a tall, shadowed stone statue in the center of the arrangement. Flames flickering in a few braziers illuminated walls painted with brilliant sapphire and scarlet, but the shadows of the temple remained deep and hid much.

"I am disappointed we had so little time together," her captor said. With that he left her, closing the wooden door, securing it with a lock. A small barred window afforded a limited view of the world outside.

Before Eleanor had time to ponder what kind of a temple had a locked door—and what exactly her captor had meant by his parting comment—she heard a snuffle. Eleanor froze, and when the sound came again, it felt as though every hair on her body stood on end. She wasn't alone.

"Cleo?"

Her own whisper sounded huge in the space, every shadow pressing closer, the flames seeming to dim. Surely that was her imagination, but even so, the idea was disquieting. There was no reply to her question, not even another snuffle.

"Imagination," she whispered to herself. Still, she moved away until she backed into a column. She recalled, with perfect clarity, her first trip into a tomb and the way she had thought the walls pressed down on her; the way it felt as if all the air left the small space. It felt like that now, as close as the canvas sack that had so recently encased her head.

Eleanor tried to calm herself and turned her attention to the temple, to the figure standing in its center. Long curved snout, slanted eyes, but not Anubis. She looked to the forked tail. The men were not Defenders of the Protectorate, then, but followers of Seth? Or were they one and the same? Finding the god of chaos was not encouraging, either way. Egyptians weren't supposed to like chaos, a childlike voice inside her protested. Her stomach flipped over and her nausea returned.

As did the snuffle.

"Auberon?"

It was not Auberon who emerged from the temple's shadows. She thought at first it might be a desert jackal, but as the beast emerged into the firelight, she saw it was no jackal. This was a wolf.

As a child in Ireland, Eleanor had kept a wolfhound as a pet, a massive animal named Oak, for he stood tall and strong like the trees. He was as gentle as he was tall and would never have hurt anyone. This animal before her was no dog. Shorter and more squat, with a sharper face and keener eyes, this animal stalked her. Brown fur brindled with gold bristled every which way as the beast moved.

She took a step to her left, meaning to place the column between herself and the wolf, but the wolf's head swung in that direction, eyes never leaving her. Those eyes—they were fathomless, and perhaps it was a trick of the firelight, but they flickered and simmered with color and heat. The pupils grew wide, a thin rim of gold coloring their outer edge.

Eleanor took another backward step and the wolf took one forward. Her parents had taught her about jackals and other feral canines, about the possibility of encountering them in the desert, but never wolves. Wolves were uncommon here, but Eleanor suspected they might keep with jackal traditions. Showing any weakness would grant the creature an opportunity to take advantage of that weakness, her father had lectured. The same might be said of humans, Eleanor remembered her mother saying.

Eleanor didn't want to appear weak, but neither did she want this wolf close to her. What was her captor thinking, putting her—

"Of course this was what he intended," she whispered.

He had known the wolf was here. Did the tribe keep wolves for dispatching those who had offended the oldest gods?

"Damnation," Eleanor spat.

The wolf's ears pricked forward, giving it an oddly youthful look, and the massive head cocked to the right, as if it were trying to determine something. Eleanor took another step backward and rounded the column, placing it between them, but felt no better for it. She was still in a much-too-small temple with a much-too-large wolf for company.

Eleanor pulled at the ropes around her wrists, but the rope only dug in more firmly. A look to the door reminded her it was locked, and if there was another way out of the temple, it lay well concealed in shadow.

"This is *not* what I had planned for my afternoon," she said and still took a step toward the door. It seemed her best bet, locked or no.

The wolf snarled at the step. Eleanor froze in her tracks. Her legs quaked as though they were not a part of her, as though something else entirely controlled them. She wasn't standing her ground—was heading for the door considered a sign of weakness? Surely preserving one's own arse was anything *but* a weakness.

Eleanor looked at the wolf, and its cautionary snarl deepened when she met its eyes. She dropped her attention to her slippers, fearing that she would present herself as a challenge. She needed to tuck her metaphorical tail and—

A sharp whistle at the barred window pushed Eleanor into motion. She turned toward the door, which placed her back to the wolf. She stepped quickly backward, *closer* to the wolf to avoid the whistle's shriek, but their proximity was short lived. The beast charged the door as men outside urged him to consume Eleanor. The solid wolf body hit the wood door until the men stopped their whistling and shouting, perhaps fearful of the enraged wolf as it bared its teeth. The door creaked under the assault, but held.

Eleanor backed deeper into the temple, her mind racing. If there was another way out, she meant to find it while the wolf was otherwise engaged, but she found no such exit. When she came back to the edge of firelight on the floor, the wolf had ceased its attack on the door. It sat on its haunches, looking somehow disappointed. The wolf raised its head and looked at Eleanor. Eleanor met the look straight on.

"If you mean to eat me," she said, "I won't go down easily." Her arms were tied behind her, she was clothed in little more than tattered nightclothes, overlarge slippers, and she had no weapon. "Not even my own boots . . . "

The wolf's ears pricked forward again, listening, and then he began to pad forward.

Eleanor's knees went weak. "If you took that as an invitation, you must forgive me, for it was not meant as such." Perhaps the wolf liked it when his food fought back.

The wolf paused near the statue and snuffled at its base, where he lifted a leg and relieved himself. Then he came forward two more steps. Had Eleanor's arms not been bound, he would have been within reach. Slowly, she dipped to her knees, thinking to treat the wolf as she might have Oak. Oak liked it when others were on his level.

The wolf closed the distance between them. Eleanor decided her end was near—she hoped it would be quick—but the beast surprised her. She felt the whisper of breath across her cheek. The wolf snuffled and buried its nose into the hair above her ear. A low growl rose between them and Eleanor's heart pounded.

"Holy God, please have—"

No more words could come as the wolf dipped his head, muzzle snuffling down her bodice before burrowing into her underarm. Eleanor flinched and tried not to haul herself away; she felt she might topple right over, arms bound as they were. The large wolf head swung up, wet nose brushing her neck as he took in her scent there, too.

His mouth was not human.

Eleanor tried to calm her breathing, afraid to meet the wolf's eyes. Would he take it as a challenge? She looked instead at his nose, wet and snuffling, and then at the bristle of whiskers and the caramel fur that spread upward along the muzzle from there. When she did meet his eyes, the pupils were not so wide as before. He was a calmer beast, gold-flecked brown eyes watching her. Familiar eyes.

"Mallory?" she whispered.

And then, she laughed. It was a low, uneven sound that caused the wolf's ears to prick again.

"I am losing my mind."

The massive head ducked, then butted against her own, almost in answer. The touch was hard, but more playful than hostile. Eleanor leaned into the wolf in an effort to steady herself. She had no doubt he could have knocked her over, and if he wanted her for dinner, she would have been such by now. The wolf didn't shy from her weight. His touch was brief, the wolf as warm as Mallory ever was before he slumped near the statue of Seth.

Eleanor exhaled in an effort to calm herself, but the glimpse of a bit of silver in the wolf's paw made her breath hitch again.

Eleanor had seen many things in her life to challenge her mind and heart, but none so curious as what happened next. Her father being Irish and her mother being Egyptian had led to a childhood full of stories rich with magic and fantastical happenings; both cultures crafted tales laden with creatures that were not wholly human. Leprechauns, fairies, the Egyptian gods themselves. There remained a sliver of humanity in the way they looked, perhaps, but there was always something strangely Other.

She thought the wolf was in pain, for it began to spasm. There was no other word for the way the body twitched against the ground, raising dust in a low cloud around it. Eleanor pulled at the ropes that bound her, but still could not loosen herself. If the animal were to go mad, she wanted her hands free.

A sound began to permeate the air around them; it was almost a growl and almost a whine—something caught between. Eleanor came to her feet and stepped closer to the wolf to see if there was something she might do, but the wolf appeared to be coming apart. Legs flailed and claws spread, the silver flashing again in the firelight. Then, the body drew back into itself. The brindled fur receded, replaced with bare human skin; claws rounded into nails, paws into hands and feet. As she watched in silent horror, the body broke itself, remade itself, fashioning a man where there had once been a wolf. A naked man. No—a naked Virgil Mallory, wearing only the silver ring around his right index finger.

Virgil shook, his back bowed as he drew his legs into his chest and wrapped his shaking arms around them. He held on to himself like he might otherwise drown. Even though he was naked, he appeared as rumpled as any of his suits, skin putting itself to rights. It was almost too fantastic, but she recalled their night in the *Nuit* and the way he had smelled her.

She felt she should turn away, give him some shred of privacy, but the idea of simply leaving him there, naked on the floor and in pain, was inconceivable. Improper or not, she looked at him and tried to decide how to help him.

"Virgil."

She imagined those ears pricking forward. He turned his head toward the sound of her voice, though his eyes stayed closed. A fine layer of sweat coated him, and he trembled as if he might fall apart again. He smelled the air.

"El—"

He couldn't get her entire name out, though he tried twice more. Eleanor shushed him and dropped to her knees at his side.

"If you can untie my wrists, you can have what's left of my robe." Her own voice was not steady, but she forced the words out, knowing only that he needed help.

Mallory couldn't sit up, though he did manage to roll over, toward Eleanor. She turned and placed her bound hands within his, trying not to fidget as he made achingly slow progress with the ropes. He was ill-acquainted with his own fingers, perhaps having to remember how to use them. When she was free, she tugged her robe off and draped it over him. His bare feet poked out, but there was no helping that; he was too tall and the robe too tattered.

He made no move to draw the robe around himself; it seemed he could only lie there and breathe, much like Eleanor had when she'd come off the horse. She dared touch him, her fingers brushing the fall of his hair back from his temple. His skin was clammy, his hair wet with sweat and blood, and Eleanor muttered a low curse. She looked around the temple until at last she stared at the statue of Seth.

"Ugly b-bugger," Mallory whispered.

Eleanor's hand slid down to his shoulder, squeezing. "Seth," she said in the same tone. She presumed Mallory meant the statue anyhow and not himself, for the wolf had been a beautiful thing. Mallory himself was not so terrible to look at, either.

A collection of clay vases ringed the base of the statue, each the same size, but with a different marking. She knew one would hold perfume, while another held oil, and another water. It was the water Virgil needed, to drink and wash both, but it had been left in offering to Seth. She was loath to touch it, not worried about incurring the god's wrath, but rather that of the people who worshipped him.

Mallory's low moan made the decision clear; she crossed to the statue, picked up the vase, and brought it back to Mallory. While Eleanor respected the gods of Egypt, Mallory was in sincere need of the water. Seth could bloody well hang.

Eleanor tore the hem of her nightgown and dampened the fabric before drawing it across Mallory's hot forehead. The water was cool, whereas he burned with fever. He managed to pull the robe more firmly around him, but even so, the line of his slim body was plainly visible beneath the floral-flecked material.

"Must be inconvenient," Eleanor said as she dunked the hem back into the water and rubbed it clean before taking another swipe at Mallory. "Surely you have a dozen tailors on staff to see to your upkeep."

She tried to keep her tone light, but question after question crowded her tongue. But now was not the time, when Mallory needed tending and the temple needed escaping. As she drew the fabric over Mallory's clenched jaw and neck and he closed his eyes, she thought of the first day she had seen him, of his carelessly tied tie, and an uneasy sob escaped her.

Mallory's hand closed around her own. She looked down at him to find him wholly focused on her. That look was still disconcerting, especially now that she had evidence as to the animal inside.

"Only one," Mallory whispered, his voice rough. "Should probably give the man an increase in his wages. He must wonder what the hell I do with all the damned clothing."

They laughed, an uneven sound in the small space, but a comfort to Eleanor. Mallory slid to a seated position on the floor and reclaimed Eleanor's hand. His fingers slid up her arm to curl around her elbow and draw her closer. She went without hesitation, thinking of the way the wolf had smelled her. Known her. Here in this small space, she relaxed in Mallory's arms and rested her head against his chest, listening to the thrum of his heart.

Then, he began to shake.

"S-so cold."

Eleanor sat up, hands moving over Mallory's arms. "You aren't cold, you're feverish," she said. She scowled when he tried to turn out of her reach, to avoid another swipe from her damp cloth. "Virgil—"

"It's—" His teeth chattered so hard that he couldn't get another word out.

He squeezed his eyes shut, in clear agony, and Eleanor felt helpless. His hands reached for things she could not see and a low moan came from him, until his fingers brushed the silver ring he wore. That seemed to calm him, but he couldn't keep hold of it with the way his hands shook, and he moaned again, shifting on the floor.

"Virgil, what can I—"

Mallory's eyes rolled open. "T-tell me." He reached for her again, shaking hands closing hard on her forearms. He pulled her closer, surprisingly strong despite the shaking. "A story. Let me—" He exhaled. "Focus."

He needed a focus. Was that what the ring did for him? Was that what the *opium* did for him? *Oh, God.*

Eleanor moved from his embrace, shushing him when he groaned at the apparent loss of her. She didn't go far, shifting only enough so she could draw his head down into her lap. Mallory continued to shake, and Eleanor drew her fingers through the dampness of his hair. With a look to the statue above them, words came to her.

"My father told me the story of Seth when I was learning to tie my own boots. Seth killed his brother, Osiris—tricked him into a coffin and dumped him into the Nile. When Isis heard that her husband was dead, she went in search of him, to properly bury him."

Her fingers tightened in Mallory's hair as his shaking grew worse. Was this withdrawal or did the beast want back out? She held him while he shuddered, while sweat beaded on his forehead. She rocked him, continuing the story as her father had told it to her.

"Children led Isis to Osiris's body, which she took home for burial. Seth feared Isis would be able to bring Osiris back from the dead—she was a crafty one—so Seth stole the body and cut it into a hundred pieces. Seth scattered the pieces into every corner of Egypt."

Back from the dead. Don't die on me, Mallory. Don't.

"Isis was furious that Seth had done such a thing," she continued. Was she imagining the way Mallory's body had begun to calm? "Isis went on another journey. Wherever she found a piece of her husband, she buried it there and made a shrine. The entire world would be marked with such shrines if Isis had her way, thus ensuring Seth would never be free of his brother."

Mallory went still in her arms. Briefly, Eleanor thought he *had* died, and the idea was like a sudden knife in her belly. But then he drew in a steadier breath and his eyes opened to meet hers. Eleanor wiped the damp cloth across his face.

"They meant for you to devour me," Eleanor said in a low tone. She didn't hear anyone outside the door now.

"Yes."

Did that tremor in his voice mean he'd been tempted at the prospect? A shiver traced its way down her spine. "What is Mistral policy? Airship destroyed and abandoned, agents taken hostage by a band of natives . . . "

"Some might say execution."

Eleanor tried to laugh, thinking back to the attack on the gallery, but she couldn't. Had Mistral done this, stranded its own people? But to what end? The simplest thing was usually true, she reminded herself. Mistral wanted the ring. To what lengths would they go to get it?

"Policy," Mallory added, clearly fighting to get each word out, "is to look for any means of escape. Gin likely sent a t-telegrapheme as the *Nuit* went down, but there's no telling if it was received." He shifted in Eleanor's lap and pushed himself up. "Heading, last known position, that we were going down."

"I've no idea where the others were taken, and saw Cleo only briefly," Eleanor said, lending Mallory a hand to help him sit upright. She kept her hand braced on his shoulder, thinking he still looked about to fall over.

"If escape proves impractical," he said, "we are to remain where we are and await extraction. Either way, our lives have been threatened, so I would recommend attempting escape rather than waiting for rescue."

Eleanor looked around the temple. It was not large, its size perhaps restricted by the quality of the canyon stone. Perhaps it had grown too soft to continue digging further in. While tombs might have a scattering of halls leading to other chambers, this temple was one room.

One room that smelled like wolf piss, she thought, her nose wrinkling.

She looked back to Mallory. "Can you control the change?" So many questions, and part of her didn't want to pry when he was clearly still in pain.

Mallory nodded, his hair brushing against his cheeks, damp strands catching in his slight beard. He went a shade paler at her question, though. "Mostly. The beast wants to come now—it's the anger."

"Anger controls it?" She shook her head before she could go off on the path of endless questions. "Let it come," she said, nodding when Mallory stared at her in plain confusion. "Let it. I'll scream bloody murder and maybe they'll come. To watch." She shuddered, for she feared they would. Maybe they would open the door. Too many maybes.

Mallory shifted again, to his knees, the floral robe falling open enough to allow Eleanor to see the scar marking his chest. A ragged, pale scar very like the one that wrapped her hand. The silence in the temple thickened. *Wolf*, Eleanor's mind whispered to her, but he was also still Mallory. Deep down, still human. Wasn't he?

"You are either amazingly brave or incredibly f-foolish," Mallory said. The shaking returned as his control slipped. "I don't—don't want you to—see."

Eleanor came to her feet. Her fingers rested against his cheek before she took a step back. "I've already seen you, Virgil. Let it come."

There was a terrible relief on Mallory's face when she spoke, and he let go of the rein he kept on the beast. Though she had witnessed his return to humanity, this was different, watching him break apart, the human Mallory consumed by the animal inside. Eleanor forced herself to hold her ground as Mallory vanished inside the shifting bones and lengthening hair. The sound of it was monstrous, bones twisting and shifting into their new forms, breath curdling into a growl. She gasped when the wolf lifted its head to look at her and threw the tattered remains of her robe from its shoulders.

She extended a hand to him again, fingers scratching his muzzle as he responded to her touch. His tongue, warm and wet and startlingly pink against her dirty fingers, tasted her palm. Eleanor's eyes sought the scars on her hand, watching as Mallory licked them. Was this the kind of creature that had bitten her that day? For so long, she thought she had dreamed that angry mouth.

"Don't actually eat me . . . " She realized they had left that critical part of the plan out and questioned if wolf-Mallory could understand her now. Did he still process information the same way?

Then, he snarled.

Eleanor took a step back. She didn't entirely believe he would eat her, but it was unnerving to stand so close to this marvelous creature, knowing that he *could easily* kill her if he wished. Summoning a scream wasn't very difficult, and she backed closer to the door as Mallory stalked closer to her.

The sudden report of revolver fire and raised voices caused Eleanor to peer through the barred window in the door. Three guards stood outside, their attention drawn to something deeper in the canyon. Eleanor could see the shadows of airships hovering over the high lip of the ruddy canyon, figures descending on lines. How like the Galerie attack, she thought as more guns fired. She wanted to be out there, lending a hand and a gun however she could.

"Mistral has arrived," Eleanor said, then looked at Mallory, whose ears cocked forward. Did he understand her? Did he understand the sounds beyond the door?

He growled shortly and stalked toward her. Eleanor held her ground this time and only stepped aside when Mallory gave her a firm nudge away from the door. A moment later, Mallory launched himself into the wooden slab of door. The hinges groaned. He bowed his head and his broad shoulder struck the door with renewed fury. Over and over, with a sound like the strike of a hammer into soft wood, Mallory threw his body into the door and when, at last, the wood cracked, he reached with his claws. He tore a ragged hole into the door. Hot afternoon daylight flooded the temple, along with the cries of their guards. Mallory greeted them with a roar.

Mallory bolted through the broken door. The splintered wood snagged through his pelt, but he didn't stop. The guards shrieked and fired their weapons, and as Eleanor crawled through the hole Mallory had left, she watched in astonishment as the guards engaged the wolf.

One of the guards broke from Mallory to meet Eleanor. He grinned, as though he felt a woman would be a simple thing to dispatch. Surely nothing compared to that snarling wolf! He crooked his fingers.

Eleanor stepped forward as he beckoned, bracing her foot against his. She lifted her fist and smashed it into his grin. His head snapped to the left, and when he righted himself, his grin was long gone.

Eleanor's father taught her how to throw a punch when she was only thirteen—would that he had taught her a year earlier, she always thought—and it was a skill that had served her well ever since. She ducked the guard's counterpunch and went under his arm, jabbing her fist sharply into his side.

"Eleanor!"

She saw Auberon beyond the guards and Cleo in the distance, but it was her revolver in Auberon's hand that most captured her attention. He threw the weapon, butt over barrel, and it landed in the dirt some distance away. Eleanor lunged for it.

The guard caught her from behind, his hand fisting into the tangle of her loose hair. She let him pull her backwards, eyes still on her revolver until Mallory came into view.

He stood atop one guard, a massive clawed paw pressing the man's head into the dirt. Mallory's jaws ripped into the man's shoulder, and blood soaked the dusty ground as the flesh came apart under tooth and claw.

"Not so fast, woman." The guard who held Eleanor hauled her roughly backwards. Eleanor exhaled and let herself go slack. She felt his hold on her ease, believing in her surrender.

She moved fast, knowing she had little time to sell the lie. Twisting in his hold and kicking out, she sent her slippered foot hard into his groin. The guard dropped like a deflated balloon, and Eleanor bolted, closing the distance between her and her revolver. She scooped the weapon from the ground and trained it on the fallen guard.

The woman with the braided silver hair stepped between Eleanor and the guard. Surprise washed through Eleanor at the sight of her and the three men behind her. One of the men appeared to be losing form—his face looked like a melting wax cast as it shifted from human to something distinctly not.

"You *will* come back," the woman said.

Eleanor ducked as the woman lunged. Her shoulder slammed into the woman's stomach and Eleanor drove her back into the three men behind her. They reached for her, just as the men had on that long-ago day. In the close space, Eleanor wielded her revolver like a cosh, slamming it into the temple of one man and the jaw of another. They fell and she ran, losing her slippers in her haste. She felt Mallory close at heel as agents waved them toward the closest airship.

A trio of agents welcomed her with a harness, a gleaming web of leather leads and bronze rings. They buckled her into the contraption before hooking the harness to a line. With a tug and a shout, they sent Eleanor careening toward the belly of the airship's gondola. There, more agents caught handfuls of her tattered nightgown as they hauled her inside.

Eleanor could only rest while the others were hauled up in similar fashion: Gin, Cleo, and Auberon with his injured arm. She realized Mallory was at her side only when she heard a low rumble. She turned toward that sound as though it were a beacon in the madness. He was still a wolf, though now wearing the harness that had been used to bring him on board.

Eleanor reached a bloodied hand out to stroke his head. His fur was matted with blood and mud and he panted, emitting a low whine as the airship lifted into the sky. She didn't suppose wolves liked to fly, their natural habitat being the ground.

Eleanor curled her fingers into his sodden jaw, and Mallory's tongue snaked out to wash her hand clean as the world below dwindled to a caramel blur.

CHAPTER NINE

Cairo, Egypt ~ September 1865

Eleanor's father lifted her down from the scratchy, stinky camel and placed her feet firmly on Egyptian soil. Eleanor crouched down, peering at the camel's feet and how they squished as the animal moved. They reminded her of a bellows without the handles, desert sand puffing around each step the beast took. She straightened and squinted as she peered through the camel's gangly legs, at the triangles that rose like black portals before them.

"Black doors!" she called. The pyramids rose tall against the setting sun, pure black at this angle, sunlight flaring gold around every straight edge. She remembered the drawings her father and Mr. Piazzi Smyth had shown her and she looked at the men now.

"It's Giza, little one," Mr. Piazzi Smyth said, peeking under the camel at her. He gave her a lopsided grin, which Eleanor quickly returned.

He was Italian, but her father said they weren't supposed to hold that against him. Not everyone could be lucky enough to be Irish, after all ("And half Egyptian!" Eleanor had cried, feeling twice as lucky with the parents she had received. Who had ever been so lucky?).

Some people *had* to come from other lands, her father told her. Eleanor was fascinated with the idea of people in other lands (Did they take baths and braid their hair?), and also the red beard that sprouted from Mr. Piazzi Smyth's cheeks and chin, but didn't cover his upper lip. She wondered how he managed that trick, if it involved a razor or simply grew as moss on a tree, clinging here but not there.

"Where do the doors go?" she asked.

She heard her mother laugh, but whatever Mr. Piazzi Smyth would have said in answer was lost as Eleanor squealed. Her father placed his dusty hands on Eleanor's cheeks.

"Da!"

Sand ran over her once neatly pressed blouse, to the toes of her boots, as

Renshaw Folley rubbed Egypt across Eleanor's brow, cheeks, and chin. She thought it felt like a blessing one would get in church and she closed her eyes, breathing in the scent of the ground and her father's hands. She coughed and nearly sneezed.

"Again!"

Immediately willing to get dirty, Eleanor rubbed her hands into the Egyptian dirt that still held the sun's heat, then pressed them over her father's face. He scrunched up his cheeks like it tickled. She reached for her mother when she moved close enough. Eleanor clasped her mother's sweaty hand within her own, pressing Egypt's dirt between them.

"Where do the doors go?" Eleanor asked again.

"Not doors, Miss Folley," Piazzi Smyth said, and drew a pack down from his own camel. "Well, not precisely." He tipped his head, though, as if he were giving the idea genuine thought. Eleanor giggled as her father lifted her from the ground and braced her against his hip.

"Pharaohs were buried inside," her father said, and they moved closer toward the pyramids, her mother following.

Eleanor's eyes widened at the idea of *dead* kings inside the pyramids. "Not under the ground?" She rested her chin against her father's shoulder as the group walked to the pyramids, the Italian showing them the way. He had explored the pyramids earlier this spring, researching a book about Giza and its marvels. She thought of her father's parents, whom she had met after a fashion; they were resting under the green grass of Ireland now, tucked into an earthy bed. She looked at the line of the pyramid, rising up against the sky.

"Above the ground," the Italian said, "so they would be cherished and admired well beyond their passing."

Eleanor held her silence the closer they got to the pyramids, curiosity taking over. She could see individual stones now, stones that were the color of the ground all around them, nearly the color of melting candy. Eleanor chewed on the tie that kept her blouse together as they stepped toward a small opening in the side of the pyramid. That was where her father set her down.

It didn't look like a regular door, for stone crumbled all around it. Bits of the writing on the walls looked chipped, too, as if someone had broken in. Still, as she followed her father inside, she could see pieces of things she recognized amid the markings.

"Owl!"

Her father only followed Piazzi Smyth deeper down the corridor. Eleanor turned back, reaching for her mother so she would not lag behind; she curled her fingers around her mother's still-dusty hand.

"What do you think, minnow?" her mother asked.

Eleanor looked up the entire corridor, thinking it went on forever and they would never reach its end. "It's quite large," she said. "And full of owls." Eleanor hooted, a sound which echoed down the corridor before them.

Her mother smiled a smile Eleanor one day might interpret to mean something wholly different than simple happiness, and they walked on in silence.

Eventually they caught up with her father and the Italian, and Eleanor grew quiet, so she could hear her parents' fervent whispers. The whispers filled the corridor and when she closed her eyes, she could picture a hundred people in conversation. Her parents talked about a place called Luxor, and another place or person that Eleanor could not understand the name of. It sounded like *Dear Ellebarie* to her, and she couldn't make heads or tails of it. She returned to her study of the walls, searching for other owls. She found them, each one peering at her, but only after tracing paths of feathers, snakes, and something that looked like lightning.

They went deeper, and Eleanor saw more owls, small suns, and many more feathers. She decided they were owl feathers and realized only then that her mother was speaking again, this time to her.

"Your grandmother had a hand here," her mother said.

Eleanor didn't know what her mother meant by that, but didn't ask. Her mother was Egyptian, as was her mother before her, so the idea of *that* grandmother having a hand here—had she placed her hands on these walls?—seemed only natural. Eleanor reached out to touch the nearest wall with its carvings, surprised that no one stopped her, not even Piazzi Smyth who fussed earlier when Eleanor had wanted to touch a camel's tail.

Her fingers splayed against the old stone, and she imagined it warm like the dirt outside. Imagined it glowing with a thousand lamps, stone turned to gold. Something like magic hummed under Eleanor's fingers, through the stone and into her. She found herself imagining a shadowed silhouette at the end of a corridor that was colored with lamplight, a silhouette that moved on four legs before standing on two.

"Daughter," this shadow said, through a mouth that wasn't human.

" . . . Da?"

"Not yet, Eleanor."

"Eleanor?" Her mother crouched beside her.

Eleanor drew her hand back, looking at her mother in confusion. She was quiet for so long, her mother eventually touched Eleanor's cheek. It was the touch of those fingers that brought Eleanor back from wherever she had been.

"I want to go," she said. She pulled her attention from the wall to look at her mother. That familiar face wiped everything else away and Eleanor felt better, but it felt like the walls were getting closer. Too many owls with peering faces. "Outside. Need out."

"I'll take her."

Her father scooped her up and Eleanor curled into his arms. She closed her eyes and fisted a hand into her father's shirt. "Out, out, out." It became a low chant between them.

Her father kissed her mother. "You go on; we'll see you when you've finished your search."

Outside could not come soon enough for Eleanor. Once under the sky, she wiggled out of her father's hands and dropped to the ground. She spied the camels all sitting in a neat row and avoided them, not wanting to be spit on again. Mr. Piazzi Smyth had been right about not touching camel tails.

"Ellie, are you quite well?"

She looked at her father when he joined her. "I was scared," she said, "but I'm better now." Better, but not perfect, because she still felt squirmy. It was like a dream, the shape and the voice, but it was also impossible, because she was very much awake.

"What scared you?"

Eleanor concentrated on the rhythm of her father's hand, smoothing slow circles over her back, and on the pretty colors of the sunset spreading over the pyramids. Both calmed her.

For the first time in her life, she didn't tell her father the complete truth. Telling him about the man crawling like a dog sounded too strange, even to her own ears. He might tell her she was talking nonsense, and she didn't want to be told that. She was afraid he wouldn't let her come back to the pyramids.

"It was too tiny, and getting darker."

"Small spaces can do that sometimes."

Eleanor crawled into her father's lap, resting her head against his shoulder. He smelled like sweat, but like oranges too, and Eleanor found this comforting beyond all things. They had eaten oranges that morning; he peeled hers for her, keeping the rind in one long ribbon. Eleanor had wrapped it around her wrist like a bracelet.

"Mum is never afraid."

Her father wiped his broad hands over her dusty cheeks. "Can I tell you a secret?"

Eleanor liked secrets very much, though she wasn't yet good at keeping them.

"Keep this one in your boot," he whispered, for he always told her where to keep such a thing. "Deep down inside, by your toes."

She nodded again.

"Sometimes, Ellie," he said, "we are all scared."

Eleanor's hand closed in her father's vest. Her forehead wrinkled as she turned that idea over in her head. She didn't like it one bit.

"You?" she clarified. "And Mummy?"

He nodded, and Eleanor's eyes sought the head of the Sphinx, washed in the first shadows of the desert after sunset. She shoved the secret down into her boot as he told her, down by her toes, tucking it under the big toe and squeezing. She wished that her father had kept his secret to himself.

Cairo, Egypt ~ October 1889

Modern Cairo spread like a disorderly circus beneath Virgil's balcony, reminding him in some ways of Paris and the Exposition. Everywhere he looked, something of interest caught his attention. After the morning call to prayer from the minaret at the end of the street roused him, Virgil opened the wood-latticed windows to let some measure of the city into his rooms.

Morning traffic filled the streets, horse-drawn carriages and supply-laden camels alike— the latter outnumbering the former by dozens—merchants and customers headed for the open-air market, a group of uniformed boys being ushered to school. The morning air carried with it the scent of camels, but beyond that, there was fresh fruit, roasting meats, and the woodsy scent of a crackling fire. Virgil hadn't been to Cairo in years, but remembered its opium dens all too well. The thought of the smoke made Virgil's hands shake, and he hardened his hold on his cup, focusing on the Turkish coffee within.

He hated that he had eased his rein on the beast. Hated more that Eleanor had seen him rip the guards apart. There was nothing to be done about it; genies let out of bottles could not be stoppered back in. It had been a relief to let the anger and the beast consume him.

Foolery, Auberon would have said had Virgil voiced *that* idea aloud.

"Foolery," Virgil whispered, still trying to convince himself he was not the beast, that the beast was not him. But it was. He knew this terrible thing the way he knew his own pulse in the night. He could close his eyes and feel his heart hammering, the steady rhythm in his throat. The beast was as much inside him as that rhythm was. Denying it was becoming impossible.

If only I had access to opium . . . if only I had not been so very angry at the idea of Eleanor being taken.

These denials no longer worked their magic. They felt empty, drained of all usefulness. The opium might make the beast sleep, but the beast was he and he was the beast. This was the only answer that made sense in the light of day.

And Eleanor had seen. She had seen and had not been afraid. *Let it come, Virgil.*

Virgil closed his eyes, marveling at that idea. When he heard the brisk knock and the squeak of the door latch behind him, he turned to find Auberon entering. His partner was tidy and crisp in a cream brocade waistcoat and matching cream trousers. His right arm was encased in what looked like sculpture, a hard case enclosing the entire forearm—no doubt the work of Dr. Fairbrass. It had been evening by the time the airship had delivered the rescued party to Cairo. Baths, food, clothing, and medical attention had been provided; clean linens and exhausted sleep soon followed for all.

Auberon nearly slammed the door behind him; the small lotus-shaped mirror beside the door rattled a complaint.

"What in the world are you wearing?" Virgil asked, rather than poke Auberon about his temper. That might wait. Goodness knew it was easier to focus on Auberon's arm and temper than his own recent indiscretions. He stepped back into the room, though left the balcony doors open to allow the morning breeze entry behind him.

"Fairbrass calls it *plaster of Paris*, if you can believe that." Auberon knocked his left knuckles against the casting and they made a solid sound, as though he knocked upon a door. "He didn't invent the stuff, but surely knows how to use it."

Auberon strode toward the coffee service and lifted the pot, though when he poured, found it quite empty. He slammed it back into place on the tray.

"Cleo is staying on the case. She's worked with the Lady all these years, so *naturally* she would stay. Cleo is staying and you've drunk all the coffee."

Virgil allowed himself a sliver of a smile, though he didn't exactly feel happy. "It was coffee or something stronger, wasn't it?" he asked, then set his cup to the side. "It's not a surprise, Cleo wanting to assist? She's good at what she does and will have impressions of the Lady we otherwise might not—"

"Don't try to cloud my mind with *logic,* of all things. You aren't helping."

Two years ago, Virgil hadn't been much help, either. What was there to say, with his friend and partner in love with another Mistral agent, an agent determined to take a post in Cairo, when Auberon was stationed in Paris. The only bit of luck that Virgil could see was that Cleo Barclay wasn't working for a rival intelligence agency. Auberon hadn't appreciated the observation. Virgil was certain he shouldn't repeat it now.

He tried to put himself in Auberon's shoes—larger though they were— and imagine how it would feel to discover that the woman you loved had not perished in a hospital after the loss of her arms, but that she had been miraculously restored. Strangely, there was revulsion at the idea of such a thing happening to Caroline. No, he didn't want to discover that.

"The coffee wasn't that good," Virgil said in a low tone as Auberon continued to fuss with the cups and saucers. Virgil set his own cup aside. "I could, however, have another pot brought, if you—"

"No." Auberon turned from the coffee service to eye Virgil himself. "How are you faring?" Before Virgil could make any reply, Auberon slipped a hand into his waistcoat. "Here." He withdrew a slim black book that he offered to Virgil.

Virgil closed his fingers around Eleanor's file and exhaled. He had believed it lost. Upon the group's separation, an overwhelming rage had consumed him. Placed within that suffocating temple, he had fallen apart, logic seeking refuge within the beast's angry mind. Yet he had known Eleanor. The sound of her voice had trickled through that animal mind to touch some still-human part of him.

"Thank you." He pondered Auberon's question and wasn't sure how to properly answer. Upon arriving at the Sirocco headquarters, he had told Auberon everything about the small temple, from his change to them bringing Eleanor for him to kill and eat (he had been tempted, he had to admit). From her bravery to her encouragement. The words that eventually came from him were not those he expected to say.

"You continue telling me this is simply what I am, *who* I am, and I continue to hope one day I will accept that as truth—that I will accept the thing I am. It was somewhat a relief, to have her see. On the *Nuit*, I worried what might happen should I change up there. And the worry only compounded the anger—anger that I could do nothing *should* the beast overtake me. And yet, if this beast *is* me, perhaps it is time to stop fighting myself."

Auberon's laugh was low, but kind. "Stubborn fool," he said. He looked up. "How often did I suggest such a thing to you?"

Virgil meant to say he didn't know, but Auberon rolled onward before he could speak.

"I don't believe either one of us could count that high." Auberon's expression remained intent on Virgil. "It is a miraculous thing, my friend."

Virgil shook the words off. "It feels like a curse. I don't know why God would ask this of me."

"Perhaps it feels like a curse because you fight it. What would happen should you embrace the idea this beast is you?" Auberon waited a beat and then added, "You cannot tell me that every saint had an easy road. That Mary herself did not question why God chose her for the miracles she worked."

"I am no saint, Auberon."

Auberon waved the denial away. "None of us are saints. If you take my words literally, you miss the deeper meaning—which I think you know. No path is easy, Virgil. Do you think my own has been without stones and pitfalls? Should I have listened to myself when I told myself I was incapable of becoming an agent of Mistral because of the color of my skin? It would have been easy to hide behind that fear, to allow it to hold me back from what I most wanted."

Virgil closed his eyes. What he most wanted. He wanted to let his human form slip away; he wanted to run on four feet through the streets of Cairo, chasing whatever birds he might rouse. Duck, he liked duck. He wanted to leap into a sun-washed lake to wash the dust from his fur. He wanted to tackle the beautiful Miss Folley and dig his teeth into her neck, to mark her as *his*. But wanting these things and realizing them were two wholly separate things, he knew

Society had questioned Eleanor's wants and, in his opinion, hers were far simpler than his own. She wanted to explore the world, had fallen in love with a man who taught her how to go where she would, and had been branded unfit because of it. She had allowed that word to press her further into the quiet spaces of her father's Nicknackatarium, where society could ignore her. Virgil knew she didn't want to be seen as a curiosity, either.

"Like knows like," Auberon said.

Virgil looked at his partner and said nothing. Auberon knew how to read Virgil's face. Even worse, Virgil let his guard down around the man. Trusted him enough to do so.

"Miss Folley didn't shy from you," Auberon pressed.

"As Cleo didn't shy from *you*," Virgil countered, taking satisfaction when Auberon squirmed. The tall man straightened from the sideboard and crossed to the latticed balcony, looking into the street. Virgil followed him, hands in pockets. "Your temper can be off-putting."

"As can your—"

"No, no, enough about my faults today," Virgil interrupted. "We have already laid my psyche bare and it's quite cold and shivering now, despite the growing heat of the day. I'm certain we have great works to accomplish and I need to know if you'll be able to handle such in her presence."

"Her?"

"The delightful Miss Barclay," Virgil said, though Auberon knew quite well exactly whom he meant. "She likes eels, you know. Despite this inherent flaw, she's intelligent in all the ways we require and those we probably don't yet realize. We do find ourselves in her homeland. Will you be able to work with her?"

Stony silence was Auberon's initial reply. He attempted to cross his arms over his chest, but the casting on his right arm made such a show difficult. "I thought I was past it," Auberon said. "The anger."

"It's not anger, it's—"

"Don't say that word."

Virgil didn't say the word. He held back, in complete understanding. Some truths needed to be confronted in small measure. "Perhaps it feels like a curse because you fight it," he murmured, giving Auberon his own words back.

Auberon only grunted in reply and turned to look at Virgil's room. It was a good room, as these things went. Much as Mistral did in Paris, Sirocco provided a townhouse for its agents, with rooms, a dining hall, and laundry services. The room was small, the bed likewise and draped with netting to keep the evening's insects at bay; the balcony was the best feature, as far as Virgil was concerned, though his newly acquired clothing that didn't involve a floral robe was running a close second.

"Have you heard from anyone this morning?" Virgil asked. He wanted to specify—it was Eleanor who concerned him most, and her reaction to him.

"No; however, I would lay wager Cleo is already with the Lady. Miss Folley should be nearby. If you're ready to head down to the archive?"

The journey to the archive could not be completed without first stopping by the dining hall. Auberon knew Virgil well enough to understand this, so fell into step beside him as Virgil detoured. Every transformation left him starving; the night before, he'd gone to the hall three times despite curious looks from local agents, and even then had still woken hungry.

Mrs. Gonne, who oversaw the operations of this dining hall, seemed to be expecting him this time around—he suspected the late evening crew had spoken of his appetite—for she moved briskly from her station near the door when Virgil and Auberon arrived, and appeared soon after with two brown packages, both slightly steaming. She offered these, along with oranges and a bundle of almonds. Her green eyes gleamed as if she were part of some great game.

"Now there's a saint," Virgil murmured to Auberon as Mrs. Gonne shooed them on their way. Virgil tucked the orange and almonds into his coat pocket and unrolled the paper bag. The fragrant scent of a meat pie hit his nose, followed by the sweeter scent of dates. He tore into the meat pie first, finding it rich with leeks, onions, and garlic. A fish pastry waited beneath that one, with three fig and date pastries stacked beneath *that*. "A saint." Today, he wasn't even going to balk at the idea of fish. He would eat most anything, if only to silence his stomach.

"I know you're hungry when you don't even make a face over my eel-jelly," Auberon said as they stepped into the brass cage of an elevator that would carry them down to the archive.

While Virgil chose the correct floor (the last one in apparent existence), Auberon spooned more eel-jelly into his mouth and, indeed, Virgil didn't even make a face. He could only presume he looked as foolish with his own repast.

The elevator was nearly silent as they rode downward, cable unspooling as gears turned and whirred above and around. Upon reaching the bottom floor, the elevator took a small stutter forward, to continue gliding upon hidden tracks, deeper and deeper into the building. It was not unlike going to the middle of the world itself, for the temperature dropped and the light in the elevator dimmed. When the elevator slowed and came to a stop, the doors opened on an unassuming sitting room, occupied by Miss Upstone. Her smile was generous and she allowed them entry without requesting to see badges or any other form of identification. Virgil noted the wrinkle of her nose as they went; while she had clearly been warned of their approach, she hadn't been informed about the eel-jelly.

The hallways were labyrinthine, curving and twisting in what Virgil still thought were secret patterns, some halls without doors, other halls with too many. All of them, however, were invitingly cool, to help preserve the artifacts; a tangle of pipes coiled over the surface of nearly every ceiling, emitting gas-cooled air.

Virgil actually found himself shivering by the time they reached Cleo's wing of rooms. They paused in the sitting room where Eleanor waited alone, save for the half-dozen mummies in glass display cases, overflow from the museum's flood reorganization. Virgil drew himself up short in surprise and doubt both, whereas Auberon strode forward to greet Eleanor with a grin as she rose from the divan.

She was dressed in trousers today, a new pair acquired here in Cairo, but still a fetching tweed. Her own brown boots had been recovered from the wreckage of the *Nuit*, as scuffed as Virgil remembered them. He liked the idea that she had shunned offers of polish. A pale blouse and a burgundy waistcoat completed her new ensemble, her hair having been pulled back to the nape of her neck. While she strove for some mastery over it, small tendrils still curled free, to brush her shoulders as she moved.

Her eyes sought Virgil's, and he found them welcoming—almost, he fancied, pleased. Her smile even deepened for him, as it moved from Auberon, revealing a faint crescent dimple in her cheek and crinkles at the corners of her eyes.

"I was wondering when you two would join us," Eleanor said, as though witnessing a man turn into a wolf was an everyday occurrence, one she brushed aside as she might a sunrise. She lifted her chin toward the two pies Virgil still carried. "I see you took an alternate route."

"Mm?" Virgil had to look down at what he carried, so distracted was he by the dimple. "Oh—these. After I—" He broke off. *Focus, Mallory, focus.* "Terribly hungry." Although now, in Eleanor's presence, his appetite for food had fled. "Would you care for one?" He extended one of the wrapped pies to her. "Date and fig." His stomach chose that moment to make a loud growl. Auberon laughed.

"I couldn't possibly," she said.

"Is Miss Barclay waiting for us?" Auberon asked, and when Eleanor said she wasn't sure, he set off in search of her.

Eleanor lowered herself to the divan and Virgil sat beside her, again offering her a pie and allowing her to refuse once more before he tucked into the last of his meal.

"After," he said once he had finished the fish pie, "I'm ravenous. The change takes rather a lot out of me." It was odd, speaking to her as though it were such a common thing, when it was anything but.

"Have you—" She broke off and rested her forearms on her thighs as she looked at him.

"You can ask what you wish." Virgil drew a handkerchief out and wiped his hands and mouth before beginning to unwrap one of the sweeter pies. "I'll answer as best I can. Some things I'm still learning myself."

"What happened to cause you to change? To become what you are? You . . ." One of her hands drifted to her own chest, indicating on herself where Virgil was scarred. "I saw a scar."

Virgil paused in the unwrapping of the fig and date pie. He set the bag and its pies on the low table before them and wiped his hands again on his handkerchief. He hadn't told the tale often, but each time, it stood as a challenge. Most didn't believe him—they didn't *want* to believe such a thing was possible.

143

"I was five years old, or thereabouts," he said. "My parents and I were visiting relatives in Paris—it was our first time in the big city. My older brother . . . " Virgil trailed off at the thought of how different Adrian had been then. "The family spent the day in Le Bois de Vincennes. My father wanted us to see the animals at the zoo. Adrian, my brother, insisted we were fine on our own, and my father believed him. We went ahead, to see what animals were on hand. I remember the peacocks. They were calling so loudly, as if upset."

Virgil was aware Eleanor did not smell like her usual soap today, but of something sweeter, something orange. Perhaps what the guest accommodations had provided her, he thought, trying not to get lost in the scent, trying to stay on track with his story.

"There was talk an animal in the zoo had broken loose. No one could explain what it was, and at the time, I could not remember. Adrian said only that it was huge and angry. Probably what had the peacocks in a twist." Virgil's mouth twitched upward, though he noted Eleanor's expression didn't change. She was intent on the story. "This beast, for lack of a better word, came out of some trees, and I remember finding myself on my back, staring at the blue sky. It went on forever; I felt almost inside the color, if that makes sense."

Eleanor's head dipped in a nod, her eyes having gone a little wider.

Virgil reminded himself to breathe. "I don't remember the pain, which is fortunate, considering the scarring. My parents tell me they nearly lost me several times in the weeks that followed." He touched his chest, his shoulder. Though he had tried through the years, he couldn't remember the tearing, the teeth. "It was years later when I first changed. I was about nine and had no idea what had happened. There was—" He broke off, not liking to think of the years that followed. "There was no one to teach me and I didn't feel I could tell my parents, not when I didn't understand it myself."

At the touch of Eleanor's hand against his own, Virgil continued. "Most people don't know. Mistral knows, for they needed to; however, sometimes I think I'm more science experiment than agent." He looked at Eleanor. He wanted to tell her that he never would have harmed her in his wolf form, but he couldn't say that. It was quite possible that when the beast took his mind—no, when his own mind transformed—he might do something he would rather not. He knew this all too well.

Eleanor's silence went on too long. He was about to give her a gentle shake, to ask what she was thinking, when she stopped him by rolling back the cuff of her blouse. She pushed the entire right sleeve up to expose the long scars marring her arm. Virgil looked down at them, slowly stroking his fingers over the bared flesh, as if in absolution. Like his own attack, what had happened to her wasn't her fault.

"Do you think . . . ?" She whispered the words and couldn't finish the question.

Virgil met her worried eyes. "I don't know," he admitted, "but I think we should talk more about it. If you're inclined. You said the mouth wasn't human."

"It wasn't," she whispered, "but I've never changed. I think I would remember something like that."

"I think you would, though early on there were times I would change and wake up the next morning somewhere other than my own bedroom, and . . . quite as you saw in the temple." He was still thankful they'd had her robe at hand. It often remained awkward, the change back into human form, when he wore nothing but his silver ring.

Eleanor's own cheeks seemed pinker, but her expression was also off. He lifted a hand, to touch her chin and bring her attention back to him. "What is it?"

"I never woke up anywhere that way," she said, but Virgil heard all the words she didn't speak. There were likely other things she couldn't explain.

Eleanor stood from the divan and rounded the low table, moving toward one of the cased mummies. Virgil stood, wanting to press her into sharing whatever it was she held back, but he suspected it would do little good.

"Old friend?" he asked when she paused beside a specific case. The label stated the mummy had been a pharaoh. The mummy looked like any of the others Virgil had seen; still partially wrapped, dried to the color of the coffee he'd had only an hour before. But the hand was partially raised, as if inviting someone to dance.

"I used to tell him my secrets," she said. "My parents would be busy and I would go to the museum, sitting beside this case. I thought that hand was magical—if I could hold it, I would know everything I needed to know." She stretched her hand out now, but it only hovered over the glass, as if afraid to touch it.

"I like to imagine what they saw," Virgil said, content with the change in subject for now. "What did those hands hold? Those feet are brittle now, but they carried this man wherever he needed to go. Some of the monuments he commissioned still stand today—can you imagine creating something that lasts so long?"

"I used to wonder the same. It's no surprise then that the pyramids are almost geometrically perfect. Imagine your descendants pointing and laughing at a mislaid stone and you'd make sure you got it right the first time."

Across the room, the elevator whirred back to life, gliding away on its tracks, and Eleanor startled. It took Virgil a second to realize that while she was curious about his ability to change into a wolf, it wasn't what had her nervous. It was being here, in this place, mere steps away from the Lady and answers about her mother.

"The Lady will wait for you," he said. "There's no need to rush this, you know."

Eleanor looked from the mummy to him, and while her expression was serene, she still seemed reluctant. "I don't want her to wait. I should be running to her, but I'm—afraid."

Virgil suspected he knew how much that one word cost her. He thought to the night on the *Nuit* and their brief conversation before the attack. How much courage had that taken her as well? She sank back onto the divan, twining her fingers together in her lap.

"I agree with a good deal of what's in my file," Eleanor said. Her voice was so low, Virgil sat beside her again to better hear her. "About my mother. I do think that she was drawn back in time with the Lady's rings, but she didn't have them all, so couldn't come back. The last time I saw the Lady, my mother vanished. As a child, I had this dream that if I ever saw the Lady again, I would vanish, too."

Virgil placed his hand over Eleanor's. She was cold, but not shaking. He squeezed her fingers, thinking back to his own childhood. The first time he saw a toad after the experience in the vineyard, he believed he would change all over again. It hadn't happened, of course, and Eleanor wouldn't vanish today—he was certain. But the worries of childhood were a difficult thing to fully banish.

"You won't vanish," he said, but the words felt inadequate.

"No," she said, "but sometimes I wish I would."

Her words made Virgil cold too, even if the idea wasn't new to him. He understood it, and that worried him all the more. To simply vanish out of this world and into another. Running down Cairo streets on four feet instead of two, giving himself up to the pleasure of simply being what he was.

Virgil looked around the room with its cases and quiet mummies. How many ghosts lingered here for Eleanor? He caught sight of Auberon lingering in the hall, his hands raised in silent question. Virgil motioned him on. The man slipped back down the hallway.

"I left this behind on a promise to my father," Eleanor said, "and now I've left him again to search for something that will hurt him." She looked at Virgil and uncertainty crossed her features. "What do you mean to do with the rings?" Eleanor's hand turned under his, palm up so that her fingers clasped his own. "We're reuniting them in order to accomplish what? You don't mean to open the Glass, do you?"

Part of Virgil wanted that, and from the tone of Eleanor's voice, he suspected the same was true for her. Who wouldn't want to see such a thing, to confirm what they believed and perhaps change the course of what the entire world knew of the Egyptians and their ways? To prove the existence of Anubis? Could one do such a thing? Was that like proving the existence of God?

"Despite their inherent value as artifacts of ancient Egypt," Virgil said in a low tone, "the rings will be destroyed. We aren't going to open anything, Eleanor."

"You've been assured of that?"

"I have." Virgil didn't like doubt, but he had lived with it every day since Caroline's death. Even the most innocent memory was tainted after discovering the truth of her. Eleanor's question was valid and it made doubt creep back in. What might Mistral do here, truly? What if they saw more benefit (profit, the cynical side of his mind whispered) in opening the Glass?

"Should the Glass exist," Virgil said, "we can't allow it to be used." No matter what he wanted, the idea of opening a portal was chilling. Portals went both ways, he reminded himself—whereas a door might be an entry on one side, so it was on the other, to anyone or anything that might be there. "Look at it this way." He forced a lightness into his voice. "We could be entirely wrong."

Eleanor's fingers squeezed his. "Touched in the head."

"Precisely. We could have no earthly idea what we're talking about, and discover that the rings are simply that—rings. Won't we feel the fools then, having moved some part of heaven and a little bit of earth to find them again?"

Eleanor's head tilted, her eyes meeting his own. "Our silver lining is that we're completely mad."

"Our garrets are entirely unfurnished."

"Windmills in the head—"

"Bollocks?" a female voice asked.

This last word was offered from the hallway, where Auberon and Cleo lingered.

"Not a game then?" Cleo asked, playing the innocent.

Virgil's hand clasped Eleanor's, and he tugged her from the divan. No games here, he feared; the Glass did exist, and every moment drew them closer to a future they could not see. If the Egyptians had it right, his heart would be weighed against a feather some day. Were that day today, Virgil feared his heart would tip the scales.

CHAPTER TEN

Cleo's office was cool, dim, and tidy, despite being packed with books, maps, and other reference materials. The top of Cleo's mahogany desk was virtually hidden beneath stacks of paper, notebooks, and an array of glass and pottery inkwells in a variety of colors, but there was an order to everything. Eleanor felt instantly at home in the space, especially when she saw the bookshelves that filled the far wall, laden to the point of sagging.

Her attention came back to the inkwells that marched in a straight line across the desk's front edge. Most were crystal or glass in hues of green, amber, and cobalt, with silver-hinged lids. Several were older: rough pottery pots without cork stoppers. None showed a speck of dust, nor did the meticulously labeled jars of sand lining the shelves behind the desk. Treasured items. Eleanor liked Cleo all the more after seeing this side of her.

"I feel a little selfish about this one," Cleo said to Eleanor as she, Auberon, and Mallory entered the office.

Gin was already there, perched on a plum couch, looking about to burst from excitement.

"I feel a little selfish about it, too," Eleanor admitted, eyeing the far door. Was the Lady through there? She suddenly didn't want any of them there when she saw the Lady. She wanted to be alone, in case the anticipation became disappointment. She didn't want anyone to see—though Mallory already had. Hadn't he? She gave his hand a firm squeeze, then released him when Cleo offered her a white mantle.

"We'll wear these inside," Cleo explained, pulling one on over her own clothing. She gave Eleanor a pair of cotton gloves, but kept her own mechanical hands uncovered. "Gentlemen, it will be only me and Miss Folley this time."

For that, Eleanor was thankful, even when Gin squirmed on the sofa and his young face showed a desire to protest. Auberon placed a hand on the man's arm before he could leap up and do just that.

"When was she last viewed?" Eleanor asked. She tugged the gloves on, then wrapped herself in the mantle, not objecting when Mallory reached a hand out to untangle the back edge of it and smooth it flat. His hand lingered on her back.

Cleo didn't have to check the files on her desk to know the answer to Eleanor's question. "Last year. A cursory exam, to determine how the body was holding up, and if she needed to be moved to a different environment. She was ship-shape, if a mummy can be said to be such," Cleo said with a widening grin. "Follow me."

Cleo crossed to the door in the far wall, but Eleanor looked back at Mallory, thinking of unfurnished garrets and all they had said before stepping in here. It was a miracle he was alive, that he had survived such an attack in his childhood. But then, she had, too.

Mallory's fingers moved briefly against her back. "Don't vanish in there."

Eleanor allowed herself a smile at that, and while she nodded, she found it difficult *not* to vanish once she stepped inside the examination room.

It was a plain room, square with more shelf-lined walls, though these contained sealed boxes, all carefully labeled in a precise hand. The air was cooler than that in Cleo's office, and electric lights gave the room a cold glow, throwing strange shadows wherever they hit the shelves and boxes. But it was the table in the middle of the room and its container that caught and held Eleanor's attention.

"I would leave you with your privacy, but Sirocco regulations won't allow me to," Cleo said as she closed the door. It latched with a soft snick. "I know this is personal for you."

Eleanor watched Cleo round the table. Her mechanical hands made no sound as she reached for the lid of the box on the table; the lights gleamed over the rotating cogs and gears that allowed her arms their normal motions, precisely-made fingers easily gripping the lid and lifting it away. Eleanor stepped toward the table and found herself looking down at a familiar body, if in unfamiliar surroundings. The Lady looked to be sleeping on her side in the Egyptian sand she had been discovered in. Muslin sheltered the body from the box edges, but Eleanor fancied it a kind of blanket, to keep her warm. It was the thought of a twelve-year-old, but she allowed herself the silliness, feeling as if she had stepped backward in time. Within the dirt that surrounded the Lady, Eleanor saw small, time-darkened beads and the curve of something that could have been a bracelet.

Everywhere she walked, she made a kind of music, her mother had told her on countless nights as she wove the story. *She strung beads herself, for she enjoyed it so.*

"All this fuss with flood and theft and they didn't damage the arm, whoever took her ring," Cleo said, gesturing to a smaller box which sat beyond the Lady. It was the box Eleanor had seen in the photograph, with its chipped edge.

"I thought she was still out there," Eleanor said. "In the dirt. I'm glad she's been here, as silly as that may sound." Safe from further damage, safe from potential floods, the Lady slept the years away in this quiet place, where not even the ticking of a clock might wake her.

"She's been quite a mystery all this time," Cleo said. "I haven't been able to find anything about her—though it would help if I had a name, a symbol, something. No tomb, no markings, nothing but the clothes and jewelry she wore." Her fingers chimed lightly together. "The linen she wore was of the finest quality. Between that and the jewelry, one has to assume she was someone of substance."

Eleanor didn't know much more than Cleo did when it came to the woman's identity, though she had her theories. Looking at the timeworn body now, Eleanor's heart skipped.

"I suppose there is a possibility," Cleo added, "she could have stolen . . . "

"But that's not how the story goes," Eleanor whispered, drawing Cleo's full regard. "My mother told me stories of this woman, of her life and her rings. How could my mother have known so much, and we so little?"

The easiest answer was that Dalila Folley had known of the ancient burial all along, perhaps since childhood, and had simply made up the stories to match what she had seen. Or perhaps the Lady had not died so long ago after all. As any Egyptologist knew, such things could be, and had been, faked. Another answer—that Dalila Folley had known about the woman because she *was* the woman—seemed both impossible and logical at the same time.

"We know next to nothing about these remains, because while I have been in charge of her, I've also been kept from her." A thread of tension ran through Cleo's voice at the admission. "The agent in this position prior to me participated in an initial exam, but upon her dismissal, her files were confiscated. I maintain certain items in this collection, Miss Folley, but admit that I know very little about them."

That no files remained from the Lady's original examination was curious to Eleanor. Anything of value could have been carried away or hidden, and with the agent who performed the examination dismissed, it didn't bode well for them discovering what, if anything, had been with the Lady. "How did Mallory arrange this?"

Cleo's gleaming fingers worked to fold over an edge of the Lady's muslin. "Director Irving and his men are presently in the Dominion of Canada, which gives us a small window of opportunity. Director Walden knows about your visit—Mallory spoke with him. He wants your help in finding the carnelian ring—but he is the only one at that level."

"The Lady is bait."

Cleo actually considered it, which proved to Eleanor that she was not wrong when it came to the agency's reputation. "Incentive, maybe."

Eleanor walked along the side of the table and peered at the Lady's calm face. It was a face Eleanor had dreamed through the years: familiar and loved, like a family member.

"You've had her for all of these years," Eleanor said, trying to remind herself that the Lady had been safe. It was foolish to be jealous of Cleo for knowing, for having some access to her. "You may not have all of the facts assembled, but surely you've formed an opinion." From the light in Cleo's eyes, Eleanor could see that was true enough. "Tell me."

Cleo released the little fold of muslin she had made and tented her fingers together. In the electric lights, her mechanical arms gleamed in shades of copper and gold, and made strange shadows across the Lady and table.

"She's unusual, to be certain. The quality of the linen, the ring, the condition of the body—all indicate an ancient death, but we have, of course, no real proof of that. No formal burial, no coffin. It appears she was tossed into the desert, or collapsed on a journey."

She was forced to flee, Dalila had told a young Eleanor. *The people feared the power of her rings, the power behind her eyes. She fled into the desert wastes and no one knew of her again. They did not mourn her loss, save for one noble lady, who hid from the people herself. The noble's time had come and gone, and so too had her friend.*

"I'm still trying to locate the original files from the time of her discovery." Cleo tilted her head. "I'm sorry—I keep forgetting that you and your mother were the ones to discover her."

Eleanor pulled the mantle closer around her shoulders. "We uncovered her, but didn't get much beyond that."

Tears turning the dust on her mother's cheeks to muddy tracks; no one believed . . . we have to get her out before the summer floods come . . . Father should see, Eleanor had said, and turned, only to see those riders. Those awful riders.

"Does she look much different to you?" Cleo asked.

Given the lighting and the box that encompassed her, the Lady *did* look different to Eleanor, but these were minor things. The condition of the body was much the same, brown like winter-thin twigs. While the world outside had marched onward, time had ceased to matter for this woman, drowsing in her muslin bed.

"No, she doesn't. Do you know why the agent in charge of the Lady was dismissed?" Eleanor asked.

"Gin will spin a grand conspiracy for you, I'm sure. That she knew too much, that the agency sought to deny the Lady's existence, that the museum did as well."

"The latter points are true enough," Eleanor said. "Every time we tried to see the body, we were told it didn't exist."

"If we could locate the original files, we could determine if there was anything else with the Lady when Sirocco took her from the sands: other artifacts or jewelry, possibly." One mechanical finger tapped against the table. "Virgil wants a radiant energy image of the Lady. It's an experimental technology to be certain, but he thinks it might tell us more about the body."

Other jewelry. Could it be Sirocco had recovered another ring and, Cleo having been kept from the entire truth, no one in their circle knew of it? The idea that other rings could be absolutely anywhere sent Eleanor's mind reeling, but she pulled it back. She told herself that there had to be logic to the madness, even if they hadn't discovered it.

"Radiant energy?"

As Cleo spoke of invisible radiant energy and photographic plates, Eleanor was reminded of her father's extractor, which could harmlessly produce a view of a dig site before extractions began. Was the technology related?

"Are you saying we'll be able to see inside the Lady?"

Cleo's head bobbed in a nod. "We have been experimenting with it on a few sealed sarcophagi, and the results have been encouraging. One can actually see inside without breaking any original seals. The equipment won't be available until tomorrow, if you take my meaning."

More secrecy, but Eleanor welcomed it. If no one knew they were examining the Lady in this manner, all the better. She hoped Director Irving stayed away long enough for them to make decent headway.

Over the course of the afternoon, she and Cleo talked at length about the Lady. Eleanor shared her childhood notebook—like her file, it had been found in the wreckage of the *Nuit*—which contained her original drawings of the dig site and the body. The images looked primitive now, drawn by a child's hand, but Cleo studied them with intent. They were the best documents she had seen from the day of the Lady's discovery.

They spoke, too, about the so-called Glass of Anubis, and its potential existence. Eleanor didn't talk about the light she had seen that day; she held back, still uncertain. It could have easily been the product of a child's traumatized mind. How much had she invented in order to move past the loss of her mother?

Cleo seemed to welcome the idea that the rings opened such a portal, and could again. It might lead to more knowledge about the ancient world, Cleo said, to discoveries they wouldn't otherwise make—it might well prove the existence of the Egyptian gods! Eleanor heard a sliver of herself in Cleo's voice; that optimism, that hope. But no one, Eleanor was coming to see, would use such a portal for benign purposes. Agents were dead, an airship downed.

Eventually, Cleo allowed the men into the examination room, wrapped in mantles and gloves so they wouldn't shed anything that could possibly contaminate the Lady. While Eleanor was pleased to see Mallory, it felt odd to have three more people in the room. She had gotten comfortable with the Lady and Cleo; during their conversation, she half expected to look up and see her mother rather than the young Egyptologist.

Gin came nose to nose with the Lady before Mallory pulled him back a polite distance. Gin prattled on about her smell, how he swore myrrh clung to her. Mallory's eyes trailed over the Lady's taut cheeks, the withered hollow of her neck. His interest in the Lady made Eleanor feel more comfortable about her own. No longer were people telling her how strange she was to pursue such an idea, but encouraged it instead. They had their own motives, of course, but she had come to believe their motivations were honest.

As the sun began to sink, they journeyed back to the hotel, the agents and Eleanor sharing a dinner at a small tavern a short distance from Sirocco's headquarters. They feasted on bread baked on sun-heated stones, fish baked in palm leaves, red wine, and spicy candied ginger. By the time Eleanor let herself into her room, she felt pleasantly drowsy and full.

She was brushing her hair out of its knot when she spied the envelope propped near the vanity's mirror. It was small, inscribed with her first name and a small drawing of a lotus. Eleanor set her hairbrush aside and plucked the envelope from the vanity. It was not sealed, the flap simply tucked inside. She withdrew a sheet of stationery to read:

We have shared the Lady,
We are trusting yet timid;
Learn a greater trust,
Climb the Great Pyramid.

Eleanor looked around the rest of her room, but saw nothing else out of place, nothing that didn't belong. What was Mallory thinking? And how had he managed to leave the note inside her locked room? She pictured him charming the staff with that smile of his—I really am quite nice, or so my mother says—leaving the note before he joined them at dinner, though he hadn't been late, had he?

So few people had climbed the pyramids to the top—Eleanor had only done it once before, and then as a child—and she picked up her hairbrush again. That was reason enough to do it.

The following morning dawned cloudy, though the day remained humid. In the depths of Sirocco's headquarters, it stayed cool and dry, and Eleanor found herself wishing she had brought a jacket. The chill began to sink through her blouse from the minute she stepped off the elevator. A long night with little sleep added to her discomfort.

She dreamed of the pyramids, but the poem-leaving Mallory didn't put in an appearance. Instead, as she worked her way up the crumbled structure, it was another hand that reached for hers at the top. This hand slid down the length of her forearm, curling familiarly around her elbow. She was pulled the rest of the way up until she stood above the entire world, looking down on small lights that were like candle flames in the dark. Breath skimmed her bare shoulder and her toes curled against the Egyptian stone.

Now, Eleanor.

It was the voice from her childhood, and Eleanor felt herself fall to pieces.

She was everywhere and nowhere all at once. Even the pyramid fell away, and she was running through an endless marsh of papyrus, the green fronds brushing her shoulders. Muddy ground squelched between her toes and the air filled her nose; she inhaled deeply and then tasted the world as a snake might, licking everything into her mouth.

There were birds nearby and fish in the deeper parts of the swamp. Birds rushed from their roosting places to take to the amber sky above. Papyrus shivered around them, and Eleanor wanted to fly with the birds, but could not, for the hand held her to the earth.

She woke in a sweat, her room entombing her in silence. Sleep was hard to find again, and when it came, was fitful.

The elevator ride to the lower level of the building was nearly as quiet and suffocating as her room. She craved companionship, even as the idea of sharing the Lady made her bristle. While alone, she felt the hand would come for her again, would cart her off, whereas being among others might give her an anchor to hook herself to.

The elevator worked soundlessly around her, depositing her into the foyer where Auberon and Mallory waited. She shivered at the chill in the air. It didn't feel like Egypt down here, but some other country far removed.

"It's always cold down here," Auberon said in apology.

Mallory headed down the corridor ahead of them, intent on putting distance between himself and Eleanor. She supposed she might be embarrassed about leaving someone a poem, too. He might also share her craving and repulsion at the idea of company.

"I imagined the opposite," Eleanor said to Auberon, "for so many tombs seem to hold the warmth of the world inside." Still, she knew it was also the memory of that dream which made her uneasy and cold. Was the dark hand that of Anubis himself? And, if so, what did he want with her?

When they reached Cleo's office, Mallory had found a clean mantle and draped it over Eleanor's shoulders. She wished she had time to ask him about the note he had left in her room, but Auberon stayed with them. The poem was a private thing, so she held her questions. Mallory didn't seem prone to poetry, but what did she truly know of the man? He kept her file close to his side, he steadied her before moving away, he hadn't smelled of opium since their journey began, he hadn't eaten her in the temple. For the time being, the last was most important.

"Thank you, Mallory," she said. "Agent."

"Mmm."

The sound Mallory made was unrevealing, but Eleanor took it for amusement. She wrapped the mantle around her and moved into the examination room, where Cleo was already at work. A young boy dressed in tidy trousers and a smudged tunic assisted her. The Egyptian boy, perhaps nine, stood on a stool at the counter, mixing chemicals in rectangular trays, humming as he worked. When they entered, he looked over his thin shoulder. His brown eyes brightened and he called out a welcome in Arabic.

"And to you, Usi," Auberon said, returning the greeting and bowing to the young boy. "It has been two years?"

"Much too long," Usi said, older than his years. He turned back to his work, mindful of measurements, his gloved hands steady at each step.

The Lady occupied the same table, the muslin drawn back to reveal her browned body. *Who are you, and why did my mother need to find you so desperately?* Eleanor hoped today would bring them answers.

Around the Lady's box sat a strange machine that Eleanor had never seen before. She presumed this was the radiant energy contraption Cleo had spoken of. It was crafted of various metals that gleamed under the room's electric lights, wires snaking from this tube to that tube and back again. The tubes were clear glass and shimmered under the lights, revealing myriad colors. Cleo made adjustments to the machine as they came in, taking hold of one handle and turning it so that the entire housing swung upward to perch above the Lady like a vulture.

"I've never seen its like," Eleanor said, wishing her father were there, for wouldn't he enjoy such a piece of machinery? She thought, too, that the patrons of the Exposition would have appreciated it.

Cleo grinned. "Isn't she beautiful!" She stroked her metal fingers down the length of the machine, as though she could actually feel its lines and curves. "And look here." She gestured beneath the table, where a curious collection of trays balanced. Then, she gestured to Usi. "Usi prepares the photographic plates and we slide them into these trays. Before they have a chance to dry, we expose the radiant energy, capturing it on the plates!"

Eleanor moved deeper into the room to take a closer look at the contraption. "This is why I deal with dead people," she said. "Modern science . . . " She trailed off.

"Seems like magic more times than not," Mallory said as he drew the door shut, effectively sealing all of them inside. "How detailed will this image be, Cleo? I heard that Tesla, and Pulyui before him, had some very good results."

Cleo allowed that was so, but couldn't guarantee anything. "We have had varying results. Sometimes the plates come out with clear images and other times they are smudged with shadows. Usi!"

"Yes, yes!" The small boy waved a hand, clearly waiting for something to happen in the trays before him, and when it did, he clapped. "Mister Auberon, your assistance, please."

The two worked together as if they had many times before. Usi handed the wet photographic plates to Auberon, who slid them with care into the trays beneath the Lady, despite his cast arm. Two plates slid into position beneath a mica-lined insulator before Cleo cranked the machine. The capacitor and discharge circuits hummed. It was like a photographic camera to Eleanor, so she came to look at each plate as a photo. Cleo took photos of every part of the Lady, from her head, to her outflung arm, to her curled feet.

Eleanor came closer to Mallory as they watched the work. This close, she could see he was shaking more than a little. "Cleo tells me that the first agent assigned to the Lady was dismissed. Do you know anything about that?"

"Mmm." Mallory crossed his arms over his chest. Whatever tremor possessed him passed. "Agent Emily Ward. The partial report I retrieved implied she engaged in inappropriate behavior with her supervisor, and thus was asked to leave her position."

Cleo snorted, but said nothing, gesturing for fresh plates from Usi and Auberon. Usi moved the exposed plates to the other side of the room, and Auberon slotted the fresh ones into the trays beneath the table. Cleo allowed the men to handle the plates, and Eleanor grew curious if her mechanical fingers might react poorly with the chemicals.

"Yet her supervisor remained in *his* position, though he likely engaged just as inappropriately?" Eleanor asked.

Mallory inclined his head in a partial nod, his entire body trembling with a new shudder. "It would seem so. Gin is attempting to locate Agent Ward's records. I'm hopeful his inherent charm will aid in the s-search."

Cautiously, Eleanor placed her hand on Mallory's arm, and his eyes met hers. She thought back to their time in the temple, how he had needed a focus. Were the tremors from wanting to transform into a wolf or from the lack of opium? She hoped they could later talk of such things. Maybe on their pyramid climb. Under her hand, though, he calmed.

"I think," Cleo said as she gestured to Auberon and Usi and the plates they readied, "this will be our last set, and once they dry, we can move back to my office and see what the Lady has revealed to us. Gentlemen, I thank you."

Cleo bowed to Auberon and Usi, the latter of whom returned the movement. Auberon only watched Cleo bow, forgetting the photographic plate he held.

"Don't drop that."

Cleo's murmured directive sent him into motion once more, sliding the last plate into place.

Eleanor was both relieved and reluctant to cover the Lady over with muslin again and watch Cleo push her back toward her normal storage area. Usi took the machine and fled, singing softly as he rolled on toward the elevator.

Back in Cleo's office, Eleanor sat beside Virgil, feeling as though she were awaiting bad news. Of course, she reasoned, anything they learned would be helpful. Wouldn't it?

With the photographic plates dry, Cleo handled them with ease, Auberon adjusting a lamp so they all could see better. The first plate Cleo held up was an image of the Lady's skull, curving bright against the darker areas of muslin around her.

"Ah, see here." Cleo's thin gold finger hovered over what looked like a thread in the image. "Her skull looks fractured."

Eleanor took a closer look at the image. The fracture ran from the base of her skull to the centerline.

"Possible cause of death?" Auberon asked.

"It would be hard to say. With the fracture being to the back of the skull, it's unlikely she sustained the injury when she fell." Cleo tilted her head. "*If* she fell. She could have been tossed into the desert and was simply unable to rise." She looked to Eleanor in silent question.

"I'm not sure how she came to be out there, either," Eleanor said. "My mother's research and notes weren't helpful there." She wanted to tell them the story her mother had given her, that this woman had fled, but the memory of such stories was still too dear to her own heart.

"And there's never been anything built on the site," Virgil added, "at least that we can determine, so it doesn't appear she was headed specifically *there*." He pointed to a bright smudge on the photographic plate, his silver ring gleaming in the light. "What is this, Cleo?"

Cleo studied the smudge on the plate. "I have no idea, although . . . " She shifted the plate to Auberon, who set it to the side while Cleo brought another one up. "Here it is again." Cleo touched the bright smudge. "It looks like something along her jawline. Something *in* her mouth?"

Eleanor stared at Cleo, uncertain what to make of that suggestion. Why would the body have anything in its mouth?

"It doesn't look like bone, see." Cleo pointed out the differences in the way bone photographed and the way the bright smudge looked. "It doesn't appear to have any blood vessels. Definitely a for—"

The door to Cleo's office burst open before she could finish, and Gin stood there, flushed and perspiring, as though he had run the entire way. In his hands, he held a small round box that might have held a hat once. Its sides were faded and brown, paper curling upward from the lid.

"You . . . are not going to . . . believe this," he said, and closed the door behind him.

Auberon came to his feet. "The director has returned?"

"No." Gin lifted the box he carried, giving it a shake. Something inside shifted with a papery sound.

"The original files?" Eleanor stood up, barely daring to hope they were.

Gin nodded, though when Auberon made to take the box, he dodged. Clearly he wanted to be the one to show off the contents. Gin's eyes met Eleanor's and he looked at her as though he had never seen her prior to this moment. Eleanor's skin prickled, a faint whisper coursing along the edge of her memory.

"You didn't always have that scar," Gin murmured and traced a line against his chin.

Eleanor's hand came up to her own chin, feeling the faint mark left there the day they had both found and lost the Lady. Those men had dragged her into the sand, biting and clawing . . .

"What a damned curious thing to say," Mallory said. He moved beside Eleanor and his arm came around her, supporting her just as she felt she might swoon. She had never swooned in her life. Terribly ladylike, she supposed, but couldn't take her eyes off Gin.

"What is in that box?" she whispered.

Gin stepped further into the room, rounding the desk to place the box upon its surface. He waited, almost like a magician about to reveal his best trick, then drew the lid off with a flourish. Everyone peered inside and at first, Eleanor found nothing odd. Mostly, it looked like stacked papers. Then Gin lifted a small brass case from the collection.

"A photograph?" Cleo guessed.

The case was the right size for a photograph one would carry with them. The photo of a loved one, an image someone wanted to keep close. The brass was worked with small flowers, forget-me-nots, curling in bright silver leaves. Despite the cake of patina upon the metal, it was a beautiful piece and familiar to Eleanor. But it couldn't be. *No.*

"This was found *with* the Lady," Gin said in a hushed tone. His long fingers pressed the leaf-shaped catch that held the case closed.

The case came open and Eleanor found herself looking at her own face. It was a younger Eleanor who peered from a thin sheet of metal, an Eleanor who hadn't yet lost her mother or disobeyed her father. She felt her entire world shift, darkness gobbling the edges of the world away until she couldn't breathe properly. How terribly ladylike, she thought.

Dublin, Ireland ~ December 1884

Four years could pass in the blink of an eye. Eleanor stood across the cobbled street from Folley's Nicknackatarium and tried to suck courage out of a cigarette. Rain poured from the sky, dribbling over the edge of the green awning above her. She didn't think she could be any colder or wetter.

How can I walk into that building? It was still an eye-catching place, the brick bulk of the Nicknackatarium situated on a busy corner; a covered porch of brick arches enclosed the display windows that were usually covered in nose- and fingerprints. The Folleys owned the house next door and rooms above, to keep a better eye on their artifacts. Lights glowed from the uppermost floor, curtains drawn against the storm.

The front door would be locked, but she still had the key. If her father hadn't changed the locks—she knew he hadn't, he wouldn't—getting inside would be no problem. Walking across the street was the problem.

Admitting defeat. Saying aloud for the first time that she hadn't found enough information to justify her continued search.

She slipped her hand into her jacket, into her blouse, and held the gold ring she had taken from Christian a few months before. She had fled and he had followed, but she'd managed to stay one step ahead of him . . . and Caroline, if that was her name.

After her near-fatal encounter with Caroline in the cathedral in Port Elizabeth, she had realized the woman had her own deadly motives. She doubted whether her alliance with Christian still existed.

Eleanor's one advantage was that she'd never mentioned this place to Christian, so he could never have given the information to Caroline. Granted, he could probably track her here, for he knew exactly whose daughter she was, but, so far, he hadn't—and she hoped he wouldn't. She exhaled.

She had loved Christian, she knew, and hated herself for it. For compromising her reputation, her future prospects—everything that hadn't mattered a whit when she was knee-deep in the Egyptian desert, but mattered now that the proper world rose up around her again. What would people say . . . what would her father say? She tried to shake those worries off, but they curled their insistent fingers into her and clung.

Still, her opinion of Christian had changed over the years. She had been allowed to see beyond the reputation, to the truth of the man, and she doubted he shared that with many. Seeing him pay for an ancient artifact rather than discover it himself had been but the first crack in his armor. It was easy to pay your way. Had Christian earned any of his renown, or simply bought it?

She drew a last smoky puff from the cigarette and dropped it into the puddle at her feet. It went out with a quick sizzle. The street was silent, appearing abandoned. Lit by hazy streetlamps, it was something from a dream. How many times had she stood here in her dreams, after all? Perhaps this was simply another.

She couldn't make herself believe that. The water dripping into her collar was too real. The rain slicked off the trees on either side of the Nicknackatarium, dripping patterns that she wanted to find sense in. Anything to delay stepping inside, where her father would roar in triumph and tell her what a foolish girl she was.

The key stuck in the lock, and Eleanor feared her father had changed the locks after all. She jerked the key out and with shaking hands dried it on her shirt. She tried again, willing her hands to steady, and nodded when it fit.

The entry was heavily shadowed, little light from the street making its way inside. The curtains had not all been pulled, so here and there, a dim sliver of gaslight painted the wood flooring. Eleanor looked up at the encased statue of Horus and felt calmed by his familiar features. An identical case stood across the aisle, empty when Eleanor had left, but now home to a statue of Osiris. She strode to his side, to look at his pale green face. She tried to find some measure of reassurance there, but finding such from Osiris would mean she was dead.

She felt dead, dead inside and alone, and wishing—as a child would—for the reassuring touch of her mother's hand against her cheek.

Backward, flow backward, O tide of the years! I am so weary of toil and of tears, toil without recompense, tears all in vain.

Eleanor closed her eyes, allowed herself to remember that touch. She whispered an apology to her mother, for failing, for abandoning the search, for—

"If you run, I'll shoot yer arse end."

Her father's familiar voice made the hair on the back of her neck stand up. She had no doubt he was holding a weapon of some sort, and she stepped away from the statue to turn and face him. He stood a short distance away, holding a sling that looked like it had come from his collection rather than a weapon that he used with any regularity.

"You know the range on those things is poor," Eleanor said, painfully aware she was dripping rain on her father's fine carpet.

"Ellie!"

Renshaw Folley dropped the sling, value be damned, and ran to her. Eleanor dropped her pack so she could wrap her arms around him as he caught her. Still strong, even for a man approaching fifty. Fifty! she thought with amazement. She had missed so much!

"Ellie, my Ellie." He feathered kisses over her wet face and smoothed her damp hair back from her cheeks.

He smelled like whiskey and like wood from the fire; like the man who had shown her so much of the world and taught her all he could. Eleanor realized she was crying. It was the last thing she wanted to do in front of him. Her father kissed the tears away, and that only made it worse. Eleanor bowed her head to his shoulder.

"Da."

The low sound that broke from him nearly took Eleanor to her knees. She held him fast and squeezed until they were both crying. He pulled back to look at her, and had only smiles for his child.

"Come on." He picked up the sling and her pack, and wrapped his free arm around her shoulders. "I was making tea when I heard the door. I hoped it was you, but after all these years—"

"I waited too long—"

"You did fine." He pressed a kiss against her temple. "I have your letters. You wait and I'll show you each one."

Eleanor was glad now that she had taken the time to write, even though at the time her cheeks burned with embarrassment as Christian chided her for writing to her "Da."

"Ellie, did you—"

He didn't finish his question. He didn't have to. It weighed between them, crouched and ready to spring like a wild animal.

"No."

Eleanor knew then she wouldn't show him the ring she wore. It would only take them back in time, to a place he didn't want to go. She saw the years around his tearing blue eyes, the wrinkles that crowded his half-frowning mouth, and she refused to do this man any more harm. Four years was time enough.

CHAPTER ELEVEN

Cairo, Egypt ~ October 1889

Virgil was not well acquainted with fainting women. When Eleanor went limp against his side, his arm snared her before she could slide to the floor. He eased her toward the leather divan and carefully settled her there.

He could hardly pull his attention from the younger image of her; the tintype had borne the years well, enclosed in its golden case, Eleanor's eyes ever-bright. She was perhaps nine, her hair longer and loose down her back. Captured outside, rolling hills stretched behind her. The hills looked grassy, which put her out of place in her pith helmet and field jacket.

Once Eleanor roused, Virgil kept his questions to himself at Cleo's insistence. The woman clicked her tongue like a mother hen and escorted Eleanor out of the offices and up to her private rooms. Virgil was left with Auberon and Gin, and the photographic case. He wanted to lose himself in those hopeful eyes, to not feel the hunger that wanted to consume him. The beast was restless, wanted out, while he wanted only the privacy of a locked room and a pipe.

He had difficulty wrapping his mind around the idea before them, that the modern photograph case had been in the grave of an ancient Egyptian. Telling himself that the body was not as old as they all presumed it to be didn't improve the situation. It raised dozens of new questions which Gin was content to spout as they came to mind.

"It couldn't possibly be her *mother*, could it?" Gin asked, pacing a track in front of Cleo's desk. He swung his arms in wide circles, restless. Virgil grew tired watching him move.

"Who *knows* what that portal does," Gin said. "It's possible she found her way back after all, by some means other than the rings? And perished *right there* after coming through? What mother *wouldn't* take a keepsake with her—*naturally* she carried her daughter's likeness!"

"What's simple is true," Auberon said, perhaps in an effort to silence Gin.

"I don't doubt Dalila Folley would have carried her daughter's likeness. When they were attacked that day, it's possible the case simply fell out of her pocket, into the grave."

Auberon's calm theory only added fuel to Gin's outlandish conspiracies.

"No, no, and no," Gin said, turning and making another pass before Cleo's desk. His hands flickered through the air now, drawing shapes only he understood. "Look at the *age* on that case. If the Lady were first unearthed, what, eighteen years ago? Granted, that's a goodly amount of time, but not enough to explain how tarnished and damn *aged* that thing looks. Add to that Miss Folley's reaction. She fainted dead away. There is nothing simple about this explanation, no."

While Virgil knew Gin had a tendency (and indeed a predilection) to exaggerate, he didn't feel the man was doing so now. Something *was* amiss, and rather than sit here and continue to be plagued by questions and Eleanor's young face, he excused himself. He encountered Cleo emerging from the elevator, and she gave him a look that would have been more familiar coming from his mother.

"She should rest, Virgil," Cleo said. "The last thing she needs is you demanding answers she cannot provide. Or those she isn't yet ready to give."

Virgil's brows drew together. "You think she knows more than she's telling us?" He wasn't sure that was the case, but then he hardly felt objective when it came to Eleanor Folley.

"I am not saying that." Cleo didn't stop Virgil when he took a step beyond her, resigned to him ignoring her admonition. "When you speak with her, do it with some courtesy. I agree we need answers, but breaking Eleanor to get them is a thing I would rather avoid."

Virgil wanted to protest, but silently acknowledged he had done such in the past, permitting the beast inside to come when cases demanded it, but this case was different. Eleanor was different. If she harbored a beast the way he did, he understood the internal conflict eating away at her. Coupled with the distress she felt over her mother, Virgil felt certain Eleanor was close to breaking all on her own.

"While I may have done so on prior cases, I don't mean to now. I only know, were it me, I would want someone nearby."

When he knocked on Eleanor's door a short time later and there was no reply, he realized it was possible she was wholly unlike him in that regard. Maybe she did not want anyone with her; perhaps that was why Cleo had returned so quickly to her office. He knocked again, this time placing an ear against the door in hopes of catching even the most muted reply.

"Eleanor."

"Go away, Mallory."

He considered her reply progress at least. "Eleanor, please. I only want to—"

The door came open without warning, and Virgil straightened before he could topple inward and looked down at Eleanor. She showed signs of crying, her eyes and cheeks reddened, but also vexation. Her entire body was coiled and ready to spring.

"Only want to what?" she asked.

Her voice was deceptively quiet in the doorway, but Virgil could see she had energy yet to spare. She was sad, but also angry and ever curious. Her childhood haunted her—and here another piece of it had been revealed.

"Talk," was the word he came up with, and when she shook her head in refusal, he plunged onward. "Or if not talk, then walk. Look at you." He gestured to her disheveled hair and rumpled clothes. He didn't suspect she was given to fainting. She likely felt out of sorts over that as well. "Let's go enjoy Cairo for a time."

Distractions had done him a world of good over the years, and he could sorely use one now. He could feel the tremors beginning in his hands again and the ache inside for the sweet smoke and its even sweeter oblivion. What alarmed him now, however, was the similar comfort being with Eleanor gave him.

"Surely you would like to see something of Cairo while you're here," he added. "A ride out to Giza—"

"I'm not prepared for—"

"Giza!" cried a new voice.

Gin announced his presence in the hallway behind them and Virgil sank against the doorframe, defeated by a single word.

"Under the moonlight, the glorious pyramids rising before us," Gin continued. "Let's climb them—are we allowed? Can we do that? We are Mistral . . . we can do what we like. Auberon! Come, we're bound for Giza!"

Gin's voice trailed away and Virgil watched Eleanor's face, not understanding what emotion flickered there. But when she at last nodded, he felt as though a knot had been undone.

"All right, Mallory," she said. "Giza."

With her concession to the journey, Virgil allowed himself a grin. "For the love of Egypt, call me Virgil, will you?" She had seen him in the altogether, had seen him as a wolf; it seemed odd for her *not* to use his given name.

Eleanor's defeat, if it could ever be called such, stiffened her spine. "I'm tired, *Virgil*," she said, stressing his name and making it abundantly clear that he had been the one to make her tired.

"You're frightened," he pressed. The words were intentional, because he wanted to see the anger flare in her, the anger he knew from his own eyes when the wolf consumed him. When the anger filled her eyes, he wasn't prepared for the gut-punch it felt like.

"I'm *not*—"

"Down to your marrow, *scared*," he said, and dared to touch her chin and the faint scar that marked it. She didn't move under his lingering touch. "The way I was in the temple, naked before you." *Naked in more than one way.*

"*Virgil*."

There was a hint of something in Eleanor's voice that he hadn't heard before, that he couldn't dare to place. Was it desperation? Was it longing? Her hand closed over his and they stood this way, doing little more than breathing as the shadows in the hallway deepened around them. Though cool, her fingers burned into his, and he pictured a fragrant smoke rising between them, a smoke that kept the beast within him at complete bay. Instead, he felt the beast reach for her and his mouth dipped toward her own.

"Virgil."

It didn't sound like a denial, especially when Eleanor's chin lifted in his hand, her mouth moving toward his. He could feel her breath, warm and unseen. She no longer smelled like hotel soap; this close, he could smell *her*, the earthy scent of her that he wanted to roll in.

The slap of a hand against his shoulder drew Virgil's attention, and he found himself looking at Gin. Gin, with a pack of gear and a grin that Virgil could have cheerfully wiped off his face with one solid fist. Gin, who smelled strangely like fresh mango and bright sunlight after the warmth of Eleanor.

"We have an accord?" Gin asked. "Pyramids by moonlight!"

An accord. Virgil looked back to Eleanor, who slipped back into her room, murmuring she needed a jacket. Virgil only wanted to stalk after her, close the door in Gin's face, and damn the rest of the world. *Down to your marrow, scared. Yes, that.*

They arrived as sunset spread its golden light across the Giza plateau. Virgil slid from his kneeling camel and helped Eleanor down from hers. He wished that either Cleo had decided to join them, or that Auberon and Gin had stayed at the townhouse. As it was, it felt like an awkward quartet to him.

The field before them was largely deserted this time of evening, but Virgil picked out two small fires burning, likely indications of archaeological teams. He saw Eleanor pause and wondered if she had seen them too, if she wished to be out there, excavating all that Giza had to give. Farther out, he spied a larger field of light, a tent rising up in shadow before it. Perhaps Bedouin. Virgil contemplated securing their camels more firmly. Camels were valuable in the desert, especially to the nomadic tribes. He tied extra knots in the lead ropes, looping them around the iron posts that had been set years ago for such a purpose.

"I was twelve my first time here," Gin said as he opened the pack he had brought and uncoiled a line of rope. "You heard about that slide of stone from the top of the Great Pyramid?" He held his hands up. "I was nearly caught in it, but truly had *nothing* to do with that one."

"And you'll have nothing to do with any such incidents *this* time," Auberon said, lengthening his strides to keep up with Gin as the smaller man picked his way toward the pyramids.

Eleanor and Virgil stayed a short distance behind, Virgil watching the agents because it was easier than watching Eleanor. "They've never shared a mission before," he said.

"They'll be lucky to survive this one," Eleanor said.

Her own stride lengthened, but Virgil kept pace with her, not wishing to find himself behind her and at the mercy of her tweed trousers. It was difficult enough walking beside her when he was keenly aware of her scent. He thought of the way she leaned into him in the hallway, the way her chin lifted to him. The slight parting of her lips. These things were more intoxicating than even opium, and he would have traded anything to find them within his hands again.

"Can you believe," she said as they walked on, "it took them roughly thirty years to build one of these?"

With some measure of difficulty, Virgil turned his attention to the pyramids before them and pictured the men who had built them, the pharaohs who had commanded it. "Thousands of men. Can you imagine, we may be walking over some of them now."

Pyramids. Dead people underfoot. Virgil tried to rein his thoughts away from Eleanor, but only came back to Eleanor in the hallway, her clothes rumpled. *Pyramids . . . the case . . . the rings . . . Focus, Mallory.* He rubbed his thumb across the silver ring he wore as the ground under their boots made a sound like crunching bones. Virgil's stomach rumbled at the very thought.

His thoughts turned to young Eleanor, imagining her in this place, so small when framed against the looming pyramids or Sphinx.

"Eleanor, that photograph—"

"I was eight," she said, which surprised him, for he was prepared for her to make more fervent denials.

"Eight," he said when she fell to silence.

Their boots crunched across more rocky ground as they walked, eyes on the pyramids before them.

"We were still in Ireland, getting ready to come here. It was my first proper pith helmet. Mother added a length of fabric to it so I would be shaded, and I insisted they take my photograph." She laughed, but Virgil heard sorrow in the sound even so. "I felt quite the princess. My mother took the photograph, though my father was close by, telling me to stand still." She imitated her father's voice, gruff and firm: "Stand still, Eleanor, or you'll blur the image."

Virgil let the silence stretch between them this time, although he wanted to ask her what it was like to see the photograph again, after so many years gone. He could guess, but it would be only that, a guess. He kept his silence, trusting Eleanor would continue. She did.

"My mother carried it with her everywhere she went. Da bought her the case in a little shop in Dublin, said the flowers reminded him of her, for while they were rounded on the edges, they were sharper along their stems. Sharper where one would be caught unawares."

"Would she have had it with her that day, Eleanor? The day you found the Lady?"

"It would have been odd for her not to have it."

Virgil pondered exactly how to bring up his next point, but to his surprise, Eleanor did it for him.

"The easiest conclusion is that it fell from her jacket during the attack," Eleanor said. "The only problem with that is, she wore it close to her skin. She didn't carry it in a pocket, as most would. She wanted it close."

"It was that important to her," Virgil said.

"She treasured little of this modern world, Virgil, much preferring the dead and their secrets. Old texts, master paintings, anything not of this century. But that case was strangely dear to her, and she took pains not to lose it."

This brought Virgil to his next point. His fingers fussed with his collar, then slid down dust-gritted lapels. Ahead, he could hear the murmur of Auberon and Gin, but his focus stayed on Eleanor. Eleanor in the hallway—*stop it, Mallory.*

"There is a test we could perform," he said, forcing his voice to stay even all the while. "We could isolate a sample of your nuclein and a sample from the Lady. Much like the radiant energy method, it's a new science, but there have been cases where the identity of a person could be— That is to say—"

"Do you think the Lady is my mother, Virgil?"

Eleanor came to a standstill. In the setting light, her eyes lost all their color, yet in their depths, he saw a small spark of the sun itself, like light across deep water. Virgil allowed himself to take Eleanor's hand. She didn't refuse.

"In all truth, Eleanor, I don't know, but I think we should explore the idea." He felt her tremble and squeezed her hands. He realized his own stopped shaking when he did.

"It doesn't necessarily aid us in the search for the rings," Eleanor said.

"No, but . . . " He looked down on her, choosing his words with care, for he didn't mean to hurt her. "I think there's more going on here than the rings. While that is one search, you've been on another—to discover what happened to your mother. And if we might solve that, I say we'd be fools not to."

"Addlepated," she said.

Virgil couldn't help but smile. "Benish," he offered.

"Cakey?"

"Mmm, pure chubs." He gave her hands another squeeze, his thumb sliding against her own.

"You really are insufferable, Virgil," she said, but by the upward slant of her mouth, he could see she was having him on. When she pulled him back into motion, moving ever toward the pyramids, she tucked her hand into the crook of his elbow.

"My mother says—"

"Are you her only child? It's no wonder she dotes on you as she does."

"Older brother, younger sister," Virgil said, quick to derail that train of thought. "You?"

"It was only ever me," Eleanor said, "so naturally I was terribly spoiled—a princess, as I said. You being wedged between two others though . . . " Her voice trailed off, she laughed, and then she said, "You aren't the oldest, the first, so everything you did, your brother had already done. And you aren't the youngest, the most engaging . . . and it being a sister that occupies that place, well, there's no way to compete. However . . . there is the entire wolf thing to consider. What *did* your parents think of it?"

"Isn't it ridiculous," he murmured, "but they still don't have the vaguest clue." He felt her curious look, but didn't look down to meet it. "The poor middle child, always striving for a shred of attention that is utterly his own. Resorts to outlandish techniques, going so far as to transform himself into a beast if his mood is foul enough."

"Virgil."

He clicked his tongue against the roof of his mouth and now did look at Eleanor, to meet her wide eyes. "One learns to live with certain regrets, yes?" He prayed he might yet learn to live with this one, but couldn't see how. When he saw the raw look in Eleanor's eyes, he knew that one did not learn. They pretended to go on well enough, but that barb was always there.

"No," she whispered.

He reached for her again as their steps slowed, his fingers tracing over the scar across her chin and then further down her neck. Though the desert was cooling around them, Eleanor radiated heat like a fire. He slid his fingers down to the chain which rested against her pulse.

"Hey, Antony! Cleopatra!"

Virgil lifted his head to look at Gin, who yelled at them across the plain. He was gesturing toward the pyramid beside him, all shadow and gangly arms.

"The pyramids wait for no man! Or woman! First one to the top doesn't pay for drinks tonight." With that, Gin launched himself toward the stones, looking rather like a spider in silhouette as he ascended.

"We could tie him to a camel with his ropes," Eleanor offered.

"We could also conquer that damn pyramid before he does. Free drinks await, after all."

Eleanor's grin told him what he needed to know, and they set out to close the distance to the pyramid. It was only when they had climbed three levels that Virgil realized the pyramid was the Great Pyramid of Khufu, the largest of them all.

Paris, France ~ August 1884

From the end of the bed, Virgil watched Caroline fold another shirt into her hard-sided case, a man's shirt although it had been tailored to fit her smaller frame. Likewise the waistcoat and jacket that followed. Everything she placed into the case appeared to belong to a man: a cigar case, pressed handkerchiefs, a handful of ties.

They rarely spoke of their individual missions, often giving only locations, and those sometimes off by an entire country. Caroline often found herself in Russia when she said Germany, China when she said India. This was an undercover mission, but Virgil didn't press for more details.

He never presumed marriage to a fellow agent would be simple. The requirements of the job itself would not allow that. There were people they could speak with, for they were not the first Mistral agents to marry, but Caroline wouldn't hear of it. Counselors intruding into their personal matters? That was more obscene than anything she could fathom.

"Should be beautiful this time of year," Virgil said in a mocking tone, and eyed the careful folds of the ties within the case. He often thought Caroline dressed better as a man than he did; her ties were always flawlessly knotted and never came undone.

Caroline looked up from the wardrobe drawers, her reflection smiling at him from the round mirror nearby. "I hope I can find some time to gather specimens."

As reticent as Caroline could be about some subjects, she was oddly expansive about others. When Virgil met her, he had had no idea she had a fondness for flora and fauna. Chiefly, it was the flora of an area that caught her interest; she could spend hours collecting flowers and pressing them flat to save. They weren't keepsakes so much as they were—as she said—specimens. She delighted in discussing them. The way one stem curled and another didn't, the way crimson might blotch one petal of an otherwise ivory tulip. These things brought out a curiosity in Caroline that Virgil hadn't otherwise seen.

Once again, the words hovered against his lips. *Darling, I'm a wolf.* What would she say? Would she demand proof? What logical woman wouldn't? Would her interest in flora and fauna provoke a curiosity about him, what he was? He shifted on the bed, lips parting. *Tell her. Say the words and trust that all will be well.*

"I'll bring you a parrot," she added, turning to place an extra shirt into her bag. One could never be too careful.

The desire to tell her passed, and Virgil plucked the top tie from her bag, winding the watered silk around his hand. "A parrot is precisely what our schedules need," he said, then gestured to the framed leaves, petals, and butterflies on the far wall of their room. "More petals, fewer parrots."

Caroline lunged for the tie he held, but Virgil held it out of her reach, which caused her to brace against the bed, her slender body notched between his legs. When she met his eyes, Virgil felt the beast inside him react. Stalk, leap, tackle, bite. Caroline touched his nose, a simple tap, but it was enough to shift Virgil's thoughts.

"We may pass over Morocco," she said and reached again for the tie.

Virgil surrendered the fabric, watching Caroline smooth it flat and fold it, placing it back into her case. Were they bound for Morocco? Could one obtain a parrot there? Part of him longed to ask her where she was going, but the other part of him knew she wouldn't tell him. It wasn't their way.

Caroline drew a blue gown from the wardrobe and a pair of gloves. She folded both into her case and then, to his surprise, pressed her mouth to his.

"I'm sorry to go," she murmured.

She smelled like lemons and pepper, and Virgil slid his hands into the short bob of her hair, digging fingers in as deeply as they would go. He swallowed

taller, ever stronger. Do you think that blight of a tower will outstand these pyramids?"

There was a touch of sorrow to her question, and Virgil touched her arm, giving her a gentle push. "I think there's room enough for both of them in this world," he said and then fell to silence, thinking that no matter how far he had gone in this world, there was always a new corner he had yet to explore. How many more wondrous things awaited them?

Every wondrous thing awaits you, so said his father in a wedding toast to him and Caroline. She had smiled the smile he had first fallen in love with; that same expression had been gifted to her own father, when he gave her a small box and wished them both well. Every wondrous thing.

"Where are you now?" Eleanor asked.

"Thinking about the breadth of the world." He ran his hand over the rough stone beneath them and thought of that small box in Caroline's hands. "I understand why these places call to you. I think I understand why even that tower has its own appeal. To some."

It was the challenge in a thing, the idea of building something taller than anyone had built before; the idea of leaving a mark that would reach into the future.

Eleanor whispered, "Do you think the Lady is my mother?"

The same question she had asked earlier, only this time Eleanor's voice didn't sound so strong. Virgil watched her fold one hand around the other.

"I have believed the Lady is a modern woman," he said, "though I have no sound evidence pointing that way—beyond your mother's photograph case now. It was only ever a feeling, and when I looked back at the accounts from you and your father that day, it fit."

Eleanor shifted on the stone, turning more toward Virgil. "Except how does my mother dig up her own body? If we say the Glass of Anubis did open, and somehow did cause a breach in time, she can't be dead and alive both, can she?"

Virgil shook his head, but it wasn't the answer he meant to give. "There may be a method in every madness, no? Least I've held to such an idea through the years. In truth, I've less held to it than dabbled with it." He felt the beast inside him stretch, yawning and rolling its eyes. If there were a method to *this* madness, he had not yet found it and mostly didn't look.

Eleanor's smile, when it came, was full of understanding. "I don't know if there is a method, Virgil. Most days, it all feels like madness. The not knowing. My father tells me that she's dead, simply that and nothing more. That we lost her that day and should move on, but there's no . . . "

"Too many questions, not enough resolution," he said. He covered her hand with his. "Someone has to dig the Lady up, so Dalila can find the ring and go back, so that she can die and someone can dig her up and . . . " Virgil drew lazy loops in the air before them. "I don't know."

"The idea that the Lady is my mother is absurd, isn't it?"

"A little frightening too," Virgil said and withdrew his hand from hers. He tried not to laugh as Gin took another misstep on the pyramid below. Auberon could no longer be seen, and Virgil wondered if he had skirted around the pyramid rather than up. "If it were my mother, I don't know what I'd be thinking."

"Tell me about *your* mother, your family. That way, I don't *have* to think."

"My mother," Virgil said with a lopsided smile. "Paragon of motherhood, should be sainted upon her death." Eleanor laughed, a pleasant sound in the otherwise quiet night. "Brother Adrian and sister Imogene—you know them as the two I am forever competing against."

"And what do they do in order to outshine you?"

What didn't they do? His fingers itched for a pipe. Ah, but he needed to speak to Adrian, no question. "Chateau Mallory, ever hear of it?" He plucked a small loose stone from those around his feet and turned it over in his fingers.

"That's your family?"

"Vintners for as long as we can remember." A memory of the toads rose in his mind, and he found himself sickened all over again. *Damn toad.*

"My father handed most of the business over to Adrian a good ten years ago, though he still takes an active part in things. One can barely pry him away from his grapes most days. Adrian lives and works on the family land. He married and has continued the Mallory line with twin boys, a little girl, and one currently on the way."

"A relief for you, no doubt."

Virgil laughed. "Oh, goodness no. I need a family, don't I? In order to rise above." The smile he flashed Eleanor was short-lived. He didn't even know if he could have a family. "Imogene surprised everyone and became a governess," he continued. "She watches after Adrian's children. For the longest time she didn't know what to do with herself, only that she wanted away from the grapes. Some part of me wanted away, too."

"And Adrian, did he want away?"

"I'm certain he did, but certain too that he felt obligated to continue what our father had continued from his father."

"How long since you've been home?"

"Too many years." His voice came out more strained than he hoped, for the idea of home was nearly suffocating. He both wanted to be there and didn't, for being there meant facing Adrian and his anger. Anger that Virgil had been able to break away and leave. "You would think I'd get there more often, based in Paris and all." He dropped the rock from his hands.

"You sound so practiced," Eleanor whispered.

Virgil bowed his head, then looked to Eleanor, whose expression was filled with understanding. He knew that soon he needed to tell her the truth of all he knew. She needed to know about Caroline, about his personal investment.

"I stayed away for four years," she said. "When you get the chance, go home."

"It is not that easy," he began to protest, but Eleanor laughed.

"The important things are never easy," she countered, reaching out to touch his hand where it rested against his leg. Her fingers traced the line of his silver ring, over skull and cross and words.

Viver disce, he thought. That was the part he had such trouble with: learning to live.

CHAPTER TWELVE

Climbing the pyramid gave Eleanor a restored sense of purpose and renewed the tie she felt to Egypt. This was a timeless place, one that even their modern world could not erase. The pyramids had stood for thousands of years and would stand for thousands more. Feeling that power beneath her feet, Eleanor calmed.

She wanted to stay atop the pyramid all night, watching the stars reel overhead and the sunrise come morning. She wanted to imagine the pyramids as doors once more, opening onto worlds she did not yet know. She wished her father were there, to christen her with Egypt all over again.

She pictured her father and Juliana climbing the pyramid, Juliana clinging to his arm the entire time. While she might scale a bookshelf in search of a particular volume, she rarely went much higher.

Instead, there was Virgil Mallory, who had begun to open himself to her. There were things he still held back—she couldn't fault him for that—and they kept their silence on the climb down.

The camels were where they had tied them, and Mallory undid his tricky knotwork with ease. The journey back to Sirocco's headquarters was one of the longest Eleanor could remember, for her thoughts would not slow. The idea of the photographic case haunted her, as did the notion the Lady was her mother. It wasn't the first time she had considered it, but it was the first time she had been faced with evidence that might support the theory.

By the time they reached the townhouse, Eleanor's mind had quieted. She took Auberon's hand as he offered it to her and slid down from the camel, who was as tired and cranky as Gin. Eleanor bade the trio of gentlemen goodnight. She promised to meet them come morning and fled to her room, despite the eager expression on Mallory's face. If he wanted to talk, she meant to make him seek her out, feeling she had already exposed too much of herself on top of the pyramid and earlier in the hallway.

Young men were not worth the trouble—didn't her father tell her that? With that idea firmly in mind, Eleanor closed and locked the door behind her. Less than an hour later, there came a soft knock.

Sleep had not arrived to carry Eleanor away the way she hoped, and she put aside her old sketchbook to stare at the door across the room. There was a long silence and then the knock came again.

It was low, but still carried, and when it came a third time, this one a bit more demanding, she slid from the bed and crossed to the door, unlatching the lock to find Mallory hovering there. His surprise was plainly evident on his face, perhaps because she had finally answered the door, or perhaps because she was wrapped in nightclothes and robe.

"I realize this is unusual," he began.

Eleanor reached through the gap in the door to take hold of Mallory by his rumpled lapel. She pulled him into the room. She closed and locked the door behind him, telling herself this was no worse than their midnight conversation on board the *Nuit—right before the airship crashed and fell to pieces.*

"It's better than you standing in the hall, knocking all night," she said. He was such a contrast, Virgil Mallory. Demanding when circumstances required it, almost shy when they didn't.

"Ah, well—" Mallory attempted to smooth the wrinkles from his jacket. She could see that his hands were shaking again, and a fine sheen of perspiration covered his forehead. "Surely I wouldn't have remained *all* night. Perhaps a mere quarter of an hour."

Eleanor moved to the liquor tantalus that crouched on the room's sideboard. The small walnut cabinet enclosed three cut-glass decanters and a plethora of small glasses. She chose two glasses and the whiskey, which she had ferreted out earlier. It was, surprisingly, Irish. She poured.

She wanted to invite him to sit, but could see that Mallory was too full of energy. She stoppered the decanter and nodded toward the other room—the bedroom—and when Mallory's eyes widened, Eleanor clicked her tongue.

"The balcony, you ninny," she said with a laugh, and moved that way, glasses of whiskey in hand. It made her question what Mallory thought of her association with Christian; did he, like so many others, think she should have been sent to a convent for the rest of her days?

When Mallory joined her he took a draught of the evening air, still redolent with smells of the marketplace twisting through the streets below. Eleanor offered Mallory a glass and he took it, clearly attempting not to drink its entire contents at one go.

"Forgive me for saying so, *Agent*," Eleanor said, "but something has you tied in knots." She sipped her whiskey and set the glass on the balcony rail, waiting for Mallory to calm.

He looked out at the city. It was a long look, from a man who had never seen Cairo before, or from one who was seeing it for the first time all over again. When he at last spoke, he looked at Eleanor, as if refusing to hide within the city's elaborate streets. In the low lamplight that flooded from her room, he looked on edge.

"One way I deal with the beast, Miss Folley, is opium, and I have not smoked for several days now."

Eleanor had the feeling he could have told her down to the very hour how long it had been since he had last smoked. She suspected, too, the admission was difficult and that those who knew of his need were few, much like those who knew about the beast.

"That isn't why I'm here, however," he said before she could make any offer of help. "That isn't what I came to tell you, in fact." He laughed, a low sound between them, and a tremor ran through him. "I have wanted to tell you for some time now, but the timing has been poor."

He paused, letting the silence draw itself out. From the street below there came the low bray of a donkey, but otherwise the quiet of the world held.

"I was recruited into Mistral after my time at the military academy and immediately met Miss Caroline Irving."

Eleanor's skin pricked with sudden heat. Mallory looked at her as though the name should be significant to her, and of course it was. It made Eleanor feel queasy, not from the whiskey, but from the idea that this was how the puzzle came together.

"At first, she was nothing more than my mentor," he continued, "and that she should have stayed." Mallory took another generous swallow of whiskey. "She was older than I, driven in her work, and respected by every agent we crossed paths with. I am not ashamed to say I fell deeply in love with her. I asked her to be my wife, and we were married after a scandalously short engagement."

Mallory set his glass beside Eleanor's, clasping his hands together as he went on to describe their marriage. It sounded like anything but a marriage, with more time apart than together. How had they possibly maintained a relationship?

Perhaps Mallory having been married should have surprised her, but somehow it didn't. Having come from a large family, it was normal for him to want a family of his own.

"Did she know?" Eleanor asked. "That you were a wolf?"

When Mallory said no, Caroline hadn't known until the end—that was the thing that surprised Eleanor most. How had he kept such a truth from his own wife?

"There were clues about her and I should have paid more attention," Mallory went on. "For a while I felt as though I was drowning in some new revelation every day—things I never saw, but that were right before my eyes. She worked for other intelligence agencies, seemingly for the highest bidder, taking jobs that even Mistral would never touch. My last mission with my partner Joel—"

Mallory's voice hitched, and Eleanor pushed his whiskey closer. "Take a breath," she said. "There's no rush."

But Mallory couldn't slow himself. "We were gathering intelligence," he said in a lower voice, one that was smoothed by the whiskey, "and Caroline was doing the same. Our paths crossed. She shot Joel and I—" There was only a slight pause before he went on. "In my anger, I let the beast consume me, and it—" A hitched pause again. "No. *I* killed her."

Eleanor reached for Mallory's hand, but he turned away, shoving his hands into his trouser pockets as he stared into the streets and across the city. Eleanor withdrew, feeling somehow unwanted, but she realized that wasn't it at all. Mallory was confessing to her—the opium, his wife's death at his hands—and how impossible it must have been for him, to first admit it to himself, and then tell another.

"Auberon and Gin know that I killed her, but they don't know what I suspect of her. They don't know because I couldn't prove anything and still I have only bits and pieces, but I hope that you—" He turned back to look at her. "Among the many trips Caroline took, there is one to Morocco. This trip seemed nothing out of the ordinary until I became acquainted with your file. You were there at the same time. You were there with Christian Hubert."

"Morocco." Eleanor lifted a hand to the ring she wore even now, curling her fingers into the fabric of her nightclothes.

Mallory withdrew a photograph from his jacket and set it on the balcony ledge between them. The wedding photograph showed Mallory with a blond-haired woman, the woman Eleanor remembered from the night flight to the Roman ruin . . . and later. How young and in love Mallory looked in the photograph, his hair neatly and carefully slicked back, eyes gleaming as he held Caroline's gloved hands within his own.

"This woman met Christian in Morocco," she said as she set her whiskey glass down and convinced her hands to stop shaking. "She gave him a ring in the tavern bar. This ring." She touched a hand to the ring she wore. "Said she knew of a ruin that she would show us. I don't know how she and Christian knew each other. Maybe you have that answer?" But at Mallory's quick headshake, she exhaled. "We camped that night in Morocco . . . and I stole the ring from Christian." Those words still wanted to stick in her throat. "They tried to find me. A month or so later, I was in Port Elizabeth and Caroline tracked me down. She was good. She nearly killed me."

How close Caroline had come, Eleanor didn't want to remember. Caroline, Virgil's wife. Virgil's dead wife.

"I have been trying to reassemble her life," Mallory said. "It hasn't been an easy thing, for her father is a director with Sirocco and may have had part in covering her trail."

"Cleo mentioned him, I think?"

Mallory reached for Eleanor's hand. She let him claim it, finding a comfort in his grip. "Forgive me for not telling you sooner. I thought I could keep this part to myself, and yet—" He laughed, a hollow sound, and then the words came in a rush. "You saw the wolf, you know my deepest shame, and every part of this mission is private and personal for you—believing the Lady might be your mother, risking your quiet, established life to return here, to this madness. You deserved the whole truth."

Eleanor held to Mallory's hand, wanting to tell him that it was all right, that *everything* was all right, but the words wouldn't come. The idea that Caroline had been Mallory's wife colored everything in new hues.

"There is one more piece to this puzzle," he added, and Eleanor laughed, as if they would never find the puzzle's end. "I don't know if it fits, but you said there are four rings. You saw all four with the Lady?"

"Yes. Always four, even in the stories my mother told me. 'The Lady wore four rings to mark her stations.' "

Mallory's thumb began to worry a path along Eleanor's thumb. She didn't mind the motion, her skin warming beneath the touch.

"At our wedding, Caroline's father gifted her with a small box. Caroline never showed me what it was. Still, it was a small box, and might well have contained a ring. Being that we can connect Caroline to the ring you wear and can further connect her father to the Lady here, it makes sense they may have had another of the rings."

It was strange to Eleanor, the idea that Caroline might have had another of the Lady's rings. It felt as though Caroline were trespassing in affairs that were none of her concern. Why was she so interested? Did she somehow have a tie to the Lady or did she, like so many others, only want the treasure? *One must preserve fair Egypt before she vanished entirely . . .*

"Most of Caroline's duties were in Cairo," Mallory continued. "Her father has always been involved with Sirocco as far as I know."

"If Christian has the carnelian ring and Caroline another from her father, that leaves the scarab around my own neck, and only a fourth to find. I would wager that Director Irving has a good idea where it is." Eleanor looked up at Mallory, who looked a measure calmer than he had earlier. "Did Caroline know what the rings might do, do you think?"

"I tend toward yes. Caroline rarely saw value in anything old—that is to say, value beyond monetary. She and her father had countless arguments about the value of Sirocco's work, being that so much of it was based around the recovery of artifacts. Director Irving values them for simply *being*, whereas Caroline always felt it was the money that mattered."

"After she—" Eleanor bit her bottom lip, considering her words. Asking about a man's dead wife, especially when he killed that wife, was rather like walking on a tightrope. "Did you find any small boxes among her possessions?"

Mallory's mouth lifted in the ghost of a smile, as if he knew the caution she took. "No."

"With Gin finding the items from the Lady's initial examination," she continued, "it makes me wonder if that ring is *here*. The Lady has been here all this time, with none outside the inner circle any the wiser about her. Why not keep the ring, too?"

The worst-case scenario was that her mother had the fourth ring, which boded well in that no one could open the Glass. Even so, that was not the outcome Eleanor wanted.

"I'll have Gin take another look around, see if we can rattle any more information from Cleo, too." Mallory's thumb slowed against her hand, drawing lazy circles. "We're here and Irving isn't and we may as well take advantage of that."

Eleanor thought of advantages and taking them where they could. The night air made itself known to her as the wind lifted off the Nile and passed over the balconies in a whisper. She took a step backward, meaning to remove herself from Mallory's reach. She did not regret her time with Christian, but she did regret the impression the rest of the world had of that time. She didn't want anyone to think poorly of Mallory, who was, even tonight, wearing the black of mourning for his wife.

Mallory's hand opened as if to let her go, but instead of withdrawing, his fingers slid over her wrist and up her forearm, rucking the fabric of her robe as they went. Eleanor felt the same tug she had felt in the hallway and reversed her course, stepping toward him as his hand slid up the back of her arm. This close, there was a different kind of awareness. Did she growl or did he?

"Miss Folley."

Was it a warning or did he want her to stop?

"Agent?" she asked and watched his mouth curve at the word. She touched his beard where it darkened his chin, and with that, he erased all distance between them. His beard was softer than she had imagined it would be, and so too was his mouth.

He seemed intent on consuming her now, even if he hadn't meant to in the temple, his mouth breaking briefly from hers to taste her cheeks, the tip of her nose, the scar that marred her chin. Mallory's fingers threaded through her hair, cupping the weight of her head as he feasted. She devoured in return.

She could not remember the last time she had been kissed, which was a poor thing indeed. If she were a lady, she would not have known this pleasure at all. It should have bothered her, that she did find pleasure in this, for weren't ladies to stay properly laced at all times? But here, she poured whiskey for a wolf, and lifted her mouth to his, and reveled in the taste and feel of him.

And the last time Mallory had kissed? Probably his wife more than five years ago, and Eleanor ached for him, too.

"We ride it out," he said against her mouth.

Those same words that he'd said to her in the desert when they fell under attack. Eleanor murmured her agreement, her own fingers having moved down his chin, to his tie where they tangled in the fabric. She gave it a gentle tug, to send the fabric spilling loose. Her fingers eased his waistcoat buttons open, so that she might slide a hand inside, around the middle of him, and up his back. She thought *he* growled that time, and his teeth caught her lower lip in a pleasant bite.

There came then a knock at the door and they paused, as though cold water had been doused over them. Eleanor met Mallory's hooded eyes and slowly, as a gentleman might, he released her lower lip. Eleanor withdrew her hand from his waistcoat and knew she didn't want a gentleman. No matter how improper, she was rather fond of this wolf.

"Miss Folley? It's Cleo." Knuckles rapped against the door again.

Eleanor was reluctant to leave him, but slid each of his waistcoat buttons back into their proper places.

"Miss Folley." His voice hitched.

"*Agent.*"

Neither could she help but touch him one more time, her fingers brushing over his lips before she finally stepped away from him.

The world felt changed, electric, and Eleanor exhaled as she unlocked the door. She pulled it open and found Cleo on the other side, a stack of photographs in her mechanical arms.

Cleo rocked on her heels and grinned at Eleanor, plainly pleased with something. "I'm terribly sorry about the hour, but I couldn't wait," she said. Then, her amber eyes flew wide.

Eleanor didn't have to follow Cleo's gaze to know Mallory had made himself known, but she still did, because looking at him had become a pleasure.

Cleo stuttered. "I-I—"

"We were sharing some theories about the Lady," Mallory said and lifted the wedding photo. Eleanor noted he didn't show Cleo the actual photograph, but its backside. Eleanor didn't miss the reserve that had returned to his eyes.

"The Lady is why I'm here," Cleo said as Eleanor allowed her into the room. Cleo lifted the photographs she held and moved toward the low table before the couch. "I wanted you both to see this as soon as possible, because I think I have discovered the right path."

Mallory and Eleanor settled onto the couch as Cleo spread out the photographs on the table before them. The first photograph Cleo showed was the familiar image of the Lady's head with the strange, pale mass lodged in the mouth. A second photograph showed a similar mass, though didn't appear to be of the Lady. A third image showed another head, this mouth filled with what appeared to be a tangle of thread.

When Cleo didn't say anything, Eleanor looked from the photographs to the scientist. "I'm not sure I understand."

"Surely you do," Cleo said encouragingly. One metal finger tapped against the tangle of thread. "Ancient Egyptians were somewhat skilled when it came to replacing teeth."

Eleanor looked at the image in a new light, because she knew this from her studies. "They used gold wire to bind false teeth into a mouth." Eleanor still had trouble digesting that idea; how anyone could have withstood such pain was beyond her, yet Mallory had shown her exactly what a body could endure.

Cleo beamed. "Precisely. This image is one such procedure." She set the image aside and lifted another. "*This* is a picture of ivory, which appears more dense than bone as it has no system of blood vessels. This was one of the earliest tests we did here, wanting to be sure we weren't going to damage a body by . . . "

Mallory cleared his throat.

Cleo trailed off. "Entirely unimportant at this juncture, but look here."

She lifted the photograph of the Lady, offering it to Eleanor. Eleanor could see the pale mass was the same. There was no blood vessel structure, so it wasn't bone or tooth. "Is this *ivory* in her mouth, then?"

Cleo nodded and then said nothing.

"Here," Mallory murmured and traced a slightly darker line on the image with a finger. "These are—teeth?"

"Artificial teeth," Cleo said, looking as though she would burst with the revelation. "Modern false teeth, in the body of a woman who—from the linen and description of the rings—otherwise dates to the New Kingdom."

"My mother never had false teeth."

It hit Eleanor, the realization that she had wanted this to be her mother after all. That they had not found Dalila Folley was impossible, their journey only having led them to a solid dead end.

She stared at the images spread before her, touching the image that should have been her mother but was likely not. It was awful and inconceivable.

Mallory shifted, leaning into her the way he so often had. Heat from his body bled into her, and Eleanor tried to find comfort in his presence and support. But the young girl who had lost her mother wanted only to cry. This revelation felt like losing her all over again.

"Eleanor, your mother may not have had false teeth," Mallory said, "but what about your grandmother?"

At Cleo's widening grin, Eleanor could only stare. She felt again that hand wrapping around her, threatening to pull her away.

Father?

Daughter.

The darkness moved. Within the dark, nothing had form—the dark was Anubis and Anubis was the dark. People had fashioned him into many forms through the centuries, from jackal to man and back again, but he was as he had ever been: older than the face of the deep, and darker than the blackest night.

Soon, daughter, soon.

CHAPTER THIRTEEN

The insistent fingers of an autumn wind pulled a shutter loose from its mooring, but it wasn't the weather that concerned her. If the radiant energy photographs spread before her were where all paths led, Eleanor found herself standing at either the end of a passage or upon a cliff's edge. Her fingers slid over the corner of an image showing the bright outline of something that should not be: modern false teeth in the mouth of an ancient Egyptian woman.

The scents of Cairo rolled into the sitting room on another inrush of air: anise, myrrh, camels, smoke. These scents were as drugs to Eleanor, nearly capable of drawing her back in time. She wanted to go, away from this room and into the guise of childhood's safety. To the known, and not the unknown spread before her.

Virgil Mallory moved from her side, crossing toward the window and its loose shutter while she remained on the couch. She had objected to the Mistral agent's very presence only a short time before—feeling he had no place in a search so private—but now did not wish even his momentary absence. Cliff's edge, she told herself. An abyss, unfathomable.

"One thing I have never been able to understand," Mallory said as he pulled the shutter to, "is why your mother was so intent on the Lady. She fashioned an entire mythology for this woman rather than simple bedtime stories. The Lady wasn't a pharaoh, wasn't a royal, so who was she? More specifically, who was she to your mother?"

Eleanor looked at Cleo Barclay as she sorted through more images. Her mechanical arms gleamed in the low lamplight, fingers carefully closing against the edge of a photo as she lifted it.

Eleanor pressed her hand against the couch, feeling not the fabric but a rough, male hand. It closed around hers with the heat of a white-hot sun burning through a cloudless Egyptian sky. She closed her eyes.

Soon, Eleanor.

It was not her mother's voice, the voice she had sought all these years, but one heavy with power and age. Was it, as she had begun to suspect, the ancient god Anubis?

As if the mere thought of his name conjured him, a sharp canine face assembled itself from the liquid black behind her eyes. Imagination, Eleanor told herself, as she had so many times before. Still, she remained unconvinced as his mouth parted to reveal gleaming fangs. Did his smile mock her doubt?

Eleanor felt the reflection of a similar expression on her lips, and she tongued the sharp fang she felt in her own mouth.

The shutter latch closed with a *click* that sounded like a revolver's trigger. It served to snap Eleanor's eyes open and her attention back to the room, where she fancied she could see the inky shadows being absorbed by the walls as the face of Anubis retreated. Eleanor ran her tongue across her teeth to reassure herself she had not just grown fangs.

"The Lady," Mallory continued, "was found buried in the middle of nowhere, but Dalila Folley knew the map of nowhere very well indeed."

Mallory sank onto the couch beside her again, and Eleanor curled into the reassuring arm he wrapped around her. She didn't care that Cleo was there to bear witness. Cleo was more intent on the questions posed by the photographs.

"There was a strange sense of relief when my mother found the Lady," Eleanor finally said, her eyes on the photographs. The day she had lost her mother was never far from mind, but pressed even closer now. They were coming closer to the truth; they had to be. "I remembered thinking that everything would be all right, because she had looked for so long, and so many people told her she was wrong. Very few respected her work or my father's—that only worsened when she vanished and he ceased his travels"

"What do you know of your grandmother?" Mallory asked. "Your mother's mother."

"I never knew her—Sagira." The name felt strange on her tongue now. "She died before I was born. My mother was raised by an aunt; her own father died when she was ten, but he was an archaeologist, too. My mother's father taught her, much as my father taught me . . . "

Eleanor felt as though a puzzle piece had fallen into place, a piece that allowed more of the overall image to become clear. But the image she saw was discomfiting. If the portal she believed in had allowed her mother to move backward through time, had it done the same for her grandmother before? Was the body in the ground indeed Dalila Folley's own mother?

Eleanor balked. The idea she had followed the same path as her mother before her was not only frightening, it was unsettling. Things she had no explanation for began to make painful sense: her father's insistence through the years, the way her mother had known where the body was, the look on Dalila's face when they had at last unearthed the Lady.

"We have no evidence—" But didn't they?

"Nothing beyond the circumstantial, but, Eleanor . . . " Mallory drew his arm from around her shoulders and made an effort to claim her hands. She pulled away, terror-stricken.

Eleanor curled her hands into fists. "Agent—"

"Eleanor, how long will you deny the obv—"

"Mallory, don't." It was a plea. Fear slammed her heart into her throat, making it impossible to think or talk.

Eleanor watched Mallory's jaw tense, but he fell silent. She suspected she knew exactly how difficult that silence was for him.

Cleo shifted on the couch, carefully gathering the radiant energy photographs into a stack, thin layers of cushioning paper between each. "I have returned the Lady to her slip in the archives," she said in a voice that was like cool balm over the conversation. "We can work from the photographs, with no one the wiser. I'll see you two in the morning?"

Eleanor crossed her arms over her chest. She felt vulnerable with this new idea before her, as if a fresh wound had been opened. She was not surprised by Cleo's sudden departure; their behavior had been dreadful.

"Cleo, please forgive me." "Me" and not Mallory because Mallory's idea was absurd, frightening . . . and true? *It cannot be. It cannot—but it can.* Panic closed a hand around her neck.

"There is nothing to forgive, Eleanor," Cleo said. "I cannot say I would be holding up nearly as well in your position."

Mallory saw Cleo to the door, and Eleanor bolted from the couch, stalking back to the balcony where she had left her whiskey. She finished it in one gulp. It burned like hellfire, bright and toxic, and she struggled for an even breath when Mallory joined her.

"Eleanor."

"Don't. Don't say it."

She wanted him to forget he had suggested the body could be that of her grandmother. She had believed for the longest time that the Lady was somehow her mother, that the mystery was that simple: her mother had traveled back in time, had lived an entire life elsewhere, only to die in the desert waste. It made no sense, the idea that her mother could dig herself up. But her grandmother? That made sense. Terrifying sense.

And if it were true? Dalila Folley remained missing. Where was she if not in that ground? Did she live yet, in some distant time they could not reach without the rings of Anubis? Would there ever be an answer?

I have grown weary of dust and decay, weary of flinging my soul-wealth away; weary of sowing for others to reap . . .

Eleanor felt the gentle brush of Mallory's fingertips against her forehead, moving a tendril of nutmeg-colored hair out of her eyes. Only then did she realize she was crying.

"I wanted it to be her," she said between choked sobs, and slumped against Mallory's chest when at last the admission was made. He tucked her into his arms as if he had done it for years and years, and rocked her as she cried, saying nothing.

When she at last quieted, the hoot of owls carried to them across the Cairo night. Eleanor realized Mallory was offering her a handkerchief. She closed her hand around the soft linen. It was still warm from his pocket when she pressed it against her eyes and cheeks.

"It only means the search isn't finished," he said, keeping her tucked beneath his chin, one hand tracing random patterns along her back. The patterns were calming, and Eleanor let herself hover there for a long while. She thought of nothing but the shapes, circles blending into infinity's figure of eight, which rounded into long coiling spirals moving inward toward her spine.

"I suppose it's childish," she said when she felt she might keep her voice on an even keel. "To want to see her again—any way that I can, even if a weathered body."

Mallory made a low sound and gave Eleanor a nudge. He guided her from the balcony to the slim bed just inside the doors. She let him escort her to the thin mattress and cover her with the colorful woven blanket from the foot of the bed. He plumped the pillows behind her, then retrieved his own whiskey from the balcony ledge. He pressed it into her hands. His hands lingered around the glass, around her hands.

"It's not childish," he said. "I think we all wish we could correct things in our past. That we might revisit people and places dear to us. There's no replacing a mother."

His voice trailed off. Mallory drew his hands away, and his expression was less than happy, one saying he understood all too well.

"Forgive me if I overstepped my bounds tonight," he said.

If he had, Eleanor wished he would do so again, be it with the kiss before Cleo's arrival or his suggestion about her grandmother.

Eleanor shook her head, wanting to reach a hand up and draw him back down to her side. She wanted to offer him another drink, another kiss, but it was too much for her right now. She felt overwhelmed by the idea of knowing him so well, by the possibility of the Lady being her own grandmother. Eleanor made only a murmur of agreement when Mallory said he would see her in the morning. She listened to the latch of the door and his footsteps retreating down the hall.

Sleep was elusive. Part of her felt certain Anubis would cart her away if she fell asleep; part of her wanted that. She finished Mallory's whiskey, then drew the insect netting around the bed. The ceiling, with its blue vault and precisely painted gold stars, was indistinct through the netting, unreal and beckoning. She listened to the distant sound of night birds outside, and felt the wash of cooling air from the open balcony doors, and still could find no rest.

Her grandmother?

Eleanor allowed herself to believe it. She saw her mother, not through her child-eyes, but through her adult eyes; saw her mother's obsession as if it were her own—for it was.

As she hounded her father through the years and insisted her mother was alive, Eleanor imagined her mother doing the same, for the sake of her own mother, Sagira. If this was true, surely Dalila had known the Lady was her mother; it explained her desperate need to claim her before time took her away.

She knew she had to contact her father. If her mother's own search had been motivated by the idea that the Lady was Sagira, surely he knew. His insistence told Eleanor he must. Would he admit it now?

When she padded down the hallway in robe and slippers, her room key secure in her pocket, it was Mallory her thoughts turned to. He had obviously considered the idea that the Lady was her grandmother for some time, and the idea that he had thoughts yet unshared made Eleanor eager to speak with him. The more her mind embraced the possibility, the less frightening it became.

She didn't pause when she passed his room, tempting as it might be. No light glowed from beneath his door, and Auberon's room was dark upon passing as well. Eleanor continued up one level in the elevator to the floor where Cleo lived.

Light glowed from beneath Cleo's door, which didn't surprise Eleanor; they had much in common when it came to work and the inability to sleep entire nights through. She knocked, only wondering after she had, if Auberon might be with her. When Cleo opened the door, however, the room was empty but for her, and she welcomed Eleanor in.

The room held a scent Eleanor came to recognize as developing chemicals for photographs. It didn't appear a likely environment for such things—it looked more like a traditional lady's parlor than a laboratory. Pastel floral prints were matched with bright stripes, lotus flowers blooming over fabric as well as erupting from black lacquer bowls around the room. The furniture was all ebony, gleaming in the lamplight. One table held an array of photographs, while another was scattered with paper. Glass inkwells—Cleo collected them—marched line after line across a bookcase.

"I didn't even look at the time," Eleanor admitted in apology as Cleo latched the door behind her.

"No apologies," Cleo said and nudged Eleanor toward the tea service occupying a low table between two wide chairs.

"When I have a project like this, I rarely sleep. My mind won't let me. It just keeps running." Cleo sat in the chair to the left of the tea, her violet caftan spreading out around her. "Sugar? Milk?"

"Just sugar."

Eleanor watched Cleo's remarkable mechanical hands deftly manage the cups, saucers, and small, steaming pot. The pot was inlaid with what looked like cloisonné lotus flowers blooming in profusion.

"I couldn't sleep, either," Eleanor said as Cleo took up a small spoon and lifted the lid from the sugar bowl. "I was thinking about the Lady being my grandmother."

Cleo's generous mouth lifted in a wide grin. "I think that idea might cause many sleepless nights. If you're interested, there is a test we could run."

"Mallory mentioned something to me, but I think I have a quicker, less experimental way to get an answer, which is why I came. I was hoping you could help."

"If I can, I will." Cleo added milk to her own tea until it was a pale and creamy brown, her spoon against the china cup the only sound in the room.

Eleanor found herself attempting to summon the courage to even broach the idea. In her room, it seemed simple enough. But if her father confirmed the identity of the Lady, what then? The idea of "what happened next" had always appealed greatly to Eleanor, but now it felt like she had approached the edge of a cliff. She could not see the bottom of the valley below.

"I need to contact my father in Paris," Eleanor said. She cradled her cup in her palms, letting the heat seep into her. "If my mother was seeking her mother, he would know. I hope he would admit it now."

With that out, other words came more easily. Eleanor rambled about her parents and their bond, the way they had always understood each other. She could remember her father being only supportive when it came to Dalila's research.

As Eleanor chatted on, Cleo moved to an ebony cabinet and opened its doors. Inside squatted a device of brass and bronze. When Eleanor moved closer, she saw it was inscribed with the letters of the alphabet, over which lay a variety of hinged needles. Wires coursed around the interface, disappearing into a wooden cabinet inscribed with the image of an inkwell. Eleanor had never seen its like.

"Will he still be at the Exposition?" Cleo asked, settling into the chair before the cabinet.

"He will."

Cleo hummed pleasantly as she cranked the machine to life, slid a sheet of paper against the needles, and tapped a message out across the engraved letters. In this regard, it seemed very like the typewriters Eleanor had seen at the Exposition. "We'll see if anyone is awake on that end at this hour. Surely there must be . . . ah!"

It didn't take long for Cleo to receive a response, something that left Eleanor a little breathless. The hinged needles moved across the sheet of paper, transferring the incoming message without the need of a spool of inked fabric ribbon. Each letter on the interface glowed as if it had been lit by a match, then dimmed as it was transferred. The type was small, precise.

"The operator says your father is in the gallery and has gone to fetch him." Cleo tilted her head as they waited and sipped at her milky tea. "If you know how to use this, I could leave you some privacy."

"I don't know how, actually," Eleanor admitted. She set her teacup down to take a closer look at the telegraph. "It's astounding, the idea that you just communicated with someone in Paris in plain language rather than telegraphy code."

"It would seem to make the world smaller," Cleo said, "and yet everywhere I travel, it remains impossibly large."

Eleanor watched the needles glide to and fro. Cleo read the words as they came through, and Eleanor had to laugh when her father expressed astonishment at hearing from her via this new technology.

"Tell him I've already seen the Lady," Eleanor said to Cleo, who transmitted the words as Eleanor spoke. Eleanor began to describe—as briefly as she could—all they had discovered, and how strange it was. When Cleo would pause, allowing for a reply (which came, but was always short, urging Eleanor onward), she saw none of this was news to her father. She felt like a fool, describing the line of bright white they had found in their radiant energy scans; felt like a child when she revealed the Lady had false teeth. He already knew.

The relationship she remembered her parents having was one of complete trust and faith. They shared everything with one another, if not with her. Her father would know the identity of the Lady, because Dalila had been desperate to find her. Dalila would have shared all she had known with him. And on her disappearance, Eleanor thought, her father had swept Dalila's research away. At her request?

"Ask him if he already knows," Eleanor said to Cleo. Her voice broke a little, and she was thankful her father couldn't hear. Cleo typed the message out and they waited for one to return.

"I've always known, Ellie," came the reply, and Eleanor felt as though she had been punched.

That he finally said it was a relief. Eleanor knew she didn't have the strength to argue with him over this—what's done was done, her years wasted when he knew the truth of what she sought, but the pain of betrayal she felt was keen. Cleo bowed her head, saying nothing, only waiting.

"My theories," she had Cleo transmit.

"More like facts," her father returned in the machine's precise type. Cleo's voice was even as she read the incoming words. "We should have told you, Eleanor—what we did was cruel, though to be fair, it did not go as we planned."

Planned. The word sent a stab of fear through Eleanor. That day in the desert, what had they planned?

"What do you mean?"

"You are very like your mother," he replied, as if he hadn't heard her question. She imagined him laughing a little at that, though Cleo didn't. "We never thought you would pursue it and yet, being her daughter, how could you not? We raised you to be curious, and I've spent God knows how many years condemning you for being just that."

Eleanor didn't know what to say—for it was all true. She held her silence, and Cleo began to read her father's words as the needles moved again.

"I met your mother when she was sixteen. I was twenty-one, and felt myself far beyond being charmed. She came to the college library, even though she was not a student. She told me the most fantastic story, and I swallowed it whole. She said that her mother had stepped back in time and she meant to find her."

It felt like winter in the room, Eleanor frozen to the floor, and while she pulled her robe closer, she said nothing. She and Cleo waited for the needles to move again.

"When we married, she allowed me to see her research. It was impressive and it changed my mind. I thought I had believed her, Ellie, but I didn't truly see until I looked at Lila's notes. Her father—your grandfather, Tau el Jabari—had been devising a way to get Sagira back."

It was a strange way to get the story, Cleo reading what came through the machine. Eleanor sat back down and Cleo continued, sounding transfixed herself.

"You know Tau was an archaeologist—Sagira went with him on his digs," Cleo read. "Tau speaks of Sagira in his journals, how she felt a connection to the land that he could not explain and envied. She would mention a temple or tomb location, and while nothing had been previously discovered there, they always found something. Under thousands of years of sand, but there nonetheless. Tau called her his lucky charm. On one dig, he found the rings. They seemed nothing extraordinary, but that night, Sagira was drawn to them. She told him she recognized them. She held them and vanished."

"And my mother?" Eleanor asked. She had to force the question out and watched as Cleo typed and transmitted. Someone had once called her a lucky charm, too.

"You are so like her, Ellie," Cleo read. "She was desperate to find the body, to understand what had happened. You must remember that about her. You were a gift to her, and she never meant to hurt you. She hoped the rings would be with her mother's body. She wanted—"

Eleanor hardly had to wait for the words to come. She wanted to use the rings. She wanted to step back in time as her mother had done.

Cleo read on. "But those men, Ellie, those riders. It was nothing we planned. You falling in harm's way. I didn't want Lila to use the rings, but could hardly deny her excavating the body. She promised she would wait, as long as she could see the body. We came to a compromise for your sake. But that day, nothing went right."

Eleanor closed her eyes. She could see it, the Glass of Anubis, opening, ripping her mother away. All these years, her father had known her theories were correct and still discounted them. He told her she was foolish, that her mother was dead. He had even gone so far as to have a memorial service, Eleanor saw now that it held a lifetime of deception.

"Eleanor?"

It was Cleo's question, bringing her back to the present "I can't—" She looked at the woman, hearing the echo of her father's voice. "Close the connection. I'm finished."

Cleo did, and offered Eleanor the sheet of paper with its precisely rendered letters. Renshaw's confession. Eleanor took the sheet, longing to crumple it.

"Thank you, Cleo. I'm sorry to have bothered you so very late," she said.

She slipped from Cleo's room and ran back to her own, cursing the apparent sloth of the elevator. She held her tears back, fighting them as she passed Auberon's room and then Mallory's. Later: she would tell them later, when she could speak without wanting to cry.

In her room, beyond the balcony door, sunrise was beginning to brighten the horizon. Throughout the city, the minarets came to life with the vibrant call to prayer. Eleanor locked her door and clutched her father's words against her chest. She muttered a prayer of her own, that she not lose her grip even as the world tilted out from under her. She shuffled into the bedroom and tossed the page onto the bed, where it covered her hairbrush.

Her hairbrush.

Eleanor lifted the page to reveal the brush where she had not left it, a crisp ivory envelope beneath it. Her attention came back to the balcony doors. She had left both standing open when she'd gone, but only one was open now.

She snatched the envelope from the bed. Who the devil had been in her room? Was Mallory playing another game? Her hands shook as she pulled the slip of hotel paper from the envelope. The same handwriting as before, though this time the language was hieratic.

You have looked now for years,
I cannot be sorry;
Your quest is ending soon,
Come to Deir el-Bahri.

Focusing on the language of the letter and not the anger that flooded through her, Eleanor knew. She knew.

Christian.

Valley of the Kings, Egypt ~ April 1882

"It's absurd."

Christian threw the sheaf of paper across the tent, where it hit the canvas wall and fluttered to the floor. Eleanor collected the pages and set them to rights. What was absurd, she thought, was the tantrum. She studied Christian in the low lamplight, his shadow thrown on the tent wall behind him.

"It's not," she said. "It looks like punctuation gone mad, yes, but there is a method here—"

"I don't need to know it." Christian stretched his long legs out before him, crossing his hands over his belly. The wicker chair he occupied creaked with the motions, more so when he shifted again to reach for his leather cigar case. He carried three cigars and was down to his last.

Eleanor wasn't accustomed to seeing this side of Christian, the side that could be defeated by something like hieratic writing. Christian wasn't one to be defeated by anything; he didn't pout, he didn't waver, he set his mind to the thing and had it done, enjoying the ride. Not this time. Could the hieratic actually have stumped him?

"This isn't like you," she said as he withdrew the cigar and snipped its end.

Christian grasped the lantern and angled it toward his cigar for lighting. He was careful to ensure the flame never touched the cigar as he rotated it in the wavering heat. His green eyes met Eleanor's, appraising, as steady as she had ever seen. Still, something was amiss.

"What I'm about to say goes no further than this room," he said. He blew a gentle breath on the lit tip of his cigar, causing the embers to glow, and set the lantern down.

Eleanor looked around the tent interior, their meager supplies stacked against one side, two bedrolls splayed on the other; the walls moved as the wind blew outside, sand whispering against the canvas.

"Such as this room is," she murmured as the peppery scent of the cigar began to fill the small space. "Who would I tell, the camels?"

She only smiled in return. Would it always be this way, a challenge at every turn? As much as she enjoyed it, it was also wearing thin.

"I'm worried," he admitted. As if allowing the cigar to serve as distraction from the truth of the conversation, he blew a breath carefully through it, then settled it into the corner of his mouth.

"You never worry, or if you do, you're well practiced at hiding it." Eleanor set the sheaf of papers to the side, away from the lantern's flickering flame.

"This is big, Eleanor," he said. "Claiming that mummy from those Germans." He rubbed his hands together, then drew the cigar from his mouth, its end glistening with spit. He rolled it between his fingers, looking excited despite his worry.

The unspoken "what ifs" that weighted Christian's words made Eleanor feel a little sick. How could he doubt this? After all they had planned, to keep that body here, in Egypt where it belonged. The Germans had been digging in the Valley for weeks, carting bits of Egypt off as they would, but this large a find—this mummy who might well be royalty—neither one could stand to see taken from its homeland.

"You're being ridiculous," she said. "We have studied that camp inside and out. You've never doubted yourself before—" She broke off. "Do you think I should stay behind?"

This would be the first raid they had attempted together. She had known Christian for six months, and while that seemed a goodly period of time to get to know a person, she still wondered if it was enough time. Did she fully trust him? Did he trust her? Maybe he thought she would muck it up and didn't know how to say such.

She had found him a great help when it came to seeking information about the Lady's rings; she thought he felt the same of her. This adventure had not been planned, but she thought they were both in accord: the mummy needed to stay in its homeland.

"Eleanor—no. I can't do this without you."

The words startled her, but no more so than what followed. She realized she was perched on the edge of her chair. The wicker creaked as she tensed. This man's opinion mattered too much to her; she wanted to be seen as worthy out here in the field, even if what they proposed was a theft of sorts.

"Every day, you amaze me," he said, leaning forward to rest his arms on his thighs. Smoke curled up from his cigar, slow and spicy. "I think I know so much and then there you are, a dozen damning steps ahead." He gestured to the papers on the ground. "That is gibberish to me, yet you read it as smoothly as your native tongue."

Only after years of study, she wanted to say, but didn't, deliberating what else Christian might admit to her. What he said made her fall into a deeper silence.

"I saw you in Cairo, before we met in the tomb," Christian said. "I asked about you; everyone praised you even if they thought you were unconventional, said you were tracking a great mystery, looking for a thing you would never find or understand. I put myself in that scribe's tomb to meet you, Eleanor. And this time, I can't do this without you. I think you are my good-luck charm," he finished with a laugh. He drew his cigar back to his lips, inhaling a mouth of smoke.

"You're even more absurd than the hieratic," she said and felt a slight thrill knowing he had watched her. She pushed her vanity to the side, because if he had observed, if he had listened to others speak of her, what did he know about the rings? "You had an amazing career before you met me, did quite well for all those years—"

" 'Quite well' has never been good enough for me."

Eleanor nodded, knowing it was true. "Agreed. But, Christian—"

"If we succeed in this, no one will know. If we fail, the world will witness it."

Eleanor suspected that no one had ever seen this side of Christian. This was not a part of himself that he revealed to anyone—and why reveal such doubt and weakness to her? Why now? Eleanor stood from her chair, crossing to his. She knelt before him and touched his hands.

"We will succeed," she said. She felt certain of it, because the alternative was impossible. Egypt could not be carted off to distant lands; Egypt and her treasures needed to stay right here.

Christian's eyes crinkled in the corners when he smiled at her. "And one day, I will write poetry in hieratic."

Eleanor said nothing, for the idea that he would write poetry in hieratic seemed a foolish thing to them both—which meant he believed the raid on the German camp would fail.

"You will write that poetry," she whispered.

Seven years later, he did.

CHAPTER FOURTEEN

Virgil lifted his eyes from his notebook to sidestep a passing Sirocco agent in the hallway and discovered Director Howard Irving standing at the hallway's end. There was no pretending he hadn't seen him, for Irving's hard eyes pinned Virgil like a butterfly to board. Virgil resisted the urge to squirm. If there was anything he liked less than eels or eel jelly, it was the icy assessment he had always found in Irving's cool blue eyes.

Irving should not have been back, Virgil thought as he closed the notebook and slid it into his jacket pocket. Yet there he stood at the end of an otherwise desolate hallway. A smile slid over Irving's face, but did not reach his eyes, and not for the first time Virgil saw Caroline's own expression there, distant and cold. Irving was impeccable as always, his suit neatly pressed, graying blond hair neatly groomed. He didn't look as though he had just weathered the long journey from the Dominion of Canada.

"Son."

It was the one word Virgil did not wish to hear from the man. Even after all this time, it made him flinch, for he and Irving had never shared a father-son relationship, despite their connection through Caroline. Irving always gave an impression of vague annoyance around Virgil. Whether it was because he presumed Virgil had taken his daughter away, no matter how clear it was that Caroline had possessed her own wants and desires, Virgil could not say.

"Howard."

Virgil extended a hand to clasp Irving's. He hadn't seen Irving in the three or so years since Caroline's funeral; while they worked for the same organization, their paths rarely had cause to cross. That they crossed now left Virgil feeling ill at ease. He wished he could fully blame that feeling on the lack of opium, but knew he couldn't. Maybe it was Irving's scent, the deep rot that followed the man wherever he went.

"Good to see you," Irving said, and withdrew his hand from Virgil's to brush his fingers down his waistcoat in an almost nervous manner. "A surprise, but good. What brings you to Cairo?"

"Tying up loose ends on a case," Virgil said and patted the notebook in his pocket. It wasn't entirely untrue. "And you? I asked when I arrived, and Agent Barclay said you were traveling."

Irving rubbed his hands together as though they were cold. "I was on a case that didn't take quite as long as anticipated. Good to catch you here, though."

Virgil allowed himself a smile, one that was likely toothier than it should have been. Caught, indeed. He felt as though his collar had shrunk, even though he wore it open against the morning's heat. How much did Irving know? Did he know that the Lady had been examined? Did he know of Cleo's assistance? When Irving stepped forward, Virgil tensed; he didn't anticipate the hug.

The beast inside Virgil growled at the contact and clawed to get out; Virgil found himself making a concerted effort to not change forms and take Irving to the floor. *What was in the box, Howard? What did you gift your daughter with on the day of our wedding?*

"Seeing you always brings Caroline right back," Irving murmured in Virgil's ear. "I still think you two are coming to dinner."

Virgil forced himself to remember the times they had gone to dinner. They weren't his favorite memories, but gave him something to quiet the wolf. Irving would take Virgil back into his study after the meal concluded, light cigars and pour brandy, and talk for hours about things that didn't matter. Caroline had been the fragile thread that held them together; otherwise, Virgil was certain he would have no need to know this man. Not even in a professional manner.

"How are you, Virgil?"

It was the same question Irving had asked at Caroline's funeral, though at that time Virgil had felt less equipped to provide a genuine answer. Now Virgil turned out of Irving's embrace, and the wolf felt but a handbreadth away.

"I'm well," he managed to say and took a step backward, not caring what Irving might think of it. Chasing what Caroline left behind, but I'm well. His thoughts shifted to Eleanor, to the comfort of her pressed against him in the Egyptian night, and he began to regain control of himself. "How are you and Sabrina?"

"Every day is a challenge." Irving said it as though Caroline's death were fresh, an occurrence from last week. Virgil looked more closely at the man and could see the fine tremor in his hands, the exhaustion that muddied his eyes. No matter where Caroline's work had taken her, Virgil reminded himself that she was this man's daughter. A blood bond would always reach beyond her treachery.

"We should have dinner, we three," Irving said. "I know Sabrina would love to see you."

Virgil wondered if Sabrina longed to talk at length about the grandchildren she had never known. He knew he was being unkind, that he could not imagine the grief these two had known. Yes, he had been Caroline's husband, and yes, her blood was on his hands even now, but Howard and Sabrina were her parents, and losing a child was something Virgil could not fully comprehend. It was something no person should ever have to know.

"You know how it is," Virgil said in a low tone. Was his voice edged with a growl? He didn't try to rein it in. "The life of a Mistral agent."

Irving laughed at that and reached a hand out to pat Virgil's shoulder. "Caroline said you were always busy with work, never had time to sit down and properly be with her, and here you are: nothing has changed."

There was a host of things Virgil wanted to say to that, but he swallowed them all when he heard Eleanor's voice behind him.

"Agent Mallory?"

Virgil didn't miss the way Irving's eyes snapped toward Eleanor. Irving would know who she was, of that Virgil was certain, for how could the director not know the young lady who had helped free the Lady from her slumber? When Irving's nostrils flared, Virgil almost took it for the scenting of prey. As though Irving were stalking her. He was not a creature like Virgil, which made it all the more curious.

"Miss Folley," Virgil said, "this is Director Irving."

As Irving moved toward her, Virgil pivoted, watching Eleanor discreetly tuck an envelope into her pocket before greeting the director. If Irving found her trousers and waistcoat odd, he said nothing; Irving was the portrait of proper etiquette, welcoming Eleanor to the Sirocco headquarters and fair Cairo.

"Miss Folley," Irving said, "a true pleasure."

Virgil thought Irving might have rocked his lips across Eleanor's knuckles had she not withdrawn her hand so quickly.

"A pleasure," she agreed, and then those warm brown eyes slid toward Virgil. "Agent, I have news. If I could have a moment of your time?"

News in addition to Irving's sudden return? When it rained, it often did pour. Virgil nodded to Eleanor, then looked to Irving. "Howard, it was good to see you, but if you will excuse me?"

For a moment, Irving looked as though he didn't intend to excuse them at all. He looked poised to protest, but held his silence. Virgil's hand rested against Eleanor's back as they moved away, out of the hallway and into the nearby library that stood empty. He closed the doors behind them, but Eleanor kept walking, appearing to want more distance between them and Irving. Virgil could hardly blame her. He followed her through the stacks and stopped when she turned to offer him the envelope he had seen earlier.

"Hieratic," he said when he unfolded the page inside and studied the collection of curves and slashes. He looked at Eleanor, then back to the page between them. "If you need a translation, you might want someone quicker and more skilled than me. *Looking for years* . . . possibly *you have looked*?"

"*You have looked now for years*," Eleanor said. "*I cannot be sorry. Your quest is ending soon, come to Deir el-Bahri.*"

Virgil's head came up, realizing she needed no translator; she already knew the words. They sent a strange chill through him. "That's a clumsy kind of poetry. What is this?"

"It's from Christian."

Virgil stared at Eleanor, thinking it possible she was making a joke, but there was no humor in her eyes.

"He left it in my room last night."

Virgil once again felt the wolf inside him straining to get out, claws pressed to flesh. He folded the poem back into its envelope, careful to not add new creases to the paper when his hands began to shake. He offered the envelope back to Eleanor, willing his hands to steady. He had no claim on this woman, though the memory of her soft mouth against his was fresh and sharp in his mind. The scent of her on the balcony, the line of her head in his hands, the taste of her blood against his tongue.

"And how," Virgil forced himself to ask, "did Hubert come to be in your room last night?"

Eleanor's eyes flew wide, anger rewriting the lines of her face. "Mallory!"

His name was almost a snarl in her mouth, and she lifted a hand, smacking his arm. Virgil captured her wrist and propelled her backward, deeper into the stacks, where the shadows fell and he could press and keep her in a corner. "How?"

"Not by my hand, if that is what you're thinking."

Relief washed over him like cold water, and then he was bowing his head, rubbing his cheek against hers as if to mark her with his scent before his mouth closed over her own. There was a short intake of breath from Eleanor—surprise? anger?—and then she reached for him in kind, hand fisting hard into his hair, not stopping him, but keeping him where he was.

Virgil growled, his mouth moving from hers. He traced a path down the line of her jaw, past the snowy fold of her collar, and into the warmth of her neck, where the intoxicating scent of her pooled. Thinking only of making his claim, he bit her, teeth pressing into flesh. The bite wasn't hard enough to puncture, but when he lifted his head, he could see his mark on her, deeply red even in the library shadows.

Eleanor lifted her hand, though not to strike him again. She covered the mark, fingers and chin trembling. Virgil thought that if they weren't pressed into the corner shelves as they were, they might both topple into a heap on the floor.

"Miss Folley, I—" He felt as though he should apologize, because as his mind began to clear, he realized what a brute he had been. He had never done such a thing to any other person. He smoothed his hands down her arms and helped her out of the corner, fully buttoning her collar to conceal the mark he had made. "You must forg—"

"Don't you dare apologize," she whispered. She held his gaze as he turned her collar down with shaking hands. "But don't you dare believe I let Christian into my room, either."

Virgil touched Eleanor's chin before he withdrew. Looking at her, one could not tell she had just almost been mauled but for the slight pinking of her mouth. It pleased him, her reaction and refusal of his apology. He nodded.

"No apologies, then," he said.

"A-are Auberon and Gin nearby?" she asked then, straightening the envelope she had entirely crumpled in her hand.

"They should be with Cleo, likely in her office." Virgil tried not to grin in amusement at the near-utter destruction of the envelope and its poem. It looked more like trash than evidence.

They walked to Cleo's office together, so that Eleanor might tell the story once and keep everyone on the same page. Virgil told himself not to be a beast, to let her explain, and to not allow anger to fill him again at the idea of Hubert in her rooms. Eleanor shared the note with the other agents, and Virgil applauded himself for his patience as Auberon and Gin each took a stab at reading the ancient writing before Eleanor simply read it for all them as she had him.

"A few days ago, there was another note," Eleanor said.

"Another note?" No matter his resolve, Virgil couldn't stop himself from bolting out of his chair at that admission. How much else might she be keeping from them? And with Irving returned! He paced a line among the chairs and tables of Cleo's sitting area. But, he decided, it was unkind of him; Eleanor hadn't withheld anything, had she? She was not like Caroline—she was not. "Forgive me. Start at the beginning."

"I was about to," she said with ill-disguised impatience. Still, her eyes were bright and Virgil was coming to know that look, half amusement, half annoyance. "This first note also contained a poem, but not in hieratic. I thought it was from you."

Virgil paused in his pacing to stare at her, while Auberon, Gin, and Cleo, all perched like birds in a row on Cleo's couch, stared at Virgil in return. There was a long silence as Eleanor's words sank in.

"Poetry," Auberon eventually said.

"From Virgil?" Gin asked.

Cleo cleared her throat, but said nothing.

Virgil silently thanked Eleanor when she pressed on. "The poem suggested climbing the Great Pyramid in an effort to trust each other more, and the following day, we went to Giza. What was I to think?"

"Reasonable enough, and considering nothing untoward happened on that jaunt . . . " Cleo agreed.

"The poet evidently did not anticipate you arriving with us," Auberon added before another heavy silence could fall, but Gin couldn't get over the idea of Virgil leaving poetry and enthusiastically said so.

"I did not leave the poem," Virgil said.

"The balcony doors were open when I—" Eleanor paused strangely, eyes flicking to Cleo and then back up to Virgil. "I contacted my father. I couldn't sleep after you two left. Cleo helped me reach him, and when I came back to my locked room, the poem was there."

"And while Virgil may be moved to write poetry," Gin said, still amused and pressing the idea, "you don't think he would scale your balcony to leave some?"

"I didn't scale the balcony," Virgil said. Did women like such dramatic displays? Did Eleanor? "That's not to say I wouldn't . . . "

Eleanor continued on, before he could. "When I traveled with Christian, I attempted to teach him hieratic. He had problems with it, but joked that one day he would write poetry in it. I think now that he has."

"And that he's guiding us to Deir el-Bahri?" Auberon asked with a headshake.

Virgil crouched beside Eleanor's chair, wanting to take her hand but not doing so. She looked down at him and gifted him with an uneasy smile. "Did you talk to your father about the Lady?" he asked.

As Virgil was coming to know Eleanor's various expressions, he knew the one crossing her face now. This was sorrow. He closed his own hand into a loose fist in an effort to not take hers, to not let the others here see such a private moment. And yet, her conversation with her father was a private thing, too.

"My father admitted that my mother believed the Lady was her own mother," Eleanor said, and related the conversation they'd had, including the original discovery of the four rings and that Sagira had vanished with them.

"And he always knew," Eleanor finished in a whisper, her eyes on Virgil alone. "He knew and he never told me, but that's for another day."

Now Virgil did touch Eleanor's hand, the rest of the people in the room be damned. "Add to this that Irving has returned," he said, swinging his look to the others. "We just parted company with him. Have you two finished poking through the collection?"

Auberon reached into his pocket and withdrew a browned and battered box. It was the size that could hold a ring, and Virgil realized he was holding his breath; he didn't release it until Auberon took the lid off to reveal a gold and lapis lazuli ring inside. Auberon met his look—even but filled with a good many things unspoken—and placed the box beside the poem on the table.

Eleanor slid out of her chair, her hand whispering free from Virgil's as she knelt. She didn't touch the box, hands coming to rest flat upon the table. Virgil was certain she had as many questions about the ring as he did, but for the moment they went unasked.

"The ring is damaged," Auberon said. "The lapis is chipped on its left side."

Even damaged, the ring was a beautiful piece of Egyptian craftsmanship. The deeply blue lapis stone nestled between ropes of carefully twisted and gleaming gold.

"Eleanor?" Virgil looked to her, still frozen before the ring. She said nothing, only nodded a confirmation; she recognized the ring. Feeling as if time were suddenly slipping away from them with Irving in the building, Virgil looked to the others. "What else have you found?"

Gin slid to the edge of the couch. "Since Auberon got the ring reveal . . . " He lifted a notebook and offered it to Virgil. "There are plenty of local legends about the Glass of Anubis. Sirocco has been collecting them for centuries. No one knows what it does or is—there are reports of light, of a portal and god-like creatures, but if anyone has gone through—in either direction—they've not been interviewed. By all accounts, it sounds dangerous—the light sets the land ablaze—"

"The information also mentions the pharaoh Hatshepsut," Cleo said, and Virgil was thankful she picked up the thread of information before Gin went on at length about the portal and its potential for danger and doom. What they needed now were simple facts, not embellishments. "Hatshepsut may have owned the rings, or known the person who did, but in either case, her temple is at Deir el-Bahri, which ties to Eleanor's poem."

They were all quiet; then each spoke at once, every voice overlapping with conflicting theories until Cleo raised hers and silenced them.

"You all have to leave immediately," Cleo said to Virgil. "If Irving is back and has seen you with Eleanor, he knows exactly what you're doing. There is only one reason to have a Folley in this building."

"We'll need transportation," Gin said, thinking ahead as he so often did. The young man moved off to arrange it without another word.

"You can't stay, either," Auberon said to Cleo. Without Gin between them on the couch, Auberon slid closer, reaching for Cleo's hand. Her metal fingers closed around his. "With Irving here and you in charge of the Lady—" Auberon's voice faltered. "He'll suspect you played a part."

"I can't go," Cleo said, shaking her head. "This is my post, and I may yet be able to do some good here."

A muscle in Auberon's jaw flexed, and Cleo drew her hand out of his. This had been their constant argument through the years. Virgil looked from them to Eleanor, still poised near the ring. His scrutiny brought her gaze to him at last, and she exhaled. She made no arguments; they could only leave before Irving prevented them from doing so.

Their belongings were few, but they all left the security of Cleo's office, returning to their rooms to pack. When Virgil finished with his own, he came to collect Eleanor. He worried he might find her unpacked and refusing to go, but her bags stood ready. She allowed him into the room, pacing a restless path between him and her luggage.

"You should have this," he said, and withdrew the lapis ring from his pocket.

"Mallory, I couldn't."

He understood the worry in her eyes. It wasn't worry that she would outright vanish with the ring in her possession, but that the memory of her mother doing so might consume her. That she might be drawn into that abyss from which she couldn't escape. It was how he often felt when the wolf pulled him down.

"Only for safekeeping," he said, and gently reached for her. "No other should have it, Eleanor."

He undid the buttons of her collar, eyeing the faint bruise that still marked her neck. He stroked the gold chain that lay against her skin, then lifted it. His hands were steady when he unfastened the clasp and added the second ring to the first.

"You aren't going to vanish, at least not without me by your side," he said as he buttoned her collar once more and smoothed it to rights. "If you go, I go. We ride this out, remember?"

Eleanor covered his hand with her own as it came to her cheek. "I couldn't do this without you," she said.

Virgil shushed her with a fleeting kiss. "You damn well could and would. You did this for years on your own." Had circumstances dictated, he had no doubt she would have flown into the face of the danger alone. He supposed it might yet come to that, but shushed that voice.

Eleanor laughed. "It's like you've always been there."

He slid his arm around the curve of her waist, drawing her closer. He supposed some would have taken offense at the sentiment, the implication that Mistral had constantly hounded her in one way or another, but he didn't. "Hampering you."

"Addling my brain with your quignogs," she returned.

"Quignogs! Making you liversick?" He rubbed his cheek into hers and looked down into her bright eyes. "My *tesorina*."

Eleanor leaned further into him at the Italian endearment—*his treasure*—which allowed him to feel the press of the rings against his own chest. Her mouth erased the world around them, until there came a sharp knock at the door and Gin calling to see if they were ready.

Virgil lifted his mouth from Eleanor's. There was no doubt in her eyes, nor in the line of her body. Whatever would come, she stood ready, as Virgil knew she would.

"Ready," she said.

CHAPTER FIFTEEN

Gin took an inordinate amount of pleasure in the fact that the ship he secured for their journey was named *The Jackal*. She was sleek, with a sharply pointed face, patinaed bronze cradling sails and balloons of cream parchment. *The Jackal* was smaller than the *Nuit*, which suited Eleanor fine. Maybe this time, they would be less of a target and would make it to their destination without being shot from the sky. Eleanor had no lack of anxiety as she boarded the ship, yet when she finally looked down upon Hatshepsut's temple crouched in the sepia sands, all worry fled.

She had only ever seen poorly rendered photographs of the temple and could only vaguely remember her parents speaking of it; the location hadn't been a consideration in the search for the Lady's rings until now. Djeser-djeseru snuggled against sharp cliffs, seeming to emerge straight from them and into the honeyed midday light. Pillared colonnades stretched the length of two tiers, dramatic, sweeping ramps leading from one to the next. It looked nearly Greek in its style with the pillars, though the roofs were flat, dusted with windswept sands.

"Have you been here before?"

Despite the seriousness of their visit, Eleanor couldn't help but grin at Mallory, who stood by her side at the observation rail. He had procured a worn leather jacket and linen scarf before their flight, but had given the scarf up to Eleanor, tucking it into the neck of her own jacket. At this elevation, the air was cool, *The Jackal* less enclosed than the *Nuit* had been. Eleanor and Mallory stood framed by one of many observation nooks; leather loops and a brass rail provided support.

"Never," she said, "which is odd, given how close the Valley of the Kings is. I've been there more times than I can count, but not here." Her eyes went back to the temple, drinking it in. "You?"

"Once," Mallory said. "On a work-related tour."

"What can we expect down there?" Auberon asked from his position beside Gin at the controls. The interior of the ship was so small, he had no need to shout; those in the control deck could easily be heard by those in the passenger cabin observation nooks.

"It's a beautiful temple," Mallory said, eyes still on it as they neared.

Eleanor took the opportunity to watch him and the light that reflected gold in his eyes. He seemed as eager as she to explore this place, and she had to remind herself they weren't on vacation. What they discovered here might lead them to her mother, to the last of the rings.

"Plenty of ruin though," Mallory added. "Be on the lookout for cobras and vipers. This remote, hopefully there won't be any wandering tourists."

As Gin began their descent, the temple looked empty, and Eleanor was thankful for that. Most who came to Egypt did it the traditional way, cruising down the Nile to see the ruins cluttering her shores from a safe distance. Wise visitors who came into the desert had guides, but Eleanor had crossed paths with more than a rogue few who thought they could tame the waste single-handed.

While Auberon and Gin secured the ship, Eleanor adjusted the veil on the pith helmet Cleo had loaned her and took the small case of gear Mallory offered. The case had a long leather strap, which she wore across her body, to leave both hands free. Mallory then offered her a brown leather holster, meant for one's belt. Inside, her own revolver was snugged.

"Mallory." She ran her fingers over the leather. "This is lovely." It was old, the leather soft enough to conform around the weapon, and slid easily onto her belt.

"Lovely," he said in a low tone, touching her chin before withdrawing as Auberon and Gin came back for their supplies. "Highly practical, that," he added, then stomped outside, every inch the wolf surveying new territory.

" . . . unless Miss Folley's poet simply wanted us out of the way," she heard Gin murmur in Mallory's wake. She looked to Gin and Auberon, each with a supply case and a canteen of water.

"What's that?" Eleanor asked, and Gin looked up.

"Could be a false trail, is all," he said as he draped his own case and canteen around his shoulders. "A trap. Might not hurt to be on our guard against such."

Eleanor's fingers sought her new holster at her belt. "We will be on guard, for all manner of things. And he's not *my* poet."

Gin hefted a leather pack and flashed Eleanor a smile that had likely charmed other women but left her feeling a little cold. "All I'm saying is, a man scales a balcony to leave two poems, he's not trifling about. He's serious—"

"About potentially acquiring a head injury," Eleanor muttered and turned from the men, refusing to believe that Christian had any emotional attachment to this scheme.

The way she had left him, taking the ring and keeping two steps ahead of him and Caroline—until Port Elizabeth—had to have left a poor taste in the man's mouth. She didn't imagine Christian as anything other than furious if they crossed paths.

Outside, as the heated wind teased Eleanor's veil over her nose, she felt something she hadn't felt since her first visit to Giza. There was anticipation—each shaded slot between the temple's pillars looking like doors to her—and so too there was dread. She recalled all too well the feeling that had come over her inside the pyramid. She had felt small and suffocated, as if all those years would consume her and leave nothing behind, not even a desiccated corpse. She hoped this temple would be different. With most of the temple open to the wide sky, she was encouraged that any claustrophobia would stay at bay.

"Eleanor?"

She opened her eyes to look at Mallory, realizing only then she had closed them at all. She had been waiting for that voice again—not Mallory's, but the voice that had long ago called her *daughter*. Mallory eased the veil from her nose, tucking it back down under her chin in the coil of the scarf she wore.

"There is always this feeling," she said, "when I go into a new place."

Mallory's grin flashed before he bent to retrieve a camera case. "I think I know that feeling well." He nodded toward the temple, and Eleanor followed him from the ship.

The air was hot and dry as they approached the temple, but Eleanor didn't unwrap her scarf; she still felt chilled and tried to tell herself it was only from the ship's flight, not from any worry attached to what they might discover. Auberon and Gin followed, one commenting about the lines of the temple while the other kept an eye on the cliffs above, looking for any danger, no matter how small. Eleanor found herself longing to draw her revolver, because the cliffs unnerved her. She could picture attackers atop them, another airship setting down, those awful whinnying mechanical horses . . .

As they drew closer to the temple, Mallory began to speak, which lightened Eleanor's mood. Much like her own father would have, Mallory told a story of the place they walked through, knowledge gleaned from Cleo and his prior work with Sirocco. He spoke of Hatshepsut, the woman who ruled as pharaoh, as if he had known her and been here when she ruled. Her temple stood empty now, but thanks to Mallory's words Eleanor could easily picture the sandstone and granite sphinxes that had once lined the ramps; could imagine the myrrh trees they were said to have brought back from an expedition to distant Punt.

At the end of the second ramp, they found a likeness of a falcon still intact, and Eleanor drew her fingers across its broad head as they passed. Gritty sand clung to her fingertips.

The traveling party also brought back incense, Mallory said, and perhaps fruit trees. Eleanor imagined flourishing gardens and pools, fancy giving flight to birds that snatched fruit from the branches. The riches the traveling party had seen and possibly brought back with them still decorated the temple walls: leopards on long leads, massive elephant tusks, towering spotted giraffes, and the myrrh trees Mallory had spoken of.

Eleanor stumbled over the loose flooring as they began to walk through the colonnades and steadied herself with a hand on the nearest pillar. The stone was rough under her fingers; she could not resist digging her fingers into the hieroglyphs that remained. She pictured the person who had carved the words, likely a man. Had he possessed any hope the words would reach into the future? Eleanor wished she could tell the carver they had.

Inside the temple, Eleanor pressed her veil against her mouth to remove the sheen of sweat beaded on her skin. The day would only get warmer, and she stuck to what little shade there was as she made her way through the pillars, loosening the scarf at last. Conversation with the others was limited; for the time being, everyone was content to revel in the building around them.

The damage intentionally inflicted after Hatshepsut's reign was extensive; where once her image had been carved, it had been chiseled away. In certain places, the image of another pharaoh overlapped Hatshepsut's own. Another mystery.

"Eleanor?"

At the touch of a hand against her arm, she turned to find Mallory, smudged with dust from his own explorations. The sunlight slanted through the pillars, painting stripes of color over his forehead and nose.

"Auberon has found something," he added, pulling her away from the image she had been looking at.

Auberon knelt in a corner deep within the colonnade. His lantern threw a blotch of light onto the wall before him, illuminating a set of hieroglyphs that Eleanor had no trouble reading. They were surrounded by an oval, the traditional cartouche.

"My grandmother's name, Sagira," Eleanor said and touched the carving before them. Part of her wanted there to be some deeper awareness when she touched the stone, but it was only stone, nothing magical. It was still beneath her fingers, warmed by the day's heat despite the shadows.

"Cartouches were reserved for royalty, weren't they?" Auberon asked.

Eleanor would have nodded, but could not draw her attention from the hieroglyphs. The Egyptians had no word for queen, nor had they known mirrors as Eleanor and the others knew them, so what the writing told her should have been impossible. She read it three times and tried to put the pieces together differently. She tried to force them into some historical sense, but could not, not around the wonder of her grandmother's name before her. Her fingers lingered in the curve of an ankh.

"They called her the Queen of the Mirror," Eleanor finally said, "but that isn't possible." However, if her grandmother's name could be upon these walls at all, how could one say what *was* possible? She drew her fingers away.

"Anubis's mirror?" Gin whispered.

Eleanor didn't answer. She couldn't. She was too stricken by the idea that her grandmother commanded such an honor. That her grandmother's name was written upon these walls at all was something that robbed Eleanor of her patience. They were close to something, very close. She could feel it pricking up her spine. Eleanor grew tired of waiting, but Sagira's name upon the wall appeared to confirm her grandmother had stepped backward in time. That she had lived a life here, had been remembered by the people.

While Auberon and Gin settled in to take rubbings of the wall, Eleanor moved deeper into the temple. She felt Mallory's eyes on her and offered him a smile. He didn't follow, seeming to understand her need to wander alone; if anyone in their group would understand, it would be him. Eleanor felt torn between laughter and tears. How many times had she explored the Valley of the Kings? And here all this sat, essentially on the other side of a broad hill. A small mark upon an ancient stone: a small mark that could have answered as many questions as it produced.

She wandered deeper into the temple, through slanting shafts of sunlight. She found carvings of dwarves, of mighty birds, and of Ma'at, spreading her generous, balancing wings over everything she could. Eleanor looked for other instances of Sagira's name, but saw none. She came around again to the temple's front row of pillars, finding a small chapel in the rightmost corner.

Its roof was still intact, and while the front pillars remained intact as well, most within the chapel had crumbled. Eleanor could see there had once been twelve of them: four rows, three pillars deep. Those that remained retained specks of paint that Eleanor longed to touch, but didn't. Some part of her wanted this to be as it was for all the days to come; she wanted this place untouched by time and hand.

A scorpion scuttled across her path and she exhaled, mindful of Mallory's earlier warning about snakes. She walked with a little more caution, but still found herself startled again when a mural of Anubis reared up on a wall before her.

The mural was worn by sunlight, wind, and time. It was little more than flecks of paint on stone, but Eleanor felt it was somehow more than that, for her heart raced at the sight of the dark god. In one hand, he held an ankh, but the other was raised, and above his palm there floated four circular daubs. The paint was chipped, but not badly enough that Eleanor couldn't easily see the colors: blue, red, yellow, and white.

Daughter.

Eleanor pushed the voice out of her head, but she felt it lingering close even so. Waiting. She took a step closer to the wall, daring to place her hand against the painting, and when she saw how perfectly it fit against the daubs of paint, she pictured her grandmother's hand there too. With her palm flat against the stone, each finger touched one of the daubs. No—

"Rings," she whispered.

"Rings," confirmed another voice.

Eleanor whirled around at the sound, drawing her revolver from its holster. There, atop a half-crumbled pillar, perched Christian Hubert.

Dublin, Ireland ~ October 1886

The wind blew hard enough to rattle every shutter Folley's Nicknackatarium and adjoining house possessed, keeping Eleanor awake long into the night. She pushed her blankets down once again and eased up onto her elbows, listening to the mournful sound of the wind as it twisted down the chimneys and through the walls. She closed her eyes and imagined that the moaning of the wind was every mummy in the Nicknackatarium coming to dreadful life, to shuffle their wrapped feet over the wood floors and shamble up the winding staircases.

This was not the way a normal young lady spent her evenings; however, Eleanor Folley was still far from normal. She pictured the wind slipping under the shutters to batter at the windows with small, insistent hands. Where the wind found a crack, it would steal inside to twirl about the house until it evaporated. She gave the rain a small voice that hummed "let me in, let me in" with each drop that began to hammer against the rooftop, and then came the thunder, which shook the bones of the house with its baritone.

Somewhere above, a shutter snapped as it came loose in the storm. Eleanor jumped at the sound and felt she was only five again as she clutched her nightgown and willed her heart to calm. She was well beyond the age of being frightened by a storm, yet something about this one had set her on edge.

She slipped out of bed, stuffing feet into slippers and wrapping her robe around her before moving toward the door. The hallway stretched in silence, the window at its end illuminated by a flash of lightning. Her father's door was closed, no light seeping from beneath. Eleanor presumed he was asleep as she turned in the other direction, toward the narrow staircase leading to the attic. If that window had come open again, she was going to have some choice words for it and the man who claimed to have repaired it.

"Crow dives through a window, ain't ever going to be the same, miss," the little man had said as he'd slid the repaired frame with its new pane into position.

"No, I daresay the crow is dead after that," she'd said. "Injured at the least." The crow in question had been injured, enough so that Eleanor had been left to finish the work the window had begun, wringing its neck and burying it at the base of a tree that grew near the River Liffey. It had been the closest bit of dirt she could find.

"The window, miss, the window!"

And what about the poor bird? Eleanor thought as she climbed the stairs. Lightning illuminated the window at the landing, its silvered light throwing everything into momentary brightness. At the attic door she could already feel the draft of wind snaking over its threshold and she scowled, pushing the door inward to fully feel the chilled air.

She and her father had spent two afternoons moving crates and other storage away from the problematic window after its repair, just in case. And here was the "just in case," she thought as she padded across the wood floor to the window that had blown inward. The curtains were soaked, and the shutter thumped incessantly against the side of the house.

Cold rain pelted Eleanor as she grabbed the shutter and pulled it closed. She secured it with a muttered curse, but the wind whipped up again, sending the shutter flying loose. Drenched and glaring, Eleanor hauled the flapping panel back into place.

"All right," she muttered, finding a length of twine in the attic to further secure the shutter. "A prayer to Saint Frances of Rome, then?" She looked heavenward, then closed the window itself, shivering with cold and wet. "Saint Frances, I beseech you to look after this window and see it stays closed this very stormy ni—"

That was when Eleanor saw the boot print illumined by another flash of lightning. Every hair seemed to stand on end as she looked at the mark on the attic floor and realized someone was in the house.

She turned her back to the window, shaking now for an entirely different reason. Every shadow took on a sinister depth; each was unknowable and might contain a dozen intruders. This was one reason the Folleys had opted to live in town; there was no telling what might befall their collection of artifacts in some isolated location. Here, they could at least provide their own security. In theory.

Eleanor reached for the nearest crate and found it not near at all, since she and her father had moved every crate in the attic. Swallowing another curse, she stepped away from the window and made it to the nearest stack of crates. She reached into the top one, pulling out the first item she came to, a rough pottery vase. She stared at it, pondering what she might do with it—she could remember excavating it, knew exactly what it was worth—and then a shadow moved. She would mash the intruder in the brainpan with it, no matter its value.

"Saint Frances," said a male voice, "is the patron saint of widows, sweetheart. Not windows."

Eleanor stiffened. Surely it wasn't—

Christian Hubert slipped out of the shadows to stand before Eleanor, dripping rain onto the attic floor. Had rats been built broad and tall, he looked like a drowned one, his mackintosh having provided little protection from the storm. Eleanor gritted her teeth together, trying to stop them from chattering. God's foot, he had to be cold, having been out in the rain, and on—

" . . . on my roof, what in the name of God were you doing on my roof, and more to the point, in my attic!" Eleanor lifted the vase, still prepared to smack him into unconsciousness if the need arose.

"It wasn't the ideal entry, no," Christian said. He shook then, like a massive dog, flinging water every which way.

Eleanor jerked as the water flew. "Get out. You have no—" She broke off, too stunned by his appearance here to properly finish a sentence. "You were breaking into my house?" There was a sentence; Eleanor felt proud of herself, vase still held at the ready as Christian took a step forward. "Stay where you are!"

"Eleanor. You're soaked to the bone."

His voice held that familiar edge, the one that said wouldn't they both rather be out of these cold, wet clothes, and discussing this over, say, whiskey, in front of a roaring fire?

"Your doing, I would point out," Eleanor said. She gestured to the window with the vase. "Had you secured the shutter, your trespass might have gone unnoticed." Though she doubted that very much, for Christian was more the kind to make it clear he had been somewhere. Especially somewhere he wasn't meant to be. He wanted people to know, after all. Wanted to bask in their exasperation and admiration alike. "What the hell are you—?"

Christian took a quick step forward, but Eleanor didn't allow him any others. She struck out with the vase, catching Christian in the jaw and sending him to the floor in a wet pile. She was stunned when the vase didn't shatter, further proving its value and the craftsmanship of the ancient Egyptians.

"Ele—Blast!" He cradled his jaw as he lay there, staring at the ceiling. She hoped his vision was swimming.

"Shall I tie you and leave you for the authorities, then?" she asked. What would he tell them? Why had he come? As Eleanor sifted through possible reasons, she could only come up with one: Christian had come to get the ring back. The ring she wore on a chain around her neck even tonight.

"Is that woman with you?" Eleanor tilted her head toward the window, but could only hear the storm rattling against the roof.

"No."

The single word came out with an emphasis that made Eleanor smile a little. She hoped his jaw was hurting him to hell and back.

"Get off my floor and out of this house." Another complete sentence. Eleanor wondered if she would soon remember how to speak in entire paragraphs. "And out of Dublin while you're at it."

"Eleanor, can't we tal—"

"No."

"You're being hysteric—"

"I'd say I have every right to be hysterical, a thief in my attic in the middle of a stormy night!"

Christian peered up at her, hand finally coming away from his jaw. "Would there be less trauma involved if the night weren't stormy?"

Eleanor flung the vase at him. The solid piece of pottery thumped off his shoulder and into a crate, where it clattered to the floor.

They only looked at each other, Eleanor filled with a fear and rage she had thought long behind her. Coming home two years ago, she believed this entire thing finished. No rings, no path, her mother well and truly lost. Now, here sat a fragment of all that had been hoped for. The man she had once thought might help her unravel all those riddles. The man she thought she had loved. Breaking into her house.

"You need to go," she whispered. "I'm surprised all this noise hasn't awakened my father." Behind her, the shutter slapped open again, sending a fresh gust of rain into the attic. "I have no intention of explaining your presence to him."

Christian picked himself up from the floor, smoothing his mac and trousers into a different mass of wet wrinkles. "Eleanor—" He winced at the motion of his jaw. "I didn't intend—"

"Don't try to placate me," she said, beginning to shiver under the continued assault of the wind and rain behind her. "Just go. This is over, Christian. Whatever you came here for . . . It's no longer yours."

Something flickered in his eyes then, perhaps annoyance because she could read him so well, even after so long apart. He opened his mouth to say more, but thought better of it. He moved toward the window, climbed onto the sill, then slid onto the slight ledge of roof. Had she been feeling generous, Eleanor might have walked him downstairs, to the front door, but all things considered, she decided he should leave as he had come. On the ledge, Christian only looked at her, as if in silent appeal.

"Close the shutter and go," she said.

He did only that; he swung both shutters inward, holding them until Eleanor tied them firmly again with the twine. By the time she had closed the window itself, Christian was making his loud, slippery descent from the roof, and by the time Eleanor had dried off and crawled back into bed, she was thankful her father slept so soundly and prayed Christian Hubert was well and truly leaving Dublin behind—forever.

Though the storm calmed and the wind quieted, Eleanor didn't sleep; she lay awake long into the night, listening for the sound of the loose shutter and the entrance of another wayward bird.

Deir-el-Bahri, Egypt ~ October 1889

Eleanor hadn't seen Christian in three years, and, physically, he had not changed much. He was imposing, made larger by the flowing Bedouin robes he wore. His white cotton *thawb* flowed down to cover his feet, while his completely unnecessary outer *bisht* was colored in wide stripes of green. His face was deeply browned, as if he had taken no shelter from the sun in years, a white *kufiya* wrapped loosely around it against the heat. The length of his robes uncurled as a snake might with his movement; he rose to stand on the pillar and lingered before dropping both booted feet to the ground. In his hands, he held a pocket watch, and snapped its case shut. The sound was loud in the small chapel, and Eleanor flinched.

"I almost didn't think you would come," he said, "but then this is your life's work, isn't it?"

Christian sounded as though he pitied her; that he wished she could move on and find something else to trouble herself with. There were days Eleanor had longed for that—to put this riddle to rest—but days like this made her reconsider. If Christian was here, her grandmother's name upon these very walls paired with evidence of Anubis's rings, she was close. If she stepped off this path, it allowed Christian unfettered access to the Glass and anything it might reveal.

"How could I resist such charming poetry?" Eleanor asked. Her voice sounded calmer than she felt, and she was proud that her gun arm didn't tremble as she kept the weapon trained on him. She was not about to call out to the others; Christian surely had weapons. He didn't appear armed, but that meant he was. At least one revolver tucked into his robes, and certainly a knife secreted somewhere—a bullet was quick, but a blade was silent. The best way to pry any information out of him was alone, when he believed he had the advantage.

She wanted to look at the image of Anubis again, but didn't dare take her eyes off Christian. She knew his ways all too well.

"Appears I learned a few things after all, hieratic among them," Christian said. He turned a slow circle to admire the chapel around them.

It annoyed Eleanor that he knew her so well—knew she wouldn't fire on him with his back turned. Still, she kept the gun on him. Its weight in her hand made her feel better, foolish as that was.

"Have you found your grandmother's name on the walls yet?"

Eleanor didn't answer, her grip tightening on her revolver as Christian prowled the perimeter of the chapel. His fingers brushed absently over the walls, and as he passed the chapel's backmost wall, Eleanor saw a break in the wall, a small access corridor flooded with sunlight. The roof was crumbling, a river of stone filling the corner. Outside, she saw a shadow move: a tethered airship.

"Toss your weapons down," Eleanor said.

Christian's hand brushed over a wall, intentionally dislodging pieces of rock and paint. "You jest," he said, content with his exploration of the wall. "You've got one trained on me, Eleanor Folley, and you're a good shot. I'm still a quick draw."

As if to prove it, he drew two revolvers from the folds of his robes. He had no trouble turning on Eleanor to level her in his sights. Eleanor braced her left hand below her right, her hands beginning to sweat around the revolver's grip.

"Fair is fair, sweetheart," he said. "And I always play fair. Remember?"

Eleanor did remember. In their early days together, he had always given her every advantage, sharing any information he could to hasten the adventure's successful end. He had always buried his fallen friends, remembered them in prayers. By the time of Morocco and Caroline, though, his interpretation of fair had changed.

"What do you want, Christian?" she asked him in a low voice. "Is Caroline with you?"

She asked the question, even knowing the woman was dead. It had its intended effect, though; Christian was the one to flinch now. The implication hovered between them that, much as in Port Elizabeth, Christian and Caroline planned to ambush her in an attempt to gain the ring. Eleanor only hoped Christian didn't know of the three other people with her. She allowed the chance of that was slim; he had likely watched them approach. He had set this entire meeting into motion, hadn't he?

Christian took a step forward and Eleanor took a step back, refusing to allow him any closer. She skirted the debris to her right, placing Christian between her and the mural of Anubis. Those four rings danced above the god's black palm, spreading light toward the painted horizon.

"Did you have a good time with Seth?"

The question drew Eleanor's attention back to Christian and set her off balance yet again. She feared her arm was about to start shaking. "What?"

"I thought you would appreciate it," he said, "though I had no idea the Defenders would take such an interest in you and your companions."

Eleanor shook her head, feeling as she had that day Caroline admitted to taking down *The Empress*. Surely she and Christian had been well suited to one another, cruel and kind by turns—though rather more of the former, Eleanor was coming to realize. She felt like a fool.

"Come now," Christian said. "You can't tell me that place didn't fascinate you. I mourn the loss of that ship, though—the *Nuit* was a beautiful piece of technology. Even in her destruction, she was."

"What do you want?" It was all Eleanor could do to ask the question again.

Her heart pounded furiously and her hands had begun to tremble. She no longer knew Christian as well as she thought. What had the years done to this man? Christian was changed in ways Eleanor would never fully comprehend.

"I thought my *wants* were clear," he said, and took another step toward her. When Eleanor elevated her aim to his face, he stopped. "I want the rings. I know you have two of them now, and while I would love to see them, it seems in poor taste to ask. I propose a race to the last ring."

Questions flooded Eleanor's mind, but none more pressing than how Christian had known she had two rings. "A race?"

"Fair is fair," he reminded her.

He lowered his revolvers, but Eleanor still didn't move hers. Her arms screamed exhaustion, but she didn't waver even as his green eyes drank her in, skimming over her in the same assessing manner he had shown in that long-ago tavern. Unlike then, no part of Eleanor fluttered, stumbled, or crumbled.

"God, Eleanor, you look delightful."

If there was an edge of melancholy to his voice, Eleanor tried not to hear it. Christian was past, he was no longer the man she had known; time had changed him and not for the better.

"And you, you look to be at the end of your rope, sir."

Eleanor tensed at the sound of Mallory's reply to Christian. His boots crunched a path through the debris as he joined Eleanor and Christian. Christian's eyes moved to a point beyond Eleanor. How long had Mallory listened? He stepped alongside her now, his two revolvers trained on Christian.

"You all right?" Mallory asked, not looking at her.

Eleanor said, "Yes," feeling relief spread through her. It wasn't that she couldn't handle Christian on her own; it was that she didn't want to. With Mallory at her side, they stood a chance of reclaiming the carnelian ring—if Christian were foolish enough to have it on his person.

"I've hardly had the time to take advantage of her, my friend, though I appreciate the compliment," Christian said and bowed shortly to Mallory from the waist. "Outnumbered and out-armed, whatever will I do? Agent Mallory, I presume."

Mallory said nothing, unless a snarl could be taken for dialogue. Eleanor had little doubt at this point that a snarl from him often conveyed more than words could, especially in instances such as this.

Christian clicked his tongue against the roof of his mouth. "This isn't playing fair, Eleanor. Two on one, and two others elsewhere in the temple."

"Coming alone seemed ill-advised," she said, and Christian laughed at that.

"Agent Mallory, I was just telling Eleanor that I would like to be fair about this."

Now Mallory was the one to laugh. "Fair, Hubert?"

Christian's attention swung back to Eleanor. "You've come so far, Eleanor, and yet I had to tell you where to come. I'm not certain you ever would have come to this place were it not for me. Being that I've done you a favor—"

Eleanor's lip curled. Curled, and she couldn't fathom it, because it didn't feel like her. It felt like that stranger part of her, like something just under the surface wanted out. "You didn't—"

"Being that I have done you a favor," Christian continued more firmly, "I think you owe me one—though I don't plan on collecting right now. No, that can wait. For now, simply a race to the final ring. You know, of course, you'll be seeing me again, for I have the carnelian."

The confession felt like a knife in Eleanor's side, confirming Mallory's initial suspicion that Christian had broken into the museum. It made her earlier denials seem foolish indeed. The rings she wore weighed heavily, as though she should have left them behind somewhere safe. But they were safe, she argued with herself; as long as she kept them, they were safe. No other should hold them—could hold them, the way she could. Had Sagira felt the same way?

"You don't know where the final ring is," Eleanor whispered, taking a chance it was true. She allowed herself to lower her revolver then and slid it back into its holster. She laughed, realizing what Christian's arrogance truly was. "This meeting wasn't for my benefit, but yours. You were hoping I would be foolish enough to guide you to the last ring."

When Christian said nothing, Eleanor felt as though the power in the room had shifted, from Christian's hand into her own. She crossed the chapel now, moving past Christian to the mural of Anubis. Did it somehow hold a clue? But in this setting, the rings were rightly with Anubis; they were not scattered, but where they should be.

"Two rings to your one," Eleanor said as she looked back at Christian. Beyond Christian, Mallory stood with revolvers still raised. Eleanor stepped out of the line of fire, rounding back toward Mallory's side. "And one of them taken right beneath your nose." She couldn't resist the jab.

"Yes," Christian said with a roll of his eyes. "It takes courage to rob a man while you kiss him."

Eleanor bristled at that, as did Mallory. His growl was plain now, and while it thrilled Eleanor in part, it also worried her. If Christian had watched them, how much did he know about Mallory? And how close was Mallory's wolf?

"Even so," Christian said, "I did admire you. It was strange to wake and find you gone. I thought you were bathing, but then I discovered the ring missing too. Math isn't my specialty, but I reached the proper conclusion, even so, didn't I?" His mouth hitched in a careless smile. "You could have gone anywhere. I was honestly surprised Caroline didn't catch you in Port Elizabeth. Guess I taught you too well."

"I learned best not to trust you," she said.

"That hurts, Eleanor." He held a hand against his side, as though physically struck. Still, his eyes were laughing.

"I don't see why." Eleanor thought back to the tavern, to Christian and Caroline exchanging the scarab ring she now wore. "What was your plan, Christian? To gather the rings and not tell me? What would you have done in the end? Gone on without me?"

"Looks like we're in this together now, plus one." Christian waved a hand toward Mallory, dismissive. "One ring to find; Anubis guiding us and the stars into perfect alignment, for he has called upon us to open his Glass."

"And then what, Hubert?" Mallory asked. His revolvers never wavered from their subject, despite the fact that Eleanor could tell he was struggling. The wolf felt close in this small chapel, Mallory's eyes shaded with too much gold, his voice thick and edged with a growl.

"What do I plan to do when the portal opens?" Christian asked. He tilted his head, and his smile was broad, bright in his sun-darkened face. "That would seem simple enough, Agent. I'll do whatever I damn well please."

With the underlying threat finally spoken, Christian lifted his revolvers, which only spurred Mallory to action. Eleanor dropped to the ground and rolled, knowing she didn't have time to draw her revolver again before Christian moved or Mallory fired. She sought to take herself out of the battle, to leave Mallory's aim unimpeded, but Christian was too quick.

He lunged forward as Mallory did; the two men collided, Mallory abandoning his revolvers to free his hands. While Christian's own guns jabbed into Mallory's gut, Mallory curled his hands into Christian's robes and threw him to the ground. Christian's guns went off, shots lodging in the ceiling, where they rained stone down on them. But the gunshots were the least of their worries. Mallory's jacket split down the back, the wolf given rein to run.

It was then Eleanor realized Christian didn't know as much as he believed he did about Mallory. He didn't know the wolf of him, because the screams that filled the chapel were true and terrified. Christian made to buck the animal off, but the wolf didn't budge, pressing Christian into the stone floor. One clawed paw rested against Christian's neck; the other lodged into his belly.

"Eleanor, run!" Christian's words were strangled, but she understood him well enough.

She didn't run. She picked herself up and moved to the pair of them, watching Christian struggle in an effort to rise. Mallory's mouth dipped close to Christian's jaw, nose snuffling as the wolf took in the terrified scent of him. Eleanor reached for Christian, beginning to search through his robes.

"Do you have it? Where is it?"

Eleanor knew she wasn't in her right mind. There was a sense of detachment, a feeling of watching herself from far away—years perhaps—as she rifled through Christian's robes in search of a ring. A ring that would lead her to Anubis, who would lead her to her mother. Just that, that was all she wanted. Just that . . .

"Eleanor—for the love of God, get this thing off me!"

"Where is it?"

Eleanor's hands fisted in Christian's robes as she gave him a hard shake. She was aware of Mallory, close and holding Christian down. She was aware, too, that Christian likely didn't have the ring on him. It made no sense, and yet she demanded that he give it to her. Some distant part of her mind remained convinced he did have it, had only slipped it into a pocket the way he had all those years ago.

Demands that made no sense to her logical mind spilled from Eleanor's lips, over and over, a broken, stammering river that ran until she rocked backward and slumped in the debris. She stared helplessly at Christian and the wolf atop him. The wolf seemed less inclined to withdraw and lowered his head to Christian's, golden eyes meeting green.

It was a writhing cobra that, at last, parted them, the snake rising from the shadow of a pillar as if to determine what had disturbed its afternoon slumber. The wolf jerked backward, and Christian took advantage of the motion to skitter back himself, until he collided against a broken pillar. He came unsteadily to his feet, holding up one hand to ward off the wolf as he stepped toward the stream of rock that spilled from the back of the chapel.

"The race is on, Eleanor," he said. Though he tried, Christian couldn't quite muster his usual arrogance; Eleanor saw he was thrown by Mallory's transformation, by her own demands.

Eleanor slid away herself, to distance herself from the snake, while Mallory took a defensive position, forelegs spread, teeth bared at both Christian and the cobra.

"You had better run for your life, Christian," Eleanor said. She came onto her feet as Mallory began to circle the debris and the cobra in an effort to reach Christian. "And I don't mean from the wolf."

With that, Christian pushed himself up and out across the spilled stone. Small stones skittered into the chapel in his wake and sent the cobra darting back into the shadows.

"Mallory! Eleanor!"

Auberon and Gin burst into the chapel, their guns drawn. Auberon's was braced over his still-cast arm, but Eleanor had no doubt he would have plugged Christian had the rogue remained. Gin made for the back of the chapel and the break in the wall alongside a still-wolfish Mallory, but Auberon drew himself up short at the sight of the wolf.

"Ah, hell."

"It was Christian," Eleanor said. Gin's revolver made a sharp report in the air outside the chapel. He returned with Mallory at heel, muttering curses that only ceased when he realized there was a wolf among them. He stared at the beast, then eyed Auberon and Eleanor.

"Ah, hell." It was all Auberon could say, and Eleanor's mouth twitched in a brief smile.

"The good news is, he doesn't know where the last ring is," she added. She looked to Mallory, still shaken by the idea of him pinning Christian to the ground. How close that fanged mouth had come to his neck, how she had seen Mallory tear such tender skin to shreds before.

Auberon holstered his revolver and looked to the wolf. Mallory paced inside the chapel, making certain his circuit involved brushing past Eleanor's legs a time or two.

"That's good?" Gin asked. "That is not good . . . not at all good."

Eleanor frowned. "Would you rather he did have it?"

Auberon slid his revolver away, watching Mallory pace. "If he did, we would at least know where to look."

Eleanor agreed; Auberon had a point.

CHAPTER SIXTEEN

Luxor, Egypt ~ October 1889

Homer may have called Luxor the City of a Hundred Gates, but Virgil needed only one. The afternoon air threatened to suffocate, but he ventured into the city streets even so. He headed for the docks where ships of sea and sky harbored, where he knew one could find an opium den tucked within the marketplace stalls, hovels, and camels if one knew where to look. He knew.

Inside the den, the first breath of air was intoxicating. Virgil's hands were shaking by the time he sat down before tray and pipe. But he hesitated, staring at the lamp and its licking flame. Slowly, fearing he would do it wrong, Virgil began to fill the pipe. He listened to the soft breathing of the person in the nook next to his. No private room here, but he didn't care. The need was like a cold blade inside him; he could feel it nick every rib as it slid downward and threatened to wake the wolf.

Still, even with the pipe properly filled, Virgil wavered. The pipe was not the one he was accustomed to, of course, but it was still finely made and rested easily in his hand. It had a pleasant weight, and he knew he had only to place flame to bowl. Yet he waited.

He closed his eyes and listened to the people around him, to the whisper of bare feet across the floor, the slow shifting of a body on a cushion, the rhythm of other pipes being cleaned, filled, drawn upon. The smoke made his eyes sting, and he became aware of a shift in his breathing, a slow inhale though his nose, an even slower exhale through his parted lips.

If Eleanor had not been in the Anubis chapel with him, he would have torn Christian Hubert limb from limb. Virgil knew this without a doubt. He would have started with the man's neck, wounding him badly enough that he couldn't struggle or get away. Next, he would move to arms, to legs, to tear apart and spill his blood onto the rock-strewn floor.

Mary, please forgive me.

It was the arrogance of the man, the assumption that he could bend Eleanor to his will, and if that failed, could shoot her. It was the threat to Eleanor—someone, he realized, he was coming to view as his territory. She was no such thing, she was her own woman, and while he knew this and respected her because of it, he had trouble disconnecting that from the wolf's instincts.

While he had been married to Caroline, he had never felt such a need to claim a person. As a man the idea was foreign, whereas in wolf form it was only right. The memory of Eleanor refusing his apology after he had marked her neck still thrilled him. It went through him as sharply as his first opium pipe had.

Virgil opened his eyes to the scene around him, to the splayed bodies which draped the rough wood floor and faded cushions. Revulsion twisted inside him at these familiar sights: the glimpse of bare thigh, the gloss of candlelight on unbound hair, the curl of hazy smoke rising upward to push against the ceiling. His body wanted the visions and slumber opium brought, but his mind was already withdrawing from it. He still wanted to run, but no longer in this way.

With a shaking hand, Virgil set the pipe down. This motion caught the eye of a passing attendant, who paused beside Virgil, kneeling to the opium tray. But when the attendant saw the set had not been touched, his eyes met Virgil's. Virgil assured the man all was proper, that he had only changed his mind.

In the street, Virgil wiped a hand across his sweaty forehead. He stood there for a long while, letting the heat of Egypt soak into him, letting the world spin as he remained still. Eventually he realized he was being watched by a pair of familiar eyes. Across the street in the shadow of a hanging tapestry, Auberon lingered, a pack worn across his torso.

Once, Virgil would have been angry, would have thought it presumptuous of this man, but that time was long since past. Now, he felt only comforted by the idea of Auberon there. Their eyes met, but Auberon made no move across the busy street. Virgil turned away, walking into the shadowed street, knowing Auberon would follow.

There was no anger now, and he focused on its absence. There was calm and there was peace, and strangely, the wolf inside lifted its head, its eyes questioning.

Mary, hold my hand, for I cannot do this alone.

Virgil began to run. Mindful of the vendors and people in profusion, he headed for the end of the street where it branched in two directions. He stripped his jacket off, giving the wolf rein the way he had in the chapel. It was almost like opening his hand and offering it to the creature, inviting it to dance.

The wolf leapt at the opportunity, literally, and as Virgil rounded a corner into a more deserted stretch of street, his feet found new purchase. Claws clattered against the stones; he felt the sunlight through his fur, and a bevy of new scents exploded in his nose. Somewhere there was roasting meat, and bird droppings splattered the stones below him. Camels smelled like prey, and the people smelled like creatures he wanted to avoid.

Ahead there lay a ruined temple, and Virgil angled his way toward it, tongue lolling out of his mouth. The air was so hot, and he wished for water, but saw none when he reached the temple. There was little rain here, a distant part of his mind told him; nothing to collect in the small depressions in the ground. Still, he found shade and took comfort in that, not so much lying down as flopping upon the hard ground. A cloud of dust rose around him, then drifted away in the cooling breeze that rolled in from the Nile.

He let the afternoon pass in this fashion: running when he wanted to, giving chase to birds if they strayed too close. He captured and devoured a rodent within the temple, but never dozed. Thus, he was awake when Auberon picked his way through the stones and perched on a tall, worn block. Auberon set his pack down, surveying the space around him, until he spied the wolf. Virgil loped to his side.

The change, when he allowed it to come, was still painful, but felt less awkward. He felt more in control this time, perhaps because he had called to the wolf without the anger consuming him. He had never felt such a thing would be possible, but here it was. He was calm and he drew back into himself because he already was himself, in either form.

"I didn't smoke," Virgil said when at last he could. He felt it was vital for Auberon to know that, considering the last time his friend had found him in a den.

Auberon opened the pack at his feet and withdrew a neatly folded stack of fresh clothing. He set these upon the stone he occupied. Socks and shoes waited in the bag. He reached for the towel first, to wipe himself reasonably clean before he started to dress.

"I did not believe you had," Auberon said quietly. "You appeared calm, but not addled, when you emerged from the den. And this . . . " He spread his hands to the temple around them, but Virgil felt the motion encompassed the afternoon Auberon had witnessed rather than the location. "You have changed. For the better."

Virgil's fingers fumbled with trousers and belt. Fingers were strange after willingly not having them all afternoon. "That remains to be seen," he said, then looked more closely at his friend. "What troubles you? Is it the wolf?"

Though Auberon smiled, Virgil felt a confession of sorts was rising toward them.

"Not that, no. If you can embrace that part of yourself at last, I can only be thankful." Auberon's large hands slid together, palms slightly lighter than the backs; it made it look as though he cupped a fragment of the sunset there, rounding it into a ball.

Virgil reached for the jacket and pulled it on before joining Auberon on the stone block he occupied. "Is it something better discussed over drinks? Has something happened with Eleanor or Cleo?"

"They are fine," Auberon assured him, though Virgil was on edge now. With Irving and Hubert both nearby, their odds weren't good. He thought back to the lapis ring Auberon had presented in Cairo, the look that weighted his eyes then. It was the same weight within Auberon's eyes now. Confessions to come.

"Would you consider us friends, Virgil?" Auberon asked. "We share a partnership, but I have always hoped—" He broke off, teeth worrying at his lower lip as he considered his next words. "My life has been a curious one. I never envisioned myself being allowed to do this work and yet here I am, traveling the world as a free man, respected by those I work with, but . . . "

Virgil didn't bother to look for a tie in the pack that Auberon had brought; he knew there wouldn't be one. Instead, he reached for Auberon's hands, covering them with one of his own.

"You are my friend, as surely as you are my partner," Virgil said. "I never hoped for that, to be frank with you. After Joel died . . . " Virgil thought of the days that had followed his death, a blur of pain. Opium had been escape even then. "I told myself it wouldn't happen again, that I wouldn't establish a friendship with a partner because there was too much to lose." He squeezed Auberon's hands, then withdrew. "You have known and accepted the truth of me since our earliest days. You have encouraged me to do the same, and I can only be thankful that God saw fit to pair you with me."

"You have done the same for me," Auberon said in a low tone, and then came the words that Virgil did not want to hear, but the words he knew he must. "Director Irving gave me the lapis ring, Virgil. Placed the box in my hand and told me to find the last one, so that our work could be finished."

Virgil's eyes did not waver from his friend and partner; he pictured the scene, Irving with another small box—the same one he had once entrusted to Caroline or another? What was Irving playing at?

"He doesn't know where the fourth ring is, but has been looking everywhere he can reach," Auberon continued. "He believes he has enlisted my assistance—believes he can trust me, since I knew about the agents who were sent to the Gallery of Machines to encourage Miss Folley's assistance."

Was this what it had been like for Eleanor to see her mother's photograph case, what it was like to learn the Lady was her own grandmother? Virgil felt not like the world had dropped out from beneath him, but that he had finally realized there had been no world at all. Only air—thin and capricious.

"He isn't going to destroy the rings," Virgil said.

"I cannot imagine that he would." Auberon unclasped his hands now, fingers rubbing lightly together. "It was better to accept the ring than to refuse it, but I realize what an awkward position this places me in. You take the instance at the Exposition, where I knew more than I said. You take my recent meeting with Irving—at his insistence, I should add. He tracked me down two nights ago. All taken together, I realize how this may reflect on me—"

"Nonsense."

Virgil wanted to leave it there and say no more, but from the sound of Auberon's voice, the man needed something more, something Virgil had never said to him before.

"Auberon—Michael." Virgil sat a little straighter on the stone block, resting his sweaty hands against his thighs. "I trust you. I find you a remarkable person—beyond your position and the color of your skin. These things don't matter, not to me. You have only ever shown me kindness and trust in return.

Had Irving offered me the ring, I would have taken it as well. Had you not taken it, this conversation likely would have come to blows. I trust you. With my secrets, with my life." His smile vanished. "With Eleanor's life."

Auberon rocked back on the stone a little, as if he had been struck. He said nothing, only looking steadily at Virgil until at last he nodded. "And that is something remarkable indeed."

Virgil looked across the temple. Shadow had begun to douse its outer limits as the sun slipped lower in the sky. "Irving knows precisely what we're doing, then." It was a dreadful realization, that.

"*Precise* is a difficult word, Virgil," Auberon said. "I believe he knows we now possess two rings, that Hubert has the third, but as to the fourth . . . Not even we can say precisely what we're doing, can we?"

A low laugh escaped Virgil. "No, we can't. Point taken." Virgil slid from the stone block, brushed his trousers off, and looked around again, as if expecting spies among the stones. "Irving gave you that ring, and Caroline . . . " He trailed off, realizing there were things Auberon didn't yet know on that front. "My eel-eating friend, let us go back to the townhouse and meet with the others. There are things you should know about fair Caroline."

Auberon grabbed the pack and headed out of the temple at Virgil's side. "Are you going to tell me she resembled her snake of a father more than I would have previously thought?"

Virgil clapped Auberon on the arm. "Among other things."

Sirocco's base in Luxor was much like that in Cairo: an older hotel, its marigold stucco walls blending seamlessly into the surrounding city. Whereas in Cairo they had lodged in small, separate rooms, here they were accorded a suite of rooms, four bedrooms fanning out from a common sitting room. The rooms were each painted with bright frescoes: four towering colossi peering out of an afternoon sky, the columns of the hypostyle hall bleeding with sunset, the hundred sphinxes lining the road to Karnak.

In the common room, a lavish spread of food spanned the tiled table between two sets of brightly colored floor cushions. Virgil thought the display looked more like a museum presentation than something to be consumed, sunflower yellow bowls overflowing with roasted vegetables and golden couscous, sky-blue plates laden with charred kebabs. Green glass platters were spread with fruit arranged in wheels of colors, cut oranges spiraling into wheels of pineapple and figs. Pottery pitchers foamed with Egyptian beer, whereas glass pitchers held water and fruit juices. Candles floated in wide bowls of water, gilding everything with more gold. The fragrant lotus on the table reminded Virgil of Cleo and that she had not joined them on this journey.

"Someone is trying to seduce us," Eleanor said in a low tone as they discovered the display. She padded in stocking feet toward the table, where she sat upon a blue cushion and studied the spread. "Still, it is a pretty gift horse, isn't it?"

Virgil followed her at a slower, more cautious pace. Gift horse was right, because Virgil couldn't erase the foolish idea that the table would burst apart—not with thirty Trojans, but something more sinister. A single Irving would do. Gin flitted from door to window and back again, looking for anything out of place, while Auberon joined Eleanor and poured a tall glass of beer for her.

"One guess," Virgil said. He chose the cushion beside Eleanor's, a deep yellow that reminded him of Irish butter.

"Got to be Irving," Gin said as he pulled a window shut and latched it. He drew the draperies across, then peered between the gap in them. "Makes a bad kind of sense. All bad."

"I feel again that I should apologize," Auberon said, shaking his head and refusing the platter of kebabs Eleanor offered. "Had I not taken the ring, we might have yet moved in secrecy."

Eleanor shook her head as Virgil made to reject that theory, too. "No," Eleanor said. "Irving came back here, Auberon. He knew well before he got here what he would find—he's not the kind to move without knowing, and there's no telling how long he's watched us. Maybe he even had a hand in the stunt at the Exposition." She offered the kebabs to Virgil, who took them with a grin.

"She's right," Virgil said. He helped himself to three kebabs, then counted those that remained on the platter. He took another two, then passed the platter on to Gin. He was ravenous and felt he could consume the entire table of food on his own. "We were foolish to presume ourselves so lucky, him being in another country. Who knows where he actually was—if he was in the Dominion of Canada, he surely made the return in a shorter time than any living man before him."

Auberon grunted, as if he hadn't considered the possibility Irving hadn't left Egypt at all.

"At least now," Eleanor offered as consolation, "Irving believes he has an in." She nodded toward Auberon as she tore a piece of flatbread in two. "If he believes you are working for him, that buys us time and hopefully keeps him off our backs. Although, if we presume Caroline was involved, Irving may have the jump on that, too. Did he know his daughter better than you did, Virgil?"

Virgil was certain he didn't like the answer he was about to give. "They were always close—I don't think she ever trusted me the way she did him. Let us presume this: that if Irving gave the lapis ring to Auberon, the lapis is also the ring he once gifted to Caroline. When she died, it came back to him—he may well have reclaimed it himself. It is unlikely Caroline had the ring with her in Russia. Her father received word of her death before I could complete the journey back to Paris. If the ring was in our home, it could have gone unnoticed by me for, well, ever. Whereas he most likely knew exactly where to look." Despite the warm of the evening, that idea chilled him. What else might she have brought into their home, if she'd been in possession of such a ring?

"So, the lady Caroline was . . . " Gin trailed off, dipping a serving spoon into a bowl filled with fire-roasted tomatoes. "Searching for the final ring all along? The Egyptian museum had the carnelian. Caroline gave Hubert the scarab in Morocco—which Eleanor later took. Irving had the lapis, and the fourth . . . "

Eleanor took a long drink of her beer, then set the glass aside. "If we presume Irving and Caroline had the lapis, and know that Caroline had another ring in Morocco, can we also presume that they, if anyone else, had access to the fourth ring?"

"It is the easiest course," Auberon said.

"Unless no one has ever known," Virgil said. "But that makes little sense. If that were the case, there wouldn't be such a fuss over these rings at all. If one were well and truly lost, the Glass could not be opened, correct?"

When everyone agreed, he continued. "So it's not lost. We just don't know where it is." He grinned—then realized that situation was not necessarily an improvement. He exhaled. "Let's go back to what Eleanor just said—the Irvings may have had access to it."

"Mmm." Eleanor touched Virgil's arm. "Let me revise that. Director Irving told Auberon he does not know where the ring is—which may or may not be true, but let's presume it is, since it's easiest. So he may not know. But what if Caroline did?"

Virgil consumed his kebabs in silence, pulling the tender lamb off the skewer and chewing thoughtfully. "If anything, I'm coming to learn Caroline was more devious than even I knew. Our line of work requires some subterfuge, and early on, I thought that was all it was. Now, however . . . " He tossed the wooden skewer into the pile that was forming in the middle of the table. "Perhaps her father believed he had a willing accomplice, much as he does Auberon here. But could Caroline have played even her father? She knew where that last ring was, but told no one—thinking she would gain the others, and . . . " Virgil scowled. "Then why give a ring to Hubert?"

Eleanor shifted on her cushion and folded her bread in half to scoop balls of fried falafel from the bowl "Christian has . . . a reputation."

Gin laughed into his beer, sending bubbles into his nose. After he finished coughing and Auberon ceased pounding on his back, he waved his arms, still laughing. "A reputation when it comes to his career and the ladies," he added. "Would Caroline have been charmed by Christian?"

Once again, Virgil felt himself at a loss. Admitting that he hadn't known his wife or what would charm her was difficult. He knew then that Caroline had never truly been his wife, his partner. In all the ways that one person could cleave to another, they never had, and he felt himself in mourning all over again for a belief he cherished, but had not actually possessed.

He looked to Eleanor, thinking he should have been reluctant to meet her gaze, but there was only patience in her eyes. "You saw them together," he said.

Eleanor didn't hesitate to shake her head, preventing Virgil's mind from running down paths he wished to avoid. "Only for one night, but even then her interest in Christian appeared manufactured. At the time, I thought Caroline was absurd, and presumed she had an interest in Christian, but it was all pretense. I think she believed his reputation, in terms of his career, could help her. She played the innocent, and part of him was likely flattered by the attention. She may have given him a ring to secure his trust."

"Did she find Christian on her own?" Auberon asked. He rested his elbows against the table, loosely clasping his hands before him. "Consider that for Mistral, the Lady has always been tied to the Folleys. It's possible Irving looked into Eleanor and found Christian. Depending on his relationship with his daughter—Virgil, you said she trusted him—it may be that Irving set Caroline in Christian's way."

Virgil finished the last of his beer and set his glass to the side. While the evening's conversation hadn't eased his mind about Caroline or her activities, it was almost comforting to put the pieces of her life together with others who could rein him in before he could contemplate paths that would have had him reaching for an opium pipe.

As it stood, he was far from drunk, but the beer had dropped a layer of gauze over everything around him. Eleanor was by his side, the candles and lotus both polluting the air with a pleasing fragrance.

Then Gin cleared his throat. "Do you think Caroline's father knew she was working for another agency?"

Silence drifted over the table, as thick as spring snow. No one was comfortable in answering; then Eleanor did.

"But was she?"

This question also went unanswered, and Eleanor sat a little straighter, resting her hand on Virgil's arm. If it was in an effort to calm him or herself, he didn't know.

Eleanor continued. "We haven't established that Caroline had agency ties outside Mistral. One of Mistral's own directors, her father, has been there at every turn, whether gifting her with a ring or possibly placing her in contact with Christian."

Virgil could only nod at the idea that Caroline acted within Mistral's circles alone. Perhaps the addition of another agency only muddied the waters; had it been Mistral all along, Caroline's actions approved and consented to by Irving himself?

"Whatever her ties," Auberon said, "it is likely her father knew her every move. They trusted each other; how could he not know?"

"And yet," Eleanor added, "Caroline was skilled when it came to disguise and manipulation." Virgil didn't mistake the caution he heard in Eleanor's words now. "Eleanor." Virgil covered Eleanor's hand with his own. He swallowed hard, thinking his tie needed loosening, but there was no tie around his neck. "All of you. I appreciate the . . . tiptoeing around this, but it's unnecessary. I did not know Caroline as I believed I did. What I do believe now is that she deceived everyone—including me, the man she married. Why would her father be any different? I think she told the truth when it suited her, and rarely did it suit."

Eleanor's fingers slid through his and gave him a firm squeeze. He knew she understood, that awful truths had been revealed about people they had both loved—and all they could do was move forward and find the final ring before either Christian or Irving did.

Christian could want the rings for himself, or he could be working in concert with Irving. If so, what did Irving intend? Had Auberon actually bought them time or had he only managed to forestall something inevitable?

A brisk knock sounded at the door, and before Virgil could rise, Gin was already on his feet and moving toward it. He opened the door to reveal a young lady Virgil didn't recognize, though she handed Gin an envelope bearing an official Sirocco seal.

"What now?" Auberon muttered.

"Urgent communiqué," Gin said. He knelt on his cushion and offered the envelope to Eleanor. "Miss Folley."

Virgil studied the envelope as Eleanor took it. The envelope was addressed to Eleanor, in a hand he did not recognize, but that told him little, other than it was not a summons from Irving. When Eleanor turned the envelope over, the official wax seal gleamed in the candlelight, revealing the spread wings of an owl. Eleanor smoothed her thumbs over it.

Messages were always sealed, even in-house, to prevent tampering en route, but the method wasn't foolproof. Wax could be reheated and eased open; Virgil knew this from experience. The seal sounded fresh when Eleanor broke it from the paper, and he prayed it was so. The evening's conversations had only heightened his sense of wariness.

He was close enough to see the handwriting upon the page when Eleanor withdrew it; it was still unfamiliar, but he saw a familiar name there: *Renshaw Folley.*

"Cleo relayed this," Eleanor said. Virgil wrapped his arm around her shoulders, Auberon and Gin and propriety be damned.

"She received a message concerning my father earlier tonight—he was the victim of an attack and has . . . "

Virgil's hold on Eleanor tightened as she trailed off. He peered down at the page before her.

"He's been taken to Hôtel-Dieu de Paris—Juliana wants me to come."

Silence descended again. There was no question they would go, and Gin leapt once more into action. "I'll see to transportation."

Virgil looked down at Eleanor as her fingers traced the carefully written words. She was oddly quiet, entirely unlike the Eleanor he had come to know. "Eleanor?"

"This isn't right," she said.

"Of course it's not, it's your father—"

"No, listen," she said. "Irving returns and gifts Auberon with one of the rings we have no other means of finding." Her eyes lingered on a nodding Auberon over the edge of the paper, then came back to Virgil. "Hubert leads us to the temple where my grandmother's name is written and challenges us to a race for the final ring. And now my father is attacked and I'm asked to return to a city I just left?"

Virgil felt cold down to his bones, as if he had been doused in ice water. "Someone wants us in Paris now." He stood from the cushions and offered Eleanor a hand up from them.

"I don't like playing the part of a chess piece," Eleanor said, but still grasped Virgil's hands and pulled herself to standing.

Virgil squeezed her hands. "But don't you know, the queen can go any direction she likes."

"Don't tell me this isn't a trap," Gin said as he returned to the room, one pack already in hand. "You may call me mad, deranged, delusional, whatever you like, but this . . . this smells as bad as eel-jelly."

Auberon clicked his tongue as he pushed himself away from the table. "Oh, it's definitely a trap," he agreed.

"It doesn't feel like Hubert's doing," Virgil said as they all moved toward their rooms.

"No," Eleanor agreed. "It doesn't."

That left only one person in Virgil's mind, he decided as he stepped from the common room and into his bedroom. Howard Irving.

CHAPTER SEVENTEEN

The cool of Paris was a stark contrast to the heat of Egypt. Where the autumn air might not have seemed cold otherwise, it now had Eleanor pulling her Mistral-purchased coat around her more firmly. *The Jackal* arrived to dismal skies and the sheen of recent rain coating everything.

Even at top speed, the flight had taken over twenty-four hours. It had been mercifully quiet, though the silence and lack of being shot from the sky gave them time to rest and ample opportunity to consider all they had learned in the days prior, which made for an uneasy atmosphere. It didn't help that worry was consuming Eleanor as she fretted over what had befallen her father. A second message from Cleo mentioned an attack after leaving the market, Renshaw found bloody on the ground. Eleanor had to wonder if the messages they received en route were from Cleo at all; she was to the point of questioning everything. Had Cleo been compromised? Was Irving overseeing her communiqués?

The attack didn't feel like Christian's doing, yet Eleanor suspected something was amiss with him too, for he wasn't his normal self in the temple chapel. Something was not right, but she didn't yet know what. Trying to unravel the constant riddle of Christian while worrying about her father was impossible.

The journey to Hôtel-Dieu seemed interminable. When at last she could see the towers of Notre Dame nearing, she began to relax, knowing her father was close. Eleanor had been to Notre Dame countless times; its towers, gargoyles, and rose windows were well known to her—but never the hospital that sprawled beside it. She would have to thank her father for the new adventure.

Eleanor slipped out of the carriage as quickly as she could—not quickly at all considering the rain-slicked cobblestones. She had considered donning a skirt to appease her father, but couldn't tolerate the idea. From the moment they had communicated in Cleo's rooms, a new path had been established. No longer would she deny who she was, not even for her father's peace of mind. She accepted Mallory's steady hand when he offered it.

"No sense in you occupying a bed here, too," Mallory said.

Auberon and Gin lingered near the carriage, taking in the church towers, the hospital roof, the shrubberies nearby. Eleanor couldn't say she was surprised that their conversation was composed of plans to ensure the hospital was secure. Their resources were slim now, as they were uncertain whom they could trust outside their circle. Director Irving possessed fathomless resources and had countless people under his command. The idea that he might attack a hospital full of patients and Augustinian nuns filled Eleanor with a loathing she could hardly contain, but she kept her composure and headed toward a knot of black-draped nuns clustered near a reception desk.

At her query as to her father, one of the sisters asked Eleanor to accompany her. Mallory stayed with the other sisters, showing his Mistral identification and explaining the delicacy of the matter before them. Eleanor left him to handle security matters and followed the small nun deeper into the hospital, then to a room occupied by four beds. Her father was in the last, near the window where he might overlook the Seine if not for Juliana pacing in front of the glass.

"Eleanor!"

Eleanor opened her arms to the woman and murmured her thanks to the sister before she left. Juliana was cold and shaking, her face lined with concern. But she calmed somewhat in Eleanor's embrace, then tugged her toward the bed, where her father slept.

"He asked me to stay for dinner," Juliana explained, "and went to the market for a few things. The market that always has those lemon drops I like so much. But he . . . " She pressed a shaking hand to her midsection. Eleanor squeezed an arm around Juliana's shoulders. "When he didn't return in his usual timely fashion," she continued, "I grew concerned and walked outside to find him—to find him—"

The man in the bed resembled Eleanor's father in only minor ways. She had to look twice before she understood this to be him, beaten and bloodied. His head was wrapped in bandages, his face a mottled purple. One hand was bandaged as well, while his other cradled a small skull. Eleanor brightened some at the sight of it, the small lynx skull he liked so well. He had told a young Eleanor it was the skull of a baby sphinx, and how she had adored it. She had spent long hours stroking a line between its empty eye sockets, as if she could conjure a jinn.

"He was on the ground," Juliana continued. "So still and bloody." She clutched Eleanor's hand within her own. "All those lemon drops spilled on the ground around him."

Eleanor opened her mouth to ask if Juliana had spoken with the police, but the question arrived in Mallory's voice, which made her mouth quirk upward.

"Have you spoken to the police?"

They both turned to look at Mallory, who joined them at the end of the bed. Juliana moved from Eleanor's side to pace the length of bed so she could fuss with Renshaw's blanket.

"I did," she confirmed, "but they aren't optimistic about catching anyone. They said he was likely attacked for his money." Here, her drawn face dared to brighten. "He won his category at the Exposition, Eleanor. The judges loved his machine, said it had a genuine and practical use in ever-expanding fields, and h-he . . . won. Din-dinner was to be our celebration."

A sob escaped Juliana. She dashed her hand over her face to remove the tears, shaking her head and smiling at Eleanor and Mallory both.

"The doctors say he will be fine, but . . . "

Everything that Juliana didn't say pressed hard and insistent against Eleanor's heart. She looked down at her father and touched her cool fingers to his temple. He might be fine, but even so remained terribly injured.

Eleanor placed a kiss against the bandages that wrapped his head. "Da?" she whispered.

She closed her hand around the hand in which he held the skull, feeling as he must have when she had been attacked that day in the desert. Bruised and trampled, his daughter's arm bitten and bleeding, his wife vanished. Her father looked so small and frail in the hospital bed, but when he opened his eyes, Eleanor felt a flare of hope.

"Lila?" he whispered.

Eleanor closed her eyes. She didn't want to be mistaken for her mother, not then. "It's me, Da. Eleanor."

"Ellie . . . " His voice was like grating gravel. "There were men, and a knife—"

"Yes, you were stabbed, you foolish man," Juliana said.

Stabbed. Eleanor hated blades—they hurt—and she looked her father over with a new interest, seeing nothing until his bandaged hand patted his wrapped chest. His ribs may well have saved his life, she thought.

"I only had . . . " Her father's bruised forehead furrowed with his scowl. "Green beans and lemon drops? Not so expensive if they wanted their own . . . "

Eleanor shushed him, Juliana fussing with the blankets again, pulling them closer around Renshaw's chest.

"You are recovering now," Eleanor told him, fighting to keep her voice even. If her father were gone, what would she do? She never thought to presume he would always be there—having lost her mother, she knew better—but this brought the realization close, that indeed someday he would go and she would be left and then . . . And then.

"You are—" Her father peered up at Eleanor in the dim afternoon light that streamed through the nearby window. "In Cairo." With that, his body began to shake from the force of his tears. "Oh, Eleanor." Her name drained him. "I'm s-sorry."

Eleanor bowed her head against his, looking down the length of the bed to Mallory, who stood there, solid and sure, his eyes heavy on them. He withdrew a handkerchief from his pocket and offered it to her.

"I'm here now, Da," she whispered. "You go on and sleep."

Eleanor took Mallory's handkerchief and dried the tears from her father's bruised cheeks. There was so much bruising; she barely touched him for fear of causing him more pain. When she withdrew from his side, Juliana settled into the chair.

"You need rest too, Eleanor," Juliana said. She closed her hand around Renshaw's and the lynx skull.

Eleanor had a denial ready at hand, but Mallory's arm sliding around her made her go silent. There was kindness there, and Eleanor wanted to lose herself: wanted to close her eyes and just drift away for a while.

"She does," Mallory agreed and tugged her back from the bed. "My fellow agents Auberon and Gin will remain here on guard, Mrs. Day," he added, "but I'm going to see that Eleanor gets some food and rest. If you need anything, you have only to ask them."

Eleanor was aware that Mallory guided her out of the room, but she felt distant, watching from afar as he guided her from the room and out of the hospital. It had been the same in those first few moments without her mother, too, that same sense of being separated from all else, floating.

Mallory didn't guide her to the carriage. He took her instead to Notre Dame, where silence and the scent of incense washed over them as they entered. Eleanor paused in the entry, feeling as though the whole of the world was shut away in here; the stillness was so encompassing, it grounded her in another place.

Eleanor had not been raised in a religious household—the Folleys were perfunctorily Catholic, but if they held to a faith, it was a faith written in the bones of the world, not in its heavens. It was a faith that ensured nothing was forgotten, even if buried for centuries.

Even so, she respected these places, and within the cathedral she dropped a knee to the floor. Mallory followed suit. They dipped their fingers into the font of holy water and crossed themselves, and by the time they took a place in the pews, Eleanor felt calmed. The holy water cooled on her forehead and fingers until it was but a memory.

"There is much we need to do," Mallory said, and reached for Eleanor's hands, enclosing them within his own, "but right now, only this." And then he prayed. "Holy Virgin Mary, you are reigning in glory with Jesus, your Son . . . "

Eleanor found a strength in Mallory's voice that she hadn't heard before. As Christian had changed, so, too, had Mallory. Something had changed within him, and it flowed through the words he murmured. He was at peace, she thought. At long last, peace. She reached for that peace, too, that she might hold it within herself and not feel the prickings of fear in this place of all places. Port Elizabeth was a long time ago, she told herself. Caroline wasn't about to appear and make a demand.

"Remember us in our sadness," she whispered along with Mallory, bowing her head above their clasped hands and closing her eyes. She knew the words, and for once believed in them with her whole heart.

"Look kindly on all who are suffering, or fighting against any difficulty. Have pity on those who are separated from someone they love."

Eleanor wasn't separated, not that, not now. She was back with her father and ever close to— She looked down at Mallory's hands around her own. His were broad, scarred, and his silver ring pressed into her as he prayed. She couldn't help but smooth a finger over the silver, over skull and bone. She remembered him bent and broken in the canyon temple, that ring glinting in the darkness. Like a small beacon.

"Have pity on the loneliness of our hearts. Have pity on the weakness of our faith and love."

She heard no weakness in Mallory's voice now. They had both fought to reach this point of peace in their journeys. Eleanor knew they were not yet finished—as much as Mallory's ring had been a point of focus in the temple, the Lady's fourth ring was such now, lost.

"Have pity on those who are weeping . . . "

" . . . on those who are praying, on those who are fearful." Mallory's hands closed around hers now, and she looked into his brown eyes, which were brightened with gleaming gold. How close was the wolf? She knew now: the wolf was always there.

"Holy Mother, please obtain for all of us hope and peace with justice," Eleanor whispered.

Mallory dipped his head and pressed his mouth briefly to hers. He was startlingly warm in the cool of the afternoon, and no longer smelled of opium, but of soap and the crisp autumn air they had flown through.

"Amen," he whispered against her lips.

"Amen."

<hr />

From Notre Dame, they took the carriage back to Mistral's Paris headquarters, where Mallory guided Eleanor to his private rooms. Eleanor suppressed a smile at the reaction of the receptionist in the lobby, the way her wide eyes tracked them up the staircase. Eleanor felt something similar, never thinking to find herself here in the course of this mission—or anything that might reach beyond the mission.

She had never pictured the place he lived—doing so would have been admitting she fostered a curiosity about him. In their first days together, he had been an agent of Mistral, something to distrust and little else. He had since become considerably more. It was a change borne out of their shared plight, and Eleanor was mindful of that; as it had been with Christian, she did not want to repeat herself with Mallory. People had speculated about her misadventures with Christian, and she didn't want to give anyone cause to do the same with Mallory.

Mallory had two rooms, the first dominated by a fireplace and gilt mirror. The walls were washed in a green paint that made Eleanor think of deep forests—all the better to run though on four bare feet—and the floor was spread with a bright rug, flowers floating on a lapis sea surrounded by a braid of gold and amber. Bookcases lined two walls, while two heavily draped windows looked out onto the Seine. Eleanor could glimpse the towers of Notre Dame, and it comforted her to know her father was close.

She got a brief look of a second room through its open door. It was plainer than the first, but both lacked personal touches of any kind. A handsome bed stood against the far wall, a wardrobe on another, a rug similar to the one in the front room also covering this oak floor. A basin gleamed in the soft afternoon light from the one window.

"I haven't required much," Mallory said in explanation, crossing the sitting room to lift a bottle of whiskey. It was the middle of the afternoon, but Eleanor welcomed the idea. "Mistral provides meals, there is a communal lavatory . . . " He trailed off, dribbling whiskey into two glasses.

"It's nothing to be ashamed of," she said when he pressed the whiskey into her hand. But glimpsing his rooms, his home, was very like getting a glimpse of Mallory, post-Caroline. There was little that was personal, little that was *him*, here. They were rooms for work and sleep alone, and she felt thankful she had been allowed to see him outside this space.

She sank onto the couch with a small groan, realizing only then how tired she was. She had not slept on the flight back to Paris, too eager to reach her father and confirm his condition. She looked at Mallory, to see the smudges beneath his own eyes. He had not slept either.

"You will forgive me—I don't have proper guest accommodations," he said.

Eleanor grinned at the formality of his words. When uneasy, he still fell back on such. She had no doubt his unease came in part from having her here—in this scant place he called home. Even though he had brought her here, it would be strange to have a woman within these walls. "I'm comfortable right here," she said and took a drink of the whiskey.

"I never have guests. Auberon's more family than guest at this point." He finished his whiskey in one gulp. "Here."

He joined her on the couch and lifted one of her boots into his lap. As though he had done it a hundred times before, his fingers pulled at the bootlaces, easing them apart. Eleanor didn't protest. She cradled her whiskey in her lap. The long days were beginning to blur together.

"You haven't had these off often since . . . On the *Nuit*, you—" He broke off as he pulled the first boot free. "Forgive me. I don't mean to . . . That is . . . " He laughed now, a low, rich sound that made Eleanor think of his advance on her in the hallway.

"We were both barefoot on the *Nuit*," she said, remembering. She felt the warmth spread through her body, but knew the whiskey wasn't to blame. It had been a long while since she had spent time alone with a man, a man who had a plain interest in her. She wriggled her freed toes; when Mallory appeared reluctant to reach for her other boot, she offered it to him. He set to work on the laces.

"Are you hungry?" he asked, sliding his finger beneath one pair of crossed lacings and then the next. "Mrs. Gonne keeps a brilliant kitchen here."

Eleanor closed her eyes; she thought of Mallory in the library, angry over the idea that Christian had been in her rooms. Angry enough that he had marked her. As his? She opened her eyes to find Mallory studying her, his eyes intent.

"I am hungry," she said, but it was not food that called to her. Still, these things that did call—the desire to know more of Mallory's mark upon her— were things that should wait. And yet, there would be no Cleo knocking upon the door this time. No Gin. No Auberon. A shiver coursed down her spine at the very idea. Was it fear or anticipation, or some heady mix of both? She wasn't sure.

Mallory tugged her second boot off and dropped it to the floor. With his fingers encircling her stocking-clad ankle, he shifted on the couch, closer to her, his mouth mere inches from her own. She wondered if he could feel her pulse and the way it pounded, having pooled into her ankle where he held her.

"You drive me to deep distraction, Miss Folley," he whispered. He moved closer, his cheek brushing hers, and she thought she could smell the dark myrrh of him, the edge of the animal wanting out. "I shall see what Mrs. Gonne has prepared today, so at least one hunger may be satisfied."

Eleanor exhaled when Mallory stepped away. He lingered, looking down at her with a hunger of his own before he crossed to the door and let himself out. She slid back into the pillows, holding her whiskey close, and listened to the retreat of his footsteps down the hallway. She listened for Mallory to come back, but when he did, she was already asleep.

⪥

Dublin, Ireland ~ Sometime in 1870

Eleven-year-old Eleanor crouched under the kitchen table and stared in rapt astonishment at the book her father had made for her. Better than even the silhouette whirligig of a few years ago, this book was a surprise each time she opened it. She was almost afraid to touch it, fearful that the delicate temple walls would crumble.

She opened the book, the back of it creaking, and the page before her sprang to life. A small paper mechanism turned within the book and its folds of paper and caused the temple to rise from the pages, to stand in three dimensions before her. She stroked a finger across the temple wall and it held.

Black lines at the base of the temple resolved themselves into people as the temple came upright; her father had left the people for her to paint if she wanted. So, too, the temple itself, with its gently bulging columns and stone-block walls. Eleanor pictured the people in colored linens, the temple walls as brilliant as sunshine.

"Ren, why can't you understand?"

Her mother's voice, from above the canopy of the kitchen table. Eleanor looked up but didn't move from her book, listening to the whisper of paper across its old surface.

"I understand exactly, Lila. Exactly what you mean to do." Her father's voice was tired, sounding the way it did when Eleanor asked one time too many to see his collection of bones.

Dalila Folley's feet had been resting flat against the floor, but she moved now, perching one foot atop the other. Eleanor watched them, comparing them to her father's feet, presently encased in ratty slippers, but pale when they were not. Where her mother was the color of rich Egyptian soil, her father was fresh cream with a sprinkling of freckles.

"I have supported this for almost ten years now, Lila. I don't know why . . . " There was a pause and a slow exhalation. "I don't know why you can't stop."

Eleanor turned the page in her book, collapsing the temple and causing a sphinx to rise in the pages that followed. There was a soft thump from the tabletop, perhaps a fist against the scarred wood. They thought she was in bed sleeping, but Eleanor had to have one last look at her magical book before sleeping, and she had left the book under the kitchen table.

"And I should stop now? Now, when I have found her?"

More papers shuffled, and Eleanor stared into the eyes of the sphinx, wishing the creature might unravel the riddle being spoken above. The folded paper remained only that, folds that might look like an ancient mouth, but were silent until she made them move.

"I have already started the process, Ren. Gaining permissions. I intend to excavate. How can you ask me to stop?" Dalila's voice broke on the edge of tears. "How?"

Eleanor watched her father's feet swing away as he maneuvered himself out of his chair. And then his knees, striking the kitchen floor when he knelt beside his wife's chair.

"I cannot bear to lose you," he whispered.

Eleanor heard the soft sound of lips against lips, and she pressed a finger over the sphinx's mouth. *Shh.*

"I cannot bear it, Lila. I thought I would be able to. I thought we would have enough time, but there is never enough, not even with the damnable Glass."

"Come with me," Dalila whispered.

He moved away from her then, faster than a man of his age should have been able to. Eleanor watched his feet stalk a path across the scarred wood floor, deeper into the kitchen.

"How can you ask that of me?"

"We could all go—"

"Absolutely not."

"Ren—"

"No."

He left the kitchen then, and Eleanor watched her mother's toes curl. She heard her mother crying, a sound that was uncommon at best from Dalila

Folley. She moved from the table a moment later, feet padding down the hall after Renshaw, and Eleanor was left alone with the paper sphinx. She lifted her finger from its mouth.

"Tell me what it means," she whispered to the sphinx, but the beast remained silent.

CHAPTER EIGHTEEN

Paris, France ~ February 1886

"Virgil?"

"Coming."

Virgil closed the small wooden chest and slid it deeper onto his wardrobe shelf, until it pressed against the back and could go no farther. He set another box in front of it, then turned to the other boxes on his bed. Two boxes, everything he had of Caroline, or at the least, everything he was willing to hand over to her parents. They didn't need what was in the smaller box, he reasoned. One box of clothing, one box of more personal items, including her framed petals and pressed leaves from her travels. He pictured Sabrina Irving hanging them in her parlor; they would make a nice pairing with the botanical prints she already possessed, spreading faded and green against the bright lemon wallpaper.

He carried the boxes into the sitting room, where Howard and Sabrina Irving perched upon his couch, the picture of grief. Both wore black, Sabrina's white-blond hair draped with a black veil; in this they matched Virgil, but in little else.

"This should be all of it," Virgil said and set the boxes on the table before them. "There was never much, with Caroline being so often away . . . "

Virgil tried to explain the lack of items, but neither Irving was bothered by the quantity of boxes. Neither seemed interested in the least, if he had to be honest with himself. Howard had mentioned cleaning out the small room Caroline kept in Cairo; had the bulk of her belongings been there? He had wanted to get these final things to her parents before moving to the rooms Mistral was so generous to provide, but Howard and Sabrina had wanted to come together. Today was their first opportunity, a day when snow silently fell beyond the windows that looked toward Notre Dame.

"Is there anything you need, Virgil, dear?"

Sabrina asked the question, but her voice sounded distant, as though she could never give him whatever he might request. She reached for one of the boxes he had brought, seemed about to open it, then pulled her black-gloved hand back into her lap.

"No," Virgil said. "There's nothing." What could any of them give one another? Not even comfort in this strange time. Virgil couldn't fathom how he was supposed to grieve for this woman, this woman he had killed.

"We won't keep you," Howard Irving said, and touched his wife's shoulder. They rose as one from the couch, Howard lifting both boxes. "As you said. Not much here."

There was never much, Virgil thought as he walked them the short distance to the door. There, Sabrina lost her tenuous control and began to weep. She reached blindly for Virgil, clutching at his arms until he pulled her into an awkward embrace.

"Oh, Virgil, she was all we had." Sabrina bent her head against Virgil's chest, and Virgil could do no more than hold her while she sobbed. "How can we—Why—?" Anything she might have said was consumed by her tears.

Virgil swallowed hard. Mistral informed him her parents had been told that Caroline died on the northern coast of Africa in the line of duty. They knew nothing of her journey to the Russian Empire or the true cause of her death. Nor had they seen her body, sealed in a lead-lined coffin. As Virgil looked over Sabrina's bent head and into Howard's eyes, he saw something that made him doubt their ignorance. Irving's eyes were hard, flinty, and while it could have been only grief, it felt like something more. Virgil told himself it was his own guilt that made him feel such. How could it not?

"One more day," Sabrina whispered. "If we could have only that. She—" Sabrina lifted her head now and smiled at Virgil through the tears that mottled her cheeks. "She mentioned children the last time we spoke."

Virgil managed a weak smile, hoping Sabrina wouldn't read the truth behind it. "We spoke of children," Virgil said. Of not having them. Of never having them.

"Come on, Sabrina, we've kept the boy long enough." Howard nodded to Virgil. "Son, I'll be seeing you."

Virgil nodded and opened the door for them, allowing them into the hallway beyond. Howard balanced the boxes in one arm, guiding Sabrina with the other. Virgil watched until they entered the elevator, then ducked back into the apartment, believing he closed the door on more than just the corridor that day.

Paris, France ~ October 1889

Now Virgil took the small wooden chest from the back of wardrobe shelf and brought it to his bed. He sat, holding the box on his lap as though it contained vipers or explosives. Nothing so dramatic, he reminded himself and opened the box.

He pulled out a copy of his and Caroline's wedding invitation, followed by the cold circle of her wedding ring. These he set aside, withdrawing a small journal (leather-bound with a tied band), a dried and yellowed rose (from Caroline's wedding bouquet), a small chandelier crystal fashioned into a pendant (a gift from Imogene, to reinforce Caroline's "sparkly.")

They were small things, things that didn't shout Caroline's name to him, but still anchored her in his mind. He took up the journal and untied the band holding it closed.

Caroline's handwriting was as precise as Mistral's own machine-written telegrams. The book was filled with a variety of meetings, only one of which Virgil was certain was true. On their wedding date, Caroline had written his name and drawn a small flower with branching grape leaves. It was so unlike her; it was the one thing that gave Virgil hope that her love hadn't been a ruse. Hadn't been another lie. Some part of her, surely, had loved him. Hadn't she?

While Eleanor slept undisturbed on the couch, Virgil stretched out on his bed, flipping through the pages he hadn't viewed in more than three years. All lies, he thought; places Caroline never went, because she was too busy pretending—

A dried flower fell out of the book with a whisper, alighting on his chest. Virgil plucked it between thumb and forefinger and realized that it wasn't a flower at all. It was a dried grape leaf.

He twirled the leaf by its stem and marveled at its presence in Caroline's journal. What's simple is true, he reminded himself as he listened to Eleanor's even breathing from the other room.

He knew, then, where the fourth ring was.

Virgil couldn't let Eleanor sleep. Not with this idea bursting to life in his mind. He paced the sitting room for a good five minutes, debating while Eleanor slept on. He set the leaf on the table and paced more; he lit a fire in the fireplace and paced a new path. Still, at last, he had to crouch beside Eleanor and shake her awake. He couldn't stand it—needed another person to share his theory. His crazy theory. Eleanor groaned a little as she came awake and muttered something about a jackal. She looked startled to find Virgil there.

"Sleeping beauty," he murmured. "I've things to show you."

"No spindles," she said as he helped her sit up.

"Never that," Virgil promised and took Eleanor's hand, opening it so that her palm lay flat. Onto it, he placed the grape leaf.

"It's a grape leaf," she said around a yawn. "Mallory . . . Virgil. I'm not fully awake, but I'm right, yes?"

Virgil settled onto the couch beside her. "You are correct. It was in Caroline's book, you see."

"Mmm." Eleanor yawned again, not bothering to cover her mouth as she still held the grape leaf. "I don't see." She leaned into Virgil, still drowsy from sleep. "It looks old. You know, one of the earliest things I ever found was the impression of a leaf pressed into a stone, and as a child, it was like a miracle, for I couldn't understand it: how a soft thing like a leaf might leave the mark of itself on something as hard as a stone."

Virgil slid an arm around Eleanor, knowing that he was coming to understand how such a thing was possible. How a soft thing like an Eleanor might leave the mark of herself on something as hard as he.

"One thing Caroline enjoyed outside of her work was flowers and plants," he said slowly. This idea was maddening, and he wanted to voice it with care. "She was always bringing home little bits from her missions. In retrospect, I suppose this was the first way I began to realize that Caroline went places other than where she said she was going. She framed a collection of them, petals and leaves. It was something I returned to her parents. But this—" He touched the leaf on Eleanor's palm. "—this ended up in a box of items I kept."

"Virgil?"

"The vineyard," Virgil said. "Chateau Mallory."

Eleanor shifted on the couch: not out of his hold, but deeper into it. She set the grape leaf on the table, then met Virgil's gaze. Waiting. He tried to order his thoughts.

"Caroline was only at the vineyard once, for the wedding. I never took her there before—there was never the opportunity, and she never wanted to go."

"Virgil, this leaf could have come from anywhere—"

"But I don't think it did." He remained excited by the idea continuing to take shape in his mind. "Caroline wasn't sentimental. She marked our wedding in her book with a grape leaf, but beyond that, everything was precise and cold. Facts only, no emotion. Taking a keepsake from where we wed makes little sense to me, unless it was also a reminder to her of something else. Something practical."

"And we were guided back here," Eleanor said. "Just so I'm certain we're operating on the same theory, you think Caroline hid a ring at the vineyard."

With the words out, Virgil could only nod. It sounded ridiculous, as ridiculous as the first time he and Eleanor had spoken of the Glass aloud, or debated if the Lady was her grandmother.

"Why would she choose the vineyard?" Eleanor asked.

"Caroline was practical. It was likely a matter of convenience—leave it there, come back when she might reclaim it safely? Was it the ring her father gifted her with at the wedding? Perhaps."

He watched Eleanor turn these ideas around, looking from him to the leaf and back again. "Do you believe Caroline loved you?" she finally asked.

The question made Virgil want to shed his human form and run. He forced himself to stay where he was. "I believe she did. In her own way." Her own way may have been alien and strange to everyone else, but everything told him that Caroline had loved him.

"I believe that, too," Eleanor said. "I didn't know her, not beyond a couple of strange encounters, but if she was career Mistral—she still married you, Virgil. What purpose does the marriage serve if not for the simple fact of love? You said she was practical—was it practical to marry a fellow agent? An agent who might one day discover her secret? It's not practical, you two marrying."

Virgil could only agree. His marriage to Caroline hadn't been practical on either side. That Eleanor believed Caroline loved him was a strange relief, and it placed him one step closer to being able to put his past with Caroline firmly to rest.

"With love comes trust," Eleanor continued. "No matter what else she did, Caroline loved you—and, as much as she could, trusted you."

Virgil rested his head against Eleanor's and allowed his eyes to close. That long-ago Russian night came back, threatening to drown him, but he held to Eleanor and stayed above the tide. "The night she died, she said she wanted to tell me. I think she was going to tell me who she really was, what she was doing."

He felt the soft touch of Eleanor's fingers against his chin and opened his eyes. Eleanor's eyes were lit by the flickering fire, gold and brown twined together.

"She trusted you, so she chose the vineyard because of you. Because of that trust."

"I loved her," Virgil said in a low tone, "but I didn't fully trust her." He felt the wolf inside him stir. "Do you believe that's possible?" When Eleanor nodded and her fingers slid into his beard, he exhaled. "I trust you, Eleanor."

Eleanor's fingers slid down the line of Virgil's jaw, down his neck to rest against the thrum of his pulse. "I trust you, Virgil."

It felt like the crossing of a threshold to Virgil. To admit to that trust; to give himself up to it and believe that she would never willingly harm him, would never willingly betray the secret of him. It felt like placing himself in her hands and not minding as she carried a part of him with her. He felt . . . safe. Knowing—always knowing—she would be his sanctuary as he was hers. Or wanted to be, if she would have him as such.

There were unanswered questions, too, as to what did or did not bide its time within Eleanor. Was she more like him than they knew?

Virgil closed the slight distance between them to capture Eleanor's mouth with his own. She was still warm from sleep and the fire, and the touch of her lips against his brought to mind the spark of lightning in a storm. So bright and potentially devastating, but he couldn't stop himself from courting the danger. When Eleanor's tongue lapped at him, tasting, he felt nearly the last thread of his control come undone.

Yet he didn't want to know the touch of her body against his own until he was certain it was a thing he could not lose, for that he knew he could not—would not—bear. He slid his hands up the length of her smooth neck, to curl his fingers into her nutmeg hair. With effort, Virgil lifted his mouth from hers.

"Come home with me, Eleanor."

* * *

"It is reckless, and believe me when I say that is the kindest word I can find at the present, Eleanor Folley." Renshaw made a great fuss of shaking his blankets, smoothing the wrinkles out, then starting anew.

Virgil couldn't fault the man's opinion, but they were already fully involved. There was no easy way out, so in Virgil's mind, they could only go forward. Forward and through to the end, and if that meant searching the vineyard from stem to stern, so be it. As the Bible told him, one did not live in the valley of the shadow, but walked through it. If this was their valley, they had to pass through.

His eyes met Eleanor's, and her smile silently told him she was still in agreement. Eleanor stood to the left of the bed, Juliana sitting to the right. The curtains at the window were mostly drawn, though a pale line of daylight snaked in to bisect Renshaw's bed across his knees. From the look on Juliana's face, it was clear she also felt Renshaw was being kind with his words, that he and Eleanor were demented to consider this mission. Virgil knew he could have asked Eleanor to stay behind, but knew also she would refuse. Surely her father understood that—and perhaps that was why he balked now.

"Mr. Folley—"

"Young man, I will thank you to keep your silence." Renshaw snapped his blankets again. "Ellie, for the love of God, I've been attacked, beaten, stabbed. Is that not enough to put you off this?"

"What would you have me do?" Eleanor asked. "Get back to my needlework and wait for Christian to claim these rings from me? And then allow him to skip off and open the Glass? Or maybe Mistral will come, with Irving leading them, and they'll open the Glass."

Renshaw's head dipped down, fingers worrying a lump of blanket in his lap. His hands were old, darkened by time spent in the sun, and yet still strong; the way he gripped the blanket proved to Virgil that even though the man was injured, he was fighting to keep his temper. How very like his daughter.

"What's the worst that could happen, should the Glass open?" Juliana asked.

Renshaw's temper burst. "Juliana Day, of all the foolish, shortsighted things you could say!" He sputtered, smoothing his hands over the blankets. "Opening a portal to the past, or who knows where? What might one do with that power?"

Anything one damn well wished, Virgil thought, remembering Hubert's words in the Anubis chapel. He felt certain the idea of losing Eleanor was also becoming a tangible possibility for Renshaw Folley. Would Eleanor, like her mother before her, choose to step through that portal?

Renshaw held up a hand when Juliana opened her mouth. "No—no. Juliana, I can picture it all too well. One person killed who should not be, one small incident—it could be anything—one change follows another, toppling like a row of dominos, then history spills every which way. And for me . . . No. I have lost my wife, and I'm not about to lose my daughter."

"You aren't going to lose me," Eleanor said, and made to reach for her father's hand. But stubbornness was winning out with Renshaw today, and he avoided the handclasp.

"No?" he asked, his eyes searching hers. "How do you determine that, Eleanor? Because you have your mother's blood within you, your grandmother's blood, Egyptian blood. It connects you to the rings, it's what will—" He broke off, going pale enough that Virgil stepped forward, thinking he ought to summon a doctor. Renshaw waved him off.

"Finish your thought then, Mr. Folley," Virgil said, coming to stand beside Eleanor at the bed.

Renshaw looked rather like a trapped animal, surrounded on all sides. Virgil sympathized with the man, knowing how difficult it could be to keep such secrets.

"Mr. Folley, if you have more information regarding the rings, we need it," Virgil said. "If anything, a lack of information could place Eleanor in more danger. We have no idea what Irving knows, but I feel certain we're already working at a disadvantage."

"Tell me," Eleanor said to her father, her tone almost pleading. Still, Virgil thought he heard an edge of anger there. A growl? "It can't get much worse than it is, Da."

Even so, Renshaw held his silence. Virgil didn't press. If the circumstances weren't enough to convince Renshaw, Virgil wasn't sure what would.

"I cannot bear to lose you," Renshaw said, and now reached for Eleanor's hand, gripping it as tears tripped down his bruised face. "The way I lost your mother. Watching her all those years, this thing consumed her." He reached toward Juliana with his other hand. Juliana took it, mindful of the bandages.

When Renshaw spoke again, his voice had regained its calm tone. "Lila had a theory. About how the rings worked. She didn't think it was a matter of simply possessing them, and one does not have to wear them."

Virgil took a step closer to Eleanor, sliding his hand along the small of her back, where her waistcoat had a loop of fabric and three buttons. He slid his fingers through the loop to hold Eleanor steady.

"You mentioned blood," he prompted Renshaw. "Egyptian blood."

"Anubis judged the deceased, to determine their worth and where they would spend eternity. Lila theorized that in order to look upon their lives, he required a measure of them. In Tau's journal, there was mention that Sagira had injured her hand. When she later held the rings, the portal opened. That day in the desert, Ellie . . . Do you remember the blood?"

Virgil felt Eleanor tense under his hand, and she nodded; one could not forget such a thing. He recalled the scars on Eleanor's arm, the way she spoke of those inhuman teeth ripping her flesh.

"Your arm," Renshaw whispered. "I don't know if your mother had your blood on her or . . . "

Virgil pictured the fingerprints on the Lady's arm, the bloody fingerprints that were likely Eleanor's. He smoothed his hand over Eleanor's back.

"You think my blood is necessary to open the Glass?" Eleanor asked her father.

"Not necessarily yours," Renshaw said, "but Egyptian blood. That was Lila's theory. Ellie, I don't want you to go, but I know . . . I understand you must." His voice was resigned now, and so, too, his expression as he looked at his daughter. "If you fail to return . . . You should make arrangements—"

"Arrangements!" Juliana cried.

"Yes, arrangements," Renshaw repeated. "Ellie may well be trapped back there if they manage to open the Glass. To my knowledge, no one has ever returned. Sagira didn't, and granted your mother can't, since she is trapped without the rings. Anything could happen to you."

Eleanor laughed, but it wasn't a sound of pleasure to Virgil's ears. "I always presumed we would be able to control the Glass," she said.

"The arrogance of youth!" Renshaw managed a laugh of his own. "I have debated all these years whether my Lila is still alive somewhere. It gave me comfort to think that she lived a full life somewhere, if not here.

I only wanted for her to be happy—even if that happiness came at such a cost."

A cost that made Virgil shudder. Dalila Folley had been willing to give up this life, her husband, her child, to reach backward in time for her own mother. And yet Eleanor was willing to risk her life as well. What was it about the Glass that called to these women?

"Juliana, the book." Renshaw released the hands he held, reaching for the leather-bound volume that Juliana handed over. "This is Tau's journal, Ellie. Perhaps it will be of use to you."

Eleanor's hands were pale against the leather cover; Virgil watched her take the journal in hand, fingers brushing over the timeworn cover. He wished then that he might peer inside her mind. What must she be thinking? Feeling? Renshaw Folley had been the answer to so many riddles across the years, but he had been an unwilling sphinx, not parting with his knowledge even in the form of riddles.

The man had his reasons, Virgil told himself, and was likely conflicted over them—as they involved a wife and a daughter. It couldn't have been easy, but neither was it easy to see the pain that crossed Eleanor's face when she peered inside the journal. How much easier her path would have been if her father had only shared what he knew. And yet, had that been Eleanor's path, Virgil felt certain he would never have encountered her. He felt a strange gratitude to the man, but kept his silence, thinking on his earlier words.

The arrogance of youth. Perhaps, Virgil thought, but they damn well had to try.

CHAPTER NINETEEN

Loire Valley ~ October 1889

Eleanor felt sick the next morning as *The Jackal* lifted into the air. It wasn't flying that caused the nausea, but the feeling that she was on a slippery slope and that her father still knew more than he was telling. Despair and grief had gripped her from the moment her father voiced her mother's theory about Egyptian blood.

She had taken his advice and made "arrangements" should she not return. Her possessions were few, and leaving them to her father and Juliana was the simplest of all courses, yet writing it down wasn't simple at all. The fact that Mallory stayed with her during the afternoon made it easier, but no simpler.

Now she leaned against Mallory as *The Jackal* soared southward toward the Loire Valley, taking advantage of his solid shoulder, which was encased in dove gray today.

She was aware of Mallory taking her hand into his at some point; she didn't stir, only threaded her fingers with his, and kept on dozing. She hoped the nausea would pass, but if anything it only deepened as they journeyed deeper into France.

"Eleanor, you should see this."

Mallory's hand squeezed hers, and she opened her eyes to the landscape around them. Beyond the windows of the airship, the valley looked like something from a painting, the trees on the hills rioting in autumn colors illuminated by late morning sun. Here and there, cottages perched between the vineyards, but it was the chateaux that stood out, rising grandly along the river Loire.

"See there—Chambord?"

Eleanor sighted along Mallory's arm to the sprawling chateau he indicated. Pale walls supported a roofline that looked like a city in miniature, so many towers and windows and curling pathways.

"We're just downriver from there . . . "

"Your neighbors?" Eleanor couldn't help but laugh a little at that and was relieved when Mallory joined in.

"They kept us humble, yes," he said. "You can see Mallory there on the right. Imogene used to think Château de Chambord was a princess's castle."

It could have been, Eleanor thought, but it was Chateau Mallory that interested her more, so she focused her attention on the smaller house, butter-colored walls rising from a tangle of golden and red-leafed trees. There even appeared to be a walled garden, containing more trees within its boundaries. The vineyards themselves spread west of the house, rolling in straight lines over more hills than Eleanor could count before *The Jackal* banked and angled toward the dock.

Eleanor thought of their conversation atop the pyramid, about coming home after long absences, and she turned her attention from the scenery to Mallory. "Are you all right?"

"From this distance, yes," Mallory said, with no trace of laughter this time.

From this distance, Eleanor thought, the house looked like a plaything; it looked safe and distant and unreal. She took in a slow breath as Gin began the airship's descent.

"My apologies, in advance, for the adventures that will no doubt befall us tonight," he added. "Mother's message said it was her Christmas miracle come early, me returning home."

Eleanor could see the tension in the way Mallory held himself. "She does think you have a way about you. They'll be happy to see you, Virgil. Family can be embarrassing, Lord knows, but they love you. I think we can endure a family meal or two."

"Remind me to be on my best behavior, will you? No snarling, no letting my temper get the better of me . . . "

"No running naked in the vineyard?" Eleanor asked. She pressed her cheek into Mallory's arm, peering up at him as he laughed.

"There was one night," he said in a low tone, "I was coming home after having been chasing rabbits, and in the vineyard, there was old Master Toms, one of the men who worked for my father. Deep into his drink at that point, but he screamed at the sight of me. Covered in mud and God only knows what else . . . Yes. No running naked in the vineyard, period."

Eleanor tried to picture that and pondered the life Mallory had led here.

Growing up was difficult enough, but growing up as part wolf? And never having told his parents. She thought of every secret her father had kept and all those that Mallory must have swallowed through the years, and knew that in some ways it must have felt like drowning.

She had little time to appreciate the dock Gin nestled the airship against before a flurry of people could be seen approaching, intent on welcoming Mallory. Even the workers securing the lines of the ship to the ground had to step back; the gangplank, fortunately, fell solidly against the dock and was fastened into place before family streamed over, nearly pulling Mallory from the ship. Eleanor waited with Auberon and Gin on the ship, but only until Mallory had crossed to the dock proper. All three then descended.

"They're quite pleased to see him," Auberon said.

"As long as we aren't bitten," Gin added.

Bitten? Eleanor looked at him in confusion, but before she could ask, she saw a sleek black dog had joined the mix of people. Mallory crouched to scratch the dog's ears and had a slobbery trail licked across his face for his efforts.

Anubis, Eleanor thought with a sharp pang, only jolted from the idea when there was a tug on her trousers and a small voice asked, "Are you Virgil's *sweetheart*?"

Eleanor looked down to find a young girl with pale blond hair streaming loose about her shoulders. She was clad in a dress colored to match her hair, but had paired it with buttoned boots that were a brilliant red. The hand that wasn't curled into Eleanor's trouser leg was wrapped around a handful of stick candies, another of which was wedged into the corner of her mouth. Wide brown eyes peered up, as if they anticipated the answers to the mysteries of the world.

"I'm Virgil's friend," Eleanor answered, deciding that "sweetheart" had not entirely been determined. Did wolves have sweethearts? "Miss Folley." She extended a hand to the young lady.

"Margarite Antoinette Mallory. I am six," she said and took Eleanor's hand before making a quick curtsey. Her adult air was maintained until Margarite could plainly no longer contain herself. "I am named for a dead queen!" She dissolved into giggles, which turned to a shriek as Mallory swung her over his shoulder.

"How could you possibly come see Miss Folley and not me?" Mallory said with a pronounced pout. Resting in his arms, Margarite tapped his nose.

"I know you, uncle, but not her," she explained. She offered Mallory a candy stick from her collection. "You should share with Miss Folley."

"I promise to." Mallory took the candy and gave Margarite a noisy, wet kiss on her cheek before setting her down. As soon as her booted feet touched the dock, she skipped off again, this time launching herself toward Auberon and Gin.

"Destined to shatter hearts across the country, if not the world," Mallory murmured, drawing Eleanor to his side. "Come on, they won't bite you."

Recalling Gin's words, she looked again to the black dog, caught once more by the thought of Anubis.

No one in the crowd did bite, but that didn't stop Eleanor's stomach from turning over throughout the introductions. Virgil's sister Imogene was nothing she had imagined, and Eleanor silently chided herself for the assumptions she had made. "Governess" put one idea in her head, that of glasses and rules and strictly pressed clothing, but after meeting Imogene, Eleanor had to laugh at herself, for she couldn't picture the young woman in anything pressed or strict. Her nephews and niece listened well to her too; Jean and Daniel, the twins, clasped hands at her direction and always stayed within her line of sight, though clearly they longed to explore the newly tethered ship.

Neither were Mallory's parents what Eleanor expected. With Mallory not having told them about his true nature, she presumed they would also be rigid in their thinking: that they wouldn't accept their son for who he was. But Eleanor saw only kindness and love in their eyes when Mallory brought her to them. They were happy to have him home, if even for only a short while.

"Mother, Father, this is Miss Folley."

Virgil's mother, a round Italian woman named Giada, had tears in her brown eyes: eyes she had given to her son, along with lips and cheekbones, and the fine line of her nose. Giada brushed her tears away and graciously welcomed Eleanor to their home. At her side, Jean Mallory also extended his welcome. His hands were Virgil's hands, with a few more years of work, strength, and love in them.

"Now you've made your mother cry," Eleanor teased Mallory, which elicited a laugh from his parents.

"I understand the two of you are here for work," Giada said, "but I'll be disappointed if you don't take a tour of the vineyard, Miss Folley. Virgil tells me you've never been to this part of France."

"Alas, you come to us after the harvest, when you can't eat straight from the vines," Jean said and clicked his tongue. "Would you look at that child."

Eleanor looked to Margarite, who was attempting to ride the large black dog as though it were a horse. She might have managed, if not for her handful of candies.

"That is Gat," Mallory said. "By all rights, that dog should be dead. I can't remember a time we didn't have him. Im got to name him—so she named him Gateau."

"My favorite thing to eat," Imogene said with a grin. "Margarite, come, you'll ruin that dress."

"Will I?" Margarite asked in a tone that Eleanor could only hear as hopeful.

Giada looped her arm through Eleanor's as the group walked toward the house. Mallory skipped ahead with Gat, throwing a stick for the dog to fetch. Though he looked at ease, Eleanor had grown to know the look of worry on him. While he played with Gat, he constantly surveyed the land around them, and Eleanor wondered if it was his brother he sought or other Mistral agents. Auberon and Gin walked at a slower pace than the main group, also inspecting the landscape. The suspicious side of Eleanor's mind was in silent agreement: if anyone from Irving's group meant trouble, there was too much cover for them to find shelter in.

"I don't care if it is work that has brought my son home, but I feel I should thank you," Giada said.

"Thank me?" Eleanor turned her attention back to the woman at her side.

"We haven't communicated often—work has kept him so busy—but in these past weeks, we have received more telegraphemes from him than we ever have, and when he mentions you—" Giada allowed a moment of silence to fall between them. "I am being entirely too forward. Virgil has a way about him, you know."

"So I have heard."

Giada stepped away, catching the twins' hands to lead them to the front steps. They skipped up them together, and Eleanor watched as though she had never seen such a thing in her life. A family this closely knit was a curious thing to her; she had missed her own so terribly. Eleanor also felt dumbstruck by the idea that Mallory had mentioned her in communications with his parents. She tried to shake it off, but couldn't stop smiling.

"Miss Folley?"

Eleanor found Mallory at her side. He drew her out of the path, allowing Auberon and Gin to precede them into the house, Margarite skipping between and around them. Mallory fisted his hands into the lapel of Eleanor's jacket, pulling it closer around her.

"You will certainly catch a chill if you stay out much longer."

Eleanor's smile widened at the sight of Mallory's nephew- and niece-tousled hair against the bright sky. Was everything more brilliant because she was keenly aware that she might not return if they opened the Glass of Anubis? Eleanor didn't know and right then didn't care to analyze it.

"I haven't once felt the cold."

⸻◈⸻

"He promised, and he knows you were due today." Giada Mallory fussed with the green and white napkins before her, and Virgil stilled her hands.

"You can fold those napkins into swans if you like, but they won't bring Adrian any sooner," he said.

Virgil looked across the table to Robin. Adrian's pregnant wife sat folding more napkins: no swans, just efficient triangles. Virgil had always been curious about this woman, this woman who could love his brother when Adrian bristled at everyone else. How had Adrian allowed her inside? Virgil supposed the *how* didn't matter, so much as the fact that he'd done it at all. Allowing someone inside was loaded with risk, and yet . . .

Robin looked up in time to catch him staring. "I can fetch him," she said.

"You'll do no such thing," Virgil said and waved her back into her chair when she made to stand. "Unless you want your child born in the vineyard."

"This entire country is a vineyard," Robin said and she laughed, a sound that put Virgil at ease. She added another folded napkin to the stack. "I walk out there every day—"

"I will go," Virgil said before the argument could go further. If Robin had been taking lessons from his mother, it might well continue until the following morning, with Adrian yet to be coaxed from the vines.

"Virgil."

He looked up to his father, who stood in the doorway, a crystal glass of amber liquid in hand. Now that he was here, it was natural; the hesitation and concern he had felt during his conversation about family with Eleanor atop the pyramid drained away, until there was only this moment, sitting with those he loved, in his childhood home.

"Father?" He could almost predict what his father meant to say, and when the words came, Virgil had trouble not grinning.

"Your brother damn well knows his way back to this house—excuse my language, ladies. You didn't travel all this way to drag your brother up here."

"Neither did I come all this way to make him feel unwelcome in his own home." Virgil stood and smoothed his coat down. "If he would be more comfortable, I can take a room at the inn up the valley—"

"You will do no such thing."

Virgil couldn't remember ever hearing such venom in his mother's voice. It sounded to Virgil as if his parents were as tired of this rift in the family as he was. He couldn't blame them.

"In any case, he and I should talk. If you will excuse me . . . " He bowed to the ladies and took his leave before anyone could stop him again.

It was strange to be in this house, but also comforting. Much of the house was as he remembered it, from its fruit-patterned wallpapers to its paintings of landscapes, still lifes, and a few ancestors. It was a comfortable home, made more so by the memories Virgil found around every corner. When he peered into the sitting room to find Eleanor with Imogene and her young charges, it was not a memory that greeted him, but a wholly new thing he could hardly understand. The sight of Eleanor in his family home made him go very still indeed.

"Fleeing the scene, are you?" Imogene asked when she spied him lingering in the doorway. The twins fluttered around her.

"Establishing that Miss Folley hasn't yet been eaten whole by you or your charges," Virgil said with a nod. It drew a laugh from Eleanor, and she crossed the room to him. She neatly avoided Margarite and walked with Virgil to the foyer.

"I'm going out after Adrian," he said with a look out the windows. He reached for a blue smock hanging from a row near the door. Vineyards could be unkind to one's clothing. "I wanted to be sure that you—" He drew the smock on, startled when Eleanor stepped forward to fasten the buttons. "—were comfortable here." His mouth tipped up, unaccustomed to such attentions.

"It's wonderful here," Eleanor said as the shriek of children and the thunder of small feet rose in the near distance, "but are you well?" She smoothed her hands down the front of his smock, then took a step back to look at him. "You appear quite fine, but . . . Adrian."

Virgil recalled their conversation on the pyramid and gave a slow nod. "Adrian. The man can't very well avoid his own home and family for the entire length of our visit, now can he? Nor can he avoid me." He thought to kiss her, for it felt as natural as breathing, but realized how terribly familiar it was—and that Margarite watched them from the end of the hall.

"Sweethearts!" she not so much whispered as shouted before she scampered away.

"You will forgive me once again, Miss Folley."

Eleanor pressed her cheek against his own. "Good luck, Agent," she murmured.

Virgil didn't have to know if she meant good luck in gaining her forgiveness or seeking Adrian out; she constantly refused to forgive him because she seemed to welcome such intrusions into her proximity. The matter of his brother would require a good deal more luck, indeed.

Virgil nodded to Auberon and Gin, who stood outside, having claimed they meant to smoke, but neither held cigar or cigarette. Virgil touched Auberon's arm, silently asking him to stay behind, while he looked to Gin. Gin, surprisingly good at shadowing a fellow agent, slipped off into the trees, his path likely matching Virgil's as he stalked his way to the vineyard, seeking a man who wanted nothing to do with him.

He found Adrian in one of the farthest fields. At the sound of his approach, Adrian stopped his work to turn and see who was coming.

"Robin? I didn't realize it was so late. Have—"

"It's not Robin," Virgil called back, trying to keep his tone light. "Do you honestly think we would allow her to come after you, about to birth that child of yours?"

Adrian said nothing. He turned his clippers back to the vines.

Virgil disliked pruning. Cutting the thousands of canes by hand was no way to spend an otherwise perfectly nice day. Pruning them, burning the end to seal against disease, tossing the pruned vine into the burn can . . . It was the kind of duty one should partake of in hell, not on earth. But Virgil said nothing; it was possible Adrian enjoyed the work after all these years.

"Mother said you were coming," Adrian said as he snipped another branch. He cut the pruned piece into two shorter lengths and tossed them into the burn can. Sparks erupted, and smoke curled into the air.

"I didn't exactly believe I would come, either," Virgil said. He stepped closer to Adrian, still leaving his brother enough room to work. "Mother won't want you at the table like that."

Adrian looked as though he had been pruning for hours, bits of vine and debris stuck to his smock and in his hair. He had grown a beard, and its brown curls were littered with debris. He looked something of a bird's nest, though Virgil wasn't about to say so. He smelled of hard work and sweat. It was a familiar scent to Virgil, one that reminded him of their father.

"Neither will Robin." Adrian looked up from the vine and exhaled. "I presume the family is gathering for dinner."

"Everyone is here." Virgil wanted to mention Eleanor, but was unsure how. So many of his memories of Adrian were tangled with their behavior at Virgil's wedding to Caroline, and he wasn't certain mentioning another woman would be wise. Would Adrian rebuke him? There was no clear path, so he stepped down the nearest one. "I've brought colleagues with me. We're—"

"You're working?" Adrian's laugh sounded like a short bark. He closed both sides of the burn can and looked at Virgil, disapproval marking every line of his face. "Can't leave it behind, can you?"

"And you?" Virgil asked, damned if he was going to let Adrian have his tantrum. He hated this. He wished it could be as it once was—the way it had been that long-ago day in the zoo, before the beast had charged out of the woods. Virgil looked up now, eyes flicking to the trees enclosing the vineyard. Gin was out there somewhere.

"Staying out to needlessly prune? That's either dedication or avoidance, Adrian. Robin has made it clear that I am to stay, so I'll be up at the house. Mother would like you to come for dinner."

I would too, Virgil thought, but didn't know how to say that. Those three words were simple, yet horribly complicated, and they lingered unsaid between the brothers.

Virgil walked away, not caring that he left Adrian alone. He damn well knew his own way back.

CHAPTER TWENTY

It was late, but Eleanor was not sleeping. She couldn't. She rarely had trouble sleeping in strange places, for such had been her childhood, traveling to here and there and back again. She knew that wasn't the problem. Every time she climbed into the beautiful bed, its carved headboard sporting a riot of carved grapes and vines, she grew uneasy. While the sheets were soft as clouds, she would have sworn she felt sand on them. She felt twelve all over again, camping in the desert with her parents and trying to shake the grit from her bedroll before sleep. This left her pacing over the pale green carpets with their cabbage roses, staring at her grandfather's journal, which lay open across the foot of the bed.

At the tapping on the balcony door, Eleanor paused in mid-step. The room was on the second floor of the house, and she thought it unlikely anyone—including Christian—had scaled the building to visit her. And Mallory would surely use the door. He had told her this room had been his own as a boy. Eleanor stayed exactly where she was, listening again over the hammer of her heartbeat. The tap came again.

Beyond the square panes of glass, the night sky was broken only by gleaming stars. There was no shadow on the balcony, which emboldened her to move again, toward the doors she unlocked and opened.

She expected autumn's cooling air, but a hot wind greeted her, pushing the doors from her hands and lifting her hair from her shoulders. Her lips became dry and cracked, and she felt as if she hadn't had a sip of water in days. It was not a French vineyard she looked out on, but, instead, a temple room. Before her stretched a rectangular pool, its inky surface reflecting the light of a half-dozen torches. In the distance, birds called to one another in the night air, and Eleanor could feel the powerful stroke of their wings as they took flight. The air they stirred poured through the temple and carried with it the stench of the underworld, black earth and sweet, rotting flesh. She knew everything here, and nothing; everything had a weight, everything had a pulse.

Her hands shook, but still she stepped forward, her foot coming down on warm stone rather than the cool balcony. Egypt's heat radiated through her, forcing the chill into retreat. Her robe whispered over the floor behind her.

At the end of the pool, she found herself making an offering to the dark god she knew lingered there. Four rings, heavier than anything she had ever held, rested in her bloodied hand, and though she didn't think it possible, she lifted them for his acceptance. Blood curled around her wrist and forearm in a crimson bracelet.

She could not look the god in the eye. Was she dreaming? She thought back to the room and her restless pacing, and decided she was perfectly awake. Awake and in France and Egypt in the same instant, offering the rings to Anubis. *But I don't have the fourth ring, so this is a dream . . . isn't it?*

"Daughter," Anubis said.

Eleanor looked at him, compelled by that word. Anubis was taller than the entire world, gold gilding every ebony edge of his body, and repugnance rolled over her. She felt helpless in his glassy eyes, a blue so dark it looked black at first glance. She blinked and saw an endless horizon. It stretched from one end of the world to the next.

She rushed toward it, knowing it was hers to claim, even if she didn't understand how. A honeyed light spilled out of Anubis's eyes, brilliant and burning as it flooded over the land. In this light, she knew everything she should not: she could feel the dead within the world, both those waiting to be weighed and those who already had been. She could taste the impure hearts Ammit had consumed after Anubis deemed them unworthy of the afterlife.

"Anubis." Eleanor spoke his name and gave him power. How many times had her father told her that naming a thing made it real, made it solid and capable? Anubis's black hand closed over her wrist. His touch was fire and ice both, and Eleanor felt he held her by her bones alone, that whatever flesh had made her into a whole body was burned away. But no—no, she saw that wasn't right. Her hand showed brindled fur and claws curling where once there had been fingers. She forced down the revulsion she felt and, in its place flooded a strange relief. She did not understand.

"Surrender them to me."

Eleanor tried to release the rings, but with his hand around her wrist, she could not move. She tried to make her other hand move, tried to pry his hand from her wrist, but Anubis would not be budged. Her hand shifted between paw and human hand, and she couldn't move either properly. Eleanor fell to her knees, and the rings spilled onto the black stone floor.

"Mine," Anubis said.

Eleanor didn't know if he meant the rings or her, because they seemed one and the same.

Against her cheek his breath was fetid. She struggled to reach one ring and felt a small victory when her fingers closed over it. She offered the ring to him, his hand now spread before her. The ring would never fit his finger, she thought, yet her blood—still coating the ring—eased its passage. This ring was silver, impressed with Anubis's own likeness that emerged as the blood funneled away.

"Soon, daughter," Anubis said. His hand reached for her, clawed fingers tangling through her hair. She bowed her head and soil cascaded over her shoulder, down to her bare feet. *Bury me, bury me here and let me rot . . .*

"Eleanor!"

She startled at the sound of her name, but could not move from Anubis's touch. The voice was familiar, and she struggled to come up with a name for it so that she might also give it power. By the time she did—Virgil!—there was a growling wolf at her side, lunging for Anubis. All four paws struck the god, but didn't send him toppling. Mallory sprang back, onto the temple floor. Anubis's hand uncoiled from Eleanor's hair. Freed, she staggered backward. She turned to run the length of the firelit pool, toward the pale green bedroom she could see at its end. It was an image from a childhood book, Alice running back up the rabbit hole as she returned to her proper world. Or had she? Which world was proper? Had Alice ever known?

"Virgil . . . Virg—"

He flopped at her side, no longer wolf but man. The warmth of an Egyptian night was consumed by the reality of France as Anubis withdrew. Eleanor kicked the balcony doors shut, as if it would keep Egypt and Anubis out. She sprawled beside Mallory on the floor. He was cold and shivering, naked but for his silver ring. Eleanor drew a blanket from the bed to cover them both. She thought her hands would be bloodied from having held the rings, but they were clean.

Mallory reached for her under the blanket, curling around her with arms and legs both. There was no politeness to his touch now, only a hungry urgency that Eleanor met with equal appetite. She stretched against him, into him, opening her mouth to his kiss. He tasted like brandy and anger and heat, and in the confusing wake of whatever they had just beheld, Eleanor could not get enough. Each taste served as a handhold to keep her from sliding back down the rabbit hole.

His hands moved down her back, tracing the line of her body beneath her thin robe and nightgown. Down and down, over the curve of her bottom, grasping her hard and fitting her against his naked body until very little of Virgil Mallory was left to Eleanor's imagination.

"Mine," Mallory said against her mouth, and it brought back the memory of Anubis. Had Anubis tried to claim her, too?

Eleanor slid her hands across Mallory's chest, across the scattering of dark hair and the scar that would forever mark him. Her fingers learned the way of his chest, shoulders and collarbones and neck, until they dug into his tangle of brown and blond hair. Her fingers—no claws, she told herself—twined into his hair to keep him where he was. Her body arched hard against him.

"Virgil."

Mallory shifted when she spoke his name, bearing her flat to the floor, where he growled. The low sound rumbled up from his belly, into chest and throat. His head nudged hers and Eleanor turned hers to the side, remembering what he had done in the library, remembering his mark upon her. The press of his teeth against her skin was tender this time.

"Eleanor."

Mallory whispered her name against her neck, then his tongue rasped over the skin he had just bitten. She felt the brief brush of his cheek against hers before he withdrew. He untangled himself from the blanket and stood.

"Damnation," he snarled. He stalked away from Eleanor, lamplight gilding his naked body.

Eleanor tried to think of something other than the naked man before her. She failed. She had seen him in the Egyptian temple, naked after his transformation from wolf to man, but there had been considerably less light. Here—

"Vir—"

"Damnable rutting beast."

The curses trailed into a steady stream of words Eleanor could not follow.

Mid-rant, Mallory appeared to realize he was still naked, his clothes strewn about the floor, and he freed the sheet from the bed. He wound it around his torso as he continued his tirade against himself.

Eleanor picked herself off the floor, tossing the blanket back to the bed. From its tangles spilled her grandfather's journal, and she picked it up. Her legs were unsteady and she didn't go far, sinking into the chair that stood beside the bed.

"Virgil."

"I am utterly repulsive." He stared at her, his expression some mixture of disgust and lust. "Loathsome. Repugnant."

His hair stood up in wild spikes, though from her own ministrations or his, Eleanor could not say. She bit her lower lip, trying not to laugh, because she didn't find Mallory repulsive in the least. He was the most fascinating person she had ever met.

"I am unfit for human company. I am revolting and should be locked away where I might not disgrace anyone with my—"

"Virgil!" Eleanor came out of the chair and crossed to his side, trying to take his hands. Each time she tried, he moved, refusing to be touched or held. "Virgil."

"Lust is a sin, Miss Folley, and this—" He reached out as though he meant to touch the mark he had left on her, but in the end refrained. "This . . . " He gestured to the room, to the ruin of his clothes and his current undressed state. "That—was lust." Mallory pointed to the floor where they had tangled. "Forgive me."

"Then you," Eleanor said, "must forgive me as well, for my heart is plainly as wanting as yours." She stared at Mallory and he stood there, looking as if he had been struck with a fist rather than words. His jaw worked, but no sound came out. "Do not tell me you were alone under that blanket."

Mallory scrubbed a hand through his hair in an effort to tame it. Slowly, it began to lie down. "Mmm."

Eleanor tried not to smile at this simple logic and failed, but it was a soft smile, one she hoped was not boastful but rather understanding.

"Mmm," she echoed. She looked past him to the bedroom door that was, thankfully, closed. She could only imagine what Margarite would have said, had she seen them tangled up. "What brings you to my room this late?"

"Damnation. What was that?" He leveled a finger toward the balcony doors.

Now they looked like doors and nothing more. Mallory strode to them and grasped the doorknobs. Eleanor wanted to tell him not to, for she felt certain they would find themselves in Egypt again, but their opening brought only a blast of cool French air. Mallory stared at the night, then thrust the doors shut once more.

"I thought I was dreaming—there were four rings in my hand, Mallory, and we don't have four rings." At his deepening frown she said, "I couldn't sleep, was pacing the floor, and then . . . Anubis."

"If you weren't sleeping, you couldn't dream."

Mallory's words left her cold. She moved to the bed and crawled back into the mess she had made of it. The sheets no longer felt gritty, only soft, if cool, and she smoothed the blanket flat. She pulled her grandfather's journal into her lap and made another attempt at explanation, to both herself and Mallory.

"I was reading because I couldn't sleep. There was a knock on the door, and when I opened it, a temple." She exhaled, thinking she could still smell the rotting underworld. She pressed her hands against her cheeks, trying to keep herself in the here and now. "I had the rings and was giving them to Anubis."

Mallory, still sheet-wrapped, crossed to the bed and sank to the edge of the mattress. "Christian said Anubis was using us to gather the rings. Do you think . . . ?" He trailed off, then lifted his sharp gaze to Eleanor. "What if you can't come back?"

The question didn't surprise her, because the sensation of standing in that temple with Anubis's soil pouring over her was still fresh in her mind. She had wanted only to be buried; everything else had been lost. Could Anubis take her away? Did he have that ability, or must one freely surrender? She considered her mother and grandmother before her, and still had no answers. Surely her mother had willingly followed Sagira's path, but Sagira's own . . .

She touched her neck, feeling the lingering mark of Mallory's bite. Mallory's eyes followed the motion.

"I can't leave this," she said, and while she believed it, she also believed in the feeling of the underworld, of the dirt piling over her. She couldn't leave either and didn't know what it meant.

As if her words had settled an ancient argument, Mallory nodded. He crawled up the length of the bed and nudged Eleanor into the pillows until

Mallory was cradled between Eleanor's legs. He ran his hands down her body to the curve of her bottom, where he held her hard against him again.

"You aren't going anywhere," he said. "And if you do go anywhere, you're going to have a companion."

Eleanor let her thoughts drift to fanciful places, where she and Mallory stepped through the Glass and were trapped in ancient Egypt, much as her mother may have been. She brushed a tangle of Mallory's hair from his cheek, fingers tracing his beard.

"Gin will be with me," she teased.

Mallory's hands tightened on her, his lips curling with what she took for an amused snarl. "Something like that." He stretched beyond her, to claim her grandfather's journal. He opened it between them and smoothed the pages flat. "Find anything of use in here?"

Eleanor looked to the pages, trying to place her attention there and not on Mallory sprawled against her.

"Quite a bit," she said and turned the page in the journal for him, to show him where she had left off. "As any good archaeologist would, Tau included illustrations of the rings."

"We're fortunate your father still had this," Mallory said, his fingers brushing over the illustrations of the Lady's rings. On the lapis ring, Tau had added a smudge of blue, and on the carnelian, a faint wash of coral.

Fortunate, but Eleanor wasn't surprised her father had kept the journal. While it may not have held sentimental value to Renshaw Folley, it was a piece of the fading past. "I don't think he could bear to destroy it."

Her grandfather Tau had made notations beside each ring, of markings, size, weights, and composition. Notes on where the rings had been found were also included—initially, the rings had been discovered together, in a shallow broken pottery bowl that had since been lost. The journal was—not surprisingly for an Egyptologist, no matter his native tongue—in French.

"God willing, we won't need that bowl," Mallory said as he read on.

Eleanor's fingers hovered over the image of the fourth ring, seeing it in detail for the first time. It was made of silver and featured a likeness of Anubis embossed into the metal. Eleanor shuddered at the pointed jackal face. It was the ring she had seen moments ago.

Mallory's fingers traced Tau's careful writing. "Listen to this. 'Sagira cut her hand on a pottery fragment this evening. The doctor says it is no matter, he isn't concerned, but there was so much blood.' And later, 'The wound is like none I have seen; it refuses to close. The doctor stitched it, yet it still weeps.' " Mallory turned deeper into the journal. " 'Dalila found me as I worked, said her mother was not in the tent. I thought she played at a game, and followed. Sagira was nowhere to be found, and later I realized that neither were the rings. A storm is rising.' "

Eleanor made Mallory read the words twice more, pressing herself into the pillows as he finished again. A chill moved up her spine, but this was not from the wind still rattling the doors. "She was there, Virgil. There when her mother vanished." She felt a scream clawing for release. How could her mother have placed her in the same situation?

"See here, how the Lady lies," her mother had said, and swept her brush over the timeworn bones in their cradle of sand.

How the Lady lies . . .

Eleanor knelt beside her mother and watched as her bedtime stories came to life, as a woman who should have been only fiction emerged from the desert.

"Maybe that's why your father fought so hard for you to place this behind you?" Mallory asked. "He knew exactly what Dalila had been through and didn't want you—"

"I used to have nightmares about it, Virgil," she interrupted. "About my mother vanishing. My father didn't want to talk about it, because she was dead, end of story."

But it had never been that.

"For the longest time, I thought I was insane, that she was really dead and I was inventing memories of that day to prove otherwise. While I think my father did try to shield me in some ways . . . I don't think it helped me."

Silence held until Mallory said, "I thought that too, you know."

Eleanor closed her grandfather's journal between them and watched Mallory's face. As distrustful as she had been of him before, she could not imagine sharing this journey with anyone else. He knew what it was to live a life of doubt, of conflict. He knew what it was to deny a thing inside himself, even as it clawed to get out. When it came, her smile was slow.

"That I was insane?"

Without the book between them, Mallory slid closer, hands encircling

Eleanor's waist. "No, but that I might have been. The first time I became the wolf." He looked to the balcony doors as if pondering something he didn't know how to say. "I pushed it away, called it a dream. I tried to run from so many things, whereas you, you tried to confront what scared you."

Eleanor touched the fall of Mallory's hair against his cheek. "Not always," she said, reminding him that she had also run, and had kept running for years on end. "I'm not running now, Virgil. Not from this or from you." The words should have embarrassed her, but when Mallory pushed up to kiss her, she could only find promise in them.

Eleanor woke abruptly to the sound of a slamming door. She stared at the room around her, watching Mallory stalk across its width. He was looking for something, his shadow prowling after him in the low lamplight. Eleanor pushed the blanket off and looked to the balcony doors. It wasn't Egypt she saw or Anubis's temple room, only the sleeping French countryside.

"Mallory?"

They had fallen asleep reading the journal, paging through more of Tau's observations, even if little more was revealed. Mallory was not yet clothed, still wrapped in the bedsheet from earlier. When she spoke his name, he looked at her only briefly, then reached for the small trunk which had carried her few belongings.

"We aren't doing this." He didn't speak the words so much as growl them. He opened the latches on the trunk, each sounding like a revolver's sharp report in the small room.

"What aren't we doing?"

Sleep still clung to Eleanor, and she had difficulty shifting her thoughts from the pleasant tangle of sleeping with Mallory to this—him clearly upset by something. His mood set her on edge, and she felt that darkness creep closer. Whether Anubis or something else, Eleanor felt it like a yawning mouth meant to consume her.

Mallory ripped open the wardrobe and reached in for Eleanor's clothing. "This. We are not staying. We are not looking for that cursed fourth ring. Let it stay lost—let it be, wherever it is. If we leave it be, all is well."

His words felt like a pendulum, set swinging by rough hands that did not care what it threw into motion. Eleanor slid to the edge of the bed, and while her bare feet pressed into the carpet, she didn't feel entirely present within the room. She felt she was on that pendulum, moving to and fro, about to fly into the darkness worming closer.

"Mallory—"

"And do not call me that!" He turned on her, his eyes ablaze with the gold of the wolf inside him. He threw handfuls of blouses and skirts into the open trunk, then stalked to the foot of the bed.

"Have you gone mad? What in hell are you—"

Mallory lunged for her, taking her roughly by the arms. Within that hold, Eleanor felt the first uncurling. The waking of the darkness inside her, an echo of Anubis's own darkness that had been content to slumber. Until now.

Soon, Eleanor.

She tried to twist out of Mallory's furious hold, but couldn't. He wouldn't let her go.

"If you think I am going to endure what your father did—mourning all those years, knowing you would rather have that life than this life—you are mad. I am not letting you go." His voice deepened until every word was edged in a snarl. "I am not letting you open the Glass, because I will not lose you, Eleanor. I will not!"

Each word felt like a carefully aimed barb, and she twisted hard to remove herself from his grasp. She slid down the length of the bed to place the carved footboard between them. She held to the wood, her legs unsteady beneath her, as Mallory's tirade continued unbroken.

"I don't care if this destroys your life's work," he said as he stalked after her. He gave her no space to move. "I don't care if the entire community laughs at your failure. I don't care."

Eleanor felt the world around her going dim. Anger closed a hard hand around her, and she tried to sidestep Mallory. But he was there, in front of her no matter which way she turned. He gave her no quarter, pressing her almost the way he had on the *Nuit*. Close, growing, demanding.

"What are you doing?" She asked the question, but feared she already knew. Mallory had told her in the temple, that anger made his beast come.

Fury strained her voice now, stole her ability to think of anything other than the hot rush of rage bubbling inside her.

"Virgil—I thought we—"

Eleanor couldn't find the words and took a staggering step back. This placed her against the wall, with nowhere else to go. Mallory would not cease, stalking toward her; the bed notched into the corner, her other side was blocked by a chest of drawers. She reached for the chest to steady herself, but saw only the line of scars up her hand, pale and ragged and—

His mouth was not human.

Now, daughter. Eleanor slid to the floor, trembling. Mallory crouched before her, his face nearing hers. He smelled angry, his wolf close to the surface, and something in her responded to that.

"You will never see your mother. You will never know. You will never have any of the answers. We are not going."

Eleanor's hand shot out, curling hard into the sheet wrapping Mallory. She held on so firmly, she heard the fabric begin to tear, but then realized it wasn't the strain on the fabric so much as the gleaming black claw that tore it. The claw from her own hand.

"Virgil, I cannot do this."

"I won't let him carry you away the way he did your mother."

Her entire body spasmed, becoming a thing she could not control. Her hand fell away from Mallory's sheet, but he caught her around the wrist. She saw the terrible understanding crossing his face and the way relief and worry both flooded him.

"Forgive me, Eleanor," he whispered.

As many times as he had asked for forgiveness, she couldn't give it now, even as she understood what he had done. He pushed her to this point to see if she was like him.

Her rage was all-consuming, closing over her the way a canvas sack had once closed over her head. The memory of the panic she had known then, coupled with the fresh anger over Mallory's ceaseless denials, swept her away.

She wondered if this was how it had been for Mallory the first time he changed. The loss of control, the realization that he could do nothing but allow it to come. A distant part of her mind thought she might eventually learn to control it, harness and use it, but for now, she could only exhale as the fury subsumed her. Her body came apart the way she had seen Mallory's do, reassembling itself into something wholly new.

The pain was a blinding fire. She screamed and was struck by the way her voice changed mid-shriek, from something human to something deeply primitive. She had heard wolves before, their howls carrying across night mountains, but this was not the cry of a wolf. This was something different, yet something familiar.

Jackal, she thought, as her bones broke apart and began to refashion themselves. She would have slumped flat to the floor had it not been for Mallory's hold on her. The heat of him still soaked through her, providing a focal point through the horror of her transforming body. She clung to that shred of warmth the way she might his hand, though now she had no hands with which to hold him.

She tried to speak his name, but couldn't do that either. Her jaw snapped and reshaped itself, and then the entire world vanished as the pain at last consumed her. The room vanished in a flood of black.

His mouth was not human.

The thought woke her, as did the scent of the man beside her. Her nose twitched, ears perking forward when he spoke.

"God, Eleanor. Forgive me for this."

She knew in some distant part of her mind that she was Eleanor, but could not say whether she forgave this man or not. What was forgiveness? In this moment, she knew only a handful of things: she was hungry, she was tired, and this man smelled like her mate.

"We had to know," he said. "Forgive me."

She rolled out of his lap, stumbling as she came to her feet on the rug. That there were too many feet was her first thought; she stood there and trembled, trying to find a thought beyond her hunger and exhaustion. She could not remember being inside, did not understand the debris scattering the floor, but she somehow knew the man. She tried to put a name to him, but could come up with nothing other than *Mate*.

Her first steps were halting, experimental as she tried to put four legs into some manner of order. Soon enough, she pranced a steady circle around Mate. Coordination was difficult, and so was attention, because a hundred new scents clamored for her notice. Nothing smelled the same but Mate.

She bowed her head and knocked it into Mate's shoulder. He laughed, a pleasant sound that made her back-step in surprise.

He reached for her slowly, tentative. She allowed him to touch her, to smooth his fingers over nose and into the fur behind her ears. Her eyes closed by half; exhaustion began to win out over hunger.

She made another two circles around him before she angled herself into his lap and flopped in an undignified heap. Something jangled loose around her neck, but she didn't look to see what. Tired, hungry, safe: these were what she knew. She stretched, yawned, and pressed herself into Mate's belly. His hands settled upon her, one at her side, the other at her neck. She slept.

The change woke her. As her body had once broken apart, it came apart again, to order itself into what it had been before. Bone and muscle shifted, hands and feet emerging from paws; the fur withdrew.

In the end, Eleanor lay naked in Mallory's lap, the rings still gleaming from their chain around her neck. He tugged the blanket from the bed, and this was distantly familiar to Eleanor, even if she couldn't form a full thought in the moment.

"Forgive me."

The words were a whisper against her temple; his lips brushed over her heated skin, and she closed her eyes. She was aware that he left and returned, but the sounds of him moving about were hushed. She was aware of the stroke of wet linen across her skin, and then of being placed back in bed. The bed that had been his as a child, where he had curled up after such transformations.

"Virgil." Her voice was ragged from screaming, his name broken on her tongue.

"I'm here. Sleep now."

Eleanor slept. She sank into the reassuring circle of Mallory's arms and slept, for once without dreaming.

CHAPTER TWENTY-ONE

"This wasn't the first Mallory vineyard here in the valley," Jean Mallory said to Eleanor the following morning as they walked through the vines. Virgil followed them at a slight distance, silently delighting in the sight of Eleanor with his father.

As Virgil Mallory was not well acquainted with fainting women, neither was he well acquainted with anything that had happened so far this day. Chief among them, waking to find Miss Eleanor Folley tangled in his arms, naked but for the rings she wore, the way she had been for most of the night.

"The first vineyard," his father continued, "was near Nantes, farther toward the coast." His gesture encompassed the west. "But the winter of 1709 was so terrible, the entire coast froze! Can you imagine? Every vineyard died. We Mallorys moved inland and have been here ever since."

Virgil tried to follow the thread of the conversation (also a thing with which he wasn't yet acquainted—to walk and talk with his father again), but his mind kept drifting to the night before. It was only right that they had been in the room that had been his own with its familiar balcony and the old mirror still in the corner. He had looked at the reflected image there a long while, he and Eleanor tangled in his old bed, before looking to her once more. Her bare shoulder had peeked above the blanket, its curve smudged with the beginnings of a bruise from the transformations.

"You have done more than well here," Eleanor said.

Virgil could hear the rough texture in her voice. He knew what that was, to have one's throat not entirely the same afterward. His eyes slid downward to the curve of tweed along her hip. Bare hip last night, he remembered, and tried to rein the memory in.

"Giada loves it here, and I wouldn't move us for all the world," Jean said, then gestured to the line of smoke that rose from further out in the vineyard. "I need to help Adrian finish this pruning work, before winter truly sets in." He glanced backward, Virgil lifting his eyes from Eleanor's trousers just in time to nod at his father. "Be sure she sees the garden."

"Oh, indeed," Virgil said.

He offered Eleanor a nod as his father moved deeper into the vines, tracing a path toward Adrian. Virgil stole a look at the hilltop where Auberon paced; somewhere, Gin also roamed.

I am not letting you go. Despite the lies he had spoken to Eleanor last night, those words were true. He would not let her step alone into the void, into whatever came when they gained the final ring. He stepped toward her now and offered her an arm. She hooked her own through it, holding to him as he guided her toward the garden.

"How are you feeling?" he asked. They hadn't had much time to talk this morning, for the children were early risers and Margarite had delighted in running up and down the hallways, singing to wake everyone. Virgil had done well to escape Eleanor's room unseen, or so he prayed.

Eleanor surprised him with a soft laugh. Her hand tightened on his arm, speaking volumes. "How were you after your first transformation?"

He grunted. His question was foolish. "A wreck."

It was only the sound of their booted feet over the paths that interrupted the silence and the occasional birdcall from the trees above. Then, "Eleanor, I must apologize for last night."

Eleanor's hand slid to the crook of his elbow. "No, Virgil. I think—" She walked a few steps in silence before saying, "I'm glad you were there. I'm glad that you—"

"I thought I might control it. I remember wishing I'd had someone with me, someone to sit with me and carry me through, and it was entirely selfish." He looked down at her, to find her attention on him. "If it were true, I didn't want you going through it alone. If it weren't, we would have a pointless argument, in which I said little that was true." He looked back to the path as they continued toward the walled garden in the distance. "The sight of Anubis, with his hands on you— The idea that he might simply take you was maddening."

Eleanor's cheek pressed into his arm. "I know."

Virgil's free hand came to cover hers. "I remember wanting a teacher so desperately, someone who knew what the hell was happening to me, and yet, I don't think I would have listened. I thought I understood everything. Eleanor, I'm sorry—I wish I understood more."

"We know more than we did yesterday," she said, her voice wavering more than a little.

Virgil felt the shaking in her hand and halted their progress to the garden. "Eleanor, of everything I said last night, one thing is true: I am not letting you go. You won't face this alone—and if we are able, you will see your mother. You will know. I only needed something to terrify you."

Eleanor freed her gloved hand to touch Virgil's cheek, and it felt like an absolution of sorts. It was more than he believed he deserved, the way it washed calm through him.

"I am terrified, Virgil. Of so many things." Her laugh broke apart into a sob. "One step at a time, we'll work this out. Together." She wiped her cheeks dry, nodding to the garden walls. "Step one, the garden."

Going slowly would have its merits, Virgil knew, and he tucked Eleanor's hand back into the bend of his elbow as they walked on. The garden was a spacious place, one Virgil remembered running through when he'd come home naked and bruised. The ancient elm still stood guard in the center of the space, spreading its thick branches out and upward. His mother kept the place orderly, no doubt easier now that she didn't have children digging holes to bury pirate loot among her flowers as he and Imogene certainly had.

And yet he was startled to see that someone had been digging holes, for he recognized the signs of it even after all this time. As he took Eleanor around the mostly fallow flowerbeds, he spied countless disruptions to the soil, divots and mounds and small footprints trailing through all.

"Do you have rodents out here?" Eleanor asked.

"Only if you can call them Margarite, Jean, and Daniel . . . " Rabbits never ventured into the garden, with its gates and walls, and they certainly didn't dig holes and fill them back in. "As children, Imogene and I often played at digging here, though—no one saw us, not even Adrian. He would come to the garden, thinking himself alone until we jumped out at him."

A private garden, where one might dig holes and hide loot, with no one else the wiser.

"At least you don't mean for us to dig up the entire vineyard," she said, amused.

Virgil looked at the ground before them with a new interest. Had Caroline been here? "We might have to overturn the entire garden, even so . . . " No one place in the garden screamed that it was more special than another; the night winds had stripped the trees nearly bare, bushes and flowers too, though low-growing evergreen dotted the paths here and there.

"These marks look fresh, though, Virgil—look at the dirt there."

The flowerbed Eleanor indicated showed signs of being disturbed. The dirt was darker than that which surrounded it, more recently overturned. "Imogene and I would never remember where we buried things," he murmured.

Footsteps crunching up the path caused Virgil to fall silent. He took a step backward and drew Eleanor beside him against the wall, holding his breath as Margarite stomped into the garden. She wore a frilly pink dress covered with a long, woolen jacket; her boots were bright yellow, and she carried a small spade and box.

"Margarite Mallory," Virgil said. Had they found their wee digger after all?

The little girl cried out at Virgil's voice and stopped in her tracks. She turned in place, ever so slowly, to stare at Virgil and Eleanor with a look of sheer terror. Her eyes were wide and round like saucers, her mouth gaping open. Virgil frowned at the box; it was empty.

"Uncle," Margarite said and tried to make a small curtsey. Her fingers, however, were turning white around the handle of her spade.

"Niece," Virgil said and bowed to her, trying not to find amusement in her outright dread. What was she about? "What do you have there?"

"Oh, Uncle—you cannot tell! You cannot!" With that, the child burst into tears.

"First your mother, now your niece," Eleanor murmured before she moved toward the young girl.

Margarite's breath hitched at the sight of Eleanor, and the girl allowed Eleanor to lead her to a nearby bench. Virgil trailed after them.

"He's simply terrible, isn't he?" Eleanor asked.

Margarite sniffled, drawing her wrist across her nose and with it a smudge of dirt. "M-maman . . . she told me not to dig in Grandmother's flowers, b-but there are no flowers!" She pointed quite firmly to the empty flowerbeds with her spade as Virgil joined them.

Virgil settled on the opposite side of Margarite, picturing the girl out here digging. Was she digging things up or burying them? Virgil wanted to rush ahead with his questions, alarmed at how quickly the agent within him came to the fore even when family—a child at that!—was involved, but when Margarite moved closer to Eleanor, Virgil told himself to bide his time. Perhaps Eleanor would have better success.

"I like t-to dig," Margarite continued, her crying beginning to cease as she found an unknown audience in Eleanor, someone to whom she might appeal. She clutched her spade close, as if refusing to be parted from it no matter what Virgil or Eleanor said.

"I like to dig, too," Eleanor said. "My father taught me how."

Margarite's eyes widened at this, and she looked at Eleanor with a renewed interest. "I don't know who taught me—maybe me! One day, I found a bracelet in the garden dirt and the next, I thought I could dig to see what else there might be, but when Maman found me, she shouted." Margarite turned toward Virgil now, abandoning her spade to clasp his hands. "She said that I ruined Grandmother's garden, and I didn't mean to. I didn't mean to."

Virgil tried not to be swayed by those small hands clutching his own. "I shall tell you a secret if you tell me one," he said, wondering if it was possible that this little garden archaeologist had unearthed what Caroline had possibly hidden here.

"Secrets?" Margarite whispered. This clearly made the entire conversation much more interesting to the girl. Virgil could hardly blame her, after all. It seemed a Mallory curse, the need to know more.

Virgil dropped his smile. "Where do you keep your treasures?"

Margarite shifted on the bench again, moving away from Virgil and abruptly into Eleanor's lap. The little girl curled there, as if afraid of Virgil's question.

"I know," Eleanor said, "that sometimes when we find treasures, it's difficult to share them with others. In some cases, though, it's good to share. Have you been to museums, mademoiselle?"

Margarite sat a little straighter in Eleanor's lap. "Oh, yes—people dug those things up?" Her expression changed, moving from wariness over Virgil's question to interest in Eleanor's revelation.

"Some of them," Eleanor said, and Margarite clapped.

"Uncle Virgil, do you want to put my treasures in a museum?"

Virgil crossed his legs as he considered her question. He wished the rings could be preserved, as he was certain Eleanor did, but given human nature, he knew such a thing would not be possible. He would be truthful with the child.

"Unfortunately not. Miss Folley and I are looking for an item, love, and we believe we have traced it to this very garden. It's quite possible that you have already encountered it on your many excavations."

Margarite squirmed a little. "And you said there would be a secret for my secret?"

Virgil grinned, unable to contain his delight over his niece's cleverness. "Indeed! A secret involving . . . " He looked around, pretending to be sure they were alone. "Your aunt."

Margarite gasped.

Virgil looked to Eleanor, who was smiling now, an echo of the grin that remained adhered to his own face. The sight of Eleanor with Margarite on her lap gave him pause, though, and made him question if Eleanor had ever wanted a family of her own. He wondered if such a thing were even possible, considering their natures.

"I keep my treasures in a box, in my room," Margarite said, unable to contain herself a minute longer. She squirmed out of Eleanor's lap and onto her knees on the bench. She knelt beside Virgil, squeezing his arm. "Surrender your secret."

Virgil laughed. "Very well. Your Aunt Imogene used to dig in this very garden, making twice as many holes as you have made."

Just when Virgil didn't think it was possible for his niece's eyes to get any wider, they did. She exhaled a soft "oh!" and then giggled madly before sliding down from the bench.

"Come, come see my treasure box." She latched on to both Eleanor and Virgil, tugging them up and onward into the house.

Margarite was proud to show Virgil and Eleanor to her room, a slightly disorganized space that held more than they would be able to sort through in one day. A rocking horse crouched in the center of the room, while a line of pinwheels decorated the sill of one window. Virgil pictured them all spinning on days when Margarite was allowed to open the window.

She went straight to her canopied bed and peered under it, retrieving a box that might rival a bank's vault. It was rigged with a complicated lock composed of bells and corded ribbons, and she bade both Virgil and Eleanor look away as she unfastened it. Several moments later, the little girl called for them to look at the treasures she had unearthed.

Virgil and Eleanor joined Margarite on the floor, peering into the wooden box. The child had found a wealth of items and, for Virgil, it was like stepping back in time, finding bits of his childhood. A small sack of coins, a bundle of dried flowers tied with a ribbon; a packet of water-damaged postage stamps, a cup decorated with golden grapes in paint; barrettes, a watch face, countless mismatched earrings.

Margarite told them where each item had come from as they went through the box, and grinned proudly when Virgil speared a silver ring onto his finger.

"I love that one, it has a dog like Gat," she said. "I found that by the Rogue Vine."

The way Margarite said it, the words had capital letters. "Rogue vine?"

"A grape that tried to get into the garden," Margarite said with a laugh.

The ring around his finger bore the likeness of Anubis. Crusted with dirt, but Anubis nonetheless, and a perfect match for the image they had seen in Tau's journal. He extended his hand and the ring to Eleanor.

She took it, but slowly, as if she felt she might yet vanish. She spat onto her fingers and rubbed them over the ring to loosen more of the dirt.

"See," Margarite said, leaning against Eleanor to point to each symbol on the ring. "A feather and a doggy—and oh, a bird, I forgot!"

"This is what we have looked for," Eleanor said, nodding to Margarite.

"Why does it make you sad?"

Virgil only realized Eleanor was crying when Margarite reached out to wipe her fingers over her cheeks. Virgil assumed that any truthful explanation might be too much for the child to understand. Yet Eleanor managed to put it so she might.

"It has been a very long search," Eleanor said, "and now it has nearly come to its end. That can be sad sometimes."

"Like hide and seek," Margarite said.

"See, this ring goes with these."

With that, Eleanor pulled out the chain she wore. The memory of Eleanor in that chain and that chain alone made Virgil shift on the bench. Margarite reached for the rings, then hesitated, only touching them when Eleanor didn't pull them away.

"Are they very old?" Margarite asked and stuck her forefinger through each of the rings, turning her hand this way and that, seeing how they looked on her.

Virgil's stomach churned at the idea of his niece being sucked away by the Glass. Four rings, he reminded himself. Four rings and Egyptian blood, so she could not be taken, but Eleanor could, and might yet.

"Older than your mother," Virgil managed to say.

"That's old!" Margarite agreed. "Let us add this one to your necklace, Miss Folley."

She helped Eleanor open the chain and watched with great patience as the ring was added. Margarite was helping Eleanor fasten the chain around her neck once more when the window shattered. Chilled air raced into the room, setting the pinwheels to spinning madly.

Margarite shrieked, and Eleanor dived atop her. The air felt suddenly heavy to Virgil, as though a storm approached. He tried to fight the memory of Anubis holding Eleanor the night before, but could not; though the sky was clear, thunder rattled the entire house, and he bit out a curse. If Anubis had come again to remind Eleanor of her duty, Virgil had a few choice words for the god. Virgil launched himself toward the window.

"Maman!" Margarite cried.

Beneath his coat, Virgil wore his revolvers, and he tossed one of them back to Eleanor. "Keep her down," he said and caught Eleanor's nod a second before someone rocketed through the broken window. It wasn't Anubis, but Christian Hubert, who landed on the floor beside Virgil. His eyes were wild with the same joy Virgil had seen in the Anubis chapel, right before everything went to hell.

"Narrow focus leaves you vulnerable," Christian said. "How many times—"

Virgil let instinct take over; he spun and elbowed Christian in the jaw. Christian's head snapped back, and he went down into the glass on the floor. Beyond Christian, he saw Eleanor and Margarite peering over the bed, the child's eyes wide and wet. Virgil knew only one thing, that he had to get Christian out of this room, away from his niece, but Eleanor realized the same thing.

"Four times, I think." Eleanor jeered as she rose from the floor, answering Christian's unfinished question. "But you're still always one step behind, aren't you?" The taunts worked. Christian leapt for Eleanor, scattering glass in his wake.

Eleanor spun out of his grip, fleeing the room, which left Christian to follow. Virgil moved without thought, vaulting over the bed with every intention of following, but it was Margarite's cry that drew him back, back to his niece who crawled into his arms, sobbing. Virgil pressed her close, praying Eleanor stayed one step ahead of Christian this time.

At the base of the stairs, Eleanor listened. Where was Imogene? Where were Virgil's parents? The house was strangely empty, and for that she was thankful as Christian's boots thundered across the floor and down the stairs after her.

She fled the house, refusing to allow Christian the opportunity to do any more damage there. She could hardly believe he had done what he had—especially with Margarite so close. Knowing Christian, he had watched the house, knew who was there. It made no sense, but then he was no longer the man Eleanor had known.

There was nothing to be done for the footsteps left behind her, by which Christian would likely track her. She rounded the house, then plunged into the vineyard with its bare vines, letting her anger take her, letting it saturate her the way it had the night before.

As she ran, she felt her human self as it was consumed by her fury. There was no less pain this time, and trying to prevent the change only resulted in more agony. She fell to the churned dirt path between the vines, crying and writhing as the jackal claimed her. Flesh already aching and bruised could do nothing but give way.

And then she was running anew, on four legs rather than two, and appearing to make good time despite the number of times she stumbled, unaccustomed to this form of locomotion.

Away. It was the one word in her head. Over and over, it repeated, like a chant, until it slowed, until she slowed and began to pick her way through the pruned vines. She found she could smell the enemy.

In this form, scent was nearly overwhelming. She could smell the ground beneath her, rich even though the growing season was past. She could smell the vines themselves, woody and, where already pruned, slightly burned. But beyond the world itself, she could smell Enemy as he approached. There was something curious about his scent—perhaps only because she had never smelled him this way—strong and nearly as dark as the dirt beneath her. But it was a different soil he smelled of, one that was somehow familiar. Ireland? This made no sense, so she ignored trying to discern its meaning; she listened.

"Eleanor, I wanted only to talk," he called out. "I apologize for being so terribly abrupt. Of course I shall replace the window."

She crouched in the dirt, noting the way her paws blended in nicely with the color. She imagined herself invisible, and pressed her nose against her paws and stilled her tail, ears perking forward.

"Cannot believe the little girl had the ring," Enemy said.

From the sound of his voice, he was a couple of rows over and approaching her position. She stayed where she was, the chain with its rings making a soft music when she lifted her head.

"I wonder how long she had it."

The sound of Enemy moving through the vines reached her; he was pushing through a row, breaking the crisp vines, the smell of him closer now. He smelled like sweat and desperation, like a thing to be taken down and gnawed to death. Slowly. She felt her lip curl and had to fight to silence her growl.

"Caroline mentioned France a time or two, but I brushed it off. She talked about so many different places, yet you ended up in Paris. Ended up here. Eleanor! I just want to talk."

She forced herself to stay where she was, nose pressed to paws, fighting the urge to leap on the approaching person. He sounded so close, so close, and she shut her eyes in an effort to get a better fix on him through scent alone. In the darkness behind her eyes, she saw a familiar face. Anubis reached for her, swift and sudden. The scent of dying flesh washed over her.

A gunshot brought her back to this world—she jerked as if she had been hit, but it was Enemy who cried out, then fled toward the ship dock, past a body that lay on the ground, horribly still. A whine escaped her, and she fled the security of the vines, running for the body. Before she could see, she smelled him: Mate's partner.

"Eleanor!"

She drew herself up short at the cry. The name was familiar to her, even in this form, and so too the voice. Mate loped toward her, his weapon held low at his side. When he reached her, he crouched down and she came to him, nuzzling the hand he extended to her. As Enemy had smelled different, so did Mate; he smelled like gunpowder, and it made her sneeze. Below that scent, there was only him, like myrrh.

She pawed at him and looked again toward the still body. When Mate moved toward it, she followed, scanning the land around them for other threats, but everything looked still. At Partner's side, she crouched. Her tail pressed into her back leg.

"Not shot," Mate said, tucking his own weapon away, hands roaming over the still body—and then Partner groaned.

"Damn," he muttered and lifted a hand to his head.

"Come on then," Mate said, easing the man up from the ground.

Partner's eyes swung toward her then, and she startled as his hand lowered. She took two steps to the side, out of his reach.

"That," Mate said, "would be Miss Folley."

"Damn," Partner whispered.

CHAPTER TWENTY-TWO

Imogene asked them to leave the vineyard, and Eleanor couldn't fault her. She couldn't get Margarite's screams out of her head, couldn't forget the way Christian had shot into the room, first with a bullet and then his body. She didn't know what had happened to him, but he was no longer the man she had traveled with. The man she had once loved. Had his search for the rings changed him so drastically? Eleanor didn't have to ask if her search had changed her, because she knew it had. But to the extent Christian had been changed? She didn't know.

Mallory managed to get her inside the house without anyone other than Auberon aware of the change that had overcome her. Once there, Eleanor cleaned herself up and set to packing. She tried to ignore the way her arms trembled and the way it felt extraordinary to walk on only two legs. How did Mallory deal with the changes? Did they become second nature the longer one endured them? She hoped she would have time to know, that he might teach her all he knew, even if his knowledge wasn't complete. It was a place to start.

When her things were packed, she came into the kitchen to find Mallory, Auberon, and Gin in hushed conversation at the table, maps spread before them. Their trunks sat nearby, and she added her own to the stack.

" . . . the issue of the final ring," Gin was saying as she settled onto the bench beside Mallory.

"We could destroy those we already possess," Auberon said. He looked little worse for his encounter with Christian, more humiliated than injured, though the cast around his arm was smudged with dirt.

All eyes swung to Eleanor at that suggestion. She withdrew the gold chain from her blouse, now heavy with three rings. After a moment's pause, she pulled the chain off and spread the rings on the table.

"For a long time," she said, "I thought about destroying the scarab." She touched the ring she had worn all these years. It was still warm from her body. "It seems the simplest way, but I can't do it. The idea of destroying something as ancient as this goes beyond everything I was raised to believe."

She could remember asking Mallory what Mistral meant to do with the rings, and remembered him telling her they would be destroyed. In her panic and worry, destruction had appeared the easiest course, if not the correct one. Anything to keep them out of Irving's hands or those even crueler.

Was it something beyond her upbringing that stayed her hand even now? Could it be the influence of Anubis? Her encounter with Anubis should have deepened her desire to have the rings leave her possession, but it hadn't; she wanted to slide those rings onto his fingers and watch him do his work. Had it been the same for her grandmother?

Under the cover of the table, Mallory's hand briefly clasped her thigh. "I don't think I could do it, either," he said.

"I must admit to a strange desire," Gin said. All eyes swung to him, and the pilot blushed straight down to the roots of his ginger hair. "To see the Glass open," he continued. "To know if it can be done, or if it even exists at all. Don't you wonder?"

"Constantly," Auberon said.

"It exists," Eleanor said and went on to speak about the day the Glass had opened for her mother. It was the first time she had spoken of it to the group as a whole, and it felt both awkward and freeing. "It looked like sunlight breaking through crystal, the way it fragments and spills. There was a voice, and a hand, both belonging to Anubis." There were raised eyebrows at this, but no one spoke, waiting for Eleanor to finish. "If my father is right and my mother's theory holds, we need more than the rings. We need me."

Mallory continued to weave the tale after Eleanor fell quiet, explaining Dalila's theory: to open what the Folleys called the Glass, it required more than mere metal.

"Egyptian blood," Gin whispered, one thin hand reaching up to encircle his own neck.

"I see only one solution," Eleanor said as Mallory finished explaining what they knew from her father, "and none of you are going to like it. I meet with Christian and make him an offer—"

"You cannot possibly—"

"What kind of offer?"

Auberon and Gin protested aloud, but Mallory held his silence, perhaps already having suspected this was coming.

"What Christian did here was abhorrent." Eleanor wanted to say more, but they already knew how terrible Christian's actions were. Placing this family in jeopardy was inexcusable.

"It only gets worse from here," Mallory agreed. "Hubert becomes more careless. He could have easily injured or killed Margarite and that . . . " Now it was Mallory struggling for calm. "Cannot happen. We need the carnelian ring, but he isn't going to simply hand it over—even to you, Eleanor."

"And what's to keep him from taking the rings we already have?" Gin asked.

Eleanor unfastened the chain. "That's why it's smartest to separate me from them." Christian was physically stronger than she, and Eleanor didn't doubt that if he wanted to ambush her and take them, he would be able to. Long ago, his tactics wouldn't have allowed such dirty play.

She slid the lapis ring from the chain and offered it to Gin. He hesitated, as if taking it meant he might vanish in a puff of smoke. When he at last took it, Eleanor moved to the ring with the Anubis mark, offering it to Auberon. He hesitated to take the ring as well, rubbing his thumb over the hieroglyphs on its surface when he finally did.

To Mallory, Eleanor gave the final ring, the scarab she had worn so long. It felt strange for it to not be around her own neck, but right that if it had to be anywhere else, it was with Mallory. She fastened it around his neck, and he tucked it down his shirt, out of sight.

"You aren't going alone," Mallory said, closing his hand around hers before she could fully withdraw.

"No," she said. "I'm not."

Christian and the *Remous* didn't prove difficult to find in the end, and Eleanor rather suspected that was his intent. As he had led them to Hatshepsut's temple, he would make himself accessible for other hints, taunts, and bargains. As she and the agents rode into the small village which crouched along the banks of the Loire River to the east of Chateau Mallory, Eleanor found it strange to see the *Remous* anchored among the few other ships at the shipyard. The ship felt like a fragment of her past, something from a hundred years ago now unearthed and hanging for all to see.

"You traveled in that thing?" Mallory asked as the carriage slowed to a halt some distance from the town proper.

Eleanor grinned at him as she slipped out of the carriage. "In my reckless youth," she said, then stepped quickly away from the agents, pretending she hadn't been in the carriage at all. Christian might have eyes anywhere, and Eleanor wanted him to presume she had come alone even if the odds of that were slim.

She moved up the street, with its gray buildings, toward the church standing at its end. Gin would see that the good Captain Hubert received her message, that she would await him in the church—an appropriate setting given their history of sanctified places, whether standing yet or in total ruin. If everything fell apart, it was also a setting that allowed her an easy escape.

Easy being relative, she thought as she walked toward the church. If something in this mission had proven easy, it usually had proven wrong as well, which kept Eleanor's guard up. Entering the thick stone walls gave her the sense of calm she always had inside a church. Her sense that she wasn't alone and would never be was stronger these days. She walked up the aisle and chose a random pew well away from any other parishioners, settling in to wait. To, for once, pray.

Eleanor folded her hands in her lap and looked to the altar. Her eyes strayed to a nearby chapel, one devoted to St. Michael. Remembering Mallory's prayers to the saint, she abandoned the pew to enter the small chapel and light a candle. She placed a coin on the square of lace spread below a soot-darkened image of the saint.

Michael, I need your strength.

She touched her fingers to the image and closed her eyes, praying that Mallory, Auberon, and Gin were safe. That Mallory's family was now out of harm's way. That Margarite would sleep without an assailant terrorizing her dreams.

"Little girl."

The two words were like a spike in Eleanor's side. She peered to her right to find Christian kneeling beside her. He lit a candle, too, and added a coin. Eleanor knew he should not be here yet. Gin could not have possibly had the time to deliver his message. Was she so predictable that Christian had known to seek her here? Had he followed their departure from the vineyard?

"I always hated you calling me that, from the first day," Eleanor said. She kept her voice low, so as not to rouse the attention of anyone in the nave.

"I think about that day more than I should," Christian said. Eleanor wondered if it was a slip or deliberate. Admitting a weakness? That was unlike Christian. "You always could surprise me," he continued. "I never imagined us here, little girl, but then that was part of the fun, wasn't it?"

Never knowing where they would go, where they would see the sun rise or set. That had been part of the fun, part of the appeal. She had joked to Mallory about her reckless youth, but so much of her time with Christian had been unthinking; they had simply gone where they wanted to.

"Christian, about yesterday . . . " She turned from the candles, but he didn't move, the shrine's candles illuminating the space between them. He crouched, immovable, and when his eyes met hers, Eleanor felt not the absence of the understanding that used to exist between them, but something else. Impatience? Frustration? Something in the set of Christian's features silently demanded she reason it out. He was giving her the time he'd never given her in their travels—allowing her to discover the puzzle's solution in her own time. This was strangely new.

"Yesterday," he prompted when she didn't continue.

Eleanor pressed her teeth together before she lost her own patience and screamed at him in the church quiet. Margarite's own screams were still too fresh in her mind, and the notion that Christian would place a child in peril—"It wasn't like you."

"Maybe you don't know me anymore," he said and now did shift his stance. He rose from the shrine and turned away from it and Eleanor both.

"I know you," she said.

Some part of her refused to believe Christian had changed so vastly in such a short span of time. Something hovered under the surface of both him and his recent actions; even if Eleanor couldn't name it, she felt it there. Silently insistent.

"The Christian I saw at Deir el-Bahri is the genuine one, the Christian who plays fair because it's more interesting that way. Charging into that little girl's bedroom wasn't fair play. Neither was the attack on my father."

Would he rise to the bait? There was a visible tightening of Christian's jaw to prove that the attack had also bothered him, which confirmed to her it hadn't been by his hand. He kept his silence.

"I want to make a deal for the carnelian," she said when he appeared unlikely to talk. "You know I have the other three."

"That isn't how this game works, and you know it. You have to claim it on your own, you and me—one on one. No Mistral. Remember how good that used to be?"

Christian moved quickly, catching her by the arm. His other hand slid over her cheek, to grip her by her neck and hold her. Eleanor tried to wrench away, but he held firm. She only kept calm because she no longer carried the rings; if he meant to search her for them, he would be sorely disappointed.

Despite the years that separated this touch from their last, Eleanor remembered the very things she didn't want to. How kind Christian could be, how gentle. Had Virgil's theory been right all along, that Christian had been motivated by his love for her? That aspect remained absurd.

"You and me, little girl. With these rings, we could go anywhere. Do anything. This is what you always wanted; to open the Glass and see your mother. I can make that happen."

It was everything she had always wanted. Traversing the world to put this grand puzzle together, confronting the thing that had taken her mother. But she didn't need a joker like Christian for that; she only needed the carnelian ring. Was it in his pocket even now? Their proximity made her calculate the odds that he hadn't been as wise as she when it came to keeping the rings at a safe distance.

"I can make that happen, Eleanor," he repeated.

Eleanor purposefully shifted the subject, back toward that which made him uncomfortable. "What happened to you, Christian? You would never endanger a child, yet yesterday you nearly killed one."

Christian released Eleanor as if she was on fire and he was in danger of being consumed. He pushed her backward, and she fought to keep her balance with the sudden shift.

"You know I always loved the exhilaration . . . the unknown of the adventure," he said as he took two steps back from her. "It takes a little more for me to experience that these days."

"There's something else here," she said and watched as another step backward placed him within the fall of light from one of the chapel's clerestory windows. The light sparked off a chain around his neck. Had he actually brought the carnelian with him?

"It would be easier if we were on the same side," Eleanor said, wondering if there were a way she could get the ring from Christian without holding him at gunpoint in a church. "But I bring more to the partnership this time, don't I? Last time, you were the one in control." And how he loved his control.

The light shifted over him as Christian took a step to his left, closer to the doorway dividing the shrine from the main cathedral. "What are you saying, Eleanor?"

That he called her by her name and not an endearment told her she was hitting near the mark, though she didn't yet know how close. She might scale the walls he had built around himself only to find herself toppling into an abyss on the other side.

"I have three rings," she said, intentionally provoking him to see where it took them. "You have only the one. I leave and you have nothing—can't open the Glass." Of course, the same could be said if he left, but she silenced that part of her mind. "I'm part Egyptian, you're not."

Christian flinched. He took a clear step backward, eyes narrowed. "What does that have— No, that can't be."

"Can't be what?" Eleanor asked.

"Little girl . . . "

She watched the curious play of emotions cross his face, having no good idea where this conversation had taken them yet. He seemed to be struggling to understand something himself, and Eleanor wanted to help him. It was then she realized how much she had missed him, not as lover but as friend and mentor. She could not count the times she longed to share a discovery with him or ask him about an ancient text.

"I've missed you," Eleanor said, surprising herself. Even Christian showed his surprise with a short bark of laughter. "Christian, thank you. You taught me so much. You're why I've come this far."

Christian closed the distance between them, long legs crossing the space in an instant. He reached for her again, but not so quickly as before. His fingers only whispered against her cheek. "You've made me proud, Eleanor, but you are why you've come this far."

In the hush of the chapel, it was more honest than anything she had heard from Christian yet, the admission from her teacher that she was more than equal to the task. She wanted to tell him all she had learned, that a remarkable thing had happened to her at the vineyard, but she stifled the words. How did a person tell someone that? *Darling, I'm a jackal* didn't just flow from one's mouth. She understood Mallory's own hesitation all too well now.

"That," Christian said, "is why it has to be one on one. I want you to take this ring from me, Eleanor, as much as I want to claim the three from you." His eyes flicked to her neck, and he chuckled. "But you seem to have left them behind. This is the challenge. You besting me. It always has been." Christian tipped Eleanor's chin up and swiftly kissed her lips, his own cool and dry.

"Christian—"

"Just a thank you, little girl," he said as he looked down at her. "Nothing more."

But there was more. Without warning, Christian's arms closed hard around Eleanor and his head snapped to the side. She stumbled under his sudden weight. What was he playing at now? But when she felt the splatter of blood against her cheek, she knew it was no game. Screams erupted from the church proper at the sound of more revolver fire.

"Christian."

Eleanor lowered him to the floor before he took the both of them over, and drew her revolver as Howard Irving stepped into the chapel. He was a different man from the one Eleanor had met in the halls of Sirocco's headquarters, less refined and more on the brink of madness. Whereas Christian was all high walls, Irving was all edges bounded by endless black. She didn't know the map of him well enough to know how far he would take a thing. Why did he want the rings? Was it only the power they promised?

"How tender you two were," Irving said. His revolver never budged from its aim on Eleanor.

Eleanor holstered her revolver with a barely contained growl and dropped her attention to Christian. She had faith that Irving wouldn't shoot her here. He needed her, didn't he? And Christian—

"Ah, God."

Irving's bullet had caught Christian in the shoulder, and hot blood flowed from him in a crimson fury. Though she pressed her hands against the tide of blood, there was no stemming it.

"You're going to be fine," Eleanor whispered to him. "Just fine." She watched Christian's lip curl in a half smile.

"You're a beautiful liar," he said. The words only made the blood rush more quickly through her fingers. His eyes rolled back, but did not close.

"I do hope the two of you said all that ever needed saying," Irving said. He took another step into the chapel and crouched some distance from them, watching, waiting. "Time to sort the wheat from the chaff."

Eleanor hadn't liked him when she saw him confronting Mallory outside Cleo's offices. He felt like oil to her, slick and on top of everything, and here, beyond the stench of Christian's spilled blood, Irving smelled like death. He smelled as though he had carried it in his hands for long distances and didn't entirely mind the task.

"Take the carnelian, Miss Folley," Irving said.

Eleanor only stared at him, her mind racing with a dozen scenarios as to how she might get out of this alive. All of them involved going through Irving and his revolver. She prayed, as clearly as she could while Christian's life fled him, that Mallory, Auberon, and Gin had by some miracle realized Irving was close. That they had realized Christian wouldn't dally, but would seek her out. And Christian . . . working with Irving?

"Caroline wasn't supposed to put the pieces together," Irving said, his hands beginning to shake. "But I don't care if you do. Now that you have all the rings, it doesn't matter."

Eleanor relaxed somewhat, feeling safe in the knowledge they had but one ring here and now. She silently thanked Christian for teaching her to be wary, for teaching her that sometimes puzzles needed to come together slowly. There was too much to thank him for; too much here at the end.

"What did Caroline do?" Eleanor whispered. She eased her hold on Christian long enough to pull her coat off, to press its ebon wool against Christian's neck. He groaned under the fresh pressure, but she took a strange comfort in the sound. Pain meant he wasn't gone. Not yet.

"My girl was too curious for her own good," Irving said. His cool blue eyes went distant, as if an old memory held him firmly in hand. "It got her killed."

Slowly, his attention returned to Eleanor. "Take the ring, Miss Folley. I won't tell you again."

Reasoning that she would have to take it sooner or later, Eleanor pulled on the chain around Christian's neck. It broke free, and she drew it into her hand. The blood-wet ring glistened in her palm, and thunder roared in her ears.

Bring them, Anubis commanded her.

"S-shoot him."

They were the last words Eleanor would hear Christian speak. Beyond the bloody ring, she sensed Irving moving. *Shoot him now, Eleanor, now.*

She released Christian and pulled her revolver, but her fingers were slick with blood and Irving was on her before she could fire. He toppled her onto the floor and though she held fiercely to the ring, it wasn't what Irving sought to claim. The butt of his own revolver slammed into her temple. Eleanor saw Christian's eyes close a moment before everything went black.

Somewhere between the Loire Valley and Egypt ~ October 1889

Shrieking horses moved in the swirling dust, more shadow than living creatures. They were slow to emerge from the clouds of dust, sand grating inside mechanical gears as they stormed toward the open grave. Eleanor lunged for the Lady, but the horses and their men were already there. The men pulled her into the loose sand, the horses careless of where they trod, be it on the Lady's fragile body or Eleanor herself. One ragged mouth closed hard around her hand, blood and slobber running into the mangled sleeve of her blouse. And everywhere, the light.

Eleanor woke, shivering. For a moment she was uncertain where she was. She forced her eyes open, and at first what she saw made no sense. The light was coming through the window at an odd angle. She tried to turn, thinking it only the continuation of a dream. She wanted to burrow deeper into the blankets, but there were no blankets, only ropes binding her to a chair. She was likewise gagged with a bundle of fabric that tasted like sour weeds. In her lap rested a cloth that oozed a bitter stench, a scent that lingered in her nose.

"I wondered when you would come around."

Irving stood a few paces distant in a hatchway—the first clue Eleanor had as to their surroundings. The cold air was the second. She looked around slowly, mindful of the way her head still pounded from the revolver strike, and saw they were on board an airship.

Panic quickly gave way to fury. She struggled against her bindings, but they were secure. She could feel the jackal close to the surface, nearly wriggling under her taut skin every time she failed to loosen the ropes. The rope burned into her skin, and she hissed at both the pain and confinement.

Breathe, daughter. She thought she heard Anubis whisper, and she forced herself to draw in the requested breath. She knew unleashing the jackal on board an unknown airship was unwise.

How long? Where were they headed? Questions calmed the beast, because they provided a focus for her attention. She decided the last question wasn't so difficult to answer when she considered recent events. Irving would surely take her back to Egypt.

"I apologize for creating a mess in that beautiful church," Irving said. He sat in the chairs that occupied the other side of the aisle, and as he did, Eleanor was startled to see Christian's body slumped against the wall. Blood soaked his shirt and jacket. She strained at the ropes again, wanting out so that she might drag Irving to the floor.

"Christian was clearly poised to become a liability," Irving continued. "We shall bury him at sea, yes?" There was no smile, only an even expression that told Eleanor nothing.

Irving shifted in the chair, unhooking the silver flask worn at his belt. He took a long, slow drink that Eleanor tried not to envy. Instead, Eleanor looked at the knife he wore at his belt and the carnelian ring around his middle finger.

"Perhaps Christian was a liability all along; I cannot say."

Irving's eyes returned to Eleanor, and a chill scampered down her spine. His face was sharp and reminded her of those men in the desert that long-ago day. He was not like them, she could not smell an animal within him, but had the look of them even so.

Eleanor looked out the arching window, where she could see only clouds below them. This view was little better, as it caused nausea to roll in a slow wave through her, but she still picked out the shape of another airship against the bright clouds. Irving's accomplices? She looked back at him, telling the jackal inside her to calm.

"We shall travel as quickly as we can, Miss Folley." Irving recapped his flask and shifted it restlessly from hand to hand. "I trust Anubis will be patient with us. After all this time he has waited, what is a few hours more?"

A few hours. Eleanor's mind raced. How long had they been airborne? How close behind were Mallory and the others? It didn't occur to her that they wouldn't follow, or wouldn't be able to follow; she simply felt they would be out there, somewhere. Behind, but still coming.

"Did you see the beautiful Anubis mural when you were there? Christian said it was astonishing, and I have no cause to doubt him."

Irving paused as if allowing for a response. Eleanor stared at him, her mouth still bound by fabric and rope. She squirmed in her seat, but whoever had tied her had done a thorough job.

"It's almost over now, Miss Folley. Almost over."

Eleanor turned her attention to the window once more, trying to determine Irving's game. Of what use were the rings or the Glass to him? Unless he shared Gin's outlook and simply wanted to see what would happen. But no, what had Irving said? Caroline was too curious for her own good.

Eleanor allowed herself to see what was truly before her. The man sitting across the aisle wasn't so much sitting as he was slumped, his shoulders rounded beneath a wrinkled shirt. His eyes appeared heavy, tired, with deep lines tracing outward. His bottom lip had been chewed until it was raw. His hands showed wear, too. His fingers whispered around the flask over and over, nails broken or gnawed, skin scratched and pink in places. No longer the hands of a gentleman, even if he did sport a very fine ring.

"I should let you tidy up . . . "

He murmured the words, as though they were an afterthought to a longer conversation. He crossed to Eleanor and knelt to loosen the ropes that bound her, though once free of the chair, she discovered she was still secured at her wrists. Outside a small room holding a basin and pitcher, Irving untied her hands and took the gag from her mouth. Eleanor lifted a hand to her jaw, feeling as though she had been struck there, so deep was the pain.

She closed the door in Irving's face and stood there, looking at the dried blood that covered her clothing. Christian's blood. She fought to keep the world from slipping away then, from giving in to the anger that wanted to claim her. It would do her no good. She had no idea how many men crewed the airship, or where they were.

Nor where Mallory was.

Eleanor cleaned up as best she could, washing the blood from her hands and face, from the cuffs of her blouse. She could do nothing about her trousers, so left them as they were, splattered with Christian's blood. Christian's blood because Irving had killed him. Killed him and—

She pushed the anger back.

"Michael, please give me strength."

A sharp knock sounded against the door. "Come now, Miss Folley, we haven't all day. There's no way out of that room other than this door."

Eleanor dried her face and hands and opened the door to stare again at Irving. Now that the exhausted old man within him had been revealed to her, she couldn't help but see him. He looked like the kind who would be more comfortable sharing cigars with her father than abducting people and bending them to his will. Christian's body was no longer present. *Christian . . .*

"I hope you don't mind I'm holding on to this." Irving lifted a hand, showing the carnelian ring that gleamed on his middle finger. She was jerked away from further thoughts of Christian Hubert.

If he meant the ring as a taunt, Eleanor let it go. It would be too easy for the jackal to pick it up and tear his throat out. Eleanor hoped she sounded perfectly at ease when she spoke. "You may as well, being that it's the only ring you possess."

Irving smiled a smile that made Eleanor's blood run cold. "This is why I do love puzzles," he said. "You may think a picture will never emerge, and then come to discover you truly did have all the pieces after all."

What had Irving done? To the rings; to Mallory, Auberon and Gin? Eleanor closed her hands into fists and strode past him, back toward the chairs. It wasn't a large airship, though larger than the *Remous*. Eleanor looked through the door into the compartment beyond the one they occupied. There seemed to be no way out of this compartment, while the other possessed a singular staircase spiraling upward.

"Don't consider it, Miss Folley," Irving said from close behind her. "You couldn't take this vessel on your own."

She turned and offered Irving words that were more confident than she actually felt. "You did speak of patience earlier."

She knew she could not, in all practicality, take this ship on her own; knew too that biding her time until they were on the ground in Egypt again would likely be her best chance for doing anything against him. She suspected Mallory and the others would know that as well—not wanting a repeat performance of the *Nuit*'s crashing. She told herself they were all right, that when conditions were better, she would see them again.

"Oh, you are awake!"

Eleanor turned toward the female voice, staring at the petite woman who entered the cabin. She was nearly Caroline Irving's mirror image with her white-blond hair and shocking blue eyes. She was dressed in a tidy ensemble which mirrored the colors of the desert, her skirts more narrow than wide. She had to be Caroline's mother, which both baffled and concerned Eleanor. What was she doing here? Eleanor might have all of the puzzle pieces before her, but couldn't yet fit them into a proper pattern.

"My wife," Irving confirmed, "Sabrina."

Eleanor said nothing as Sabrina strode forward and clasped Eleanor's hands. It took an effort not to pull her hands away, to not recoil from the woman's clammy grip.

"Miss Eleanor Folley, what a genuine pleasure it is to meet you at last." Sabrina's smile was kinder than it had a right to be, but then Eleanor supposed this woman fully understood her husband's plan. His madness. "I cannot thank you enough for your continued cooperation in this endeavor. Why, without you and the rings, we would be at a complete loss!"

"It was more coercion than cooperation, Mrs. Irving," Eleanor said and then did free her hands with one firm tug. "Perhaps you can elaborate on exactly what you want of me." But Eleanor felt she knew, knew as surely as she had when her father had first told her about her mother's theory.

Sabrina Irving settled herself into a chair, tucking her feet under her skirts. "Only your blood, dear," she said. "Only your blood."

CHAPTER TWENTY-THREE

The Loire Valley, France ~ October 1889

Of all the things Virgil Mallory was indeed acquainted with, he wished he could eliminate this item from the list. The gruesome sight of bright blood spilled across the chapel's marble floor made him draw up short. Auberon stepped into the saint's chapel, but Virgil couldn't make himself do it, not at first.

Instead, his hand curled around the ring in his pocket. He didn't know whether the blood on the chapel floor was Eleanor's, but if it was—

The fury that took hold of him left his hands shaking. He focused on Auberon and the way his partner moved around the chapel in an attempt to ascertain what had happened there. He paused before a bloody handprint that marked the floor. Small enough to be Eleanor's hand, Virgil thought, and met Auberon's steady gaze. He tightened his hold on the ring.

"Don't lose your focus," Auberon said. "I need you on this."

Virgil stepped into the chapel and silently prayed for calm and reason, but the closer he came to the blood, the more disturbed he felt. He told himself Gin was scouting outside, that danger would not arrive unannounced yet again, but the wolf wanted out. He wanted to track Hubert and Irving and—

What had he told Auberon—that he meant to embrace the wolf, that it was not a thing separate from him, but part of him. To that end, could he tap into the wolf's senses even in his human form? There was still so much he didn't know and hadn't experimented with. He eyed the splatter of blood against the gray stone, then crouched beside Auberon.

The chapel smelled of beeswax and incense. He guessed the incense had not been burned here in the last day, and tried to reach beyond those lingering scents. There—there it was. The blood had a strange musky note to it, and no typical iron overtone. It smelled like a dying animal to him, a thing easily traceable if it stayed on the ground. He looked to the droplets of blood that led out of the chapel. No footprints.

"It doesn't smell like Eleanor," Virgil said. He realized such a statement might sound foolish, but Auberon only relaxed.

"All right. She comes to the church," Auberon said, pacing a circle around the pool of blood. "Comes into the chapel, where she waits. We know Hubert was either already here or en route, because by the time we reach the shipyards, he's nowhere to be found and we have only a handful of Irving's men in his place."

"Two handfuls, if you want to be precise about it," Virgil said, rubbing a hand across his jaw. It still ached from the punches he had taken. Not giving in to the wolf during the fight had been a challenge, one he struggled against as intently as he had the men in their effort to claim the rings.

"Eleanor wouldn't have fired on Hubert without good cause, and not here," Virgil said, "but this . . ." He trailed off as he reached for one of the bloody handprints. He spread his hand above it, knowing well the size of Eleanor's hands. "It's messy, as if it was not planned . . . Hubert would not intend to be shot, of course, but . . ."

"Perhaps they weren't alone, as we were not," Auberon said. "Let us presume that Christian arrived with the fourth ring, and let us presume that he presumed Eleanor would come with those she had. Perhaps he still has a certain faith in her, based on what he knows of her from the past."

"And while we're doing all this presuming?" Virgil asked.

"Let us also presume that another interested party, say one Howard Irving, made presumptions of his own, and presumed to take advantage of this curious meeting—in addition to leaving men at our presumed destination, in case Miss Folley was wise enough to not bring the rings with her."

Virgil grunted, but looked around the chapel again. "Someone carried the bleeding party out of this room," he said. "If it's Christian's blood, she could not have carried him. If it's Irving's, she still couldn't have carried him, but I would wager we would be looking at a body now, and not simply blood." Virgil looked to the small altar, the image of Michael, and the coins scattered over the lace.

Eleanor would not have been so reckless as to shoot Christian here of all places. He remembered enfolding her hands within his own as they had prayed at Notre Dame and knew she would not desecrate a church. But what might Irving do if he believed all four rings were in this chapel?

"Irving has taken them to Egypt."

The words came from Virgil and Auberon in the same instant. It comforted Virgil to know he wasn't alone in the belief.

All roads led back to Egypt, where this adventure had begun with the unearthing of the Lady. Even before that: Virgil thought of Tau's journal and Sagira's own encounter with the rings. What had it been like for Tau to lose her? His journal had maintained a scientific distance from such emotions. What had it then been for Renshaw Folley to face the possibility of losing his own wife—and then his daughter—to this thing? Virgil could say only what it was to face the loss of Eleanor to Anubis and his Glass. It was a thing he would wish on no other man.

Virgil followed Auberon from the chapel, but not without a final glance to the bloody handprint on the stone floor. He wouldn't lose Eleanor to this; if she went, he would do everything in his power to go with her.

Deir el-Bahri, Egypt ~ October 1889

Irving was in a fouler mood when the airship set down just outside of Deir el-Bahri. He stalked from the ship, leaving Eleanor in the hands of a tall man who was disinclined to give her his name. Still, he was more muscle than the petite Sabrina Irving, whom Eleanor might have overpowered to escape. The lackey held her wrists—bound once more—keeping to the shade of the airship.

"What's all that about?" Eleanor asked Sabrina as Irving met the pilot of one of the accompanying airships. He gestured wildly, cursed, and at last struck the man hard across the face. The pilot crumpled to the ground, and Eleanor flinched.

"I won't apologize for him," Sabrina whispered.

Eleanor looked to Irving's wife at her side, hearing a strange tone in her voice. Her scent said that she wasn't afraid, but rather sad.

"Soon," Sabrina continued in that same whisper. Despite the heat of the afternoon, she wrapped her arms around herself and shivered. "This will pass and she will be returned to us and every terrible thing we have all endured will be forgotten. You will see."

Eleanor felt suddenly cold herself. "She?"

Eleanor asked, but deep down, feared she already knew. The *she* in question had to be Caroline, Sabrina's daughter. As to being returned, Eleanor looked toward Hatshepsut's temple and felt the growing presence of Anubis. It seemed to spread outward from his chapel, a cold that pierced the Egyptian afternoon.

"Sabrina, this won't—"

"You shut your mouth!"

Sabrina's hand cracked hard across Eleanor's cheek. Eleanor bit her cheek under the impact and tasted blood. The blow was so hard she staggered and would have fallen were it not for the man holding her roped hands. She saw two of him for a moment, and spat blood onto the ground.

"Leaping straight to resurrecting the dead, then," Eleanor said, "and you'll tamper with time later?"

"You . . . " Sabrina's voice trembled now. and she closed her hand into a fist. "Shut. Your. Mouth."

Eleanor did fall to silence, only because she didn't know what else to say. The idea of resurrecting a dead daughter was staggering, and the more she tried to hold on to it, the more it slipped away.

She lifted her eyes from Irving's wife to the ramps leading to Hatshepsut's temple. Though the wind whipped her hair across her face, Eleanor could see a long shape resting at the top of the final ramp. A coffin, still coated with dirt.

"Oh, God," she whispered, feeling her legs begin to tremble. How could Irving have done this to his wife? Given her this hope? Or had it been Sabrina who concocted the plan? "Sabrina. This won't work. You must know that."

Sabrina began to walk toward the coffin and temple; the man holding to Eleanor pulled her along after as though she were a dog on a lead.

"I know nothing of the sort," Sabrina said. "Anubis had the power of life and death—"

"He—" Eleanor was at a loss for words. Anubis had been considered the god of the underworld, but surely he couldn't bring a person back from death? Isis perhaps, collecting a person the way she had the pieces of her slain husband, but not Anubis. "Sabrina, he can't—"

"Caroline has paid enough for the double life she led! She has suffered enough . . . we all have."

The anguish in Sabrina's voice was far too familiar to Eleanor. What was it about mothers and daughters; Dalila had pursued Sagira, she had pursued her own mother and now here stood Sabrina, still grieving for her dead daughter, convinced she had found a way to bring her back.

Eleanor's vision blurred with tears, tears that were whipped away by another hot uprush of wind. While the air was warm, Eleanor was so chilled by the idea Sabrina had voiced she would have sworn they were walking through a winter's day in Dublin.

"You knew?" Eleanor stopped walking and stumbled when the man pulled her back into motion, up the ramp. "About your daughter's deceit?"

"Who do you think she took her orders from?" Sabrina continued to march up the ramp; strands of her fair hair whipped out of her chignon, whisking behind her in the wind. "Who did she report to?"

Her voice hitched, and then her revelations ceased as she reached the coffin. Sabrina fell to her knees in front of it, bending over to embrace the dirty wood.

Eleanor looked away. Of all the ways this could have gone from bad to worse, this was the one she hadn't imagined. This was the thing she never would have believed, and perhaps should have always looked toward first. Mothers, daughters, unbreakable bonds. What lengths would she have once gone to, to get her mother back? To embrace her again and know that everything and everyone was back where it was meant to be?

She was pulled from her thoughts when the man holding her rope transferred it to another set of hands. Irving. Irving, who had controlled his daughter to her destruction. Eleanor didn't presume she could convince the man his methods were insane, not having had any luck with his wife, but the words still came.

"Caroline is dead, Irving. Let her rest."

Irving's hand across her cheek was harder than his wife's. Eleanor did fall this time, spitting more blood onto the dusty ground as her knees cracked against the stone. Her hands splayed in the dirt, ropes biting into her wrists.

"If I have to beat every drop of your blood from your body, I will, Miss Folley. I would rather it not come to that, all things being—"

Whatever Irving had been about to say was cut off. He joined Eleanor in the dust, sprawling flat on the stony ground in an inelegant heap. Eleanor stared at him, his wide eyes, and then heard gunfire. Hope lodged in her heart.

"Howard!"

Eleanor thought the gates to the underworld had been opened or that she was hallucinating, for strange figures began to emerge from Hatshepsut's temple. The people were wrapped entirely in black cloth, and as they moved, Eleanor spied the jeweled bird masks she had seen during the attack on the *Galerie des Machines*. The birdmen came to Irving, raising rifles to defend the temple and the Irvings' position. The rifles roared, over and over, toward two more arriving airships.

Eleanor reached for Irving and the knife he wore at his waist, her sharp elbow in his ribs sending him toppling. She pulled the knife free and sliced across Irving's midsection. Sabrina cried out and lunged for her husband. Eleanor let them tussle so she could exchange her grip on the knife and turn it against the ropes that bound her.

"Your boys aren't coming, Irving!"

It was a familiar voice that growled above the thundering rifles, and Eleanor's head jerked up. Familiar people crossed the dusty plain before the temple. Auberon, Gin, and—

"Virgil," she whispered.

The relief that flooded through her was short-lived as she ducked to avoid the crossfire of Mallory's incoming party and Irving's. She worked the knife between the ropes again and began to saw.

"Bastard."

The curse came from Irving, and he leapt upon her, wrestling her to the ground in an attempt to reclaim the knife. The knife stuck in the ropes, and the angle of Eleanor's hands wouldn't allow her to pull it free. She watched Irving's hands close effortlessly around the familiar hilt, but instead of pulling the blade toward him to free it from the ropes, he pushed inward.

With his weight against her, Eleanor could not avoid the blade as it slid into her side. The pain was sharp and bright, but doubly so when Irving ripped the blade free. Eleanor screamed as Irving lunged for her again.

"It's your blood we need, girl," he said and jabbed again.

Eleanor rolled to dodge the second thrust. Irving found himself suddenly beyond her and turned for another attack. For an older man, he moved well, but then the desire to return his daughter to life was foremost in his mind; surely it would keep him moving, no matter the circumstances.

Irving came at her a third time, and Eleanor stayed low, meaning to kick his legs out from under him. But it was Mallory who lunged into Irving's side, throwing the man off his feet. Human Mallory, but growling. Eleanor heard the sickening smack of Irving's head against the side of Caroline's casket as he went down. The bloodied knife spilled from his grip.

Eleanor crawled to Irving's side. The man was motionless, but his chest still rose with labored breaths, telling her he lived. She grasped his hand and then the carnelian ring he wore. She tugged it free and slid away from him.

"No." Irving stirred and tried to lift his hand to reclaim the ring, but Mallory kicked his arm back down.

Blood from her hands coated the ring, making its passage smooth as she slid it onto her own finger for safekeeping. Eleanor shuddered at the memory of placing the bloody ring on Anubis's finger. The world before her swam, darkness threatening to pull her away.

It was Mallory who pulled her away before anything else could. They staggered from Irving and the incoherent screams from Sabrina Irving's mouth, down the temple ramp and into the chaos that ruled the dusty plain. Irving might not have had all his men, but those he did have were unwilling to surrender, a good match to those Mallory had brought. Mallory pulled Eleanor toward the airships as if he meant for them to make their escape.

"Virgil—" The knife wound in her side throbbed with every frantic heartbeat. "They mean to bring Caroline back." Mallory didn't turn or stop, and she didn't know if he had heard her. She tried to slow his pace, but could not; onward he trudged toward the airships.

"Virgil." Her voice broke on a sob.

He guided her free of the immediate chaos and then turned to her, to press his hand against her bleeding side. The warmth of his hand sank through her, and she took a slow, steady breath.

Dust coated Mallory, blood freckled a path across his face and jaw, and she saw tears brightening his eyes. It hit her then, what the idea of Caroline coming back would mean to him, Caroline's husband.

Backward, flow backward, O tide of the years! I am so weary of toil and of tears . . .

"Oh, Virgil."

All the words Eleanor meant to say stuck in her throat. It couldn't be done, surely he knew that the way she did. No matter how much he might want such a thing—he had to know.

"They have to know that cannot happen."

Mallory's words echoed her thoughts, and it took her a heartbeat to realize that he had spoken them instead of her. After stripping the remains of the ropes that had bound her from her wrists, Mallory pressed a bundle into her hands. She looked down to see the Lady's three rings.

"My *tesorina*," he whispered.

"We ride it out," she said.

With shaking hands, Eleanor freed the rings from their gold chain, sliding them onto the fingers of her left hand one by one. They fit as though they had been made for her hand and felt strangely familiar as each settled into place. The carnelian sat upon her middle finger, the lapis and gold scarab following to the left. The silver band ringed her forefinger much the way Mallory's silver ring did his.

Mallory's hands were damp with her blood when they closed over hers, over the rings. And then the world went black.

Nothing existed except the rings and the fiery pain that came with each heartbeat. Eleanor could no longer feel Mallory's hands on hers, only the hot metal of the rings against her blood-damp flesh. She feared the metal would sink down to her bones the way Anubis's touch had seemed to, feared that she wouldn't know what to do to get them out of this black space, but then—

There came the gleam of light.

The light was familiar, piercing the darkness from a singular distant point. This point expanded and the pain in her hand receded, the light dancing the way Egyptian sunlight did when it sank between shadowed pyramids. Shadows moved within the light, one of them her own.

She was smaller, only twelve, kneeling in the Egyptian sand to brush it back from the Lady. The shadows became fluid, ink moving through golden light as Eleanor grew to meet Christian in the artisan's tomb.

Despair washed through her, as sharp as the knife wound she now bore. Though she couldn't see them, she felt the squeeze of Mallory's hands around hers. Felt, too, a presence at their backs; this presence swept a hand across the light, and more shadow images flared into life. Eleanor watched shadow-Mallory bending over Caroline's dead body. Regrets spilled from him like rain to wash the forms away.

Eleanor blinked, and time rushed forward and then back once more, showing her more shadowed images from her life and Mallory's. There were instances she could hardly separate: seeing herself walk down a street in Morocco, where Mallory sprawled and asked about a blue parrot. She felt his sorrow as he packed away Caroline's belongings, and then her own delight when she encountered Mallory on the upper deck of the *Nuit*, barefoot. She tasted the opium smoke as he took it in, dizzyingly sweet to him, and then the bitter tang of a toad.

The sweet scent of orange blossoms seeped through the light. With this scent came a black hand. Eleanor found she no longer feared this hand; Anubis did not reach for her, only expanded the range of light and the images it held. Eleanor saw her mother and Sagira both—one swept away, the other following.

"Virgil," she whispered.

"Eleanor, look."

His hand slid under her chin, guiding her attention upward. Toward what should have been the sky, the light of the Glass diminished. There came the soft whisper of balsam-scented branches around them. Near their feet, a peacock dipped its beak into a pool of moonlit water, and in the near distance—

A flawless Djeser-djeseru rose against the moon-washed cliffs, braziers of fire turning each pillar into a living flame. Rows of sphinxes flanked the ramps toward the temple, and the ramps were filled with—people. People should not have been remarkable, but they were, because they should not have existed. They had in the past, but not now. Not now, unless—

Eleanor couldn't finish a proper thought. She leaned into Mallory, hoping the trees would conceal them, but they had already been seen.

Dalila Folley strode toward them amid the moonlit myrrh.

CHAPTER TWENTY-FOUR

Djeser-djeseru, Kmet ~ Sometime between Year 12 and Year 22
of the reign of Maatkare Hatshepsut-khenmetamun

Years before, when she first began her quest, Eleanor told herself a story. Each night before bed and on days when she felt the path toward truth vanishing before her, Eleanor told herself a story so she wouldn't lose her will. She closed her eyes and thought of the tale her mother shared, but here the story became her own, crafted by her own hands.

It was a familiar story, beginning much like the one Dalila had shared with a young Eleanor, about a forgotten lady in the desert. These women longed to be found, for no life should be spent withering beneath Egypt's vast deserts. These women wanted to be discovered, unburied, brushed off; wanted to feel the sunlight on their bones; wanted to be remembered.

Eleanor had told herself Dalila wanted to be found as much as Eleanor wanted to find her. Where Eleanor possessed a singular need to know what happened to her mother, Eleanor told herself Dalila possessed an opposite and equal need to have her daughter know.

Now Eleanor realized that while the Lady had not been a bedtime story, the tales she had spun about her own mother had been. Not that Dalila's life had not ended that day in the desert—this was true enough—but that Dalila had kept any affection for the family she had left behind. Time and tide had changed Dalila Folley, just as they had changed Eleanor.

Dalila Folley strode closer, trailed by two other women. The myrrh branches parted against their sun-browned shoulders with fragrant whispers. White linen draped Dalila, a many-pleated cloak over a dress, and gold gleamed at her wrists, neck, and ears. Dalila's head was covered by a wig of gleaming onyx braids, her face painted; the outlines that began at her eyes trailed over her cheeks, branching outward to her ears and down to her jaw like tree roots.

Eleanor wanted to brush it off as a dream—it would have been easier that way—but the touch of the night air on her cheeks was real enough, the moon burning bright and clear overhead. Eleanor laced her fingers with Mallory's, wanting to ensure that he didn't step away to allow them the privacy he might think they needed. But Mallory only moved enough to press his handkerchief over Eleanor's still-bleeding side.

"Daughter."

It was a voice Eleanor had not heard in eighteen years. Even though it stumbled as if English were unfamiliar, Eleanor would have known the sound of it anywhere. Part of her still wanted to fling herself into her mother's arms, but the larger part of her held back. She left. She wanted to be here, in the past, and she left. Left me. Da. Everything. But as with Sabrina outside the temple, it was no longer anger that glossed those thoughts; it was sorrow.

"Mother."

Beyond all else, she remained that, and Eleanor wanted to weep for the loss she still felt. She gritted her teeth together and looked beyond her mother, to the two women behind her. Eleanor was astonished to recognize one of them—the woman from the canyon with the braided, bound silver hair. The woman who had wanted Cleo for study. Eleanor's mouth grew dry.

"Come," Dalila said, "and let us clean you up." She nodded toward the press of Mallory's hand and the bloody handkerchief. Dalila's words were slow as she struggled to find them. "You and your friends."

Despite the wound she was painfully aware of, the child within Eleanor wanted to protest, to stomp a foot and scream no. She wanted to speak with her mother, wanted to unravel the questions that had plagued her for eighteen years. Instead, she followed her mother's gaze.

"Friends?" she murmured.

Through the myrrh trees, others approached. Auberon and Gin, Irving and Sabrina, and Cleo too. Cleo carried a small case, and Eleanor stared in silence.

"I'm not allowing Mallory anywhere near a needle," Cleo said as she came to Eleanor's side.

Only when Cleo took hold of Eleanor's arm did Eleanor realize how unsteady she was on her feet. She was aware of the pain, the blood, but had trouble thinking beyond the fact she had found her mother.

"Come then," Dalila said and turned, guiding them through the trees.

They walked up ramps that were only partly familiar to Eleanor; here they were whole and gleaming rather than crumbling into dust. As they approached the temple, the people there stepped back, some going to their knees as the group passed. Eleanor held to Mallory and Cleo, wondering at Mallory's silence. But then, what did a person say about such a thing? Eleanor could hardly marshal her own thoughts and emotions. When she sought logical explanations, the mere sight of her mother obliterated them.

Dalila led them into the temple, between the flame-lit columns and into a private room. Eleanor opened her mouth to protest when her mother made to leave—the fear that Dalila would vanish was overwhelming and childish, but there even so. Dalila didn't leave the room, only spoke to the woman Eleanor recognized from the canyon in hushed tones.

"Please take your rest here," Dalila said, finally addressing Eleanor. "There will be food and drink, and also time." Dalila's eyes pinned Eleanor at that final word. Eleanor could only nod.

Eleanor settled onto a low settee as Mallory took a bowl from another servant and passed it to Cleo. Eleanor felt frozen, as though movement required too much thought. She was almost thankful when her mother and her attendants left the room, for she felt she could breathe again.

"When you returned to Cairo," Cleo said to Auberon as she helped Eleanor lie down, "I had no idea you intended to bring me to such a wondrous place."

"I do endeavor to surprise you," Auberon said. He unfolded a length of clean linen and offered it to Cleo. He then set to threading one of the fine needles within the small case Cleo had brought with her.

Cleo unbuttoned Eleanor's waistcoat and rolled up the bloody hem of her blouse to expose the vicious wound that spread below Eleanor's ribs. Irving had struck her well, leaving her bloody and bruised. Cleo dunked the clean linen into the bowl, and it came back out the color of dark wine. Eleanor flinched when Cleo began to clean the wound and squeezed Mallory's hand, finding him too quiet by far.

"Say something," Eleanor said, and Mallory laughed low. He lifted her bloody hand and pressed his lips against the rings she still wore.

"When I saw the blood in the chapel—" He broke off and bowed his head. He rested his forehead against her hand in a long moment of silence.

Eleanor exhaled, for St. Michael's chapel felt like ages ago. The memory of Christian dying on the floor came back in a rush, and then she was crying as she tried to explain to them all that had happened. Exhaustion and fear pulled at her equally, but so did relief that they were here and safe. "The Irvings are outside," Gin reported as he joined them in the small room. He crossed to the settee and crouched beside Auberon, rocking from foot to foot as if keeping still were impossible. "There is a casket. Mrs. Irving said . . . " He trailed off.

"They think Anubis can bring Caroline back to life," Mallory finished. Auberon and Cleo looked at him as though they'd both been struck between the eyes.

"What?" Cleo whispered. "You aren't telling me that they're going to attempt that?" Though she was plainly surprised, her mechanical hands remained steady as she took the needle from Auberon and began to stitch Eleanor's now-clean wound. Eleanor winced. No chloroform this time.

"I couldn't say what they mean to attempt," Mallory said. He kissed Eleanor's hand again. "Being that the Glass exists, and we are here, it would be logical that Anubis himself exists as well."

Eleanor was filled with the intense desire to leave. She wanted off the settee and out of this too-small room. If Mallory wanted Caroline brought back from the dead— She couldn't finish the thought, because only madness lay that way.

A frown creased Mallory's forehead; then his eyes met Eleanor's. His hand tightened around hers, even though she was still coated in her own blood. "They have to know that cannot happen. That it shouldn't. Death is a line that should only be crossed one way. And even if it could be countered, who would want that?" His thumb stroked slowly over Eleanor's. "I don't want her back, Eleanor."

Eleanor supposed that someday, her emotions and thoughts would order themselves properly. That she would eventually be blessed with a clarity of both. For now, this was not the case. As much as she had wanted to leave this room only moments ago, she now wanted the others gone, so she and Mallory might be alone, so she could slide her arms around him and allow herself to want everything they might have beyond this place and time.

It was Mallory who bent down despite the others in the room and covered her mouth with his own. Eleanor could taste a trace of tears between them, but if they were hers or his, she did not know. When they parted, she knew it didn't matter; they were two halves of the same confused thing: what was his was also hers.

Cleo bent her head to her task, her mechanical arms steady and gentle as she worked to mend the wound in Eleanor's side. When she had finished, she helped Eleanor sit up and wrapped another length of clean linen around Eleanor's ribs and abdomen.

"Here."

Auberon offered a fresh basin of water, and Eleanor set to washing the blood from her hands. The lamplight shimmered across the surface of the water as she washed, reminding her of the light that had broken through the darkness. She cleaned the blood from each ring, rubbing the markings with her thumb, and found herself not wanting to take them off.

"What are you thinking?"

Eleanor looked up at Mallory's question, finding the others had moved toward the edges of the room. They looked out onto the thriving plain before the temple. Cleo gestured to the pools and trees, while Gin complained they obscured the potential field of battle.

"I'm thinking that these rings are not mine and need to be returned," she said.

Mallory slid a hand into the basin of water to help her clean the last of the blood from the markings on each ring. "You don't want to stay?"

The idea was absurd to Eleanor, and she stared at Mallory in confusion before saying, "I don't belong here, Virgil. It was never about staying for me. It was about knowing what happened to my mother. I wanted . . . " She withdrew her hands from the water and dried them on another square of linen. "I always thought she would want to come back with me, not that I would stay. If we can get home, that's where we belong."

"We." Mallory's mouth curled upward.

"We." She touched Mallory's shirt collar, the fabric rumpled beyond all recourse. "If I never have time to say it again, thank you for coming back to the exhibition after I told you no."

Mallory brushed his cheek against hers. "I have the persistence of a cat chasing a mouse, or so my mother says. If she knew the truth, she would revise that to include a dog somehow."

"Mothers," Eleanor whispered, knowing that hers was just outside. There was much yet to say, to hear.

With her wound tended to, Eleanor and Mallory left the small room for the terrace outside. Dalila looked to be holding court, with her attendants and priests gathered around her. The Irvings lingered near Caroline's coffin, holding each other. Eleanor didn't care to imagine what this was like for them, so didn't. She couldn't, not when her thoughts were in revolt. It was too much.

Another person drew Eleanor's attention, a woman Eleanor had only seen photographs of. If, she supposed, she didn't count unearthing her body outside Giza when she was twelve. Her grandmother, Sagira el Jabari, was among the crowd, beautifully regal and completely alive.

"My dear daughter of my daughter," Sagira said, stepping out from the others. "You look like your photograph, even now." Her grandmother's English was even rustier than Dalila's. For all Eleanor knew, she may never have been fluent before her journey to the past. So much Eleanor did not know.

Sagira moved toward the group with the sound of rustling bells and shells. Sagira gathered Eleanor's hands into her own and took a long look at her.

The Lady, as flesh and bone and blood, and Eleanor could only stare, thinking of Sagira's body in the desert, given no proper burial. What would have led to such an end? What would make her flee this place? Here and now, she was beautiful, unlike the image Eleanor had often held in her mind, that of a smooth-faced woman immortalized in ancient stone. She was a living woman, time having made its mark upon her. Lines from laughter and tears spread outward from her expressive brown eyes. Her mouth pursed in surprise when she saw the rings, bent fingers reaching cautiously toward them. Eleanor extended her hand, seeing a similarity to her grandmother's fingers in her own. This realization was like a prick of electricity down her spine.

"Oh." Sagira's fingers played lightly over the rings Eleanor wore. "I never thought I see them again. When Dalila come to me, she left one ring . . . on the other side, much to the . . . dismay . . . of Defenders."

"Defenders of the Protectorate?" Mallory asked.

Sagira's piercing eyes swung to him. "Indeed, young man. They come through and were as trapped as my daughter was." She laughed in obvious amusement and freed Eleanor's hands. "It give them a new, better admiration for their country."

It would also explain why such a group had existed for so very long, Eleanor thought. Men—some of whom were also jackals—desperate to keep Egypt's treasures for Egypt.

"You should have these back in your care," Eleanor said and moved to take the rings from her fingers. Sagira held up a hand.

"No. I am not she you must entrust these to."

Eleanor bristled at the idea of what Sagira meant. Did they belong to Anubis? Was it true that if his Glass existed, then he must? What did such a thing mean for every god the world gave name to?

"Eleanor," Dalila said. "Walk with me among the trees. We have much to discuss."

Her mother's voice drew her out of the more troubling questions that wanted to drown her. She looked at Mallory, wanting him to join the conversation, but Sagira laughed.

"Go with your mother. I know how to entertain these men." Sagira's kohl-lined eyes fell on Auberon and Gin.

Gin's expression welcomed the idea of entertainment, whereas Sabrina Irving looked about to be sick. Despite everything, Eleanor's heart went out to the woman.

Eleanor followed her mother into the lower court, where myrrh trees flourished. They bordered T-shaped pools, making small, shaded havens. The number of people who congregated in them astonished Eleanor; it felt like they were all waiting for something.

"We have awaited you, daughter," Dalila said as if she could read Eleanor's thoughts. She guided Eleanor toward a wall decorated with carvings that Eleanor had only seen in their ruin. They stood fresh and new now, vibrant colors crisp against the stone.

"There were . . . " Dalila struggled to find the correct word. "Portents. Your grandmother could almost always still feel the rings, so long did she wear them."

"Portents?" Eleanor asked.

Dalila inclined her head, a gesture Eleanor wished she could say she remembered, but her mother's bearing was utterly new to her: regal, reserved, and unknown.

"You gave Akila a curious look, daughter. Is she known to you? She is a Defender and walks between the worlds, by rituals known only to her and her people."

Eleanor realized she meant the silver-haired woman. "She . . . " Eleanor felt at a loss for words. The people in the canyon had been Defenders? She would never live that down with Mallory, and regretted doubting Christian's word—but how could she not?

She reached a cautious hand out to the wall closest to them, to touch the image of Hatshepsut shown as a sphinx trampling her enemies. Eleanor was uncertain of what she should say to her mother. All this time, all this distance, and there Eleanor stood, tongue-tied.

"It took me the longest time," Dalila finally said. "To touch any part of this world. I thought anything I did touch might send me back, but the days passed, and I realized I had no way to open the Glass."

"But you didn't want to come back." It wasn't a question.

"I did not," she agreed.

Hearing the admission was less terrible than Eleanor had feared it would be.

"There is no easy way to say that I never felt a part of that world," Dalila said. She reached a hand toward Eleanor, perhaps meaning to stroke it over her hair, but pulled back before she could. "I did miss you."

The words, when at last they came, spilled in a rush from Eleanor. She let them come as they would, before she lost both the nerve and the opportunity.

"I've spent my life looking for you. I had always hoped to have this conversation and now, here I stand and have no clue what to say to you. When I was younger, I used to think I would bring you home to Da and that everything would mend itself. But look at you." Eleanor looked at her mother, a woman who looked like she had been born here. "You're already home."

Dalila's onyx braids whispered against her shoulders. "I will remain with Sagira and the pharaoh and serve them both as long as I am able." There was only the briefest of pauses before she asked, "How is Ren?"

Eleanor pressed a hand to her aching side and debated how to answer the question. Her father was not the man her mother had married, nor the man who had lost her. Eleanor looked back to the temple, where she saw Mallory crossing toward the huddled Irvings. Howard held fast to Sabrina, defensive in the face of Mallory's approach. Marriage, Eleanor decided, was entirely too complicated.

"I think the honest answer would break your heart," Eleanor eventually said.

She looked back to her mother; those eyes evaded Eleanor's, bright teeth biting into a plump lower lip. That expression was familiar, the look Dalila had always held before breaking something open. Equal parts anticipation and dread.

"Tell me you have not spent your life the way I spent mine."

"There was only ever you," Eleanor said. The same despair she had known countless times over the course of this journey welled up inside her. She didn't want to be angry, but was. Angry and sad both—wasn't that what her father had said? "I had to know. Da said you were dead. Over and over he told me you were gone." Eleanor's voice broke, thinking of him in his hospital bed, a similar wound in his side.

"I meant to say goodbye, Eleanor. After we found the Lady." Dalila's voice took on a new urgency, and she turned toward Eleanor, reaching out to grip her arm now. The touch made Eleanor flinch where once it would have flooded her with comfort. "I would not be so cruel as to leave you without a word, you must know that."

"But you still planned to go!" Eleanor hated the way she sounded—like a child. And yet how much of her still was the child who had witnessed her mother vanishing that day? That little girl who stood bleeding in the desert as she lost everything she had known.

"I did." Dalila released Eleanor and turned away. "None of this is fair. I never intended for you to lose me like that, Eleanor. I wanted you to understand that I had never felt a part of that world, so long as my mother was in this one. I never wanted you to know that same ache."

Eleanor laughed, a hollow sound that broke from her like a bark. "How could I not? It was all I ever knew."

"Those men—"

"Don't put this on them." Eleanor's voice was rough as she turned on her mother. "You wanted this, no matter what actually occurred."

Dalila looked to the star-spangled sky arching over them. "I thought your father would explain. I never thought you would search—"

"And don't you dare place this on his shoulders, either. He tried. He told me you died that day."

"Perhaps I did, Eleanor. At least the mother you knew died." Dalila trailed her fingers over the carvings on the temple wall, sand whispering out of the nooks as she went. "I have not spoken English in years. This world has shaped me into someone else, into Dalila el Jabari, daughter of the Queen of the Mirror."

"Better 'mirror' than 'rabbit hole'?" Eleanor's words were bitter as she thought of her grandmother's name written on the temple walls. It made a strange sense now, that two women from the future had given Hatshepsut's people the notion for the portal Anubis could open.

Eleanor knew the woman she had looked for all these years was truly gone, lost that day in the desert. It wasn't a matter of her mother not loving her, or not loving her enough; they had shared a journey, Dalila searching for her own mother as Eleanor had searched for hers. Eleanor knew her mother understood the pain and the longing better than anyone else ever could.

"I do love you, my daughter, but my place is here."

At the touch of a familiar hand against her shoulder, Eleanor turned into her mother's arms. The embrace was awkward, the child in Eleanor trying to hold the mother who had vanished so long ago. She smelled different, of lotus and oil and the paints that decorated her skin, but deep down, when Eleanor closed her eyes and shut the rest of this world away, she found that Dalila still smelled like her mother. Like home.

Home. Where she belonged.

Eleanor extracted herself from the embrace and looked at the woman before her a long moment. Dalila did not flinch under the study, but looked at Eleanor in kind. Eleanor was curious what her mother thought, but did not ask. She wasn't sure she wanted to know; Eleanor had spent her life much as her own mother had, chasing a thing that didn't want chasing. What would she think of her daughter's masculine clothing? What would she think of the woman her daughter had become? Eleanor wanted to tell her mother about Virgil, about wandering the Egyptian halls of the Louvre, and of the mechanical pterodactyls in the Exposition's gallery hall, but she knew these were matters that no longer concerned Dalila el Jabari.

"Is it possible to get home from here?" Eleanor extended her hand, the rings winking in the moonlight.

"You command the Glass," Dalila said as if this were an ordinary function of life here. She took hold of Eleanor's hand to brush a thumb over the rings. "Anubis has judged you, my daughter, and he will send you home." Dalila's expression suddenly filled with mischief. "After you return his rings to him."

⟫━⟪

Virgil stared at the dust-coated casket and the Irvings who stood nearby, and gritted his teeth. It should never have come to this, their daughter unearthed from her resting place, but Virgil had trouble censuring them, for what would he do if it were his own child? To be confronted with the miraculous and magical every day, yet not be able to have his heart's desire, could not have been an easy thing for Howard Irving. To see the possibility that lay beyond grief, to imagine Caroline whole and living once more: how tempting a thing it must be to a father.

Virgil touched the silver ring he wore. There had been times he wished his life might be lived over again, that he could change decisions he had made; that he might take back the night on the train and see Caroline again. But one look at Eleanor told him that was no way to live. He watched her speak, some distance away, with her mother. Eleanor's face showed, at first, pain . . . and then slow understanding.

No one stopped him when he approached Howard and Sabrina. They looked at him with matching expressions—though not expressions he would have expected. They both smiled.

"Your lady friend must give the rings to Anubis," Howard said, drawing himself to his full height. "We also require an audience with him."

Virgil stared at Howard and Sabrina and clasped his hands to stop himself from giving them both a hard shake. Did Irving believe it was so simple? That they could petition Anubis and Caroline would return like abducted Persephone having been freed from Hades's hellish clutches?

"Caroline is dead, and you should let her rest." Virgil was certain he had never said those words aloud before. Speaking them now was a relief, as if he were finally setting a weight down.

"Have you?" Sabrina asked him in a whisper.

The question caught Virgil off guard, and he said nothing. If his silence damned him, then so be it, but the satisfied smirk on Sabrina's face told him she wouldn't hear whatever he said. The Irvings wanted their daughter back,

334

come hell or high water. Or, Virgil considered, come hell or Ammit, the monster who sat ever-ready to devour an unworthy soul.

"You are a curiosity, Virgil Mallory," Howard said, so softly that none around them might hear. "You are also an abomination, a creature I have never understood even if I have employed your foul kind in my work. Yet there were nights I prayed our Caroline would come back, even as such a monster. We slept near her grave with the hope she would, but she never did. You were chosen, you took her, and yet she never . . . " He trailed off and scrubbed his shaking hand across his mouth. "I had to find other ways."

"Do you still taste her blood in your mouth in the night, Mallory?" asked Sabrina.

The idea of Caroline's parents sleeping beside her grave horrified Virgil. It came as no surprise that Howard knew his true nature, given his Mistral ties, but that they knew of his role in Caroline's death—that was something of a shock.

The idea that Irving had employed Virgil's "kind" in his work turned Virgil's thoughts to the train and Caroline's freshly dead body. The jackals— had Irving sent them to escort his daughter in her own perilous work? They could have carried word of Virgil's involvement back to Irving easily enough. Irving used people as he saw fit, no matter their nature.

"Anubis will see," Sabrina said. She rocked back and forth and wrapped her arms around herself. "Anubis will understand all that has happened. He will see you for what you are, Mallory—never a son to us, never a husband to Caroline. A foul creature guided by his own needs. He will see the wrong life was taken. All will be made right."

In the early days after Caroline's death, Virgil had believed those things, especially the notion he had never been a proper husband to her. He had spent long nights questioning how he might have done everything differently, how he might have replayed the entire hand he'd been dealt. He had, for lack of a better description, indeed lay awake with the taste of Caroline's blood still in his mouth. Sabrina would have enjoyed his guilt, he was certain.

Those nights had given way to hazy days where he struggled to make amends for all he had done, for all he hadn't managed to do. If he had found better methods to control the beast; if he had sought a teacher; if he had not let his blind rage consume him that night. If, if, if. But this game had only shown Virgil that the world was imperfect, for he could play it with Caroline's actions, too. And if her own father had known of her duplicitous nature, surely he bore a measure of the blame himself.

Placing blame helped no one, Virgil knew. He had made what amends he could.

As for bringing Caroline back to life, that was surely an impossible feat, even for Anubis.

"You will never know what I went through after Caroline's death," Virgil told them. "Even if I told you, you would not care or believe. I loved her, but that means little in the face of your own love for her and your loss. I wished for so many things with her, only to be denied because Caroline's work always took her away."

Was it doubt that flickered over Sabrina's face? He saw the brief drop of her eyes, from his face to her own clutched hands. Virgil didn't know what to take it for. He knew that in the end, his words would be discarded; they would forever side with their daughter, which was as it should have been. But to say the words for his own benefit and relief— He swallowed hard and attended to that task. This confession. The wolf inside him curled close.

"When I realized it was her on that train—" His voice broke, but he felt no shame. He gave himself up to the feeling of loss all over again, and—word by word—began to finally set it aside. "It was too late. There was no going back. Her blood was on my hands, and that will be a thing I will forever live with." Live with, but it won't strangle me. No more. For my sake and Eleanor's. "To have killed the woman I loved was a thing I could not comprehend."

"Thou shalt not," Sabrina whispered.

Perhaps she was saying he would never understand it; perhaps she was reminding him of God's commandments. Either way, Virgil agreed.

"I had no idea you knew I had killed her. If I had, I would have prayed that one day you would both forgive me. But now I see that it isn't you I need forgiveness from. It's myself. Nothing can replace a child—but you also never knew me. Never knew the true me, who loved Caroline and mourned her, and now, finally, moves on."

Virgil looked at the casket again, not wanting to think on what remained inside. He stroked his fingers over the solid wood. "As wrong as everything went, this is not the way to repair it. I have let Caroline rest, and now you must."

"An abomination moves on," Howard spat the words. "To that knickknack bunter who does as she will, the rest of the world be damned? What a fine way to honor the memory of your dead wife."

"You will never speak of Miss Folley in those terms again." The wolf inside him pressed to get out, to stretch its jaws around Howard's neck. "I pray you will both be able to heal, but attempting to bring Caroline back isn't the way."

With that, Virgil turned away from them and, even when Sabrina screamed after him, he kept walking. Down the temple's ramp and away from the guilt and shame he had felt in their presence through the years; away from every bad memory and blue parrot and mistake. He could only move forward.

Forward to Eleanor, who had left her mother and now stood at the edge of a lower ramp. She extended a hand to him when he neared. He slid his hands around hers, trying to understand the look in her brown eyes. Reflected firelight danced there, but, strangely, no tears.

"I wasted so much time," Eleanor whispered. "Please tell me that from here on, we never look to the past and wish for what might have been."

Virgil bowed his head and kissed Eleanor's fingers. When he looked at her again, his smile was gentle. "Mirrors are difficult, showing you what lies behind, but glass . . . " He thought of the swirling light and the images he had seen—Eleanor's past twined with his. "You can look through glass, beyond the reflection. You can look ahead."

"Maybe that's the trick of it." Eleanor slipped her hand free of his, to slide her arm inside his jacket and around his waist as she burrowed close. "I am to return the rings to Anubis. I can't do it alone."

"You can," Virgil said, "but I will be there, *tesorina*. Trust in that."

Dalila and Sagira and a host of robed priests guided them to the Anubis chapel. No longer the ruin Eleanor had seen in modern times, the space was as it should be, pillars supporting a lapis-blue ceiling painted with golden stars. Every wall was intact and also brightly painted, the mural of Anubis reaching out of the wall toward Eleanor as they approached.

But as she drew closer, she realized it was no mural. The creature standing before the wall was as dark as night, towering nearly to the ceiling. He smelled of rot and life in the same instant, like the cold, flooding Nile.

Behind Anubis stood a large black horse with gleaming green eyes. Eleanor couldn't put the horse into any context—it wasn't part of the Anubis history she knew. On the other side of Anubis was a more familiar creature, the squat beast that was part crocodile, part lion, and part hippopotamus. Ammit was all hunger and snapping jaws.

Dalila, Sagira, and the priests dropped to their knees before Anubis, and Eleanor slowly followed suit. She could not quite force herself to bow as the others did, for she couldn't pry her eyes off Anubis. He was unlike anything she had seen, even in the dreams he had invaded.

"God's trousers," Mallory whispered.

Anubis was massive, his ears flicking against the star-painted ceiling above. His skin gleamed as if oiled, lapis and gold shimmering in the wide necklace draping his neck and chest. Eleanor looked for a seam, something that might indicate a mask, but there was none. Everything she saw and smelled told her this creature was real and here and looking at her with his blue-black eyes. Anubis's fingers brushed her chin and curled lightly around her neck. Eleanor took a stuttering breath as his flooded-Nile scent rolled over her, as his fingers conveyed both his strength and heat.

Mallory growled.

Anubis laughed. The sound rolled through the chapel, shaking every wall.

"Be calmed, wolf," Anubis said, his black eyes taking in Mallory before he looked back to Eleanor. "Daughter." His hand moved down to hers, fingers brushing over the rings. He made no demand for them, and before Eleanor could offer them, Anubis's sharp face snapped up, his attention on the entrance of the chapel.

The Irvings picked their way through the columns to stand behind Eleanor. Eleanor spied Auberon, Gin, and Cleo pressed to the back wall of the chapel, their expressions as shocked as she herself felt.

"Great Anubis, I come to ask for the life of my daughter. For the life of Caroline June Irving." Howard Irving's voice didn't tremble as he spoke; in fact, he sounded as though this was all merely a formality and that he was dearly tired of the entire thing.

Eleanor looked back at Anubis. With one hand, Anubis gathered dust from the ground. Within the broad valley of his black palm, Caroline took shape, small and perfectly wrought in dust. Sabrina gasped.

"This one," Anubis said, "has been weighed and long ago given to Ammit. She did not live true. She tainted even her life-mate, who could have been her hope and salvation." He exhaled a low breath across his palm, and the dust of Caroline scattered to every corner of the chapel.

Anubis said nothing more. The silence in the chapel was broken only by Sabrina's sobs.

"Daughter, my rings."

With shaking hands, Eleanor released Mallory and pulled the rings from her own fingers. She did not know how the rings would fit upon Anubis's large fingers, but as the metal had changed to accommodate her, so too did it for Anubis. The metal shifted in her grasp, feeling like flesh and not metal at all. The rings also appeared to know their place; each slid easily onto the god's fingers. Eleanor hesitated to step away. Instead, she lifted a hand to his cheek. She wanted to touch the creature who had so plagued her, wanted to believe there was nothing here to fear.

Anubis's muzzle was warm to the touch, much as Mallory's own when he was a wolf. Eleanor gave the god before her a scratch under the chin, realizing how absolutely foolish it was. But when Anubis stretched into the touch, finding the pleasure of a puppy in the affection, she couldn't say who was more the fool.

"Daughter," Anubis said again, and Eleanor felt the jackal within her leap.

Behind Anubis, the strange horse stamped a hoof, and Eleanor looked at him. His ebon hide streamed with water, which pattered to the floor, sending rivulets through the dust and columns. Was it the Nile, or another river that overflowed him? It could have been any wet place where a waterhorse might frolic. Within the steed's green eyes, Eleanor saw a familiar imp, a man she had traveled part of the world with, a man who had always been more content with mischief than violence.

"Hubert?" The whispered question came from Mallory. Eleanor dropped her hand from Anubis, because she didn't know the answer. Waterhorses came from Ireland, though; her parents had told her stories of them, too, saying once that her own wolfhound was such a creature, made smaller so she might take him everywhere she would.

"I would have guided him to Osiris, daughter," Anubis said, "but his path is elsewhere."

With that, Anubis stepped past Eleanor and Mallory. The god reached one hand down, snatching both Irvings from the chapel floor. Sabrina shrieked anew and struggled in his grasp. Everyone scattered back as Anubis held firm to the couple.

"You come to be weighed," Anubis said.

The ground shifted under Anubis's passage, dust clouding the air in a golden haze. The chapel walls shimmered away, and Anubis claimed his position by the golden scales that assembled themselves out of the chapel's dust. A feather already rested on one side.

Eleanor stared as Anubis plucked the hearts out of both Howard and Sabrina. She expected blood, gore, but the hearts came seamlessly away, dry and dusty. A sizable crack ran through the center of Howard's heart, whereas Sabrina's was withered, almost gray. The Irvings stared at their own hearts as Eleanor did, transfixed.

Ammit paced and snapped her glistening jaws more furiously as Anubis set Sabrina's withered heart onto his brilliant scales. Other gods made themselves known then, emerging with whispers from the dust suspended in the air: green-skinned Osiris, pale Isis beside dark Seth, sharp-beaked Thoth.

"We are hallucinating," Eleanor whispered as she took a step backward, lodging herself firmly against Virgil.

"I keep telling myself that, but not even while smoking opium have I seen such things," Virgil whispered back. His arm slid around her.

Bright images filled the space where once walls had stood, the light of the Glass coalescing into images that moved through the air. Eleanor watched Sabrina Irving's life unfold, each image crystal-bright as the Glass spun it. Everything Sabrina did was for the only child she would bear, her daughter Caroline. No matter how awful, Sabrina saw the acts as selfless, wholly for Caroline's benefit. If she had a hand in taking another's life, she saw it adding to Caroline's life. The scale did not agree.

The withered heart dipped the scale downward, heavier than Ma'at's feather. Anubis plucked the heart from his scale and without expression tossed it to Ammit. She caught it in her crocodile jaws, her squat hippopotamus body shuddering with pleasure as she consumed the filthy thing.

Sabrina cried out. "You cannot—"

But her protest was silenced as she crumbled to dust, a small trickle out of

Anubis's hand. Howard, still firmly in the god's grip, tried to reach for her, but his hands met only dust. It blossomed in a cloud around him, then into the Egyptian sky.

Howard closed his eyes as Anubis took his heart to weigh. Like his wife's before him, Howard's heart dipped the golden scale, but this heart was heavier, to the point it moved the entire chapel. Under the weight of Irving's love for his daughter and his devious work, the columns shifted and the ground cracked, sending Eleanor and Mallory to their knees in a cloud of dust.

Mallory could not have gone far, but Eleanor realized he was no longer at her side. The heat of burning oil from spilled lamps surrounded her, brightening the curve of a shoulder within the dust. She reached out. Her fingers brushed the smooth-skinned flank of Ammit, and with a gasp, Eleanor withdrew. The whinny of a horse and splashing water carried through the cries of the priests and others. Eleanor pushed to her feet and stepped into Mallory.

"Eleanor!"

She grabbed his hands as he grabbed hers. Dust made their palms slick, but she held firm, refusing to lose him in the confusion again. The entire world was unsteady beneath their feet, the chapel continuing to buckle as sharp streams of light pierced the dust around them. Instinctively she pulled Mallory toward the light.

She wanted to say goodbye to her mother, her grandmother, but knew deep down that she already had. The past was in the past, and she needed to leave it there. Their place was here, as surely as hers was elsewhere.

Everything faded. Eleanor knew the comforting touch of Mallory's hands as the light dwindled to a pinprick and the clouded dust evaporated. She closed her eyes and turned her face into Mallory's neck. He smelled of myrrh and wine and dust, of places long since buried under sand. For once, she didn't want a shovel.

When Eleanor found the courage to open her eyes, the temple stood once more in ruin around them.

CHAPTER TWENTY-FIVE

Paris, France ~ 31 October, 1889

"I do not believe this outrage."

"Believe it."

Eleanor tucked the wool blanket more firmly around her father's knees. Her father's annoyed-and-yet-not tone amused her for the first time in a long while, and she fought the smile that wanted to come. They had much ground to cover, she knew; many wounds still needed healing, but she prayed that now they actually could heal, now that everything was spread on the table before them.

"You are staying in." She brushed a kiss over his cheek, then stepped back. He looked somehow smaller and perhaps, she thought, more human than he had in her youth. "Juliana will be here and—"

"I wanted to view the fireworks, Ellie."

"And so you may." Eleanor gestured to the window of their rented rooms, where she had left the draperies open. "There is absolutely no sense in you running all over the Exposition grounds and exhausting yourself."

"And you?" Her father made a disgusted noise. "You're no better. You should be home, resting and healing."

Eleanor's hand went instinctively to her side, which was still tender, yet healing well. "Your wounds were considerably more grave, good sir," she said. If her father thought she was going to miss the final night of the Exposition, he truly didn't know her. She planned to run all over the Exposition grounds and exhaust herself before the night was through. After such explorations, Mallory had asked her to accompany him to services at Notre Dame.

"Hmph." He snorted and snuggled deeper into his chair, where he appeared wholly content despite his grumblings.

Eleanor moved from her father's chair at the sound of a knock on the door. It was strange to her that this room and the city beyond had not changed when so much else had.

They had returned to Paris only three days prior, and Eleanor swore she could still taste the temple dust on her lips. Yet here, the Exposition went on; people boggled at the machines and inventions on an hourly basis, the mechanical pterodactyls had been returned to their graceful flights, and children continued to displace shells from their displays, thinking of nothing and nowhere beyond this place. Eleanor wished her own thoughts might be so easily distracted, but they continued to stray backward in time, to the sight of her mother in that garden—her mother content and in her place at last.

Juliana squealed at Eleanor's appearance when Eleanor opened the door. "Ah, look at you! Did the mask arrive?"

Eleanor stepped back, the hem of her black cloak whispering over the ground. She had kept her dress and cloak simple, wanting the mask to draw all of the attention. "Just this morning." She gestured to the table as Juliana entered, to the jackal mask perched upon a stack of books.

It was a brown papier-mâché face, smudged here and there with gold paint. Small ears, one pierced with a thin gold ring, perked atop the head, while oval slits would allow her to see out. Eleanor had tried it on earlier to confirm the fit, which was perfect. And strangely, it felt right.

Not telling her father and Juliana about her true nature also felt right, at least for the time being. She didn't remotely understand it herself—there was so much yet to learn!—and she wanted to know more before she told them. She needed to know more. *Saint Michael, give me strength to learn the truth of myself . . .*

"Absurd!" her father grumbled from his chair.

"You hush," Juliana said as she lifted the mask to give it a closer inspection.

Eleanor closed the door as her friend and father exchanged barbs. "Perhaps this evening alone will give the two of you time to talk," Eleanor said, giving them a gentle nudge in the direction she rather hoped they would take. She prayed her father would be able to truly let Dalila go now—even as she knew such a thing would take time.

"Talk?" he asked.

"I don't know what you mean," Juliana said and returned the mask to its place. She brushed her hands over her jacket, then slowly began to unbutton it, as if only now deciding to stay.

"Whatever could I have to say?" her father continued.

Eleanor picked up the mask. "I'm sure you can think of something," she murmured, then kissed Juliana's cheek. "I will be terribly late in coming home, if I come home at all."

"When one keeps such dreadful company," Juliana said with a grin, "one can hardly presume otherwise."

Eleanor left them, moving down the stairs and into the night, which was cool but not yet unbearable. The sky was clear and star-splattered, the trees still decked with leaves of orange and gold. She paused long enough to tie her mask into place, then moved toward the Exposition, toward the food vendors and the beautiful fountain in front of the Große Gallery.

The Exposition remained as lively as ever. People still thronged to see the sights, many in costume for the final evening's celebrations. More extravagant international fashions were on display tonight than she had seen over the course of the Exposition. The vendors remained as varied as the sprawling fair itself, foods from Spain, England, and Italy scenting the night air; it was a veritable feast for every sense, even if Eleanor declined the eels.

Word was that some of the displays would be turned into bonfires; some vendors were shocked by the very idea, for who had the wealth to burn such things, whereas others wondered aloud if the dreadful tower Eiffel had assembled would be melted down as well.

"Pray thee, good miss, a soul cake?"

She turned at the sound of Mallory's voice. They had not told each other their costumes for the evening, though she supposed he would know her under her jackal mask after all. She had speculated he would find a wolf mask, but it was a large papier-mâché toad head that perched upon his shoulders. He had chosen his green suit to pair with it. She noted the rumpled tie circling his neck.

"Do toads eat cake, then, Mister Toad?" she asked. She kept hold of the bags that contained the pies and cakes, not yet surrendering them.

"That's Agent Toad to you, Miss," came the reply. He lifted the toad head off his shoulders and grinned at her. His eyes were gleaming in a way she had only seen twice before. Eleanor blushed to know precisely what occupied his mind. It wasn't cake.

"Agent Toad," she murmured, then surrendered the bags of treats so she could untie her own mask.

Mallory guided her to nearby benches, where they took seats and he doled out the food. The meat pies were still steaming as they unwrapped them, fragrant between them in the cold air.

"Someone told me they meant to melt Eiffel's tower," Mallory said around a rather large bite of pie. "Can you imagine our luck should that be the case?"

Eleanor glanced up at the tower, gleaming against the night sky. The beacon at the tower's uppermost point still streamed over the Exposition, clear and bright. "I would think it rather messy," she eventually said. "I predict it shall stay, ever a thorn in your side."

Mallory drew his handkerchief out to wipe his mouth, looking at Eleanor across the open bag which still contained their sweet cakes. "Speaking of sides, how is yours, Miss Folley?"

They had not seen each other in three days, and the separation had been nearly unbearable to Eleanor after having spent the prior two weeks rarely outside Mallory's company. The days had been filled with long meetings and recitations over the adventures they had experienced. Director Walden, while firmly grounded in their court, wanted to ensure that everyone was clear on what had happened. He was almost amused when the stories matched up, puzzle pieces locking easily together.

The holes in Mistral's own files were patched with equal ease, as Irving's covert activities helped explain them. Likewise, his personal doings led them to other Mistral agents who had not been quite so honest in their dealings throughout the years. No one showed any surprise when the Irvings didn't arrive to defend themselves. Walden compared it to a nightmare fleeing the light of a new day.

"Healing well," Eleanor said. "I have seen Cleo, who took me to Dr. Fairbrass, and both are pleased with me—though how could they not be?" She sat straighter and tilted her head. "Considering my beauty and charm?"

"God, I have missed you," Mallory said with a laugh as he polished off his pie.

Eleanor's smile deepened. Would she ever grow tired of hearing that? "You found time for that, despite the meetings and explanations, followed by more meetings and explanations?"

She had not minded the meetings so much, for they gave her the hope that Mistral would put itself back to rights and become the organization she always felt it could be. Director Walden had invited her to assist, for so many of the Egyptian artifacts Irving had handled were in doubt now; were they genuine, had they been stolen? There was much yet to discover, and Eleanor hoped to be a part of it.

"Indeed so," he said, and wiped his hands on his handkerchief. "I was even in touch with Adrian, and we have agreed to find a way forward." Mallory stared at the handkerchief for a good long while, so long that Eleanor nearly asked him what he saw in the smudges of gravy there. Did they hold the key to all resolutions with his brother?

When Mallory looked at her again, his look was certain, as steady as she had seen it. "Miss Folley, I have a proposition for you."

"Dreadful company, indeed," she murmured and shook her head when Mallory gave her a curious look. "Pray continue, Agent Toad." After all they had been through—

"Considering all that we have been through of late . . . "

Could he read minds now? Eleanor supposed she would have to better mind her thoughts if that were the case.

" . . . and seeing how extraordinarily well we have gotten along . . . "

Eleanor thought of the ways they had argued, of the ways they had nearly devoured one another, and had to agree it was indeed extraordinary.

" . . . and also taking into consideration the apparent attraction"—and here his eyes fell again to his splotched handkerchief—"we both have for myth and artifact—"

"Agent Toad." Mallory's eyes came up at her interruption, and she pursed her lips, holding back the bulk of her amusement. "Have you noticed that when you are particularly invested in something, you tend to sound like an archaeologist reciting a paper on the precise construct of dust found within an otherwise empty tomb?"

Mallory tilted his head. "Truly?" He folded his handkerchief, then proceeded to shove it into his jacket pocket. "I had hoped this would be infinitely more intriguing than that." He sat straighter on the bench, looking directly at her. "Miss Folley, I am proposing a courtship. Being that you are of age and that I am of age, and that we share an attraction for one another, in addition to our love of adventure and—"

Eleanor's heart skipped. "Mallory—"

"I have decided—"

"Mallory—"

He pushed forward, plucking at his rumpled tie now. "I have decided—decided rather a while ago, I should hasten to add—that my heart has . . . "

He fell to silence when Eleanor's hand covered his above his tie. She nudged his fingers away, then loosened his tie with one certain tug.

"So formal," she whispered and pulled the length of fabric free from his collar. The tie was warm from him, as everything that touched him must surely be. She could not imagine a person who radiated more heat than Virgil Mallory.

"Miss Folley, is it the delivery of the proposition that vexes you, or the proposition itself?"

She folded his tie into her hand and tucked it with equal care into her own cloak pocket. Later, she thought, she would look back on this and be astonished she had kept her mind as well as she did, when inside she felt as though she were falling to pieces. Pieces which only Mallory knew how to reassemble properly, after he had cleared the dust and dirt with fingers and breath.

"Soul cake, missus?"

The sudden trio of voices at Eleanor's side startled her, proving her less steady than she believed. She laughed out loud and without thinking gave the bag of cakes to the trio of children, their faces brightly painted. As they scampered on their way, Mallory slid closer to her on the bench.

"You have me reconsidering the entire proposal," he murmured. "You've just given away perfectly good cake."

Eleanor leaned into Mallory's side, and his arm came around her shoulders to keep her close. "You aren't asking out of obligation, are you?" she whispered. It had been a tiring two weeks, and much had changed for both of them. "I only ask because the night I changed into . . . " She laughed softly. "Oh, whatever I am . . . "

Mallory's free hand came up to cup Eleanor's cheek. "A beautiful jackal," he said. "Daughter of Anubis. My *tesorina*, if I might be so bold." His fingers stroked down the curve of her cheek, over her jaw, and down to the thrum of her pulse in her neck. "No obligation. On either side, Eleanor. Should you not feel—"

Eleanor's finger over Mallory's mouth silenced him. His treasure. She wouldn't let him debate, wouldn't let him go down that path. "I accept your proposition, Agent Toad," she said.

Mallory's mouth curled up beneath her finger. "I won't move your hairbrush."

She smiled too, under the press of Mallory's mouth, opening herself to him and the possibility that lay ahead of them. If they could leave the shadows of the past behind, there was no one Eleanor would rather walk ahead with—no matter where the path curved or fell apart.

"But will you write me poetry?" she asked when he lifted his mouth to drop a kiss on her nose.

He moved closer and brushed his cheek against hers, marking her in all the ways he might, despite little goblins running to and fro. He laughed, low and dark. As the night sky above them erupted in explosions of violet, gold, and blue, Eleanor closed her eyes. It was not Anubis's face that rose in the darkness for once; it was Mallory's.

"Every day, Eleanor. Every day."

⇐◆⇒

Howth, Ireland ~ October 1929

Clear moonlight washed the treeless cliffs, ocean waves pounding far below. Eleanor could hear their roar and shivered as she drew her robe around her. Winter would be upon them soon.

She moved through the house barefoot. Her feet ached with the coming of the cold, even though doctors told her it was normal. She was an old woman, they said; did she think she could run as she had when she was young?

The back door stood open an inch, and she pushed it wide, stepping into the garden. All the flowers were sleeping now, but come summer, the garden would be a riot of color. She looked over the fenced-in space and frowned; was it only the lack of warmth in bed beside her that had woken her, or—

A wolf's lonesome cry carried over the fields, reaching down into her bones. She knew that cry, and even now it made her smile. Once more and twice more, the cry came, and by the time it sounded yet again, she was at the edge of the garden, nightgown discarded on the back fence alongside Virgil's robe.

She ran. Slower and more cautiously than she had once, but she ran, letting her human self fall away until she was bounding on four legs through long and fragrant grasses that led to the curl of the river, where the ground grew soft and bore the mark of her mate. She followed the gurgling water, leapt over stones, and watched the moonlight spread outward in rings across the surface of the lake as the touch of a nose and tongue broke the water's surface.

The wolf lifted his head, water dripping from his silvered jaw, and howled one final time before leading the small jackal in yet another chase. His shoulder dipped to the ground, tail wagging in the air. Then he leapt away from the water and into the long grass, until she was running by his side, as she ever had, as she ever would.

ACKNOWLEDGEMENTS

To my readers, be it first or last draft: Deva Fagan, Michael Mazour, Jennifer Kahng, Aimee Li, J. Anderson Coats, Anna C. Bowling, J. Kathleen Cheney, and Kenneth Kao. For plying me with virtual cake and avocados, Beth Wodzinski. For always going above and beyond, Sean Wallace, Paula Guran, and Natalie Luhrs.

To they who know what I know not: Sophia Kelly Shultz for all things Egypt; Mary Robinette Kowal for etiquette and protocol; Lazarus Avery for weaponry; and Joseph O'Flaherty for matters concerning Ireland, Catholicism, and wolves.

For endless conversations about the naming of things, for suggestions as to what may hide within cases and nooks, for images of parchment and bronze airships, and monsters howling on opium winds, one can only thank the muse—should such a creature exist.

ABOUT THE AUTHOR

E. Catherine Tobler is a Sturgeon Award finalist and the senior editor at *Shimmer Magazine*. Among others, her fiction has appeared in *Clarkesworld*, *Lady Churchill's Rosebud Wristlet*, and multiple times previously in *Beneath Ceaseless Skies*. For more, visit www.ecatherine.com